APEX
III
THE EXLIAN SYNDROME SERIES

BOOKS BY SETH RING

THE EXLIAN SYNDROME SERIES

Advent

Dark Dawn

Apex

Evolution (coming in 2025)

Shattered Glory (coming in 2026)

Light's Ascension (coming in 2026)

THE IRON TYRANT SERIES

Chain of Feathers

Crow's Fortune

Healing Skies

THE SOUL CALLER SERIES

Soul Caller 1

Soul Caller 2

THE DREAMER'S THRONE SERIES

Dreamer's Throne 1

Dreamer's Throne 2

Dreamer's Throne 3

Dreamer's Throne 4

THE NOVA TERRA SERIES

Mad Master Alchemist

THE TOWER SERIES

Forgemaster

Reforged

Arcanist

Ignition

Bloodline

Avatar

Challenger

Marauder

THE BATTLE MAGE FARMER SERIES

Domestication

Germination

Cultivation

Fermentation

Transformation

Preservation

Separation

Conservation

Culmination

THE TITAN SERIES

Nova Terra: Titan

Nova Terra: Greymane

Nova Terra: Kingbreaker

Nova Terra: Guardian

Nova Terra: Liberator

Nova Terra: Earthshaper

Nova Terra: Stormbringer

Nova Terra: Stone King

Nova Terra: Catalyst

Nova Terra: Worldbearer

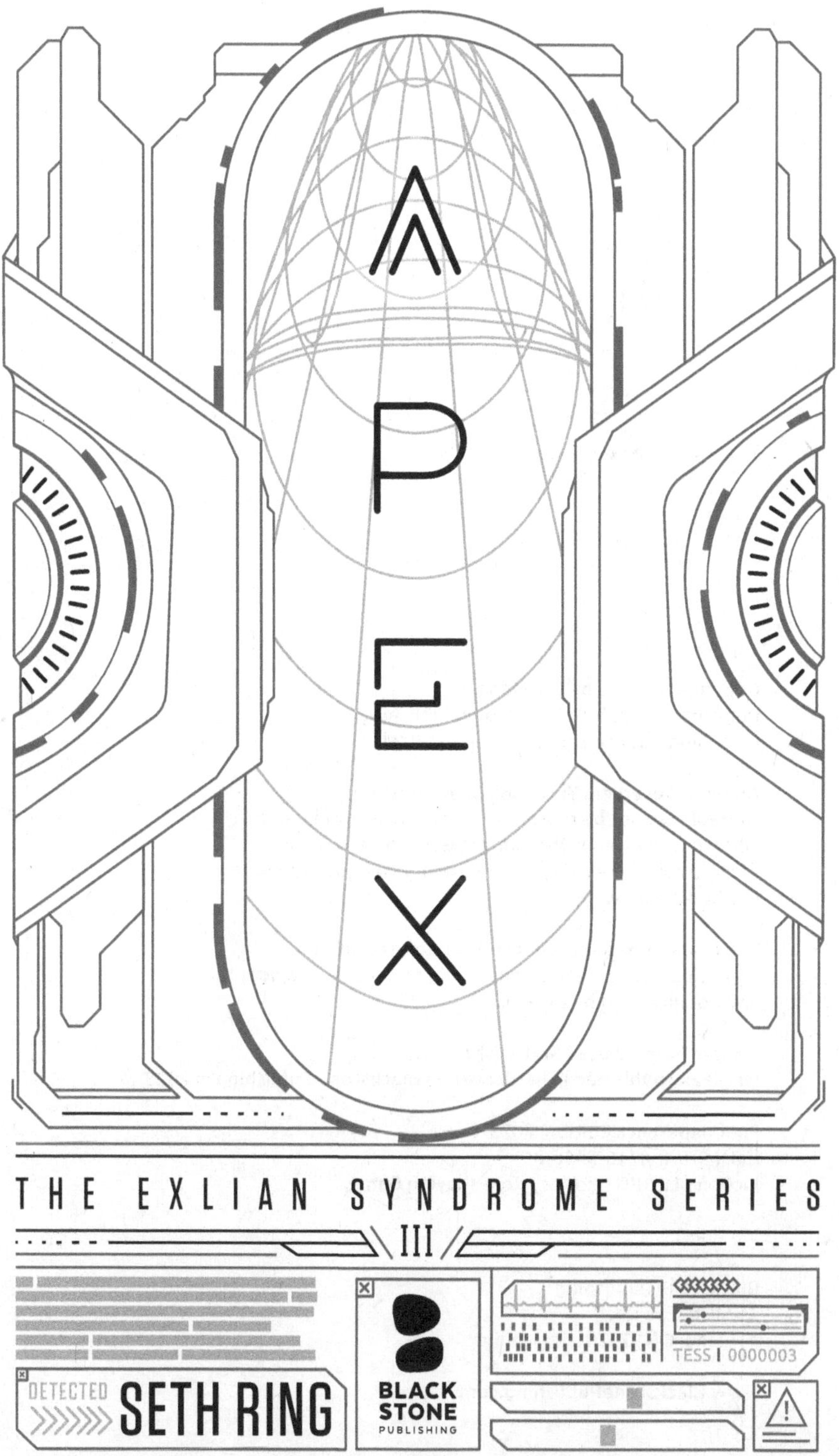

APEX

THE EXLIAN SYNDROME SERIES

III

Published in 2025 by Blackstone Publishing
Cover and book design by by Larissa Ezell

Printed in the United States of America
Originally published in hardcover by Blackstone Publishing in 2025

First paperback edition: 2025
ISBN 979-8-8746-9496-8
Fiction / LitRPG (Literary Role-Playing Game)

Version 1

Blackstone Publishing
31 Mistletoe Rd.
Ashland, OR 97520

www.BlackstonePublishing.com

THE EXLIAN SYNDROME SERIES

The clang of the prison guard's baton against the wooden bars rang in Mark Fields's ears, but the guard wasn't here for him, so there was no point in paying attention. Instead, he kept his eyes closed and focused on his meditation. He wasn't exactly sure how much time had passed since he had been brought down into the depths of Gray Rock Prison, but his best guess was a week. The large room he was in remained pitch black unless the guards had to enter, which they only did to deliver his food once a day or to pull one of the other prisoners from a cage.

There were six cages in the room, and apart from his, only one was still occupied. Once a prisoner was taken from a cage, which seemed to happen around once a day, they didn't return, and though he was idly curious, Mark figured he would find out what was happening to them soon enough. Mark carefully regulated his breathing as he concentrated on erasing the sensations he was feeling from his mind, seeking to sink deeper into his meditative state. The damp air that brought a chill to his skin, the clomp of the guards' boots that echoed in his ears, the rough flagstone that pressed into his legs, and the bite of the shackles on his wrists—after focusing on each feeling for a moment, he erased it from his perception, his mind filling with the state of his body.

The disorientation brought about by the mana running through him left him so weak that he could hardly sit up straight. A sharp clang intruded into his thoughts, and with a sigh he abandoned his attempts. Glancing toward the door that had just closed, Mark could feel the slow, simmering anger in his chest reaching a boiling point. After leaving the Black Mountain Battalion and returning to New Emery, Mark had been seized almost immediately upon entering the city and thrown into Gray Rock Prison on fabricated charges. All the rights he was supposed to have, including the right to counsel and a fair trial, had been denied, and now he was stuck in the middle of a prison deep underground, waiting for who knew what.

Time slipped past again: How much, Mark had no idea, but one moment he was alone, and the next he saw Mime sitting in front of him. With a weak grin, he reached out and tried to pet her. Unfortunately, the shackles drained too much of his strength, and he could barely lift his arm before it fell back. Mime shook her head as if disappointed. It stung, but Mark could only give half a shrug, unsure how to explain it to her.

The weak become prey to the strong.

Jerking in surprise, Mark looked around, wondering where the voice had come from.

If you want to avoid being prey, you must become strong.

It took him a moment to realize that the voice, so clear that he'd assumed someone was talking to him, was actually coming from inside him. It rose from his heart and echoed in his mind, transforming into a reverberating roar. Mark, for all his disorientation, wasn't stupid, and he focused on Mime, still staring at him in the darkness.

Those above you treat you like prey, only because they have not learned to fear your claws.

With a grimace, Mark leaned forward, struggling to lift his hand. "Bit too late, Mime. I don't have claws anymore."

The man and cat looked at each other, and then Mime opened her mouth, and a gleaming black orb appeared on her tongue. Mark's eyes went wide. He had assumed Mime had swallowed the Exlian nest and digested it to improve her own abilities, yet here it was. She placed it on the ground and rolled it toward him with her paw.

Claws can be regrown. You have allowed your enemies to strip yours for the time being, but you can get them back if you are willing.

The nest was pitch black, but Mark could see it clearly even in the dark room. It called to him with a faint and ethereal temptation that played across his mind like music and made his mouth water. The sense was so slight that he had never noticed it before, but in the absolute silence and darkness of the prison, Mark's awareness was unusually sharp.

No one is coming to save you, and if you would stand against your foes, you must grow in power. Consume the nest. Break your shackles. Regrow your claws and become the hunter.

Mime's words stoked the anger simmering in Mark's belly, and his expression hardened. He had no clear idea who his foes were, though he was starting to suspect Andre Javesi might be involved. Regardless, he was stuck in a prison with shackles on his hands and feet, and Mime was right. No one was coming to save him. Apart from Jason, no one even knew that he had been thrown in prison. His master wasn't around, and Mark genuinely doubted that anyone would be coming to help him out. If he was going to get out of this situation, he would have to rely on himself.

Focusing as best he could, he reached out with a shaking arm and grabbed the nest. As he lifted it, he could feel something squirming inside. Gritting his teeth, he stared at the nest for a long moment, his mind ablaze. He had no idea what this would do to him, no idea what kind of monster he would become if he consumed it, but at this point, he wasn't sure if he cared. Without hesitating any further, Mark tossed the black marble into his mouth and swallowed it in one gulp.

He felt the hard marble slide down his throat, and then a supernova went off in his stomach. Mana rampaged through his body, bringing terrible pain with it, yet Mark had the strange sense that it was guided destruction. The mana current intended to stop his empowered abilities faltered in the face of the nest's absolute power, and Mark felt his body's regeneration start to kick in.

Big drops of sweat appeared on his skin, and though he couldn't see them in the darkness, he could smell a hint of blood as they emerged. Unable to maintain his seated position, he flopped onto his back, his muscles twitching violently as the mana from the nest raged through him.

Embrace the pain. It brings with it the power you need.

The voice brought Mark a measure of comfort, and as he leaned into the pain racking his limbs, he discovered that doing so helped with how quickly the mana soaked his muscles and bones. For some reason the process brought the corpses he had dismembered with his master to mind, and unconsciously, Mark started guiding the mana through his body according to the paths that Master Abrams had pointed out. This only increased the pain, but Mark's mind was too hazy to care.

Time blurred, and suddenly, Mark snapped to awareness. The pain was gone, and he found himself lying on his back in the middle of the cage, his body covered in grime. There was no mana rampaging through his body, and Mime had vanished. Had he imagined everything? Mark could tell that his body had a ravenous resilience that hadn't been there before, and even his mind seemed to have been reinforced, bringing his memories into even greater clarity. It was as if every one of his cells were desperate for nourishment, but rather than starving or eating each other, they remained completely stable.

After a moment of lying on the floor, Mark pushed himself up, moving slowly to conserve energy. His body was covered in grime and more than a little blood that had been expelled through his pores during the transformation he had just gone through. Mime was nowhere in sight, but Mark didn't care. She could clearly come and go as she wanted, and she was always around when he needed her, so there wasn't anything to worry about. Instead, Mark's thoughts were occupied by his new, clear memories.

Analyzing everything that had happened to him over the last few weeks, Mark's mind turned to Master Abrams. His master had vanished before Mark was carted off to Gray Rock, and Mark couldn't shake the unsettling feeling that something was wrong. He didn't know if it was intuition or something else, but whenever he thought of Master Abrams, a dull ache filled his chest. His only consolation was that Abrams was more than capable of taking care of himself, so he was probably fine.

With a clang the door opened again, interrupting Mark's thoughts as a beam of light spilled across the floor. A guard carried in a tray and placed it on the ground outside the cage. After making sure that Mark was far enough back, he picked up a loaf of bread and a bowl of thick stew and slid them through the bars. When the door closed, Mark finally moved, crawling across the floor to the food. The bread and stew weren't good, but they were sustenance, and Mark didn't leave a single crumb behind. He had been a bit surprised to see how generous the prison was with its portions. Though it made sense when he considered how much more fuel empowered bodies required.

Slowly he sat up, his body weak. The shackles on his arms and legs were still working as they had before, filling his body with a chaotic flow of mana that brought about a deep fatigue. Sensing something curious, Mark glanced down at the bracelet on his right wrist. The hazy feeling started to solidify, and faint glowing lines began to appear on the shackle. The lines shifted and moved as they coursed around the shackle in a twisting loop. Mark's forehead furrowed.

As his eyes traced the lines, he saw they extended into his own body, or more accurately, extended from it, running along the needle that poked out of the metal shackle and pierced into his skin. As they ran up his arm, the lines began to spread out, dividing into thousands of smaller lines that formed an always-shifting web.

"Is that . . . is that mana?"

Mark's whispered question rang loudly in the darkness. Looking at his other wrist, he saw lines appearing on it as well. Shocked and more than a little excited, he turned his gaze to the bars and soon perceived the same lines running through them, reinforcing the thick metal.

There was no question in Mark's mind now about what he was seeing. Somehow, he was able to observe the flow of mana in the world around him, which should have been completely impossible. Mark had always been taught that mana was fundamentally invisible, impossible to see with the naked eye, and almost impossible to see with any sort of equipment. It could be detected but never observed . . . yet Mark was able to not just see it but see it clearly.

The longer he looked at the mana flowing from his arm into the shackle, the more familiarity he felt with it. It looked almost like a string, and he had the strangest sensation that if he willed, he'd be able to reach out and touch it. Curious, Mark did exactly that, stretching out his left index finger to tap one of the lines of mana on his right wrist. Though he knew full well he wasn't actually touching anything, Mark felt slight resistance when his finger intersected with the line, and then the mana shifted its path, flowing around his finger.

For the briefest of moments, the flow of mana was disrupted, and Mark felt the weakness that had been plaguing him fade. Almost immediately, the line of mana reconnected, and the weakness returned, but he was so shocked by what he had just done that he didn't even register it. When he recovered from his surprise, he didn't continue with his experiments, afraid of attracting the guards' attention. After all, they were probably monitoring the shackles, so if Mark suddenly turned his off, it was likely to attract attention.

Instead of continuing to play with the shifting mana, he sat back and began considering what he was experiencing. The nest he had swallowed had focused entirely on external mana control, and that seemed to be what Mark was now tapping into. He hadn't been sure if by absorbing the nest he would be able to pick up another ability, yet that was exactly what had happened. Unfortunately, the guards had stripped him of his activator, but he had the faint sense that the empty slot in his genetic memory ability had been filled.

Of course, understanding the ability would take a lot more work and exploration, but if Mark's assumptions were correct, he had just picked up a truly astonishing power. Affecting mana was something that only energy controllers could do—though from what he understood, they couldn't actually shape mana freely but instead pulled it together or dispersed it in preset patterns.

The nest had exercised almost complete control over the entirety of the underground facility at Felwer Mine and had been able to not only power up but even direct the facility's defenses. Even a fraction of that power would make Mark a force to be reckoned with. He had never heard of anybody who could directly control the flow of mana . . .

Focusing on the web of mana running through his body that was disrupting his abilities, Mark poked at it and watched the mana shift around his finger. On a whim, he tried to will the mana that had just moved to remain in place as he pulled his finger away, and for a moment it did. He was so surprised that he lost focus and the mana shifted back to where it had been before.

Excited by his discovery, Mark continued to experiment on his body, trying to manipulate the mana the shackles were spreading. Once a day the guards would come in, interrupting his tests, but they didn't seem to notice anything different about him, and after banging on his cage with their clubs, they'd toss down the food they brought and then leave, shutting him in the darkness again.

Mark soon found that while he could affect the flow of mana in his body, doing so used up mental energy, and after a few minutes, his head would start to feel tight. If he persisted, it would begin to ache, and any further attempts to control mana would produce a splitting headache. After he rested, the ache would fade and he could use his power again, and Mark soon fell into a steady rhythm of practicing his mana control and resting.

Though he wasn't sure about the passage of time, Mark could tell that everything about him was changing. His decision to consume the Exlian nest that Mime had squirreled away had been born of equal parts ambition and anger. It didn't take a genius to figure out that his unjust imprisonment had been engineered by someone who had it out for him, and Andre Javesi, city councilman and the father of one of Mark's best friends, Noah, was clearly involved. Though he had played the good guy, showing up after Mark had been stewing for a few days and offering a devil's bargain, Mark wasn't fooled. Rather than take it, Mark had opted for jail, which was how he'd ended up with cuffs on his ankles and wrists.

The more he interacted with the shackles, the clearer Mark's sense of how they worked became. Their function was simple. They disrupted the mana that flowed naturally through his body by forcing it into a wide, chaotic web. This web prevented his powers from activating and continually threatened his balance, disorienting him.

Mark soon found a trick that helped. So long as he concentrated on the mana and willed it to calm down, the effect would lessen. This didn't erase the disorientation completely, but it reduced it enough that he could regain control of his body. Doing so took every ounce of his concentration at first, but then he had a stroke of genius. Rather than maintain his focus, he used the quantum clone ability he had picked up from his former lieutenant to partition off a small piece of his mind, setting it to the task while freeing up the majority of his brain to work on other things.

This was a trick he had discovered back in the mine, and it allowed him to maintain the level of concentration he needed to be able to operate his body normally while also thinking about and doing other things. The first time he tried using a mental clone to manipulate the mana flow from the shackles, he found it worked tenuously at best and often accidentally broke his concentration, causing weakness to flood back through him. The longer he practiced, however, the more adept he became, and soon he felt confident in his ability to keep the disorientation at bay.

Slowly climbing to his feet, Mark took a moment to adjust to standing up. This wasn't the first time he had done so, but every time he did, he found himself needing to recalibrate his balance to avoid pitching over onto his face. It was one thing to get used to the disorienting effect of the shackles while sitting, and entirely another to do it while standing.

Mark had discovered that while the mana web the shackles produced left him feeling weak, it didn't stop him from accessing his abilities. He wasn't sure exactly why this was, but he welcomed it wholeheartedly. He was wary of being watched, as undoubtedly there were cameras hidden somewhere in the room, but he had tested his transformational ability while hiding his arm and was excited to discover that it still worked, allowing him to shift his arms into bone blades.

He had yet to try his null field ability, but he was confident that would work, as he could feel the strange pocket of energy that would void the mana in the surrounding area lurking in the back of his neck. His quantum clones still worked perfectly as well, though Mark hadn't tried making a visible clone, only a mental one to help him keep focused. His regeneration worked also, which meant that Mark, to all intents and purposes, still had access to all his powers. He could only imagine what would happen to him if the warden or the prison guards found out.

On shaky feet, he began to practice his martial arts to calm himself down and keep himself from going crazy in the deep darkness. The more he practiced, the smoother his wobbly stance became, and after a few days he felt like he had fully grasped the trick to maintaining his balance. Mark slowly rotated between manipulating the mana in his body, practicing his martial arts, and resting quietly at the center of the room. A few times the two guards who had brought his bread and stew paused to watch him through the bars.

"He's a bit young to be in here, isn't he?" one of the guards whispered. "What's he in here for?"

"Not sure, but it's gotta be murder, or something like it," the other guard said, much less interested. "That's the only reason people get tossed in here."

"Hard to believe somebody that young would kill someone else in cold blood."

Mark ignored the two guards, focusing on maintaining his concentration. He knew it was a waste of time to try to defend himself against the guards' slander. When he heard the door close behind them and the room was plunged into darkness once more, he let out a long breath.

An hour later, after he had eaten and done his stretches, Mark was just considering what test to run next when the door banged open again and he heard the tromp of boots. There were four people this time, three guards and an officer, and they stopped in front of Mark's cage. The only light in the room came in from the doorway, casting the guards' shadows across Mark. Slowly, he opened his eyes and stood up. Anytime this officer arrived, someone was removed from a cage, and since Mark was the last person in this room, he figured it was his turn next.

"Time to go," the officer said, and with a click, the metal door swung open.

Before the guards could step into the cage to grab him, Mark strolled out, causing all the guards to take a wary step back. The officer had an ugly look on his face, and Mark could see him glancing at the shackles on Mark's limbs, clearly wondering why they were not working properly. Not wanting to be a threat, Mark stood in place quietly. After glancing at him, the officer didn't ask any questions and just waved for Mark to follow. He led the way out of the room, down a short hallway filled with light, and into a small office, where he took a seat at a desk.

"Mark Fields?"

The officer looked Mark up and down a couple of times and then consulted his paper. There was a flash of confusion and even something resembling sympathy in his eyes, but by the time he looked up, they were indifferent once more.

"Yes."

"Your body has stabilized sufficiently that you'll be moved to the Tomb in the next batch. We're assigning you to a two-month stay in holding center 7B until then. You'll have a bunkmate whose name is Arthur, and he'll show you the ropes. Stay out of trouble and you won't get thrown back in solitary. Any questions?"

"What is the Tomb?"

Looking him over, the officer smirked and lifted Mark's profile. "It's where everyone who the world considers dead goes. But don't worry, you'll still be able to contribute to society."

The officer waved his hand, and two of the large, burly guards escorted Mark out of the room, down the hall, and into an enclosed car that shot along a rail like a high-speed train. At this point, Mark knew that they were no longer under Gray Rock Prison, but where they were, he had no idea. When it stopped, Mark was brought to a guard post, past which was a large common room where roughly one hundred prisoners lounged around. Some sat by the wall on stools, while others chatted in small groups at the scattered tables. When the guards came out, bringing Mark with them, the prisoners hardly paid them any attention, though Mark could feel more than one gaze lingering on him when he wasn't looking.

Mark's cell was roughly twelve feet wide and eighteen feet long. It wasn't a large space but was enough for a toilet, a sink, and a set of bunk beds. The door was hanging open, much like the doors to the other cells Mark had seen on his way there, and they seemed to be remotely controlled. After pointing at the bed, one of the guards grunted that this was where Mark would stay. Without another word, the two guards left, and Mark took a deep breath and sat down on the lower bunk. He had been there for a few minutes when another prisoner wandered in, eyes narrowing as he sized up Mark. He wore the same dull-gray uniform that Mark wore, but somehow it seemed to fit him better, leading Mark to wonder if the clothing had been modified.

"I'm Arthur," the prisoner said. "You must be Mark."

"Yes, sir. Mark Fields."

With a smirk, Arthur shook his head. "You better cut that right out, kid, especially if you want to survive in here."

This time, it was Mark's turn to narrow his eyes. So far, the only time he had spent in Gray Rock was in the cage he had been tossed into, and though initially some of the other prisoners had been rather belligerent, that hadn't lasted. Mark could only imagine, however, what throwing a bunch of empowered criminals together into a prison would do. It didn't frighten him, but he also had no desire to get caught up in fights, so he nodded. "Thanks for the advice."

"Don't worry about it. I'm assuming they've put you in here because they want to give you a chance to get used to everything. If they'd given you anybody else as a roommate, you'd likely end up stabbed before the night was through."

His forehead wrinkling, Mark glanced out at the central room, where the other prisoners were gathered. "Is it really that dangerous?"

"It is when you're on the bottom of the heap, and believe me, everyone who comes in as fresh meat is on the bottom of the heap."

Just then, there was a loud chime, and everyone began to wander toward the end of the common room. Walking to the door of their cell, Arthur gestured for Mark to follow him. "Come on, that's the dinner bell. Let's go get some food. I can answer some of your questions along the way. Maybe introduce you to some people it'd be good to know."

Getting up, Mark joined Arthur, and they followed the crowd. Nobody moved particularly quickly, and Mark could sense an intense wariness among the prisoners as they were funneled into a narrow hallway. They were currently underground, and he didn't see any clocks, so he had to take it for granted that Arthur was telling the truth and that the chime he had heard was the dinner bell. He still had no idea how much time had passed since his arrest or whether any of his friends had any idea where he was. The whole process had happened so quickly Mark wasn't sure what to think.

The cafeteria was massive, nearly four times the size of the large room his cell connected to, and the line snaked all the way around the outside of the room. Thankfully it moved quite quickly, and once they got up to the counter, Mark understood why. There was no selection, and as each prisoner stepped up to the counter, they were handed a tray with a plate of food portioned into small, separate sections and a drink in a blue bottle.

After getting his food, Arthur led Mark to one of the long tables to sit down. As they walked through the cafeteria, Arthur occasionally nodded to other prisoners and received nods in return. For the most part, everyone kept their heads down and focused on eating, and as they took their seats, Arthur opened his bottle and took a drink. "The food's good, at least as far as prison food goes, but you're going to want to eat fast."

Sensing the slight tension in Arthur's voice, Mark picked up his fork and glanced around. "Why, is something going to happen?"

"Just keep your head down and eat your food," Arthur said.

Mark's biofuel was starting to run low again, so he began shoveling food into his mouth. Either Arthur's palate was seriously warped or he had just been flat-out lying, because the food was disgusting. Mark almost spat out the first bite he put into his mouth, despite the fact that he was used to sucking down tubes of nutrient paste without any trouble. This tasted at least a dozen times worse, but Mark could feel the nutrients it contained immediately breaking down in his body and replenishing his starving cells.

In truth, Mark didn't actually care how bad something tasted, as what he needed was energy, and energy in a high volume. Within a couple of minutes, he had slurped up every bit of food on his plate and finished his drink as well. Arthur, who was less than a quarter of the way through his plate, gave Mark a bemused look. "Hungry much?"

"Starved."

"I wondered about that," Arthur said. "You're looking a bit thin around the cheekbones. Here, I eat too much anyway. You can have this."

Mark hesitated for a moment as Arthur pushed his tray across the table, and then, with a nod, grabbed it. Arthur watched him, occasionally taking a sip from his bottle, while surreptitiously glancing to the right and to the left every once in a while. As he finished the extra food, Mark was going to ask what Arthur was looking for, and then he saw it. Around four tables away, a small group of prisoners stood up as another prisoner came walking by. No words were exchanged, though Mark caught the fierce glance between them, before two of the prisoners who had stood up jumped the other man.

They wielded no weapons and used no powers, but Mark could hear the heavy thwack of an empowered fist slamming into the prisoner's cheekbone. Almost immediately, the surrounding empowered jumped up and ran, heading away from the fight as fast as possible. Vaulting over the table, the third prisoner in the group joined in the scrap, and for a moment, the air was filled with flying fists and sharp curses as the four fought one another fiercely.

Arthur let out a sigh and put down his bottle. "Well, you picked an exciting day to come into the prison."

"What's going on?" Mark asked, still watching the fight.

"Nothing particularly important. Likely a fight over commissary goods. The result will be rather annoying, though: Since it's more than two people, we'll likely have to stay in the cell for a couple of days."

A large, empty area had formed around the four prisoners who were fighting, or rather the three prisoners beating the tar out of the fourth. Looking around, Mark noticed that the guards were conspicuously absent.

"Shouldn't somebody step in?" he asked.

"What for?" came the callous reply. "The guards don't discriminate between people who attack and people who defend themselves. If you're involved at all, you get to be involved in the punishment too."

"But he might die," Mark said, his eyes fixed on the now-unconscious prisoner still being pummeled.

"So the world will have one less murderer." Arthur shrugged. "No one in here is innocent."

Just as Mark thought that might actually be the outcome, a loud horn blast filled the air, and a few dozen guards with light armor rushed in, carrying small shields and batons that crackled with energy. The prisoners quickly moved aside, but the guards applied the batons liberally to anyone in their way, and when they arrived at the group of three still kicking at the unconscious man they had assaulted, they fell on them without mercy.

Mark heard the faint crack of a bone snapping and the shriek that accompanied it. A moment later, the shriek cut off as a few of the guards beat the three prisoners who had launched the attack into unconsciousness. A couple of minutes later, all the prisoners had been subdued and unceremoniously dragged out of the room.

"They'll get a bit of basic medical attention and then be thrown into solitary," Arthur said. "Long story short, it's absolutely not worth it to get caught up in the fights."

"You said that fight was over commissary goods? What's that?"

"Ah, to be young again," Arthur said, patting Mark on the shoulder. "Come on, we'll head back to the cell and settle down. Take a good look around, because it'll be the last time that you'll see the outside for the next two days. Mark my words."

The doors to the cafeteria were opened once the guards had exited, and Mark followed Arthur at a casual pace back to the cell.

"You're on the top bunk," Arthur said. "I'm down here. I know you don't have any stuff right now, but you can keep your things in that basket. Just remember that they get searched every week, so if you have anything that you don't want the guards to find, that's not the place for it. Now, I feel like we were talking about something. What was it?"

"You were going to help me understand why the commissary was worth starting a fight over."

Sitting down on his bed and unlacing his boots, Arthur pulled them off and began to massage his left foot. "Prison life is pretty simple, especially here in Gray Rock. You just experienced dinnertime. Breakfast happens in the morning and is announced with a horn that has two blasts. Dinner happens in the evening, one blast. We don't get lunch, but believe me, as filling as the food is, there's not really any need for it."

Mark, of course, begged to differ, but he didn't want to contradict Arthur, so he just nodded along.

"Apart from eating, people spend their time doing one of two things. You can either laze around, or you can get a job. There are a variety of things that the prison will allow us to do, and if you apply for and are accepted to one of those jobs, well, you can earn a bit of credit. The labor we do is mostly unskilled, though there are a few jobs for people with particular talents, so if you've got one, make sure you let the quartermaster know. He's in charge of assigning people to tasks."

After putting his foot down, Arthur kicked off his other boot and began to massage his right foot. "Of course, if working isn't your thing, you can just hang out, though I don't recommend it, as it often leads to trouble. Regardless of what you decide, if you have the credits to spare, you can go to the commissary. It's open for each block once a week. Our day is Tuesday, which is about three days from now. Commissary is really like any other kind of market. You can buy what you need so long as you have the money. Of course, this is prison, but you can still find some nice things. Otherwise, that's about it. The best thing to do, if you want to survive in Gray Rock, is to keep your head down and stay out of other people's way."

Mark, who had been planning on doing exactly that, at least for the time being, nodded. "Sounds good to me."

Just then, a loud chime sounded, and with a rumble, the doors began to shut. Mark was slightly surprised to see that nobody had stayed out in the center of the room; it appeared that everyone had gone back into their cells. As if able to guess what he was thinking, Arthur laughed and got up, walking over to the bars and leaning against them, looking out into the central room.

"It won't take you long to pick up the unspoken rules," he said. "We'll be in here for the next two days because of the fight, and then they'll let us wander around again. But since we've got a couple of days to kill, I'm really curious how someone as young as you ended up in here."

Smiling slightly, Mark shrugged. "It's a pretty long and complicated story, and I'm not sure that I even have all the details of it. It's been a bit of a whirlwind."

Giving Mark an appraising look, Arthur nodded. "You came from the military?"

"Yes, Engineering Corps."

"Huh. Maybe that's one of the reasons they tossed you in here with me. I was in the Engineering Corps too. Well, it's nice to have another wrench head here to talk to. There aren't very many of us in the prison. Few of the crimes engineers commit are bad enough to land us in Gray Rock."

Turning, Arthur flashed a smile at Mark. "I know it goes without saying, but you'll need to be careful of the people you meet in here. For the most part, everybody's on good behavior. Except, of course, for the occasional dustup, like the one you just saw. But at the end of the day, there isn't a single person in this facility that isn't a stone-cold killer inside."

Seeing Arthur tapping himself on the chest, Mark's eyes narrowed. "That include you?"

"Of course it does," Arthur replied. "When I say 'everybody,' I mean everybody. You only get into Gray Rock if your crime is bad. But a surprising number of us just want to live out the rest of our lives in peace and quiet so we can avoid being buried in the Tomb."

Perking up, Mark leaned forward. "The officer who sent me here mentioned the Tomb and a batch going there soon. But he didn't tell me what it is."

Walking back to his bed, Arthur flopped down on it.

"The Tomb is the real reason that people who come to Gray Rock don't ever leave," he said, his voice lowering to a hushed whisper. "It's a massive facility underground where the real criminals go. Mass murderers and people like that. This part of the prison is a cakewalk in comparison. They send a convoy down to the Tomb once every three months to drop off prisoners, and getting called up right before the convoy goes down is called a death knell."

Just as Arthur had predicted, the doors to their cell didn't open for a day and a half. During that time, Arthur and Mark had plenty to chat about. Arthur was an easy conversationalist, seemed more than happy to share insights about the prison, and knew how to avoid sensitive topics. Over the course of the day, Mark learned that Arthur was a D-ranked empowered with B-ranked telekinesis. Of course, the shackles he wore prevented Arthur from being able to access his ability, and when Mark asked if any prisoners in Gray Rock could still use their abilities, Arthur snorted and shook his head. "Do you know what kind of havoc that would cause? Of course, there are certain categories of power that simply can't be blocked. Endurance, physical strength, things like that. And if you run into those sorts of prisoners, pray that you don't get into a fight."

Mark was sitting on the floor against the wall across from the bed, and hearing the annoyance in Arthur's voice, he leaned forward with a grin. "That sounds like a story."

Rolling his eyes, Arthur snorted again. "I've had my fair share of run-ins, but believe me, as much as you can avoid them, you want to. Thankfully, most of those people have been sent to the Tomb already, so it's unlikely you'll ever run into them."

Mark still hadn't mentioned to Arthur that he was going to

be heading to the Tomb with the next prisoner convoy, but he was eager to find out as much as he could before he went, so he pressed Arthur for more information. "Do you have particular people like that in mind?"

Glancing at Mark, Arthur nodded. "A couple of the gang leaders fall into those categories. Rock of the Syndicate and Coriolis, the leader of Viper Clan, are two good examples. Both of them have mainly physical power sets, which makes them especially dangerous. Rock has strength and endurance, while Coriolis has an unbelievable level of agility."

"Those were the two main gangs you mentioned, right? The Syndicate and Viper Clan?"

"Yes. And if I were you, I'd steer clear of all that nonsense. There's no faster way to get yourself into a bind than start messing with the gangs. Actually, your bunk used to belong to someone who didn't heed my advice."

"What happened to him?"

With a savage grin, Arthur raked his thumb across his throat. "He started working for one of the gangs as an informant. Another gang found out and didn't like it. And do you know what the penalty for killing another prisoner is?" Arthur sat up from where he had been lying on his bed and began to pull his boots on. "A month of solitary."

"Wait, that's it?"

"That's it."

Stamping his feet down into his boots, Arthur stood without bothering to lace them. As he stretched, a loud horn echoed through the prison, and the doors to their cells slid open.

"Come on, we better get some exercise. It's important to move around while you can, because you never know when they'll lock down everything again."

Jumping up, Mark followed Arthur out into the large central

room. Other prisoners had started to drift out of their cells as well. As they walked, Arthur began to introduce Mark to the various amenities the prison offered.

"Guard post. You'll head there if you need to talk to the guards about something, or if you need access to the infirmary. You've already seen the cafeteria, and we'll head there in a couple of hours when they blow the dinner horn. Through that door is where you'll find the commissary. You can only get in on your day, so tomorrow I'll take you in and show you around, and we can talk to Paul about getting you a job and a credit account. There's a gym through there, but I'd steer clear of it, as that's where the Syndicate hangs out."

"What does the Syndicate do?"

"Protection, racketeering, smuggling, you name it. They're involved in everything you can imagine organized crime might be. The guards turn a blind eye to most of their activities, since some of the higher-ups are on the take. Unless things get too violent, of course."

As they finished their tour and headed back toward their cell, a group of prisoners suddenly stood from where they had been seated at one of the tables and headed in Mark and Arthur's direction. Hearing a groan from Arthur, Mark took a better look at the prisoners and realized that all of them wore their uniforms with the right sleeves rolled up.

"Viper Clan," Arthur said under his breath. "Let me handle this." Stepping forward, he lifted his hands. "Hold on."

"Get out of the way, Arthur. We want to talk to the new blood."

"Can't you at least give him time to settle in?"

"No. Orders are orders, and these ones come from up top. If you don't get out of the way, you're going to have a problem with us."

His face paling, Arthur opened his mouth to say something,

but Mark reached out and grabbed his shoulder, pulling him back.

"It's all right," Mark said, giving Arthur a reassuring glance. "I'm sure these fine gentlemen are just here to make friends."

A couple of the prisoners smirked, but the man in the lead, who was bald and had a snake tattoo running up his neck and onto his cheek, gave Mark an appraising glance.

"You'd do well to become our friend, new blood. My name is Asp. I represent Coriolis of the Viper Clan. We're looking for someone to do a small favor for us, and we thought you might be interested."

"What kind of small favor?" Mark asked, scanning the men behind Asp. They all looked tough, but the sort of tough that came from posturing and hanging around other humans. To Mark, it smelled like weakness.

"There's someone who's been a bit of an annoyance, speaking of things they shouldn't," Asp said, his eyes drifting past Mark to land on Arthur. "We'd like you to help us do something about it. You know, make sure his mouth stays shut. We don't care how you do it, just that you do."

With a nasty smile on his lips, Asp's wrist twisted, and a short metal spike appeared in his palm, glinting gray in the bright lights.

Arthur had taken a step back, his expression hard, but while they had been talking, another group of Viper Clan thugs had drifted around behind them, sealing off Arthur's retreat.

"You want me to kill my bunkmate?" Mark asked, staring at Asp like he was crazy.

Taking a step forward, Asp flashed a nasty smile. "If that's what it'll take to keep his mouth shut, then that's what you're going to have to do."

Considering it for a moment, Mark reached out and took the metal spike from Asp's hand. He sensed Arthur tensing, as if he were about to make a run for it, but before he could, Mark shook his head and held up the makeshift weapon Asp had handed him. "And I'm supposed to do it with this piece of junk? You have to be joking."

Holding the shiv in his fingers, Mark flicked it, and the end of the weapon sheared clean off, clattering to the ground. The sound was so sudden that most of the thugs jumped in surprise. Dropping the now-dull metal stick in Asp's palm, Mark took a step forward, his own gaze growing hard.

"I'm new to this whole thing, so I don't quite understand whatever power dynamic you think you have going on. But if you approach me like this again or make any more of these idiotic requests, I'll take whatever weapon you have and use it to sew your lips shut. Don't bother me with this kind of nonsense anymore."

Mark had fully expected Asp to flare up. Instead, his face neutral, Asp nodded and took a step back.

"Fine," he said, holding up his hands. "I got it, loud and clear."

Taking another step back, he flashed a grin that didn't reach his eyes. "Since you're new here, I'll enlighten you on a small rule that your buddy Arthur probably didn't tell you. You only get one chance."

As he finished speaking, he gestured, and one of the thugs behind him transformed into a blur as he darted around Mark. Pivoting, he stabbed the metal spike he held toward the back of Mark's head. Though Mark was caught off guard by the attack, his response was instantaneous. His right foot slid forward, and his body leaned out of the way of the stab. With his weight swinging forward, he spun on his heel and his hands came up. There was no hesitation in his movements, and as his left palm deflected the stab, his right hand shot out, two fingers pointed. His counterattack landed as the prisoner was shifting forward, and his two fingers pierced a hole through the attacker's throat.

Before the prisoner realized he had been struck, Mark's foot snapped out, kicking the prisoner's ankle sharply to knock his feet out from under him. That combined with the tug on his arm forced the attacker horizontal, and then gravity took hold and he slammed face-first into the ground. The movement was so smooth and fluid that no one registered it until after the attacker had crashed to the ground and blood began pouring out of the hole in his throat. With a twist of his wrist, Mark flicked the blood from the ends of his fingers and looked down at the dying prisoner impassively.

Suddenly, a loud siren ripped through the shocked silence, and the doors that led out to the guard post burst open. A dozen guards in riot gear raced in, their eyes scanning for threats. The other prisoners, shocked by the sudden death, weren't moving, so it took the guards a moment to figure out where the problem was, and it wasn't until they saw the growing pool of blood under the unmoving prisoner's body that they rushed over. By the time they arrived, the prisoner who had attacked Mark had bled out, and as they gathered around, they seemed at a loss.

"What happened here?" the guard captain asked, his eyes sweeping the gathered prisoners.

No matter where he looked, however, all he got was neutral stares and the occasional shrug. Mark, who had fully expected the others to turn him in, was surprised. When he glanced at Asp, he found the Viper Clan lieutenant glaring at him with hate-filled eyes, but when the guard captain asked Asp what happened, his expression became blank and he muttered something noncommittal. Obviously, no matter how much they disliked each other, the prisoners had no interest in helping the guards.

Despite this, it was clear to the guards what was going on, especially after they had reviewed the footage of the incident. At the captain's command Mark was seized and dragged to a holding cell similar to the one he had originally been stuffed into. He was escorted there by six wary guards who all kept their shields up as Mark walked between them. After throwing Mark in the cell, they left, plunging the room into darkness.

Blinking as his eyes adjusted to the lack of light, Mark looked around. There was one other person locked up in the cage across from him. The man hopped up and walked to the bars of his cage, peering through them at Mark.

"Nice of you to come keep me company. I've been bored out of my mind."

With a mirthless smile, Mark shrugged. "I wasn't given much of a choice."

"Ha, I understand that. I'm never given much of a choice either. What did you do, kill someone?" Seeing Mark's short nod, the man let out a loud laugh. "You know, sometimes you just have to. Some people just have that look about them. You know, you look at their face and you think to yourself, 'You'd be much better as a corpse.'"

Accompanying his morbid words with a wide grin, the man tapped on the bars. "Let me guess, they've got you on 7B. Well, you won't be there for long if you make a habit of killing people. Soon, you'll be assigned deeper. But don't worry, that's where the real fun is. I'm Joker, by the way."

As the prisoner spoke, Mark could feel a subtle shift in the air around him, though it was hard to place exactly what was going on. Joker was clearly genuinely mad, but as dangerous as the man seemed, his easy smile carried a warm congeniality that made it hard for Mark to resist responding.

"Mark."

"What a boring name. Don't worry. Once you come to the Tomb, we'll get you a cool name. Like mine. Joker. Isn't it cool? I got it because I love telling jokes. And not because I once dressed up in a clown suit made of other people's skin."

After pausing for a second, Joker burst out laughing again. "Ha, that was a joke. You should have seen your face."

Chuckling, Joker stepped away from the bars and sat down. "Anyway, nice to meet you, Mark. I'm only in here for another day or so, and after that, you'll be on your own. Unless, of course, one of the others decides to pop in for a visit. You know, it's getting harder these days to coordinate our stays. Finding tickets is becoming a bit of a challenge."

Joker continued to prattle on for a while, but as Mark had stopped responding, he eventually fell silent. Mark genuinely didn't know what to make of the madman, though he was starting to believe Arthur's claim that no one in the prison was good. Just as Joker had said, the next day, he was escorted from the cages. As he left, he gave Mark a wink and a wave, and then Mark was alone. For the next week, he remained by himself except when his food arrived. Then a couple of guards entered the room and unlocked his cage, much to his surprise. They escorted him to an office, where he found himself facing a colonel.

The colonel gave Mark a long, hard look and shook his head. "Prisoner Fields, the first time you were put in solitary, it was to give you a chance to get used to your shackles, as they can be quite disorienting. This time, however, it was assigned as punishment for killing another prisoner. Normally, the punishment would be considerably more severe, but in this case, after reviewing the footage, it has been determined that you were acting in self-defense. Still, killing other prisoners is not allowed. And if it happens again, self-defense or not, you will find the punishment significantly more severe. Now, you will be escorted back to your cell, and I sincerely hope that I will not see you again."

"Thank you, sir," Mark said, bowing his head slightly.

Clearly irritated, the officer waved him off, and Mark was escorted back through the tunnel to the common room. A few people glanced his way when he stepped inside, and as Mark scanned the prisoners sitting at the tables, most of them gave him wary looks. He couldn't blame them, of course, and had he been in their position, he would have been wary too. Mark didn't see Arthur or Asp, though he did spot a few people from Viper Clan across the room. For a moment, he considered walking over, but then, deciding it was a better idea to keep his head down, he turned and headed for his cell. Arthur was sitting on the bed when he walked in, and the older man jumped up, his eyes wide as he stared at Mark. Noticing the black eye and puffy lip Arthur was sporting, Mark greeted him with a smile and wave.

Arthur goggled at him. "How . . . ? What are you . . . ? I thought you'd still have at least a couple of weeks."

"Me too." Mark shrugged. "I guess they let me out for good behavior."

"You killed somebody. They don't give good behavior for that."

Scratching his chin, Mark shrugged again. "They said self-defense, which it was. He attacked me, and it's not my fault my combat instincts are honed to perfection."

The lightness in Mark's tone seemed to put Arthur at ease, and with a chuckle, he suddenly grinned and stepped forward, patting Mark on the shoulder. "And some combat instincts those were. I didn't even see you move, and then bam, he was on the floor. What was that?"

"Martial technique. It's called the Cutting Palm."

"Huh, I didn't think martial techniques worked against empowered."

"This one does," Mark said. "What happened to your eye?"

"Ran into somebody's fist," Arthur said, taking a seat back on the bed, as Mark crouched against the wall across from him. "The Viper Clan didn't like that you had downed one of their members. Asp must have felt like he had lost face or something, because they threw their weight around for a couple of days. I got dragged into one of the fights and ended up like this."

"What happened to them?" Mark asked, his eyes narrowing.

"Most of them are in the infirmary," Arthur said, his voice turning hard. "The other gangs didn't particularly appreciate Asp's attempts to reassert his authority."

"Do you think I'll have more trouble?"

"You? On this floor? Not even a chance. Nobody's going to risk having you poke a hole through their throat. But you have to watch yourself because if anyone else dies, you might get slated for the Tomb. So you better be careful."

"About that. I think I'm already headed there. On next month's convoy."

Arthur's face paled, and he stared at Mark for a long moment. "I'm sorry."

"No need," Mark said with a shrug. "It was actually decided from the beginning. They just stuck me here to have me wait. But speaking of the Tomb, I ran into somebody named Joker in the cells who brought it up." When Arthur's expression twisted at the mention of Joker's name, a bad feeling rose in Mark's heart.

Taking a moment before he responded, Arthur scratched his head. "Joker is bad news. But it doesn't make sense that you saw him out here. He was sent to the Tomb a few years ago. Rumor is he was a really dangerous serial killer when he was loose. I'm not saying you are lying, of course, but maybe it was a copycat on the way to the Tomb?"

Frowning, Mark slowly paced back and forth in the cell, trying to make sense of what Arthur was saying. After a few minutes he still couldn't come up with a clear answer, so he turned his attention to the original matter. "Now that you know I'm on my way to the Tomb, can you tell me a bit more about it?"

"Sure, at least what I know. The Tomb is actually a giant research facility of sorts, one that is run entirely by prisoners."

Mark could hear the clear fear in Arthur's voice. "What do you mean by 'run by prisoners'? How does that work?"

"There are no guards in the Tomb," Arthur said with a shrug. "The most powerful empowered criminals have been sent there. The rumors are that the only rule is strength, and if you want something, you have to have the power to take it. Of course, that doesn't mean there isn't some order. The most powerful have a council of sorts, and they establish the rules for the Tomb. In order to survive, they trade with the government of New Emery and ensure that the rest of the criminals stay in the Tomb. I don't know much more than that, but even before I was tossed in here, I heard that there are black markets where you can get all sorts of wild things and that most of the black market items come from the Tomb."

"Do you know who runs the Tomb? Or at least who is on that council?" Mark asked.

"I know that the major gangs all have areas there that they control. The Syndicate and Viper Clan each have presence, but other than that, I don't know. Typically, once prisoners head down to the Tomb, they don't come back, so I have no idea what the facility even looks like. What I do know is that only the strong survive down there. I've heard that people will kill you as soon as they look at you. It's not like up here, where order is generally maintained. If you're assigned to the Tomb, it's a free-for-all."

The next few days were relatively quiet, and Mark found himself slowly settling into prison life. Not wanting to draw any more attention than he had already, he spent most of his time in his cell, meditating or practicing the Cutting Palm. He found it slightly frustrating that he couldn't practice his abilities, especially the new mana control ability he had gotten from the nest. One day, after a quiet breakfast, he headed back to his cell and heard some whispers behind him. Word had clearly gotten out that he was on his way to the Tomb, and no one wanted to associate with him for fear they might suddenly find themselves thrown into the prisoner convoy with him.

Mark tried not to let it bother him, but he was starting to feel quite stifled and was even beginning to look forward to going to the Tomb. He was finding the prison more and more oppressive every moment, and he felt as if his senses were beginning to dull. He had realized that he would rather throw himself headfirst into danger than spend the rest of his life in this tepid environment.

When he arrived back at his cell, he found two people there. Arthur was standing at the back of the cell, holding something behind his back, while Asp was leaning against the bars, clearly waiting for him. When Mark walked up, Asp straightened. Though the signs of the beating he had received were fading, he still sported a gnarly purple bruise on the side of his cheek, where somebody had clearly tried to kick his face in.

Raising his eyebrow, Mark walked past Asp into the cell. "Here to ask me for another favor?"

Mark's voice wasn't aggressive, but Asp still took a slight step back, staying well out of arm's reach.

"No, I wasn't lying when I said there was only one chance. You've made your stance clear. I'm just here to make our stance clear too."

"No need," Mark said with a wave. "I'm not going to be around long. It's clear that I'm not suited to, well, this place, so I'm heading down to the Tomb in a week."

Asp's face paled, and he took another step back. "I know. And that's why I'm here. You chose not to join the Viper Clan, and you've been marked. That means that they'll try to kill you when you get to the Tomb. After I reported what happened, they told me not to worry about it, which means they've set their sights on making you a ticket."

Joker had used that word too, and Mark didn't know what it meant, but he could tell it wasn't positive.

"Thanks for the warning," Mark said, giving Asp a long look.

He had no idea why the gangster would decide to warn him, but he suspected that Asp was probably putting himself in danger to do it, which was something Mark wouldn't forget. Even if this was Asp's method of self-preservation, it still was a major favor in Mark's book. For a long moment, Asp didn't say anything, his face pale as he stared at Mark. And then, with a sharp nod, he turned and left. Mark watched him go and straightened up. When he turned around, Arthur was slipping the metal pipe he had been holding back into its hiding place.

"You really are nuts," he said, giving Mark a disbelieving look. "You seem like you're actually eager to go to the Tomb."

Mark flashed a lopsided smile. "It's just a bit boring up here, and from what everybody's said, the Tomb is much more exciting. I've no desire to waste away here for the rest of my life. If I'm going to be stuck in Gray Rock until I die, I may as well go out with a bang, right?"

It was a sentiment that Arthur obviously didn't share, and for the next few days, he seemed to be quietly avoiding Mark. On the third day, a guard came to get Mark and brought him to the office, where the officer in charge of the floor waved a paper in Mark's direction.

"You are being transferred," he said. "You're heading down to the ninth floor. Gather whatever things you have. It's time to go."

"I'm ready now, sir," Mark said, spreading his hands. "I don't actually have anything but what I'm wearing."

Escorted by a squad of four guards, Mark was brought to an elevator, which plunged down through the earth. When the door opened, he was escorted through a heavily guarded gate and loaded onto a railcar. Half a dozen other people were in cages there already, and after Mark was locked in his own cage, the guards hurried off the train and it began to move. From where he sat, Mark could see that the others were heavily restrained, and all but one sat motionless. That last prisoner was clearly insane, constantly throwing himself against the bars of his cage. Each time he did, there was a flash of lightning and the stench of scorched flesh filled the cabin.

The train car moved smoothly, and after close to half an hour, in which they switched directions a dozen times, the car came to a stop. With a click, the door slid open, revealing a dozen prisoners, who peered into the car, doing a quick count.

"Looks like everyone is here. We have seven fresh meat. One mad dog, five chattels, and what looks like a free agent."

Listening to the prisoners talk, Mark didn't say anything. He was the only prisoner on the train who wasn't muzzled, but until he knew more about his situation, he didn't think it wise to draw attention. One by one the cages were unloaded from the train car, and Mark saw hundreds of crates of other goods being unloaded as well. The crazy prisoner they had referred to as the mad dog had been carted off, and a group of prisoners was arguing over a list while gesturing in the direction of the other cages, which gave Mark the chance to look around. After some time, they finally reached a decision, and one by one the cages were opened. Each time, the prisoners entered, subdued the person in the cage, and carried them off. It wasn't particularly hard, since they were already heavily bound, and soon Mark was the only one left.

A large prisoner who looked almost as wide as he was tall had been standing nearby and leering at Mark for the last twenty minutes, and now, as Mark's cage opened, he suddenly pounced, squeezing himself into the cage. Mark could tell the man was stronger than him from the unrestrained aura that poured off his body, and he quickly tried to back up out of reach, only to be stopped by the bars of the cage. The man's eyes lit up, and he licked his lips as he stared at Mark and slowly reached his hand out. "Don't run, boy. I'm your new master."

A tremendous number of thoughts ran through Mark's head in that instant, but one thought superseded them all. This man had to die. No sooner had the man finished speaking than Mark sprang forward, one hand slicing at the inside of the man's wrist while his other hand shot toward his throat. At the last moment, the man's expression twisted and he slapped his own hand sideways with tremendous force. Mark barely managed to twist out of the way in the confines of the cage, but it still wasn't enough. Though the slap didn't touch him, Mark was still thrown back against the bars with bone-shaking force, his own attacks disrupted.

Lips pulling back to reveal his teeth, the man claiming to be Mark's new master pressed even farther into the cage as his hand clamped down on Mark's ankle. There was a crunch as his bones fractured under the tight grip, and dreadful pain shot up Mark's leg, but he didn't even twitch as he glared up at his attacker. Mind working furiously, Mark suddenly noticed a necklace around the man's neck, and a wild thought filled him.

The man was working to stick his other arm into the cage, while at the same time he pulled on Mark's leg, trying to drag him out. Rather than continue to resist, Mark shoved off the bars, practically flying into his attacker's chest. His leg was throbbing, but he ignored it as he attacked with both hands, targeting the necklace around the man's neck. With one hand he grabbed it, and with his other, he stabbed at the man's head.

When Mark's fingers connected, his attacker's skin glistened with a glimmering light as the mana fused into it blocked the attack. It was like striking steel, and Mark found his fingers glancing off, leaving faint red lines behind. Even as the man let out an evil chuckle and let go of Mark's ankle to reach for his back, Mark didn't stop. He struck again, this time targeting the man's eye, but his real attack came from the hand wrapped around the necklace.

Mark had noticed that the lines of mana running from the man's shackles were quite orderly, a clear sign that the man had figured out how to work within the disruptive flow the mana web produced. Mark knew from his experiments after eating the nest that any disruption to those lines would produce intense disorientation, and that was exactly what he focused on. With his hand wrapped around the necklace and his knuckles pushing into his opponent's throat, Mark focused his will on the orderly lines of mana, throwing them into disarray. As the mana trickling through the large man's body began to dance, a groan escaped his mouth, and his large body suddenly sagged as the mana inside him ran wild. Seizing his opportunity, Mark stabbed again, and this time his fingers weren't blocked. Rather than bounce off mana-reinforced skin, they tore through his would-be master's head, causing him to scream and thrash. As he gave a mighty heave to try to break free of the cage, the large man was unable to shake Mark free, and no matter how he retreated, Mark was right there.

By the third stab, Mark was covered in blood, but he didn't stop as he targeted vitals. He laid open his opponent's cheek and neck and even stabbed through his eye, blinding him and tearing a bloody gash across the man's head. From the first moment, Mark had realized that this was a life-and-death situation, and he was determined to choose life, even if it meant that his attacker had to die. There was a gurgle from the man's throat, and Mark felt a hand pawing weakly at his back, but he was supremely focused. His hand rose and fell once more, and the man went still. Releasing his grip on the necklace, Mark jumped back, his mind working furiously as he tried to anticipate what would come next. There were still a dozen other prisoners outside the cage, and Mark could hear them shouting. They had seen him attack through the bars, so there was no going back now.

"What's going on?"

"I think Gereg is dead. Look at all that blood."

"Ha, did he really just get killed? Drag him out of there."

Unable to gauge the situation from the flippant way the others were speaking, Mark watched warily as they grabbed the large man's legs and tugged him free from the cage's entrance. He was currently soaked in crimson blood and undoubtedly presented a savage picture, but the men didn't spare him more than half a glance. One of them heaved Gereg over, examined the wounds on the corpse's face and neck, and then nodded. "He is dead, all right."

Another of the men, a thin man who looked a lot like a vulture, stepped forward with gleaming eyes, rubbing his hands together.

"He's got a class-two apartment, doesn't he? It'll be empty now."

"You'll need his ID, and it's the kid's."

The man who'd responded was heavily muscled, and his body exuded a faint sense of power that overcame the suppression of his shackles, similar to the feeling that Gereg had given off, making Mark think that he was probably B ranked. The vulturelike man paused for a moment and then turned toward Mark, a threatening look in his eyes. Mark returned his stare evenly, then suddenly smiled. He wasn't sure what it was, since the situation he was in was genuinely terrible, but something about his current environment made his savage side incredibly happy. Under the measured gazes of the gathered prisoners, Mark walked out of the cage and stopped next to Gereg's corpse. "How do I collect his ID?"

Giving Mark an appraising look, the muscle-bound prisoner gestured to Gereg's watch. Mark had been so focused on surviving that he hadn't noticed that all the prisoners present were wearing watches.

"You killed him, so you can claim his citizenship slot. That comes with the authority to wear a watch."

Mark crouched to pull the watch from the corpse's arm, but he kept half an eye on the vulturelike prisoner, who was still staring at him with an openly hostile gaze. As Mark adjusted the band to fit on his wrist, the crowd started to disperse, and the vulturelike prisoner went with them, glancing back at Mark a couple of times. Only the muscle-bound prisoner remained.

The watch functioned exactly like other watches that Mark had used, though it didn't seem to be connected to the InfoWeb. At least, not the InfoWeb that Mark was used to. The Tomb had its own network, and Mark found everything from stores and services to forums, just like the regular InfoWeb had.

Once Mark had finished searching Gereg's body, the waiting prisoner gestured for him to follow. Mark observed him quietly as they walked. Like Mark, he had shackles around his wrists and ankles, but he moved with the steady assurance of someone who knew how to deal with the disruption they caused. When Mark examined him closely, he saw that the web of mana had been calmed, though Mark wasn't sure how.

The Tomb was located in a massive cavern at least a few miles long with a ceiling that loomed a mile overhead. The cavern extended down into the darkness like an endless abyss that might swallow everything at any moment. The Tomb itself was a gigantic, sprawling complex that filled almost the entire cavern.

Mark could see a few thin rail lines just like the one that he had come in on stretching out from the complex to thin tunnels in the cavern wall, but otherwise, the facility seemed to be floating freely in the air. It was disconcerting, to say the least, and Mark couldn't help but draw a sharp breath. The prisoner escorting him, clearly used to seeing such responses, didn't say a word as he let Mark take in the view.

They were currently standing on a separate platform connected to one of the rail lines, and Mark could see the prisoners completely deconstructing the train. It came apart in neat pieces that were stacked up and carried by cart to the edge of their floating platform, where there were smaller, detachable platforms. Peering out over the edge, Mark saw that the Tomb extended down into the pit, which seemed to have no end, continuing until it was swallowed in darkness.

"Come along. I'll send you to the Tomb and give you the introduction."

Seeing the skeptical look Mark gave him, the muscle-bound prisoner chuckled mirthlessly and held up his hands.

"Look at your watch. See that green light? That means you've been registered as a new citizen. If anyone tries to do anything to you before that light turns off, they'll lose their own citizenship. Think of it as a twelve-hour grace period. At the same time, it will make you a target for any chattels in the Tomb who fancy getting themselves a spot on the citizenship roll. As for why I'm telling you all this? If I give you the full introduction, I'll get paid one hundred merits, which is too much to pass up for such an easy job. Come on, I'll take you to the Tomb and show you where Gereg was staying. My name is Henry, by the way."

"What about his body?"

Shaking his head, Henry pointed toward the Tomb. In the distance, Mark could see a couple of dots flying across the abyss toward them. "Reapers are already on their way. His body will be turned over to Maestro for research. Even in death we get to contribute to humanity."

Mark wasn't able to detect any irony in Henry's words, and he couldn't help but wonder if most of the prisoners had a similar outlook. Walking to the edge of the platform they were on, Henry punched a code into a keypad, and with a grinding sound, the entire platform detached and began to move out across the gap toward the hanging complex.

In the distance, Mark could see hundreds of prisoners, though most of them weren't dressed like the prisoners on the seventh floor. The only way Mark could tell they were prisoners was by the shackles around their wrists. He didn't spot any guards, though as they got closer, he did notice a large metal figure that stood absolutely still at the corner of a street. All the prisoners who walked by gave it a wide berth, and occasionally, the large robot's eyes would flash as if scanning those who walked past.

It took almost fifteen minutes for the slow-moving platform to connect to the complex, and when it did, Henry punched in a code to lock it in place and gestured for Mark to follow him. "This is the Tomb. Everyone here is either chattel, a citizen, or an overseer. Chattels have no rights, and that is what you would have become if Gereg had managed to keep control over you. There are a limited number of citizen slots, and as a citizen you have the right to lease property, own goods, et cetera. Of course, if someone kills you, they get all your things, because everything you own is tied to your citizen ID."

"What happens if I collect multiple IDs?"

Mark's question was met with a cautious glance and a step farther away. "You can transfer property between IDs and then turn in extra IDs to the administrators for merits."

Though Mark wasn't planning on running around and collecting more citizen IDs, he had a strong suspicion that he would end up with a few.

As they walked through the Tomb, Mark looked around, observing the prisoners who walked this way and that. Most of them kept their heads down and hurried along, their wrists conspicuously bare. For every fifty prisoners without IDs, Mark spotted one prisoner, or rather citizen, who had a watch, and when he remarked on it, Henry nodded.

"The ratio is close to one citizen for every sixty chattels. This is where your apartment is."

Henry brought Mark to a building that looked a lot like a set of apartments he would have expected to see on the surface, and using his watch, Mark was able to open the door. The apartment he had inherited was on the fifth floor, and after going up the elevator, he found himself in a moderately sized set of rooms with the tackiest decorations he had ever seen. There was a bedroom with a massive bed that took up almost the entire room, a bathroom with a tub-and-shower combo, and a combined kitchen and living room with a large couch. Mark had expected the apartments to be more like the cell that he had stayed in on the seventh floor, so having multiple rooms came as a pleasant surprise. To Mark, it didn't feel like a prison at all, and that thought was further confirmed when he opened the closet and saw the wide range of oversize clothing that Gereg had left behind.

"I'd recommend taking some time to sort through Gereg's stuff," Henry said. "You'll find more information on your watch, but the most important rule is pretty simple. Never mess with Maestro's robots."

Giving Henry a quizzical look, Mark closed the closet door and took a seat on the couch.

"Maestro is the true ruler of the Tomb. He's the only S-ranked empowered down here, and he makes the robots."

"S ranked? How on earth are they keeping him trapped here?"

"Trapped?" Henry shook his head, a strange expression on his face. "Maestro isn't trapped. He created the Tomb. They wouldn't let him conduct his research on the surface, so he made the Tomb. Now he trades the results of his research with the government on the surface for supplies, and they send him prisoners for his experiments. He only cares about his experiments, so as long as you don't bother him or disrupt something he is working on, you shouldn't have any issues."

"What about gangs? I've heard there are different forces down here."

Henry leaned against the table and tapped himself on the chest with a smile. "There are. The League runs things, but there are only two main groups you'll want to be aware of. First, the

Syndicate, which I am part of. We are mostly involved in things like moving goods, and we control most of the shops in the Tomb. Our leader, Rock, is one of the A-ranked empowered in the League. Then the Viper Clan runs the gambling houses and the brothels. They're a mean bunch if you are on their bad side. Coriolis, their leader, is in the League as well. Then there are a few others, but those are the big ones. Speaking of factions, I recommend you find one to work with. Gereg was a member of the Syndicate, like me, so the citizen ID you hold belongs to us."

Hearing the implicit threat in Henry's words, Mark sat up, his gaze growing hard, and Henry quickly held up his hands. "Slow down. There is no need to attack me. The boss is pretty strict about these things, but if you get another citizen ID, you can turn this one in, and everything will be fine. Or you can just join us."

Relaxing, Mark gave Henry an amused look. "Let me guess, there is a recruitment bonus?"

"Heh, yeah. I get two hundred merits. But you get benefits as well. Not only will you get access to our network, but you get a measure of protection. There are also jobs that you can only get if you are associated with the Syndicate."

Holding up his hand to forestall Henry's pitch, Mark shook his head. "I'm not planning on joining anyone at the moment, but I'd love to leave the option open."

"Most people do," Henry said, his smile turning into a sneer. "But if you decide to go your own way, that's it. There are no second chances in the Tomb. If you don't join now, you'll have missed your shot."

Unshaken by Henry's aggressive tone, Mark shrugged. "That's what I've heard. Regardless, while I appreciate your help, I'm still not looking to join a group at the moment. I'll let you know if something changes."

Giving Mark a hard look, Henry shook his head. "Then we have nothing more to talk about. You can find more information on your watch. This is the end of what I'm responsible for. Good luck."

After Henry left, Mark opened his new watch and began to browse through the network, looking for anything that might help him get his bearings. The watch had three main functions: communication, navigation, and employment. Opening up the navigation function, Mark spent a little bit of time looking at the maps until he found the building where he was currently. It was on the outskirts of the complex, near some shops.

The third section, employment, was the one that interested Mark the most. It listed a tremendous number of jobs, though as Mark scrolled through them, his expression grew grimmer and grimmer. These were not normal jobs, not the sorts of jobs Mark would expect up on the surface, or even the jobs he would expect in a prison. He paused to click on one of them:

> Test subjects wanted. Looking for three C-ranked empowered for experimental medicine trial. Reward: 200 merits.

Merits, the currency used in the prison, could be earned for doing all sorts of things, but most of the requests were similar to this one, some sort of testing of experimental drugs or participation in scientific research. Those weren't the only requests, however, and Mark found others for everything from labor to combat to weapons testing to dancing and playing instruments. As he scrolled through, a couple caught his eye. He had no interest in participating in any of the scientific testing, but there was a request for an alchemical helper, someone to assist an alchemist in the creation of potions, as well as a request for people to fight in an arena.

He still hadn't fully gotten his head around the fact that the

Tomb wasn't really a prison at all. There were no guards to speak of, and the prisoners were largely free to do whatever they wanted. Of course, all the prisoners were still wearing their shackles, locking away their abilities, but otherwise, they seemed completely free. A bit more searching through the job requests proved that Mark's suspicion was right. Everything in the city cost merits, and if Mark wanted to stay in the apartment he had been assigned, he would have to pay 1,000 merits every month. Food cost merits as well, as did all the clothing and other goods in the shops.

Checking his watch, Mark saw that he still had eleven hours until the green light clicked off, so he decided to explore a little. Leaving the apartment as it was, he headed down to the ground floor and walked out onto the street. He passed another resident on the way out and could feel the prisoner's eyes following him down the block, clearly curious. Stopping at the corner, Mark spent a moment watching as people hurried this way and that. The vast majority had no watch, and Mark saw more than one person looking in his direction.

Mark didn't have any particular destination in mind. For the next few hours, he simply wandered around the streets near his apartment. For the most part, everything was calm. However, Mark did occasionally see groups of empowered individuals pushing their way through the crowds.

Those from the Viper Clan were easy to spot, as they all wore their right sleeves rolled up to reveal snake tattoos on their arms. The members of the Syndicate were a bit harder to identify, though Mark noticed that many of them wore red or black bandannas around their necks. He did his best to steer clear, moving to the side of the street every time they came by. For the most part, nobody paid him much mind.

Just as he was about to head back to his apartment, Mark sensed someone closing in behind him, moving quickly. He had just stepped around a corner into a side street when he saw three people walking out in front of him. Turning to glance back, he saw three more cutting off his retreat.

There were four men and two women, and all of them bore the hard, dangerous look common in the Tomb. None of them were wearing watches, and from the way they stared at Mark's wrist, it was clear that they were here for his citizenship.

Assessing their strength, Mark was fairly confident that they were all D or C ranked, as none of them carried an aura strong enough to suppress the shackles. What they did carry, however, was weapons: pipes, blades, and even a chain wrapped around a fist. Scratching his cheek, Mark watched calmly as they closed in.

One of the women stepped forward, extending the knife she held to point at Mark's chest. "Drop the watch and you can walk away!"

There was a faint tremble to her voice, though it wasn't fear. As Mark's eyes scanned her, he saw a poorly healed wound at her neck that she had tried to cover up with a handkerchief. She noticed his gaze and let out an angry shriek, lunging forward as she slashed her blade at him. Immediately, the others jumped into action as well. Mark responded by deflecting the blade coming toward his chest and jabbing rapidly, leaving three bloody holes: one in the woman's chest, the second in her throat, and the third in her temple. She fell to the ground even as the others arrived next to him.

Shifting his hands into their bone blade form, Mark blocked the other attacks, his fingers carving through the weapons with ease. Everything had happened so quickly that they'd had no time to register the death of their companion. When they finally did, their weapons lay in pieces at their feet. Mark had fully intended to resolve the conflict without killing, but clearly, that wasn't an option here in the Tomb.

One of the attackers had managed to land a blow on Mark's shoulder, tearing his skin open. But within moments, the wound had sealed back up, and Mark had returned the favor, his fingers leaving a gash on the man's cheek. With their weapons destroyed and the imminent threat of death, the five attackers scrambled backward, trying to retreat.

Capitalizing on his momentum, Mark took two of the attackers to the ground and then turned to deal with the others, only to find they had fled. He abandoned his thoughts of giving chase and turned to consider the terrified man and woman he had subdued. Standing over them, Mark looked them over properly for the first time. They were dressed in what could only be described as rags. What had once been crisp, clean prison uniforms were now dirty and torn. Their limbs were weak, their skin taut across their bones. They'd attacked so quickly that Mark hadn't gotten a good look. But now, as they lay trembling on the ground at his feet, he could tell that undernourishment and the constant disruption of the mana in their bodies had weakened them. Both of them stared at Mark in despair as he crouched and held out his watch. "Did you attack me because of this?"

The woman on the ground nodded mutely, and the man stammered out, "Yes."

"What were you going to do with it? After all, only one person can keep it, and there were six of you."

Seeing their eyes dart toward the rapidly cooling corpse that lay to the side, Mark looked over and realized that the woman he had killed looked quite a bit different from the others. Though she was still thin, it didn't look as if she had missed as many meals. And the clothing she wore, though worn, wasn't the prison uniform. It seemed as if she had been a bit better off than the two people Mark had captured.

"She hired us. We really didn't mean any harm."

Even as he spoke the words, the man's voice faltered. They had attacked Mark with weapons, giving the lie to his statement. Though in a certain way, the twisted logic made sense. They were trying to survive. He seemed like an easy mark. Putting the two together, while he didn't approve, he certainly understood why they had decided to launch their attack. The question was, What should he do with them? After looking them over, Mark sighed and gestured for them to leave. Unable to believe their luck, they scrambled backward and then crawled to their feet before running out of the alleyway as fast as they possibly could.

As they fled, Mark turned his attention to the woman's corpse and searched it. Though she had no watch, he did come up with a card that held merits. He had seen information about merit cards in the introduction to the Tomb. They served as ways of transferring merits, without them being tied to somebody's account, and could be checked with a watch. Holding the card up to the top of his watch, he heard a beep and saw that it contained 553 merits, which he soon added to his account. Though not enough to rent an apartment for a month, that would be more than sufficient to keep someone fed.

Mark was feeling rather peckish, but after he finished searching the corpse and stood up, a thought struck him. Why waste money on food when sustenance was readily available? As Mark turned away, he waved his hand, and his shadow began to stretch and ripple. Tendrils extended, pouncing gleefully on the woman's corpse, and as Mark walked out of the alley, a faint crunching sound echoed from the walls behind him.

By the time he got home, his biofuel was nearly full, and as he unlocked his door and settled onto his couch, he found himself conflicted. Mark wasn't naive enough to think that he'd be able to survive in the Tomb without getting his hands dirty. But the casual ease with which he had just killed and devoured that woman set off warning bells in his head.

He'd first discovered the two distinct sides of his mind that now waged a subtle war for dominance out in the wilderness. Up on the surface, among the people of New Emery, his rational, human mind was stronger. After all, society had clear and strict rules that made it easier for him to suppress his more monstrous urges. He had thought that when leaving the wilderness he had left those urges behind, but now, in the darkness of the Tomb, he could feel his monstrous side starting to stretch and grow once more.

To an extent, he felt that adjusting his actions to meet the requirements of his environment was natural. He had done so out in the wilderness, and it seemed appropriate to do now. The problem was that he wasn't sure whether he'd ever be able to go back if he began walking down that path, unleashing his more monstrous urges and listening to the devilish voice whispering in his ear. Some paths, once trodden, were impossible to retrace.

He had no desire to give up his humanity, but he could sense just how hard it was going to be to live in the Tomb without embracing his monstrous side.

Feeling something soft nudge his hand, he glanced down

and saw Mime crawling onto his lap. She gave him a satisfied smile, licked her lips, and then snuggled down. Watching her close her eyes, Mark scratched her side, the turmoil in his mind and heart beginning to calm. In truth, no matter how much he thought about these issues, no matter how much he tried to determine the best path, he still had to live. It was one thing to hold an idealistic view, another to survive. Mark wanted to do both, and though he wasn't exactly confident he'd be able to, the only way to know was to try.

Resolving to take things as they came, Mark closed his eyes. His life was nowhere close to what he had imagined it would be a year ago or even six months ago, but he was still alive, and no matter where he was, he was determined to thrive. The apartment was calm and quiet, and Mark slowly drifted off to sleep, lulled by Mime's soft breaths.

Mark woke to a pounding on his door. He was disoriented for a moment and, looking around the apartment, tried to remember where he was. Another round of knocking, accompanied by a muffled shout, jerked him from his confusion. Mime had moved to the back of the couch, and now she lifted her head and gave Mark an annoyed look, as if asking if he was going to get the door.

"Yeah, yeah, I'm going."

Pulling himself up off the couch, Mark stretched and headed for the door. The pounding sounded for the third time, then cut off as Mark turned the handle and pulled the door open. There were three men in the hall outside, and when they saw Mark, they stared at him in confusion. "Is Gereg here?"

Blinking, Mark took a moment to remember who that was.

"No," he said, then held up his wrist to show his watch.

There was no green light on it anymore, as twelve hours had passed since Mark had inherited it, and as soon as they saw the watch, the men's faces twisted. The predominant emotion was annoyance, though one of the men looked rather angry, and his stance shifted forward slightly.

Noticing his tensed muscles, Mark slowly raised his eyebrows. "Was he a friend of yours?"

One of the other men shook his head. "No, he was just going to be helping us with something, and he was late."

"I'm afraid that is my fault," Mark said with a shrug.

The other men looked at each other, and then the one who had originally spoken shrugged too. "What's done is done, but I wonder, any chance you're interested in a job? It's pretty easy, but we're on a bit of a time crunch, and we need a fourth."

It was rather disconcerting how quickly they adapted to the new situation, but Mark could only suppose that this wasn't actually that uncommon. Killing was clearly a normal part of life in the Tomb, and it made sense that if Mark could eliminate Gereg, he was probably strong enough to help them with whatever their job was.

"What did you have in mind?" Mark asked.

Exchanging glances again, the men seemed to come to some sort of unspoken agreement, and the one who had been talking tapped his watch, sending a file to Mark.

"Viper Clan and the Syndicate are in the middle of a turf war. It's created a bit of a no-man's-land. Well, we spotted some goods being stored in one of the warehouses. Nobody will notice if a crate goes missing. They'll think it just got destroyed in the fight. Gereg was going to act as backup for us, ensuring our ability to escape if anything goes south."

Looking over the information that had been sent over, Mark's eyes narrowed. "And who does this crate belong to?"

"Viper Clan."

"Sure, I'm in."

Mark figured that since he had already made enemies with the Viper Clan, he might as well go all the way.

Breaking out in a smile, the man introduced himself and the others. "The name's Carson. This is Louis and Kai. Welcome to the team."

"My name's Mark."

"Well, it's nice to meet you, Mark. I hope you're ready for some action, because we don't have long."

"We're already an hour late," Kai said, jumping in. He had looked angry earlier, but now he seemed to have calmed down considerably.

Glancing back at Mime, still on the couch, Mark shut the door and locked it, then followed Carson, Louis, and Kai out of the building. None of the three spoke, and Mark kept his silence as well. This was the first time he'd ever done anything like this, so he wasn't quite sure what to do. He figured he'd be okay as long as he took his cues from the other three, but he was also ready to bail as soon as things went south.

It took almost an hour to get to the building where the crates were stored. As they got close, Carson slowed down.

"We have a way in," he said, "a grate on the second floor. What we need you to do is hang out outside the warehouse. If you hear a loud whistle, we need you to cause a commotion, preferably at the front of the building. That'll buy us time to slip out the back."

Holding up his hand, Mark looked at the three men in turn before addressing Carson. "We haven't yet discussed my compensation."

Carson frowned and then shrugged. "We were going to pay Gereg three hundred fifty merits."

Mark highly doubted that; he assumed Carson had just chopped that number in half. But rather than argue, he just nodded. Considering he would be the one exposed if things went sour, he didn't think that was nearly enough. At the same time, with no frame of reference for what a job like this should cost, he didn't have much choice but to go along with it.

Once he was in position, Carson, Lewis, and Kai crept toward the building. Mark hesitated for a moment, then tore a strip from his prison shirt. He wrapped it around his face, making a makeshift mask. He even took off his watch and tucked it away safely, leaving nothing visible on his body that could identify him. Just because he had been hired to run out and create a disturbance didn't mean that he'd be foolish about it. The last thing he wanted was for the guards to be able to identify him later.

For almost half an hour, Mark waited, his eyes never leaving the front door of the building. Occasionally, he could see guards going past, making their rounds. And just when he thought nothing would happen, he heard a sharp whistle and saw the guards at the warehouse springing into action.

Mark jumped up from where he had been crouched and took off running, heading straight for the front of the warehouse. He hit the large metal-and-glass door at full speed, lowering his shoulder at the last moment as he slammed through. There was a loud crash as the glass shattered and the metal twisted, and Mark found himself inside a foyer.

There were three guards there, all sporting the distinctive snake tattoo of Viper Clan, and they attacked immediately, racing toward Mark with their mana swords drawn. Not wanting to tangle with the mana-enhanced edges of the swords, Mark ducked past the first slash and jabbed with his right hand, wounding the first attacker's wrist. As the man yelped and jerked backward, Mark spun, catching the dropped mana sword with his left hand and lifting it to block a second slash.

Wielding the sword in his left hand and the razor-sharp fingers of his right, Mark matched the two other guards blow for blow. He could hear shouting in the distance, and then a fourth guard burst through the doors from inside. Mark could see more behind him, pressing to get through, and rather than be surrounded, he darted forward, launching an attack against the guard who had just stepped from the hall.

Backpedaling quickly, the guard ran into his companions, who were trying to come the opposite direction, and for a moment, confusion reigned. A lot more guards were coming, and Mark was starting to get the feeling that Carson hadn't been entirely truthful about how easy the job would be.

Glad that he had elected to wear a mask, Mark blocked a slash and dodged a kick, launching counterattacks that drove the guards back. While none of his attackers had access to their abilities, they were still empowered, and that made them faster and stronger than any human had a right to be. Most of them were only D ranked, though a couple seemed to be just as strong and fast as Mark, and it wasn't long before Mark was forced to abandon his position in front of the hallway, allowing more of the guards to flood into the room.

Deciding he had bought the others enough time, Mark turned and ran, sprinting out of the building and heading for a nearby alley. With a loud shout, the guards started to give chase, but he turned and hurled the mana sword he had picked up, forcing them to duck back inside. By the time they had rushed out, he was gone.

Unsure if the guards could track him, Mark spent the next hour getting thoroughly lost in the twisting maze of streets. Along the way, he stopped to buy something to eat, to replenish the biofuel he had lost. Once he was sure no one was following him, he sent a message to Carson, asking where they should meet up. Almost forty-five minutes later, he still hadn't received a reply, and Mark's eyes narrowed. He sent another message, but this one failed to deliver, meaning Carson had blocked him.

Closing his eyes, Mark let out a long breath. He should have expected something like this. Opening his map, he saw that he was about half an hour from his apartment, but rather than head back, he instead looked around until he found a bar. Unlike the prison above, the Tomb had practically everything a person could want, including alcohol, and there were at least a dozen different bars scattered throughout the facility.

Mark chose a bar close to his apartment and headed over. The bar was located on the second floor of a building, above a general store that sold groceries, along with a number of other odds and ends. Climbing the stairs that led to the second-story bar, Mark saw a mountain of a human standing next to the door. The bouncer looked him over, then nodded and jerked his head at the entrance when Mark held up his watch.

One of the things that Mark had noticed about the Tomb was that those without citizenship were not allowed to enter most of the buildings. Bars were reserved for citizens, as were shops and practically everything else in the Tomb. This forced noncitizens, or chattels, to rely on citizens if they wanted to survive.

Pushing open the door, Mark stepped into the dimly lit room, his eyes scanning the space. There was a U-shaped bar in the middle of the room and dozens of small tables scattered in the corners. A stage took up one wall, and a woman sat on a stool in the middle of it, strumming a guitar. There weren't many people in the bar, but those who were present eyed Mark as he walked over to the bartender. "I'm looking for someone."

"Let me guess. Tall, dark, handsome? We all are, dear."

The bartender flashed a smile, amused by her own joke. Not in the mood to joke around, Mark shook his head and described Carson. "Tan skin, blond hair. About forty-five. Blue eyes and a large nose that looks like a chunk was taken off the end. Goes by the name Carson and runs with two others, Louis and Kai."

Giving Mark an appraising look, the bartender put down the glass she had just filled and wiped her hands on a bar towel. "Information on where people are costs more than just money, kid. I'm going to assume you are new to the Tomb; otherwise someone else would have beaten this lesson into you already. If you want to access the black network, you need a recommendation. We don't sell information to every schmo off the street, especially not important information like this."

Frowning, Mark leaned on the bar. "And where do I get a recommendation?"

"Talk to one of the gangs or an enforcer. They can recommend you."

Glancing over his shoulder, Mark saw that the massive bouncer had stepped into the bar and was watching him like a hawk. He hadn't seen the bartender signal the man, which meant that they were quite used to situations like this. Not wanting to cause any trouble, he lifted his hands and nodded. "Got it. I'll get a recommendation."

With finding out directly no longer an option, Mark headed back toward his apartment. Along the way, he found a shop that sold clothing and bought a new shirt, replacing the one he had torn. While he was there, he asked the shopkeeper if they bought used clothing. It turned out they did, providing him with a way to get rid of the clothing in his closets. He ended up with an extra 700 merits from the sale, bringing the total number of merits in his account up to nearly 6,000. Between what Gereg had left behind and what he had earned in the last couple of days, Mark had more than enough money.

That evening, Mark sat on his couch in his now-emptier apartment, trying to quell his racing mind. Mime, who seemed to sense the complexity of his thoughts, crawled up on his lap, nudging him with her nose until he began scratching her under the chin. The feeling of her silky-smooth fur brought a smile to his face and helped him calm down. Something about the normalcy of his surroundings caused Mark to lower his defenses, and as soon as he did, thoughts of his brother and friends crashed down on him.

There had been no contact between Mark and his brother since he had seen Joe before being deployed, and Mark wondered if Joe knew that he had been put in jail. If he did, would Joe even care? Mark could clearly remember the anger in his brother's eyes at their last parting, and the memory weighed heavily on him. It was entirely possible that Mark would die down here in the Tomb, and Joe would never learn what had happened to him.

Mark's friends were undoubtedly in the dark as well. Even Noah, whose father had come to see Mark when he was first sent to Gray Rock, probably didn't have a clue about Mark's whereabouts. After all, Mark had never heard of the Tomb when he was on the surface, and he wouldn't be at all surprised if his friends hadn't either.

Thanks to Mime's comforting presence, Mark was able to keep himself relatively calm, but that began to change when Mark started to remember his master, Abrams.

For whatever reason, Master Abrams's absence before Mark was hauled into the prison weighed especially heavily on his mind. For the most part, Mark was able to ignore his unease when he was keeping himself busy, but in quiet moments like this, he found the weight that settled on his chest almost too much to bear. The mystery of the note his master had left continually came back to Mark, along with a confusing tangle of thoughts about his friends. Did any of them know what had happened? Or had he just vanished completely from their world?

Were they worried about him? He could imagine Sky fretting over his disappearance, but if he knew Phoenix, she'd be digging to try to find out what had happened. They'd had a date for that night, and when he hadn't shown up, she would undoubtedly have started asking questions. Mark could only pray that it didn't lead her into trouble, though given her family's influence, she shouldn't be in any danger. Leaning his head back, he stared at the ceiling blankly until Mime nipped at his fingers, which had stopped their scratching. With a soft laugh, he straightened up and resumed petting Mime.

"I hope you're all doing well," Mark whispered, closing his eyes.

Though Mark had more than enough merits to live for a long

while, that didn't mean he was planning on lazing around. He had been combing through the job boards every chance he got, and an ad for an alchemical assistant had caught his eye. Deciding to check it out, he sent in an application and the next morning headed toward the center of the Tomb. Just like in New Emery, the Tomb was organized with the most important buildings in the center and the residences surrounding them. It took Mark close to an hour to walk to the building listed on the job posting, and along the way he saw two fights, a robbery, and hundreds of chattels lying in the streets, too weak to move.

It was hard for Mark to reconcile just how different the Tomb was from New Emery, but the more he thought about it, the more he realized that they were not that different at all. Everything that he saw down here was happening up above as well, just hidden behind a veneer of civility and order. The main difference was that now it was right in Mark's face.

The thought stuck with him as he opened the door and walked into an alchemist's shop, where he caught sight of half a dozen alchemical materials that were illegal to sell in New Emery. On the surface, they would have been hidden in a back room and only sold to a specific clientele. Down here, they were thrown on the shelf with everything else.

The door let out a chime, and a moment later a large figure stomped out of the back room. Seven feet tall and made of bluish metal, a large robot stared down at Mark through red eyes. "You are Mark Fields. Prisoner 79956312. You have applied to work as an alchemical assistant."

The robot spoke in a flat, factual tone, leaving no room for Mark to dispute what it said.

"I did."

"Good. I am Alchemical Robot 773. You will call me Mr. Robot. We will start work now."

"Yes, sir."

The robot, who had started to turn away from Mark, paused, and his head swung back toward Mark. "My name is not 'sir.' You will call me Mr. Robot."

"Yes, Mr. Robot."

Mr. Robot led Mark into the back room, where a full alchemy lab was set up. A number of potions were already being brewed, and Mr. Robot sent Mark a list of ingredients that needed to be added, along with the specific timing and conditions for each. None of the potions were particularly complicated, and Mark had made two of them before, though the other two were new.

"If you fail to complete these potions, you will pay the cost of the ingredients in merits. If you succeed, you will receive half of the cost of the ingredients in merits. Wake me when the potions have been completed."

With those words, Mr. Robot walked over to the corner and stood silently, his glowing red eyes dimming slightly. Left in the middle of the workshop, Mark took a deep breath and looked around. He hadn't anticipated being thrown in the deep end like this, but in retrospect, alchemists were a rare group, and they were likely even more rare among the prisoners in the Tomb. That meant that Mark's talents were quite valuable, which explained the rather ridiculous reward that Mr. Robot was offering for each completed potion. Mark had more than enough credits to pay up if a few of the potions failed, but he wasn't planning on letting that happen. Rubbing his hands together, he grinned. Time to get to work.

The first step was to review the recipes for the two potions that Mark had never encountered before. These were a good bit more complicated than the healing and stamina potions Mr. Robot also wanted him to make.

The first, called Liquid Lunch, appeared to be a fasting potion.

It would not only pack nutrients into the drinker's body but also remove their desire to eat by suppressing their appetite. Potions like this weren't uncommon, though typically prolonged use wasn't encouraged. Still, it looked fairly straightforward to Mark. After reading it a couple of times, he put it down and picked up the fourth recipe.

It was by far the most complicated of the four potions, and Mark's eyes slowly narrowed as he looked it over. There was no description for the potion, just its name—Blur—the list of ingredients, and some rough instructions for putting it together. After he mentally reviewed the ingredients' effects, Mark was relatively sure that this potion was intended to speed up cognition. However, it wouldn't speed up mental clarity as well, making him wonder what exactly it was for. Figuring he could ask Mr. Robot after waking him up, Mark shrugged, put the recipe down, and started on the easiest of the potions, the stamina potion.

There was something comforting about practicing alchemy, and Mark had soon immersed himself in this feeling. Measuring out the ingredients precisely, mixing them together with the application of heat, and monitoring the exact timing of each step allowed him to temporarily forget that he was working in a prison, deep underground, and not in Master Abrams's workshop, where he had first learned alchemy.

It was almost an hour before the stamina potion was ready, and after he had finished, he paused to have it assessed, wanting to make sure that it was up to his standard. After perusing the readout the assessment machine spat out, Mark frowned. Though the potion met the minimum standards, the poor quality of the ingredients had dragged the entire thing down by a grade. Still, it counted as a pass, so Mark placed the potion with the readout underneath it on the table next to Mr. Robot's inert form and headed back to start working on the healing potion.

This took even longer, in large part because Mark was especially meticulous about the ingredients he selected. Rather than just throw them all together, he carefully went through them one by one, doing his best to understand their specific features. Every ingredient was assigned a grade according to the level of potions it could be used in, but not all ingredients were created equal, and some were more effective than others, depending on how they had been harvested. That was one of the reasons alchemical butchers existed in the first place, as they were able to produce higher-grade versions of common ingredients due to their unique method of retrieval.

As Mark studied a stalk of grass meant for the healing potion, he noticed a now-familiar sight. It contained trace amounts of mana. Curious, he picked up a second stalk, comparing the two. Almost immediately, he noticed a difference in the amount of mana each contained.

Taken aback, he picked up a third stalk and then a fourth. Every single one had a different amount of mana inside it. When he shifted in his seat, one of the stalks brushed against the edge of an alchemical machine, and Mark saw the mana it contained dim slightly. Freezing, he stared at the grass and then slowly extended it. As soon as its tip brushed up against the metal machine, the mana faded again, drawn out through the edge of the leaf.

He knew that metal wasn't good for mana-infused items, as it tended to conduct the mana away. But now he was able to see exactly how that worked. Putting the stalk down, Mark thought for a moment and selected another that was already dim. He looked it over carefully, noticing dozens of small abrasions on the stem. This one had clearly been plucked with significantly less care than the others, and he suspected that was why it contained less mana.

Fixing his mind on the remaining mana, Mark did his best to hold it in place and then, reaching out, brushed the stalk against the edge of the machine. He felt the mana's impulse, a tangible desire to rush out and fill up the metal. But then the mana ran up against his desire for it to stay, and hesitated. Ultimately, the mana didn't move, though each time he brushed the stalk against the side of the machine, he felt the instinctive pull.

Putting the grass down, Mark scratched his head. His level of mana control was rudimentary at best, but with constant practice, it was getting stronger. Reaching out, he touched one of the leaves and used his finger to guide the mana it contained toward the top. The mana moved with his finger, and he found it much easier to control that way than with his mind alone.

Curious, he overlapped two of the leaves, then tried to gather the mana from one and inject it into the other. When he got to the edge of the first leaf, however, he felt resistance, as if an invisible barrier were keeping the mana contained. Thinking for a moment, Mark pinned the mana in place, then made a small incision on each leaf, smiling as he felt the mana trying to escape through the holes.

He found it tremendously difficult to keep the mana locked in place after creating these new exits, and a dull ache started to thrum in the back of his skull. He ignored it and brought his fingers together, guiding the mana in each leaf toward the other. Rough work, and despite his best efforts, the majority of the mana evaporated. But Mark was ecstatic to find that some had indeed transferred between leaves.

He had no idea what exactly he would use this newfound ability to do, but Mark figured that the more he knew about how mana behaved and how far his control of it could go, the better off he would be. He had a sneaking suspicion that this ability, gained from the Exlian nest, absolutely dwarfed every other ability he had, and he was determined to plumb its secrets.

Keeping ahold of the stalk that had been charged with extra mana to prevent it from leaking out, Mark got to work on the healing potion. As he worked, he paid careful attention to how the mana moved in it, and occasionally tried to nudge the mana in the different ingredients to blend together a bit faster. A couple of times, he nearly ruined the potion because he was so intent on understanding how the mana moved.

When he was finished with the healing potion, he was pleased to see it assessed as high quality, a step above a normal healing potion. Though the difference between a standard healing potion and a high-quality healing potion was so infinitesimally small that it wouldn't actually matter to the person drinking it, for Mark, it was as if a whole new world were starting to open up.

Healing and stamina potions each had a single effect: healing damage done to the body and restoring energy. And because both of them simply converted power that already existed in the drinker's body into either regenerative ability or more energy, the only improvement a high-quality version of one of those potions could produce was a slightly faster application of the power.

However, for many potions, a high-quality version could be sold for almost twice the price. Of course, Mark wasn't foolish enough to believe that just because he had created one high-quality potion, he'd be able to repeat the process on other potions. Especially when it was his first time encountering the ingredients.

Having completed both the stamina and healing potions, Mark turned his attention to the other two. Of them, the fasting potion was easier. But Mark was much more interested in the Blur potion, as it required fewer ingredients. After reviewing the recipe again, Mark set out all the ingredients and carefully examined each one.

Getting to know the mana inside them, he was starting to understand that not only did the amount of mana differ, but its qualities differed as well. In some of the ingredients, the mana was light and airy, a sort of ethereal mist. Any damage to the skin of the ingredient would cause the mana to leak out like a popped balloon. In other ingredients, particularly minerals and earths, it was heavier and firmer, and it moved like molasses.

Potions tended to favor ingredients that were all of the same kind, and Blur strongly favored the first type. All but one of the ingredients carried much lighter mana, making Mark wonder if that was one of the requirements for creating a successful potion. After all, the ingredients did have to mix together, and not only the physical components but the mana they contained had to blend . . . He assumed that it would be easier to blend mana from two objects that were similar in temperament as well as intensity.

Getting out some base to serve as the foundation for his potion, Mark paused and glanced at it. It had almost no mana in it, just the mana originally contained in the water and a trace amount from the salt. But curiously, he could sense stickiness in the liquid, and as he carefully observed the first of his ingredients mixing with the base, Mark realized that this was what was keeping the mana from simply escaping into the air. Base acted as a sort of glue, holding the mana together so that it could be mixed to produce the potion the alchemist wanted.

It took Mark a full four hours to complete the Blur potion, in part because he was taking a considerable amount of time to carefully observe and theorize about the fundamental process of alchemy. When appropriate, he would pause and consider his previous experiences, trying to understand them in light of the new information that he was getting. Ultimately, the potion he produced was barely standard, but Mark didn't mind, as succeeding on the first try with a new recipe was practically unheard of.

A few steps had almost tripped him up, but able to see the interaction between the mana and the ingredients, Mark had been able to catch the problems before they spiraled out of control. By now, he had been in the workshop for close to ten hours, but Mark wasn't about to stop. He still had one potion to go and was full of energy.

Unlike the Blur potion, Liquid Lunch was made from heavier materials that carried a thicker quality to their mana, which, in Mark's mind, made absolute sense. After all, this was a fasting potion, designed to suppress appetite and provide long-term energy. With this in mind, Mark began brewing it.

About halfway through, he accidentally left it on the heat too long and ruined it, transforming the mixture into a disgusting mess. Unperturbed, Mark cleaned up all his tools, got another batch of ingredients out, and started again. This time he managed to finish the potion after three hours of exacting work. Of course, he wouldn't make any money from it, as he'd have to pay for the ingredients of his failed first attempt and would only receive half that amount for the successful one. Mark, who felt as if he had just spent the most profitable fifteen hours of his life, didn't care one bit.

Arranging the successful fasting potion on the table with

the failed potion next to it, Mark stepped close to Mr. Robot and coughed lightly. "Ahem. Excuse me, sir. I mean, Mr. Robot."

There was a hum, and Mr. Robot's red eyes blinked back to life. "You have finished."

"I have." Mark gestured to the potions. "If you'd like to inspect them."

The tall metal man stepped over to the table and picked up the stamina potion, examined it carefully for a moment, scanned the readout, and then nodded. "This potion is sufficient."

With a whir a plate in his chest opened, revealing a gap. Curious, Mark watched as Mr. Robot stuck the potion inside, and the plate closed. Mana shimmered in the robot's chest as he turned to examine the healing potion. It, too, was picked up, the assessment was scanned, and the potion was shoved into Mr. Robot's chest. Mark, who was watching him carefully, was stunned to see that the other potion wasn't there. Instead, the hole had been empty before Mr. Robot stuck the second one in.

There was another flash of mana, and Mr. Robot picked up the failed Liquid Lunch. "This potion is not active. It is a failure. You will be charged the cost of ingredients in merits."

Placing the ruined potion to the side, he picked up the successful Liquid Lunch, examined it, and with a sharp nod placed it in his chest, which was, once again, empty. This time, when he activated the mana in his chest, Mark was watching extra closely. He saw mana race through a complex pattern, too detailed to understand at a glance. And as it vanished, he got the sense that the potion was gone. This was confirmed when the Blur potion, having passed Mr. Robot's assessment, was placed in his chest where the Liquid Lunch potion had been a moment earlier.

By this point, Mark was dumbfounded. He wasn't unfamiliar with robots, but he had never seen one with a teleportation chamber in its chest. Further, while there were empowered who had the ability to move objects through space at will, Mark had never heard of technology being able to do the same thing. Yet clearly, that was exactly what Mr. Robot was doing. Though he desperately wanted to inquire, Mark hesitated when facing Mr. Robot's dispassionate gaze.

"You have passed the assessment. One potion was deemed a failure. The others were successes. I've assessed the number of ingredients present in the workshop and confirmed three of your potions were made on your first attempt and one was made on your second. You will receive a total of two hundred merits for each potion whose quality is tier one, seven hundred fifty merits per tier-two potion, and two thousand merits per tier-three potion. The workshop will cover the cost of five failed tier-one potions, one and a half failed tier-two potions, and half of a failed tier-three potion. You will be responsible for other ingredients. These work terms are acceptable to you, and you will indicate your agreement."

Here, Mr. Robot paused, looming threateningly over Mark, who quickly nodded. It might have been his imagination, but he felt as if Mr. Robot relaxed slightly.

"Additionally, you will be responsible for arranging, procuring, and organizing ingredients. Each week, you will be assigned a potion quota that includes the number and type of each potion required. Your first quota will be assigned tomorrow. You will leave now and be back tomorrow at seven a.m."

Realizing he was being dismissed, Mark held up his hand.

"You have a question."

"Yes, I do have a question."

"That is what I stated."

"Right. My question is, Can I use the workshop to create potions above and beyond the quota?"

"Yes. The workshop is free for your use, but you are responsible for procuring your own ingredients. Any ingredient belonging to the shop that you use will be charged at twice the market rate in merits."

Gulping, Mark nodded. "Got it. I'll make sure to bring my own ingredients."

The room lapsed into silence as Mr. Robot simply stared at Mark, and after a moment, getting the hint, Mark said goodbye and left the workshop. When he stepped out into the store, he saw somebody was there browsing through the potions, but the woman didn't look up, so Mark just slipped out the door and headed for his apartment. His mind was still abuzz with everything he had learned about mana and its interaction with alchemy, and he couldn't wait to get back to it the following day.

Of course, as much as he would have loved to just bury himself in alchemy, Mark still had other things to deal with. The first was figuring out how to get a recommendation so that he could access the black network. According to the bartender at the bar near his house, Mark would only be able to get such a recommendation from one of the gangs or an enforcer. Unfortunately, neither was going to be easy. Mark had already turned down both of the major gangs, who had each made it very clear that he was giving up his only chance of joining them. Mark was quite confident that they wouldn't be interested in giving a recommendation to somebody who wasn't on their side, which only left finding an enforcer. The problem was, enforcers would likely be even harder to convince than the gangs.

Over the past few days Mark had come to an understanding of how the Tomb operated. At the top was an enigmatic figure who went by the name of Maestro, and the robots that patrolled the streets and much of the technology that existed in the Tomb were the results of his work. And from what Henry had said, this entire place was Maestro's playground.

Underneath him were five individuals: the leaders of both Viper Clan and the Syndicate, and then three individual empowered known collectively as the enforcers. Their role in the Tomb's hierarchy was to make sure that the few rules that existed were followed, and they did so with brutal efficiency, killing any prisoner who stepped out of line.

Stepping around a corner near his apartment, Mark spotted a familiar figure hanging out at the other end of the street. Louis, one of Carson's men. As Mark approached, he saw Kai step out of a building and join Louis. Mark didn't hesitate as he walked straight toward them. He was just crossing the street when Louis spotted him and said something, causing Kai to turn around. On recognizing Mark, Kai let out a laugh and shook his head.

"Well, if it isn't our friend," he said with a smirk. "You know, I never did catch your name."

Mark looked between the two men and then held out his hand. "Three hundred fifty merits," he said calmly.

"That's a funny name. Louis, have you ever heard a name like that?"

"I don't think that's his name, Kai. After all, you'd have to be damaged in the head to walk around with a name like that."

"Well, I'm pretty convinced he is damaged in the head," Kai said, spitting on the ground at Mark's feet. "Where else would he get the courage to walk up to us like this?"

Mark moved so quickly Kai didn't see it coming. One moment, Mark was standing there with his hand out. And the next, his fist was buried in Kai's solar plexus. To Mark, it felt like he was punching a brick wall, and he could feel the skin on his fist breaking as he rammed into Kai's hard skin, but from the way Kai gasped for breath, he had still managed to achieve his objective.

Realizing that Kai was stronger than he had assumed and suspecting Louis was too, Mark narrowed his eyes and opened his fist.

No matter how hard Kai's skin was, Mark was positive that his fingers would be able to slice right through it. As his arm transformed into a bone blade, he saw Louis stepping around his companion, a murderous expression on his face. Just as Mark was about to cut Kai's heart out of his chest, he heard a shout and paused. The door to the building they were standing in front of opened, and Carson came running down the steps. "Hey, there you are."

Kai staggered backward, and Louis hesitated as Carson came to a stop in front of Mark.

"We tried going back to your apartment today, but you weren't there. You never came to meet us either. You're here about your payment, right? Well, I got it right here. A bit extra too, since you did such a good job."

With a flick, Carson pulled out a card, which he held in the air for Mark to see. Mark silently held out his watch. After Carson tapped it, Mark felt his wrist vibrate as the merits were transferred over.

"Thanks again for your help. You provided a great distraction. We were able to get out without any trouble. I hope you were too. Tell me, if we have other jobs like that, would you be interested? Now that we know how reliable you are, you'll get paid more for them too."

Taking a step back, Mark shook his head. "Not at the moment, but thanks. It was nice working with you."

Mark had no idea what had caused Carson's sudden change of heart, as it was clear that neither Lewis nor Kai had expected Mark to get anything. But it was hard to hit a smiling face. And since he had gotten paid, Mark decided to just hold it in. Before he rounded the corner, he glanced back and saw the three men huddled together. Kai was gesturing wildly in his direction, but Carson seemed much calmer. They were no doubt talking about him, and Mark had a sneaking suspicion that his trouble with them wasn't over. But as long as they stayed out of his way, he'd be content to live and let live . . .

As he walked back to his apartment, Mark clenched his fist. In the heat of the moment, he had moved decisively, overwhelmed by a sort of instinctive desire to dominate. But now, as his adrenaline calmed down, Mark found himself disconcerted. Since being thrown into Gray Rock and especially after consuming the nest, he'd killed multiple people with barely a thought. It seemed as if as soon as he entered danger, all his emotions fled to the recesses of his mind, leaving nothing but a cold, calculating rationality behind.

While such a state was excellent for combat, Mark was quickly realizing that it had its downsides too. It made him overeager to attack rather than try to resolve situations more peacefully. At first, he had thought that it was the influence of the Exlian abilities he had consumed, but he didn't have the blind rage and overwhelming hunger that most Exlian exhibited.

Mark remembered the strange humanoid monster he had seen out in the wilderness. It lacked the mindless drive of other Exlian he had observed and, in a sense, operated more like a regular human than an Exlian. Much like the nest, which hadn't attacked him blindly, as Mark had anticipated it would.

Opening the door to his apartment, he saw Mime sitting on the kitchen table, licking her paw. She looked up and gave him a nod, then went back to cleaning herself as Mark walked to the fridge and opened it up. It was empty, reminding him of another task he needed to take care of. "Want to go grocery shopping?"

Perking up, Mime nodded and hopped up onto his shoulder, where she sat, her tail lashing eagerly. The grocery store was only a couple of blocks away, and though he glanced up at the bar that sat above it, Mark didn't bother going in. Instead, heading into the store, he filled up a cart, focusing on getting high-energy foods and things he thought Mime might like.

"My brother would yell at me for not getting more vegetables," he said, eyeing the bags of carrots.

Ultimately, he decided in favor of more steak instead. The fact that there was a grocery store in the heart of Gray Rock Prison still left him rather dumbfounded. But Mark was slowly coming to accept that the Tomb operated like any city, albeit one with insane prices. After spending close to 400 merits to buy enough groceries to last the week, Mark packed them up and headed for home.

As soon as he stepped out of the door, he could feel multiple gazes latching onto him. As he walked down the street, they followed. The first group jumped him when he got to the alleyway that led to his building: ten half-starved chattels who stared at Mark as if they wanted to eat him as much as the groceries he carried. With a sigh, he put the groceries down in a pile at his feet.

"Do me a favor and look after these," he said to Mime, who nodded and hopped down from his shoulder, perching on top of them.

Cracking his knuckles, Mark strode forward. Less than a minute later, the alleyway was filled with groans. More conscious of his instinctive desire to completely eliminate threats, Mark did his best to pull his punches. Though by the time he had finished, everyone lying on the ground was wounded, one of them badly enough that if he didn't get treatment soon, he'd probably die. Biting his lip, Mark stared down at the man moaning on the ground and then shook his head resolutely, reminding himself that the only people in the Tomb were people who had committed enough crimes to be thrown in here. When he turned around, he saw Mime licking her lips. Beyond her were a few scattered limbs, the remnants of a group that had tried to sneak up and swipe some of the groceries she was guarding. Taking a deep breath, Mark walked over and crouched next to her. He reached out a hand and stroked the fur on her head, causing Mime to close her eyes happily.

"Thanks for keeping everything safe," Mark said, still feeling quite conflicted in his heart.

There was nothing he could do for the injured, so he gathered up his groceries and, with Mime in tow, headed to his apartment.

When Mark walked back that way the following morning, heading for the center of town to take up his job with Mr. Robot, the only signs of any struggle were a few dried bloodstains on the ground. The rules of the Tomb were strict: Bodies were sent to Maestro's lab. Mark had a strong sense that the Reapers, the robots who collected them, weren't particularly picky when it came to how dead those bodies had to be.

Much like in New Emery, the closer to the center of the Tomb one got, the brighter the lights were. As the Tomb was entirely hidden from the sun, Mark had no way of knowing if the time on his watch was actually accurate. Of course, it didn't particularly matter to him what time it was on the surface. After all, the Tomb was completely isolated, and there was no interaction between the two, at least by all public appearances.

Mr. Robot was standing in the front of the store, and his eyes lit up immediately when Mark walked in. "You have arrived. Good. Inside the workshop, you will find the production list. Completed potions should be placed on the table on the right side of the entryway. Failed potions should be placed on the left."

With a hum, he powered down, his eyes going dim once more, and Mark was left to his own devices. Walking past Mr. Robot, Mark stepped into the workshop and spotted a piece of paper on the right-hand table. It listed the potions he needed to make over the course of the week, including twenty healing potions, twenty stamina potions, ten Liquid Lunches, and ten Blurs. Noticing a number for an ingredient supplier at the bottom of the list, Mark dialed it, and a rather round-faced man popped up on the virtual screen a moment later.

"Kelly's Alchemical Supply. Who is this, and how did you get my number?"

Taken aback, Mark introduced himself and explained why he was calling.

"Mr. Robot, huh? So you're the new employee. Sure, I can send you some ingredients. It'll take me a couple of days, though. It'll be faster if you come yourself. Just make sure you bring a cart or something."

"Where are you located?" Mark asked, his eyes narrowing.

With a grin, the supplier, who Mark assumed was Kelly, gave him an address only a couple of blocks away. Figuring it wouldn't be too much trouble to go and get the ingredients himself, Mark agreed, and half an hour later he was standing outside a building with a large garage door that had *Kelly's Alchemical Supply* scrawled on the wall. There was a rattle, and a large metal door rolled up.

"Come on in. I'll show you what you're getting."

Stepping into the warehouse, Mark looked around and saw a couple of heavily muscled men moving crates around. He had to admit he was quite curious where the Tomb got all its alchemical supplies from, but he didn't feel like it would be wise to start digging, so he followed Kelly in silence.

Kelly went to a large stack of boxes, one of which was open. Dozens of stalks of grass were laid out in neat rows in the box, and grabbing one, he twiddled it between his fingers as he held it out for Mark to see.

"You're lucky I like precision, because this is prime stuff that you're getting," Kelly said, peering at Mark.

Mark didn't respond, because he was busy examining the grass's mana content. Though a bit lighter than he would have liked, it was still acceptable, and after hesitating for a moment, he nodded. Tossing it back in the box, Kelly closed it up.

"We can charge it to the account, but the deposit has to be paid up front," he said. "Two thousand merits."

Realizing he should have gotten more information from Mr. Robot about how purchasing supplies normally went, Mark hesitated for a moment. He could afford the fee, but his experiences in the Tomb made him rather skeptical. Kelly didn't care and just held out his hand. Finally, Mark reluctantly sent over a payment of 2,000 merits to Kelly's watch. His misgivings only grew deeper as Kelly's eyes gleamed and he flashed a wide smile.

"We'll get these boxes loaded for you. Free of charge," the merchant said, and soon Mark was walking back down the road with four crates stacked on his cart.

He made it back to the shop unmolested, which he found quite astounding, considering the number of people who had been staring at him from the nearby alleyways, and after carrying the boxes in, he opened them up and began to sort through the ingredients. The first few stalks of grass were fine, but as he picked up the fourth, Mark paused. On the surface, the stalk looked absolutely perfect. In fact, it looked even better than the one that Kelly had shown him. Inside, however, was a different story, as there was no mana.

Mark's lips tightened as he picked up another stalk. It was the same. Perfect on the outside, but manaless. The only reason alchemy worked was the mana contained in the ingredients, so stalks of grass like this were entirely useless. The farther into the crate Mark went, the colder his expression became. Of every ten stalks of grass, maybe one had traces of mana, but even those were barely usable. Nine out of ten had no mana at all, and as Mark opened up the other boxes, he quickly found the same to be true in them.

His first thought was that he had been scammed. After all, the average alchemist, especially a young one, would naturally have an abysmal success rate, which meant that when their potions failed, they wouldn't find it out of the ordinary, even though the failure would be due to faulty ingredients rather than a lack of skill.

That gave him pause: Was it possible that Kelly simply didn't know himself? After all, if you couldn't sense mana like Mark could, it would be almost impossible to tell the good grass from the bad without attempting to make potions with them. Looking at the worthless materials spread out on the tables, Mark thought for a moment and then dialed Kelly's number. Nobody picked up.

Taking a deep breath to keep himself calm, Mark carefully repackaged everything in the crates and wheeled them back out of the store, heading toward Kelly's. When he got there, the door was shut, but it opened up after he banged on it, and a heavily muscled man covered in tattoos leered at him. "What do you want?"

"I want to talk to Kelly," Mark said, glancing around.

"Do you have an appointment?"

"No, but—"

"Then get out of here. Come back when you have an appointment."

Stepping back, the large man started to pull down the door, but Mark stepped forward and grabbed it.

"Let me rephrase that," he said. "Get Kelly and bring him out. There's a problem with the goods he sold me."

"Those are dangerous words, kid."

Hearing Kelly's voice, Mark looked past the thug who was glaring at him and saw the merchant walking over.

"After all, a business's reputation is its lifeblood, and if you go slandering like that, things aren't going to turn out well for you."

"You're correct," Mark said. "A business's reputation is its lifeblood, which is why it makes me so unhappy that you've sold me a batch of defective goods. If you're not willing to make this right, then give me my deposit back, and you can have your ingredients."

Smirking, Kelly shook his head. "Unfortunately, I don't remember a deposit, and those don't look like my goods."

Still holding on to the metal door, Mark took a deep breath and nodded. "In that case, it must be my mistake."

Kelly had clearly expected a fight, and as Mark stepped back and pulled his cart away, the merchant stared after him, a frown on his face. Mark quietly pulled the cart down the street, a wry smile slipping across his lips.

"It's harder to adjust than I thought," he said to himself.

Returning to the shop, Mark put the boxes at the side of the room and then sat down, his mind churning over his options. Clearly, he had been taken for a sucker, and this wasn't the first time.

Just then, Mr. Robot poked his head in the door. "You have a problem."

Amused by the matter-of-fact statement, Mark shrugged. "It's not much of a problem, and it'll be resolved by tomorrow."

For a long moment, Mr. Robot stared at Mark. Then he nodded and returned to the shop, where he powered off. Mark spent the rest of the afternoon looking through Mr. Robot's recipes, doing his best to memorize the ones that seemed interesting. After the shop closed for the evening, Mark headed back to his apartment, where he made dinner for himself and Mime.

After he had finished and cleaned up the dishes, he looked outside and saw the city's lights starting to go out. It had surprised him the first night he was here when he saw the lights clicking off one by one. But to a certain extent, it made sense. Rather than run the lights twenty-four seven, the Tomb simulated a day-and-night cycle, which helped keep everyone on a similar schedule.

As the city darkened, he glanced at Mime. "You want to do some hunting?"

Perking up, Mime nodded emphatically. Together, they stepped out the door, and Mark slowly made his way through the city, sticking to the shadows cast by the streetlights. In truth, there wasn't much difference between the Tomb in the daytime and the Tomb after the lights were shut off. The same number of people lurked about the alleyways, and a couple of times, Mark saw groups of chattels eyeing him up. Why they didn't decide to ambush him, he wasn't quite sure, but it might have had something to do with the ice-cold expression on his face.

His destination was Kelly's Alchemical Supply, and when he got close, he turned off the main street, walking quietly through the alleyways toward the back of the building. As he walked, he tied his makeshift mask around his head.

When he stepped into the alleyway next to the building, two chattels who were hanging out there froze. Mark didn't even spare them a glance, and as soon as he had walked past them, they scrambled in the other direction, not wanting anything to do with whatever was about to go down. Pausing by the side of the building, Mark reached out his fingers, touching the wall, and began scanning his psychic network. It was much harder to spot humans than Exlian, but after a few careful sweeps, he identified five people inside, one of whom was walking toward the outer door.

Realizing he might have had a stroke of luck, Mark backed up, hiding himself among the debris scattered in the alley. Less than a minute later, the door opened, and the large tattooed man from that afternoon poked his head out and looked around. Wedging the door open, he stepped outside and got out a cigarette. As he looked down, fumbling for his lighter, Mark attacked with his null field blazing to eliminate any external defenses.

Mark's fingers made short work of the man's throat. With a stunned gurgle, he fell to the ground. Not giving himself a chance to think about the fact that he had just murdered a man in cold blood, Mark stepped to the door and glanced inside. Seeing nobody, he paused for a moment. His shadow wriggled, and a moment later, the corpse was gone, along with everything on him.

After glancing through the door again, Mark stepped in and clicked it shut behind him, canceling his null field at the same time so as not to accidentally alert anyone. The warehouse was around three thousand feet in length and easily that wide, if not a bit wider. It was full of shelves with dozens of boxes stacked to the ceiling. Mark kept low as he crept forward, his eyes scanning for enemies.

Spotting another thug crouched in one of the rows, looking at a couple of boxes on the bottom shelf, Mark approached on quiet feet. Some sixth sense must have warned the thug that someone was behind him, because he suddenly spun around, his mouth opening like he was going to yell. Mark grabbed at him, his fingers brushing against the thug's arm. As soon as he made contact, Mark pressed his will forward, causing the faint web of mana in the prisoner to go crazy, completely disorienting him.

As the thug collapsed to the ground, Mark was on him, his fingers piercing the man's heart. Hearing a rustle, one of the others called out, but when the guard walked around the corner, there was nothing but an empty aisle.

"Huh, must have been a rat." With a shrug, the guard turned around, oblivious to the silver line falling toward him. Mark, concealed among the boxes on a nearby shelf, watched in awe as Mime's attack bisected the man neatly. The attack was so sharp that the guard didn't even realize he had been killed. He took a step forward, a strange expression crossing his face, before his head tumbled from his shoulders.

Mark was on him in an instant, his shadow enveloping the corpse before the smell of blood could spread. As the shadow began to devour it, Mark peeked around the corner. His sweeps through the psychic network revealed three more people in the building, including one sitting in the center of the warehouse, where a desk had been set up.

Mark glanced at Mime, who nodded. A moment later, he felt a blurry wave shroud him as Mime extended her stealth ability to cover him as well. On silent feet, he crept forward, heading not for the center of the warehouse but for one of the other guards. Mime split off, heading in the opposite direction.

Mark found it amazing how clearly he and Mime instinctively understood each other. He began to wonder if their connection went far beyond the owner-pet relationship he had first assumed. Mime's ability to communicate directly in his head, their mutual understanding with just a glance, and their near-perfect coordination during fights were clear evidence that their connection was far deeper. However, there would be time to consider that later. At the moment, Mark's entire focus was on eliminating the guard in front of him.

All the prisoners in the Tomb that Mark had seen wore

shackles on their wrists and ankles, which prevented them from using their abilities. Mark had discovered, however, that some prisoners were better at suppressing the disorienting mana field the shackles produced. As he peeked between a couple of boxes, watching the guard strolling by in the next aisle over, Mark saw something interesting.

For most of the prisoners, the web of mana that produced the disorienting effect was spread relatively evenly throughout the body. Its effect was often suppressed by the prisoner's physical strength, which left them feeling exhausted, while also preventing their powers from activating. In this prisoner, however, not only had the web been suppressed, but the threads of mana that made it up had been compressed, forming only a few faint lines that linked the shackles together, while leaving the majority of the prisoner's body free from the effect of the mana. This was very similar to what Mark had done in his own body.

As the guard stepped around the corner and into the light, Mark saw that his skin bore a bronze sheen. He also carried a mana blade at his waist, and his hand rested on the weapon's handle. He seemed spooked, his eyes darting this way and that, searching the shadows for any sign of an enemy.

Eyes narrowing, Mark launched himself forward, hoping to catch the guard by surprise. Whether it was a shift in the air or something else, the guard's eyes widened and he spun around, drawing his mana blade with a smooth motion. Mark didn't hesitate, and as he arrived in front of the guard, his null field rolled out, blanketing the entire area in the strange energy that dispersed mana.

The guard, not realizing that his mana blade had lost its edge, raked it across Mark's arm, but the dull metal simply bounced off Mark's bone blade forearm. As the guard's mouth opened wide to shout, Mark stuffed his fingers straight down the man's throat, cutting through the back of his head and severing his spine.

Though he managed to prevent the guard from yelling, he wasn't able to stop the mana blade from clattering to the floor as the guard's body spasmed. The sound was loud, and Mark immediately heard someone stirring in the center of the warehouse. Deactivating the null field, Mark retreated, bringing the guard's body with him. As he hid, he saw Mime trotting over, licking her lips.

Mark reached out with his psychic network, finding only one person remaining in the warehouse. They were currently heading in his direction, and peeking past the corner of a shelf, Mark saw Kelly clutching a mana sword in his hands and looking around nervously as he walked down the aisle.

Mark backed up, Mime hopping onto his shoulder as he made his way toward the edge of the warehouse and circled around. He could hear Kelly continuing to call out in the distance as he strolled toward the desk, where he found stacks of paper and a terminal. He took a seat in the single chair and waited quietly until Kelly hurried back.

As soon as he spotted Mark sitting in his chair with Mime on his lap, Kelly froze, staring in shock at the strange person who had suddenly appeared. "Who are you?"

Ignoring the outburst, Mark stroked Mime and watched Kelly. To his credit, the merchant calmed down quickly, and apart from glancing around, as if hoping his minions might pop back up, he faced Mark squarely. "What do you want? If it's merits, I can give it to you. If it's a rare good, I can get it for you."

Shaking his head, Mark stood up. "You sold a batch of defective goods yesterday."

"Wait, is this about the ingredients that I sold that kid?" Kelly said, lifting his hand.

"So you knew they were defective."

Mark's tone was light, but as he stepped forward, Kelly took a quick step back. "Hold on, we can talk about this."

His voice was frantic, but Mark could see the crafty look in Kelly's eyes. As Kelly reached for his watch, no doubt intending to send some sort of distress signal, Mark lunged forward, grabbing the merchant's hand tightly.

As he activated his null field, the mana surrounding them bled away, creating a dead space where no messages could be sent, and Mark launched his attack. Recognizing something was wrong, Kelly let out a roar and tore his hand free from Mark's grasp. At the same time, he thrust out his other palm, forcing Mark to dodge, as a violent wind was kicked up. Realizing that Kelly was a strength-based empowered, Mark slipped away, his hand lacerating Kelly's side. Fury blazed through the merchant's eyes, and he spun with surprising quickness, launching a devastating punch at Mark's head.

Mark leaned back, and his foot shot out, slamming into Kelly's thigh to prevent him from moving forward. The blow only stopped Kelly for a moment before he surged forward again, his fists flying. Every strike he unleashed stirred up great wind, and Mark was forced to scramble away, knowing that if he got hit by even a single punch, he'd be in trouble.

Their fight took them across the warehouse, and as Mark swerved around crates, Kelly went straight through them, caring little for the product they contained as he bulldozed his way forward. Cursing, Kelly finally pulled up short, his breath heaving as he glared at Mark. As they paused, Kelly suddenly threw himself backward, clearly intending to get away, but Mark stayed with him. Triumph bloomed in Kelly's eyes, and having successfully baited Mark in, he stepped forward, unleashing a fierce punch. Mark had been expecting it and slipped around, his own attack tearing at Kelly's wrist. His goal was to take off the brute's watch, ensuring that he wouldn't be able to call for backup. The attack sliced through the band of the watch, then continued on, digging deep into Kelly's wrist and tearing through the shackle the merchant wore. Yelping with pain, Kelly jerked his hand back as both his watch and shackle clattered to the floor. With hate-filled eyes, he glared at Mark. Then, catching sight of the ruined shackle, he blanched. "No, no, no!"

Diving for the mangled piece of metal, he tried to grab it, but Mark was a step faster and kicked it to the side. As it spun out of the range of the null field, there was a sharp beep, and Kelly let out a terrified scream. His eyes wild, he leaped for Mark, who was forced to skip backward. One of Kelly's heavy fists blasted through a post supporting a metal shelf, causing the entire thing to sag. Heavy boxes began to slide and shift, and Mark took off in a sprint as the shelf began to collapse. One of the crates slammed down on Kelly, driving him to a knee, but he didn't care. With a frantic growl, he turned and rushed after Mark, who continued to retreat.

"You! I'll kill you!"

Kelly's enraged roars filled the warehouse, but Mark was too fast for him and was able to stay out of his reach as he was chased around. Kelly seemed to have lost control of himself, and Mark had no idea why, until he heard a loud hum, and then the wall of the warehouse exploded inward.

Spinning around, Kelly stared in horror as four large robots floated in through the wide gap they had created. They were as tall as a man and hovered a few feet off the ground. They each had four large mechanical limbs that ended in heavy claws, and when he saw them, Kelly began to back up. These were the Reapers, tasked with collecting the bodies of those who died in the Tomb. Ducking behind a shelf, Mark watched as they rapidly spread out to surround Kelly. It was then that he remembered Henry's clear warning to never lose his shackles.

A mechanical voice that sounded an awful lot like Mr. Robot's rang out. "Morris Kelly, Prisoner 98325679, you have been found in violation of the Prisoner Code. You will be reassigned as a test subject."

"No, it—"

Kelly didn't manage to finish his sentence as one of the Reapers extended an arm toward him. Mark felt a flash of mana, and the three remaining shackles lit up, causing a surge of mana to run through Kelly. His words turned into a garbled scream, and he collapsed to the ground, his body twitching as mana coursed through him.

One of the Reapers floated over to where the discarded shackle lay and picked it up, while another effortlessly lifted Kelly's body. The third and fourth Reaper spun slowly, scanning the warehouse. One of them paused as its sensors picked up Mark, and for a tense moment, it stared at him.

"Mark Fields, Prisoner 79956312. No registered violations. Flag applied."

With that, it continued to scan, and Mark let out the breath he had been unknowingly holding. As quickly as they had come, the Reapers left, flying out of the hole they'd punched in the side of the warehouse, leaving Mark alone in the ruins.

Looking around at the alchemical ingredients scattered across the floor, Mark felt a twinge of pain. He had no doubt that scavengers would soon descend on the warehouse, and he didn't want to be here when they arrived. Unfortunately, he wouldn't be able to carry much. Sensing his dilemma, Mime trotted out from her hiding place and opened her mouth. One after another, five watches dropped on the ground in front of her.

"Wait, are those the guards' watches?"

Mime flashed a self-satisfied smile and nodded.

"How?"

Mark looked at his shadow, then at Mime, and then back at his shadow. His shadow had devoured all but one of the guards, and yet their watches had ended up with Mime . . .

"So how much can you store?" Mark asked.

Mime considered the question for a moment and then hopped up onto a large crate, which she patted with her paw.

"Mime, that's amazing. How do you fit it inside you? I mean, do you have to swallow it? Wait, no. I guess I can take it in my shadow, right?"

Mime nodded and made an enveloping motion with her front paws. Picking up the watches, Mark looked around.

"All right, we probably don't have much time before scavengers show up," he said, fixing his makeshift mask back around his face. "Let's get what we need and get out of here."

By the time Mark had finished going through the ingredients he needed and transferring them all to a new crate, he could sense dozens of people gathering. He had no desire to get into a fight, so after commanding his shadow to absorb the crate, Mark sneaked out the back door. Close to twenty-five people were standing in the alleyway, clearly waiting for a command to go inside. When they saw Mark, they all froze. Doing his best to appear nonchalant, Mark jerked a thumb over his shoulder.

"No one is here, but you'll want to get in there quick," he said. "There were probably thirty people out front, all waiting to see if it's clear. If you head in now, you could probably get the upper hand."

He could feel their eyes raking over him, but he didn't appear to be carrying anything, so they didn't stop him as he strolled through them toward the end of the alley. As soon as he stepped around the corner, Mark took off, running as fast as he possibly could. He didn't head to the alchemy shop, instead spending the next hour and a half getting lost in the maze of streets. He couldn't sense anyone following him, and when, two hours later, he made it back to his apartment, he was pretty sure that he had gotten off scot-free.

As he shut and locked the door, Mark could feel his nerves jumping. He had originally intended to go in, eliminate the guards, and threaten Kelly in order to get his money back. Instead, he had accidentally gotten Kelly dragged off and the entire business shut down.

Glancing down at the shackles on his wrists, Mark felt a hint of danger. The Reapers made the hair on the back of his neck stand up, and while he was confident that he would be able to fight one of them, there was absolutely no way he could take on multiple. Of course, they had managed to subdue Kelly, since he still had three of the shackles on, which wouldn't work against Mark's null field. That brought a question to mind. Would his null field work in deactivating the robots? It was something to test, but Mark wasn't quite sure how he could without alerting the powers that be of his ability.

Checking his watch, he lay down to catch a few hours of sleep, since he had to report to the alchemy shop at seven. When he arrived the next morning, he saw that the entire end of the street where Kelly's Alchemical Supply was located had been cordoned off, and half a dozen large robots stood outside it.

He still had a few minutes before he needed to start, so Mark wandered over. The robots didn't react to his presence, though he assumed that if he stepped over the line they had drawn, that wouldn't be the case. A number of other people were hanging about, watching the goings-on, and Mark tapped one of them on the shoulder.

"What?" the man snarled, looking over his shoulder.

When he caught sight of Mark, however—and more importantly, the watch on his wrist—his expression changed, and he quickly groveled. "I'm sorry, sir. I didn't see you there. What can I help you with?"

Rather put off by the abrupt change in attitude, Mark gestured to the cordoned-off warehouse. "What happened here?"

"A raid, or some sort of fight," the man said with a half shrug, indicating that he didn't know much about what was going on. "Word is that Kelly got hauled down to the labs. People said they heard his screaming. Then the Reapers showed up. They dragged him off, still alive, the poor sod."

"He deserved it," another man said, spitting on the ground.

The man who had been speaking to Mark rolled his eyes. "He

was tightfisted, sure. But getting turned into a living experiment? I don't know if anybody deserves that."

Deciding it would be better not to hang around, Mark put ten merits on a card and tossed it to the man who had answered his questions. He then headed back to the shop. When he walked in, Mr. Robot was looming behind the desk, his beady red eyes fixed on Mark. For a moment, Mark thought he'd get a question about last evening's activities. But Mr. Robot just gave him a sharp nod and went dormant.

Walking into the back workshop, Mark carefully shut the door and paused. He glanced down at his shadow, then scratched his head. Last night, he'd asked the shadow to envelop the crate without consuming it, but he had no idea how to get it back out. Thinking for a moment, he tried picturing the crate appearing on the ground in front of him. His shadow boiled and surged to cover that part of the floor. A moment later, it retreated, and sitting there was the wooden crate.

"Well, that's incredible," Mark muttered.

Taking the lid off, Mark saw the rows of ingredients he had tossed inside. He had gathered everything he needed for this week's potions and more. Licking his lips, Mark began sorting them out and putting them into their respective containers. Occasionally, he would glance over at the boxes of manaless ingredients. Finally, curiosity took hold of him.

Retrieving one of the inert stalks of grass, Mark took a mana-filled stalk of the same kind and examined them side by side. A crazy idea started to brew. The difference between the two stalks was that one held mana and the other didn't. Otherwise, they were exactly identical, at least as far as Mark could tell. The mana contained in the stalk of grass felt to him like a soft cloud, slightly wet, but delicate enough that a gust of wind might blow it away.

Sitting down, Mark held the two stalks of grass in his hands and began to concentrate, trying to express mana through his palm and into the inert piece of grass. It took him a moment to get the hang of it, but it wasn't long before a faint trickle of mana was leaving his body and filling the grass. Immediately, he noticed a problem. His mana was different from the cloudy, soft mana that the other piece of grass contained. It was sharper and heavier, and it moved more like molten metal than mist. Almost immediately, the stalk of grass began to wither, brown spots appearing on its leaves and stem, as the thick mana destroyed it from the inside. Rather than trying to withdraw his mana and salvage the grass, Mark just watched it, paying careful attention to how his mana destroyed it.

"Fundamentally, the principle is sound," he mused. "I just need to figure out how to change my mana. Or maybe that's the wrong approach. Maybe what I need to do is pull in mana from other sources, rather than using my own."

Biting his lip, Mark threw away the ruined piece of grass and carefully recorded what he had seen. Though he wanted to continue with the experiments, he only had six days left to make all the potions, so he spent the rest of his day working on stamina potions.

For the next few days, all he did was alchemy, and four days later, he had successfully finished all sixty potions. The more he practiced, the better he got, and the majority of his potions were tier two, earning him a tidy profit. Over those four days, he also called around to a number of other suppliers, since Kelly's warehouse was still cordoned off. Having learned his lesson, he handpicked the ingredients he would take, looking through them one by one. When one of the suppliers complained at how long it was taking, Mark simply shrugged and told him to talk to Mr. Robot. That shut the merchant right up, and after Mark had finished and arranged for the delivery, he found himself with some free time.

Since he still had multiple crates of defective ingredients, Mark began his experiments again, working on manipulating the mana into the right consistency to keep the plants from being destroyed. When Mark announced he was done, Mr. Robot stomped into the workshop, examined the potions one by one, and then sent Mark 26,150 merits. Stunned by how much he had earned in a week, Mark celebrated with another trip to the grocery store, this time picking out some of the more expensive food he had avoided during his last shopping trip.

When he got back to his apartment, however, he found a man leaning against the wall in front of his door. With an armful of groceries, Mark stopped well out of arm's reach.

As the man straightened up, he said, "The name's Jemson. I'm your landlord. Rent's due."

"And how much is rent?" Mark asked.

"Two thousand merits."

Raising his eyebrows at the sudden increase in cost, Mark put his groceries down and tapped his watch, sending the payment over. Jemson, surprised at how quickly Mark had paid, licked his lips.

"Actually," he started, but Mark reached in his pocket and pulled out the bundle of watches he had tied together, cutting Jemson off mid-sentence.

"Somebody mentioned that I could turn these in to the administrators or one of the enforcers. I was wondering if you knew where that was."

Swallowing whatever words he had been about to say, Jemson nodded. "The central admin building. Downtown."

"Thanks, I appreciate it," Mark said with a smile. "Also, I wonder if you could help me. Is it possible to set up autopay for my rent? You know, so it comes out every month."

Jemson took a step back as Mark walked closer.

"We don't have anything like that. No," the landlord said, shaking his head.

"Well, if you could work on it, that'd be really convenient. I'm sure it's annoying to have to go around and knock on everybody's door. This would probably save you quite a bit of headache."

With a nod, Mark opened his door and stepped into his apartment as Jemson gave him a sickly smile.

Mark had been considering what to do with the watches for a while, and while he could take them to the administrative building, another idea was starting to brew in his mind. The next day, since he didn't have any potions to brew and there was still one more day before he would get his new production list, Mark headed for the central administrative building. The closer he got to the center of the Tomb, the more robots he saw, and each one's eyes followed him as he passed by. Unsure what was going on, Mark kept his head down and walked swiftly, not wanting to draw any attention.

At the central administrative building, he entered through the wide double doors and found himself in a large foyer, brightly lit by mana lights, with a marble floor inlaid with an abstract symbol that looked a little bit like an octopus holding wands in each of its eight legs. Had he not known he was underground in the Tomb, Mark would have sworn he was in one of the government buildings of New Emery. Even the people who walked through the building didn't look like prisoners, and he noticed more than one who lacked shackles. Most of these people were dressed in lab coats and had the look of administrators or scientists.

"May I help you with anything?"

Hearing a voice at his elbow, Mark turned and found one of these administrators standing next to him. Behind the administrator, a large robot watched Mark carefully.

"I have a couple questions," Mark said, "about property and the rules of the Tomb."

Frowning faintly, the administrator tapped on his watch, and the eyes of the robot behind him flashed. Though Mark couldn't see what was happening, he assumed that the administrator was pulling up his profile. After all, the robot seemed to have immediate access, likely through the sensors contained in the shackles.

"Ah, you've just been assigned to the Tomb a week ago, and you already have a job as an alchemist. Impressive."

It was slightly disconcerting how much information the administrator had on him, but Mark pushed the discontent down and nodded respectfully. "Yes, sir."

Scrolling farther down, the administrator suddenly paused and then looked up at Mark. "Are you here about the warehouse incident?"

Mark had, in fact, come to inquire about the warehouse. However, he had a sneaking suspicion that what the administrator was discussing and what he was interested in were two different things. Tentatively, he nodded, and the administrator gestured for him to follow. He was led to a small room with a simple desk. After the robot had squeezed in through the door behind them, the administrator shut the door and took a seat. With a few taps on his watch, he projected Mark's file onto the table so that they could both see it.

"Presence at the scene of a break-in is not, in and of itself, a violation. But the fact that you were wearing a mask when Morris Kelly was found in violation for removing his shackle got you flagged. The cost to remove a simple flag like this is ten thousand merits. If it was a violation, it depends on what kind of violation it is," the administrator said, chuckling. "There are a couple of different categories. A simple flag is ten thousand, a moderate flag is fifty thousand, a severe flag one hundred fifty thousand, and a nonexecutable violation is five hundred thousand. Of course, if you get tagged with an executable violation—for instance, removing one of your shackles or harming one of the robots—you'll be immediately processed. There is no recourse for that."

Taking a deep breath, Mark nodded. "Got it."

"So would you like me to clear it? I see that you have merits in your account."

"Before we do that," Mark said, "I was wondering, is it possible to buy property in the Tomb? Or rather, can I start a business?"

"What sort of business did you have in mind?"

"Well . . ." Mark bit his lip as he considered how to approach the subject. "Kelly and I were in the middle of negotiations when there was an accident and his shackle came off. I was wondering what it would cost to maybe take over his business."

For a long moment, the administrator didn't say anything. Then, rubbing his face, he shrugged.

"Businesses aren't a matter of paying," he said. "At least, not as far as the administration is concerned. All you need to do is put in an application. I happen to know that there are already a number of other applications that have been submitted. Three from Viper Clan, two from the Syndicate, and six from other individuals. You're welcome to put in an application, and the administration will award the contract to whoever it thinks is most appropriate. That's something that I can help you with if you need."

"Thank you," Mark said, dipping his head. "If you wouldn't mind, I'd like to do that and get rid of my simple flag."

"Sure, we'll need to fill out some information, including why you think you're the best person to run Kelly's Alchemical Supply."

An hour later, when Mark walked out of the administrative building, his application submitted and his simple flag cleared, he found the robots didn't pay any special attention to him. Feeling quite relieved, he headed toward Mr. Robot's shop. In truth, he had no anticipation of being awarded the contract for the alchemy supply store but figured it was worth applying for regardless. He had been asked to provide a reference and had put down Mr. Robot, earning himself a curious glance from the administrator.

About a block from Mr. Robot's shop, Mark saw a group of people step out of an alleyway and spread out in front of him. Not wanting to walk straight through them, Mark started to cross the street, but one of them called out to him. "Excuse me, can we have a moment of your time?"

Pausing, Mark examined the group closely. There were two women and a man, and the one who had spoken to Mark was tall, blond, and quite pretty. Yet despite her beauty, something about her caused Mark's senses to tingle, a faint sense of danger that he hadn't encountered in anyone he had met in the Tomb so far. Before he could figure out what it was, she took a step closer and, clasping her hands in front of her chest, bowed. "The Prophet would like to speak to you."

Thrown off, Mark gave her a strange look and stepped back. "Who?"

"The Prophet."

For a moment, Mark and the woman stared at each other, and then Mark shook his head. "I'm sorry, I am a bit busy at the moment. Maybe another time."

Her companions bristled, and one of them, a tall, athletic-looking man, started to step forward, but the pretty blond held up her hand to stop him. "Very well, we will return another time."

Bowing again, with the same clasped-hands gesture, she turned and led her companions away, leaving Mark scratching his head. He had no idea who this prophet was supposed to be, and after racking his brain to try to figure it out, he could only shrug and walk the remaining block to Mr. Robot's alchemical store.

A couple of people were browsing through the potions when he entered the store, but they paid him no mind, and neither did Mr. Robot. Heading into the workshop, Mark continued with his experiments, attempting to shift the structure of the mana he was controlling. He was making steady progress, though excruciatingly slow, but he didn't mind particularly, as he assumed he'd have plenty of time on his hands going forward.

Mark had been doing his best not to think about the fact that he would likely never make it out of the Tomb, and when the thought did creep into his mind, he resolutely forced himself to banish it. Once he was established, then he would think about it, but until then, worrying about whether he would be able to escape was a fool's errand.

When it came time to close up for the evening, Mr. Robot appeared and handed him a new production list. The same as the first week, though it listed fifteen Blurs instead of ten. After Mark had looked over the list, Mr. Robot produced another piece of paper. "You have applied to operate the business once known as Kelly's Alchemical Supply. You put my name on the application as your reference. Your application has been approved."

His eyes going wide, Mark grabbed the paper Mr. Robot held out and scanned it. It was simple in both its language and content, informing him that the administration had approved his application, and he was now in charge of the warehouse and a number of supply channels.

Mark, who had only applied on a whim, with no anticipation of actually being awarded the business, swallowed as he read the terms listed in bold lettering at the bottom. Every month, he would have to give the administration 40 percent of the business's profits or 100,000 merits, whichever was larger.

Mr. Robot regarded Mark for a second and then, without saying another word, turned and stalked out of the room. Mark hurried to finish cleaning up and practically ran down the street. When he arrived at the warehouse, he saw that the writing that had been scrawled on the side of the building had been scrubbed off, and the giant hole that had been blown in the wall had been repaired. The doors were locked tight, but as he scanned his watch, they opened with a beep, and stepping inside, Mark pulled up short.

The inside of the warehouse was a wreck, with broken and twisted shelves and cracked boxes. Almost everything of value had been stripped out by scavengers, and Mark suddenly had a sinking feeling that he had just thrown himself headfirst into a pit.

As he walked through the destroyed warehouse, Mark could feel his stomach clenching. He had a month to come up with 100,000 merits, which meant that he had to get this alchemy supply store back up and running as fast as possible. Thankfully, included in the contract were the supply points where Mark could find material, as well as a long list of previous customers.

Taking a deep breath, Mark walked to the destroyed desk and hunted around for the chair. One of its legs was snapped off, but he balanced it on the edge of the collapsed desk and took a seat. His fight with Kelly had completely destroyed the area, and no effort had been made to clean it up.

Rubbing his cheek, Mark suddenly laughed at the absurdity of it all. Still, no matter how absurd, he had to deal with the circumstances in front of him, and as he thought through the pros and cons of his situation, he quickly came up with a workable plan.

The majority of the goods left behind were duds, and Mark was beginning to wonder if that was just the case across the board. No wonder alchemists had such a low success rate, if they couldn't tell the difference between mana-active ingredients and inactive ingredients that looked identical. If he had to guess, he suspected that the difference between apprentice alchemists and full alchemists was a sort of instinctive sixth sense for which ingredients would actually work and which would not.

To a certain degree, Mark was thankful that the scavengers had cleaned out the warehouse. This meant he wouldn't have to try to sell the inert materials and instead would be able to stock and sell active ingredients. Thinking for a moment, Mark went and opened up the large garage door and looked around the street. When he spotted a group of seven chattels hanging out nearby, he gestured for them to come over. "You gentlemen looking for work?"

The men's eyes lit up, and they hurried forward. "Yes, yes, we are."

The one who spoke was the man Mark had talked to before. He quickly bobbed his head, likely remembering the merits Mark had given him.

"A hundred merits, however you want to split them, if you clean up the warehouse."

Without a word, all seven of them immediately got to work,

clearing out the ruined boxes and piling them up in the back of the warehouse. Boxes that still held ingredients or were in good enough shape to be used were stacked in the other corners. While they were working, Mark took note of which shelves had to be pulled down and directed the men to take them apart and pile them up to be sold off for scrap. Almost a third of the shelves had to be pulled down, but Mark had no intention of replacing them, so the warehouse ended up a good bit emptier. They worked most of the night, and by the time morning came, all the men were exhausted. Mark handed over the hundred merits, along with an extra hundred.

"Do me a favor: After you guys have gotten breakfast, keep an eye on the warehouse. I'll be gone for a little while, and I'd like to make sure nothing happens to it."

"Of course, yes, boss."

Eager to please, the men all bowed repeatedly as Mark locked up and headed to Mr. Robot's shop. He spent most of the day making potions, clearing his whole quota of stamina potions and the majority of the healing potions he needed to make as well. He worked with absolute focus, keeping himself entirely locked in to ensure the highest-quality potions possible. Apart from one healing potion, all of them were tier two, and Mark was quite pleased. He fully intended to complete Mr. Robot's production requirements in two days instead of four, as that would give him five days to work on the alchemy supply business.

That evening, after getting back to his apartment and tumbling into bed, he spent a few minutes looking for an apartment closer to Mr. Robot's shop. The only one he found was almost four times more expensive, which he simply couldn't afford. Deciding that he could just sleep in the warehouse, which would help with security as well, Mark bundled up his bed the next morning and carried it through the streets, earning himself quite a few strange looks.

When he got to the warehouse, he found a couple of the men

he had paid to watch it lurking outside, and they hurried forward to help him with the mattress. After placing it in an empty corner, Mark called the men together again, paid them another 200 merits, and asked them to knock together a small room using the broken boards and scrap metal from the shelves. A few of them scratched their heads and looked at each other, but their leader, who had introduced himself as Albert, quickly took the merits and pushed the others toward the piles of scrap.

Mark had absolutely no expectation of coming back to anything even remotely impressive, but after spending the day finishing off the rest of the potions, he returned to find a neat little partition at one end of the warehouse. Around two hundred square feet had been blocked off to build a sturdy little office. Rather bemused, Mark found Albert lurking nearby, looking rather nervous. "Did you build this?"

Albert hurried to nod. "Yes, sir. I did. Well, with the others' help, of course."

"Have you done much building before?" Mark asked, squinting at the surprisingly robust-looking structure.

"Yes, sir. That was my job before, well, before I was moved down here."

"How did you get moved down here?" Mark asked. It was an impolite question, and Albert flinched when he heard it, but after a moment, he sighed and shrugged.

"I had a rival, sir, a competing businessman. He was empowered, just like me, and he muscled into some of my business. I lost one too many big contracts to him and got sick of seeing his face." With a grimace, Albert shrugged. "One night, we were both at the club, and, well, there were some words. One thing led to another, and when I woke up, I was in Gray Rock. I spent a couple of years on the sixth floor and then got tangled up with the Syndicate. That landed me down here."

"Ah, I see. Stay here."

Walking into the room, Mark saw the bed had been placed in the corner, and a makeshift desk had been set up nearby. There was nothing else in the room, but when Mark envisioned a watch on the desk, his shadow crawled up and deposited one of the five watches he had gathered from the warehouse guards. Picking it up, he walked back out of the room and tossed it to Albert, who stared at it in shock.

"I'm going to loan this to you," Mark said. "In return, you're going to work for me, guarding the warehouse and helping out. Your companions can stick around too. Pay will be five hundred merits a month for anybody who has a watch, and one hundred merits a month for anybody who doesn't. But if anybody does a good job, there are more watches where that one came from."

Albert, his eyes wide, quickly nodded and slipped the watch onto his wrist with trembling fingers. As he locked it in place, relief seemed to wash over him.

"We're going to be getting supplies soon and opening for business by the end of the week. If you can find material, you can build another bunkhouse in the corner over there. Just move these shelves down, and anybody who works here is allowed to stay."

"Thank you, sir."

Waving him off, Mark walked back into the office and sat down at the small desk. After going through the list of wholesale suppliers the administrators had attached to his appointment document, Mark picked the one he liked and called to make an appointment.

The following morning, he found himself standing outside a nondescript office near the central administration building. At eight o'clock, the door opened, and a massive man squeezed out. Close to eight feet tall and as broad as a barn door, the man looked Mark over, checked his watch, and then gestured for him to come in. As Mark stepped past him, he marveled at the size of the brute's hand. He imagined the giant could likely squeeze him in half without much effort. When he stepped inside the building, Mark came face-to-face with a middle-aged woman dressed in a severe gray suit with a short bob. She peered at Mark from behind steel-rimmed glasses, her eyes weighing him, as if determining exactly how much value he had.

"You must be Mark. My name is Viola Carice. I am in charge of the Western Supply Channel. Please have a seat."

Ms. Carice spoke in short, clipped sentences, and every word sent a shiver down Mark's spine. He was absolutely certain that the woman in front of him was A ranked, and probably at the high end—he could practically feel the aura radiating from her. It was something he had only ever experienced with his brother before Joe had burned out, and between the massive brute outside and the realization that Ms. Carice could squash him like a bug, Mark was suddenly reminded that no matter how powerful he was, he still wasn't at the top of the pile. As Mark sat down on the edge of a chair, Ms. Carice sat across from him and crossed her legs.

"Kelly was one of our larger clients," she said briskly. "But from what I understand, you have taken over his business."

Surprised he'd chosen the same supplier as Kelly, Mark nodded as Ms. Carice handed over a folder.

"Inside you'll find our contract; you'll sign it and we'll be done here."

Keeping his expression carefully neutral, Mark opened up the contract. Though she frowned with impatience, Ms. Carice didn't stop him and remained silent until he had finished reading.

"Well," she asked, "do you need a pen, or did you bring your own?"

The further Mark had read through the contract, the deeper the furrow between his brows had grown, and at Ms. Carice's question, he let out a sigh, his expression easing.

"This contract will bankrupt me within a month," he said, shaking his head. "Which means you won't get paid."

"I always get paid."

With a wry smile, Mark shrugged. "There has to be money for you to get paid. Even if you chopped me up and sold me off for parts, you wouldn't get your money back. The volume that Kelly was doing isn't something that I can match, at least in the short term. However, I am willing to sign this contract . . . with two stipulations."

"I don't think you're in a position to be asking for stipulations," Ms. Carice said, her eyes narrowing behind her glasses.

The pressure Mark felt was intense, and as Ms. Carice stared at him, a bead of sweat rolled down the back of his neck. Still, he kept his expression even as he held up two fingers.

"First stipulation is that we increase the size of the contract, but that we do it gradually. I'd rather work with a single supplier than multiple."

Taken aback, as that sounded like exactly the opposite of what Mark had initially suggested, Ms. Carice tilted her head as Mark continued.

"Second stipulation. I want to select the goods and have the right to turn away any material that isn't up to my standards."

Watching the flash of realization in Ms. Carice's eyes, Mark knew that she had figured out what he was suggesting.

"You want to compete on quality, not quantity," she said.

"Correct. Rather than running a wholesale business selling cheap ingredients with an incredibly questionable success rate, I want to run a business that sells guaranteed ingredients."

"'Guarantee' is a strong word."

"My eyes are good."

"They'll have to be if you want to survive after making someone a promise like that."

Leaning forward, Mark smiled with what he hoped was a confident air. "Ms. Carice, I'm an alchemist. If I'm being honest, I only submitted for this business on a whim, and I have a sneaking suspicion that my employer had a lot more to do with me getting it than anything I said on the application. I'm confident in my ability to pick ingredients, and if you're willing to let me do that, then I think we can come to a very profitable arrangement."

"Can you back up your words?"

"Sure." Mark leaned back in his seat, crossing his legs, mirroring Ms. Carice's attitude. "It's simple enough. Do you have an alchemist? Let me pick the ingredients that each of us use, and I'll guarantee your alchemist fails to brew the potion."

Slowly, Ms. Carice's eyebrows rose, and for a long moment she stared at Mark, as if she wanted to see what was inside his head. "Crusher."

The giant brute, who had been standing quietly in the corner, perked up. "Yes, Ms. Carice?"

"Go ask Master Peller to meet us in the workshop."

"Yes, ma'am."

Getting up, Ms. Carice gestured for Mark to follow her through a set of double doors and down a long hallway. At the end of the hall was what looked like an office complex, and Mark saw numerous white-coated individuals running around. Most of them paid no attention to Mark, but all of them paused to greet Ms. Carice. She took Mark to a small workshop, and a few moments later, Crusher and an elderly man Mark assumed was Master Peller arrived.

"I hope this is important, Ms. Carice. The research that I'm working on is at a critical juncture and cannot be delayed."

"It shouldn't take up much of your time, Master Peller. Allow me to introduce you to Mark Fields, a budding alchemist and a potential partner of ours. He has claimed to have a rather interesting ability, one that could be immensely profitable if he is telling the truth. I'm hoping that you can assist us in testing whether he is."

"Oh?" Master Peller looked at Mark. "And what sort of ability is this?"

"He claims to be able to tell whether ingredients will create a successful potion before the potion is even brewed."

Frowning, Master Peller looked at Mark, then at Ms. Carice. "He's a little bit young to be a master alchemist, isn't he? And even if he is, so what? Any master alchemist can do that."

Holding up his hands, Mark shook his head. "I'm not a master alchemist, sir. In fact, I haven't even taken the alchemist examination. I'm not technically an alchemist at all."

Master Peller shook his head. "Then what are we even here

for?" he asked Ms. Carice, who was staring at Mark in shock.

She quickly tapped her watch, likely pulling up Mark's profile, and read over it. When she got to the end, she looked at Mark again. "But you're employed by Mr. Robot, making potions?"

"Well, yes," Mark said. "But I still haven't taken the actual alchemist test. I don't have a license or anything. I was planning on it at some point."

Hearing Mark's words, it was Master Peller's turn to look shocked. "Wait, you work with Mr. Robot, and you say you can pick out material with one hundred percent accuracy?"

"I'm not sure about one hundred percent," Mark said, hedging his bets. "But I'm fairly confident that I can pick out ingredients with at least ninety percent accuracy."

"Ha! Seventy-five percent accuracy is the best any master can do, including myself," Master Peller said. "So if you can actually pick out ingredients at ninety percent accuracy, that is, well, that'll be astounding. Come, I have to see this for myself."

His other experiments forgotten, Master Peller rushed over to a shelf of ingredients and quickly selected enough for ten healing potions.

"Healing potions are the easiest," he said, as he laid the ingredients out. "And my success rate with them is above seventy-five percent. Now, tell me, which of these sets of ingredients are going to fail?"

Suddenly feeling a bit nervous, Mark stepped forward and began to examine the ingredients one by one, Ms. Carice and Master Peller both watching him like hawks. At first, he started by picking up an ingredient and concentrating on it, but soon he realized that merely focusing his gaze on each ingredient in turn was enough to see how much mana it had inside.

In the third set of ingredients, he found an inert stalk, then another in the sixth. In the eighth batch, he saw a piece of mushroom that lacked any mana, and in the ninth, he saw a set of leaves whose mana was thick and heavy, a far cry from the light, cloudy mana that it should have had.

Pointing out the third, sixth, and eighth batches, Mark shook his head. "These three won't work. The potions will fail. The ninth batch could fail too. There's something wrong with these leaves, though I'm not exactly sure what."

Ms. Carice looked at Master Peller, who let out a laugh. "Ha! Would you look at that!" Picking up the leaves from the ninth batch, he waved them in the air. "You can actually tell the difference between silver stem leaves that have been grown in wet conditions and silver stem leaves that have been grown in dry conditions. Incredible."

Noticing the confusion on Mark's face, Master Peller patted Mark on the shoulder. "The silver stem plant is one of the few that absorbs different characteristics depending on where it's grown. For healing potions, silver stem leaves grown in wet conditions are necessary. A silver stem leaf from an arid environment will only ever be able to produce a tier-zero or tier-one potion. It will be impossible to make a better potion with the leaf, so you're correct in saying that something would be off about this potion. In fact, most alchemists will simply fail to make a potion with this sort of leaf at all."

"What about the others?" Ms. Carice asked, her expression intense.

Shrugging, Master Peller cleared away the ingredients for the ninth potion.

"We won't know until we try and make them," he said. "You said third, sixth, and eighth? I'll use those ingredients and see if I can succeed. If I can, it'll mean you aren't telling the truth. My success rate is better than seventy-five percent, so I should be able to succeed in at least two of these potions. Come, let's give it a try."

Rubbing his hands together, Master Peller began preparing the ingredients for the first potion. Mark watched intently. This was the first time he had ever seen another alchemist at work, and though his master had taught him a few tricks, he found himself enthralled by the ease with which Master Peller worked. His movements were smooth and sure, his measurements exact and without second thoughts. Twenty minutes later, he had already finished the first potion. He stuck it in the assessment machine and then began to prepare the ingredients for the second potion while the machine worked. Ms. Carice was there and ready to grab the readout as soon as it appeared. After scanning it, she handed it to Master Peller, who took it and grimaced.

"A failure," he said, glancing at Mark.

For his second potion, he took a little bit more time, working carefully with the ingredients to ensure absolute accuracy. Yet when the assessment machine spat out the report, he once again grimaced. "Another failure."

By this time, it was clear that he was taking this personally. The last potion took almost three times as long as the first. Mark watched carefully as Master Peller mixed the ingredients together. He could see the individual strands of mana captured by the base blending together. The other two potions were still full of mana, as each had only one inert ingredient. However, because that ingredient was the grass necessary for activating the healing effect of the potion, drinking the potion would infuse mana into the body but not activate a person's regenerative ability.

Mark was curious about this third potion, however, as it had the grass but lacked a mana-active mushroom. As he watched, Mark suddenly noticed something fascinating. Whether it was a natural phenomenon or due to the care with which Master Peller was working, Mark noticed that the mushroom began to absorb mana from some of the other materials before they mixed together, like a dry sponge. A flash of insight raced through Mark's mind like lightning—anytime he had tried to put mana into an inert ingredient, he did so by injecting it directly into the center. But the result was always the same. The ingredient would wither and die as his mana burned through it. Now, however, he was seeing the mushroom successfully capture ambient mana from its surroundings.

As Master Peller finished brewing the potion, Mark was lost in his thoughts, revising his theories about inert ingredients. The beep of the assessment machine knocked him free from his musings. The master alchemist stared at the assessment for a moment and then, with a groan, handed it to Ms. Carice. She read it and raised an eyebrow. "Isn't this good? It's a successful potion."

"Successful? That's not successful," Master Peller grumbled. "That's a tier-zero potion. If I sold something like this, I'd lose my master's license. That might be good for an apprentice, but for any licensed alchemist, that's considered a failure."

Seeing Ms. Carice look over at him, Mark shrugged.

"I mentioned that I'm only ninety percent accurate," he said. "But an easy way to tell would be to use the other six sets of ingredients. If Master Peller can make potions out of all of them, then it should prove that my senses are as accurate as I'm claiming."

Ms. Carice looked at Master Peller, who nodded. "We've already come this far; we might as well go all the way. Let's see if he's right."

Two hours later, staring at the seven tier-three healing potions, Master Peller groaned.

"Can you tell me how you do it?" he asked Mark.

Mark just shrugged. "It has something to do with my power, I think. I have uncommonly sharp senses. I can't tell you specifically what it is about the ingredients that triggers it, but pretty much as soon as I look at something, I can tell whether it'll work or not."

"Natural-born alchemist," Master Peller muttered and shook his head. "No wonder Mr. Robot hired you."

Ms. Carice was still looking at the reports, and as she reached the last one, she put it down on the table. "Master Peller, what is your assessment?"

"Either the kid has a trick that is undetectable, or he's telling the truth," Master Peller said with a shrug. "He didn't touch any of the ingredients that failed, and he was able to correctly identify which ones would work and which wouldn't."

"What about the eighth potion? I know you said that you consider a tier-zero healing potion a failure, but technically that one succeeded."

Grimacing, Master Peller shrugged. "He said himself that he doesn't have a one hundred percent success rate. With something like healing potions, it doesn't particularly matter if your success rate is only at seventy-five percent, as the ingredients are cheap. But when you get into the expensive potions, where each set of ingredients costs one hundred thousand merits or more, having a ninety percent accuracy in being able to determine success or failure . . ." He let his words hang in the air and shrugged again.

With a decisive nod, Ms. Carice turned to Mark and held out her hand. "We have a deal."

Though slightly worried his hand would be crushed, Mark took a deep breath and shook.

The specific details were ironed out over the next hour, and by the time Mark returned to the warehouse, he had already selected his first batch of goods for delivery and spent 20,000 merits of his own money to buy them. If he could sell all of them, he would make a cool 250,000 merits, more than enough to both pay the administration and buy more materials. It was a gamble, of course, as he wasn't sure if he'd actually be able to sell them. But that concern evaporated as calls started to come in.

He fielded the first few calls himself, and when he gave the price, most of the customers just laughed. Mark was charging four times more for each of the ingredients than Kelly had been. Undeterred, he continued to give the same price. On his sixth call, the potential customer, frustrated, asked him if he was crazy.

"No," Mark said. "The price is because all the goods have been guaranteed. If you have a competent alchemist, using our ingredients will increase their odds of success to at least ninety percent."

The other side of the call was quiet for a long moment. "I'm sorry, did you say ninety percent?"

"Yes," Mark said. "Or your money back."

There was another long moment of silence, and then the customer agreed. "Fine, but I want it in writing."

"Of course. You'll have to come to the warehouse to pick up your goods, but as long as you have a licensed alchemist creating your potions, we guarantee a ninety percent success rate using our ingredients."

Though clearly skeptical, the customer agreed, and an hour later Mark had made his first sale. Three hours after that, the customer was back, along with a slightly frazzled-looking woman whose stained fingers marked her as an alchemist. She fidgeted uncontrollably as the customer tried to haggle with Mark, but he stuck to his guns and soon had sold almost a quarter of his stock.

Mark figured the word would get out eventually, and sure enough, two days later, another alchemist showed up and made a huge order. Within the week, Mark's inventory was almost completely gone, and he had to head back to talk to Ms. Carice about getting more ingredients.

Soon, Mark's life had settled into a steady rhythm. A couple of days a week, he would go to Mr. Robot's shop, where he would brew potions using the ingredients supplied by Ms. Carice. The rest of his time was spent either packing orders for customers or selecting ingredients from Ms. Carice's warehouse.

Mark was careful to always mix in a few duds, just to make sure that no one else had a 100 percent success rate with their potions. At the same time, he continued to experiment, trying to figure out how to manipulate mana in such a way that the inert ingredients could absorb it. After all, the world contained nearly endless mana, and if Mark could discover a way to make inert ingredients active, he'd be able to print money.

Albert and his friends were quite a help to Mark, and they soon handled most of the sales and moving of material. And as the weeks ticked by, Mark handed out the other four watches, along with two more he had picked up after some thieves had broken in to try to swipe some of the ingredients. Seeing how easily Mark had eliminated the two thieves, Albert and the others felt even more eager to stick with Mark, and soon life had settled into a predictable, if mundane, pace.

When the first month had ended, Mark personally delivered the 920,000-merit fee he owed the administrative offices, which was 40 percent of his 2.3-million-merit profit. He had always known alchemy was a tremendously profitable field, but just how quickly he amassed merits stunned him. More and more customers were rushing to buy from him, and Mark quickly realized that he was going to have to raise his prices if he wanted to stay in business.

The problem wasn't with his customers. Rather, the problem was that there simply weren't enough mana-active ingredients to fulfill the desire. Over the course of the month, Mark had discovered that only one in every ten ingredients had active mana, while the others were inert. This meant that the vast majority of potions simply failed, which in turn drove up the cost of potions and made it tremendously expensive to run an alchemy shop.

What Mark was doing, in essence, was pulling out those active ingredients while leaving the inactive ones for other alchemy suppliers, who couldn't tell the difference. Their customers, in turn, saw a plunge in their success rates and soon began to look for other suppliers. Mark first noticed this problem when half a dozen men showed up at his warehouse, along with their steely-eyed leader. Mark met them at the door, and after looking him up and down, the leader introduced himself. "The name's Harrow, of Harrow's Alchemy Warehouse."

"Pleasure to meet you."

"Oh, that depends on how this conversation goes."

Mark's eyes narrowed imperceptibly, and he took a step back. "Come on in."

As the men entered the warehouse, Mark assessed them. He felt he was getting rather good at determining an empowered's strength just from looking at them, thanks to his ability to sense the density of mana in their bodies.

Given the shackles, most of the people who held power in the Tomb were brutes, speedsters, or paragons of some sort. Physically oriented passive powers reigned supreme. Mark was still wary, however, as the shackles didn't prevent him from using his abilities, and he could only imagine that some other empowered could do so as well.

But regardless of whether the men in front of him still had access to their powers, Mark could measure the amount of mana in their bodies to determine their rank. Harrow, the leader, looked to be B ranked, while the rest of the thugs were C ranked like Mark.

Over the last week, Albert had scrounged up some chairs, so Mark invited Harrow to sit down. The others elected to stand in a rough half circle behind Harrow. Albert and the others had started lurking nearby, shooting slightly worried glances in Mark's direction, so he waved his hand and told them to be about their business.

Once they had gone, he took a seat across from Harrow. "So how can I help you?"

Harrow leaned forward, pinning Mark with a hard stare. "You can help us by shutting your business down."

Mark didn't respond for a brief moment, as if he were genuinely considering Harrow's words. Then he shook his head. "I can't do that. The contract I'm in won't allow it."

"We can buy out your contract."

Raising his eyebrows, Mark shifted in his seat, getting more comfortable. "Who exactly is 'we'?"

"I'm here representing myself," Harrow said as he straightened, "but also the Syndicate. Of the eight wholesalers, the

Syndicate controls four, and at first we were content to live and let live. However, your recent actions have harmed our bottom line, and my bosses are not too pleased with that."

"I'm sorry to hear that, but that is how business competition goes. We compete on price and quality of goods. My price is five or six times yours, easily, and it'll probably be going up again soon."

A frustrated look flashed across Harrow's face, and his fist balled. He restrained himself, however, and nodded heavily. "You're not wrong, but let me give you a piece of wisdom. Down here in the Tomb, things are solved differently. Sure, we can't stop you from setting a price, and if customers prefer your goods to ours, then that's what they prefer. However, we have other ways of ensuring your business doesn't go smoothly."

Sitting up, Mark looked at Harrow seriously for a moment, then glanced at the heavyset men behind him. "Why don't we cut to the chase? I'm sure you're not here to just try and intimidate me out of business. What is it you actually want?"

"What I want, what we want, is for you to come under the Syndicate. Currently, you have no backing, which means that your business will fall prey to one of the gangs or merchant groups. I'm sure that you've already started to feel the probing, people poking around to try and find your weaknesses."

"I have."

With a mirthless smile, Harrow tapped himself on the chest. "Well, your options are to be taken over by one of them or join us, and if you're taken over by one of them, I can guarantee that your business isn't going to survive long. We simply can't afford to have anyone cut into our business like this."

"What are the benefits?" Mark asked.

"First and foremost, protection. We'll keep the other groups off your back. Second, recommendations to get you access to all the special services the Tomb can offer. Of course, there are obligations too. You'll give a cut of your business to the Syndicate, and you'll work with the vendors we tell you to work with."

"I'm going to need more than that," Mark said, shaking his head and leaning back.

Harrow's gaze grew hard. "I don't think you understand the position you're in."

Holding up his hand, Mark interrupted him. "I understand the position I'm in just fine. Look, you might think it'll be easy to come in and take over my business. And sure, you could drive me out, insert somebody here, and keep it going for at least as long as there's ingredients in the warehouse. But what's unique about this business is me. And without me, you're going to find yourself in exactly the same position you were before. You're right that I've been starting to see other people poke around. And truth be told, you're not the first person to come and make an offer. So far, I've rejected everybody else. But I'm not entirely opposed to working with the Syndicate."

"You should be."

The voice came from the door, and when Harrow heard it, he lunged to his feet and spun around, his jaw set with anger. A woman, standing six feet five, with shoulders as broad as a bus, strolled into the warehouse. She wore a short vest that left her arms and midriff exposed, and tight leather pants that showed off her heavily muscled legs. A snake tattoo coiled up her right arm and onto her shoulder, then extended around her throat and up onto the side of her shaved skull.

"So you're Mark," she said, completely ignoring Harrow as she came to a stop a dozen feet from where Mark was sitting.

She only had two people with her, both smaller but with the hard looks of professional killers.

"And you are?"

"The name's Python. I'm an underboss for Viper Clan. And

when I heard that Harrow was coming to chat, I thought it'd be a good time to drop in and make a counteroffer. The Syndicate is too stuffy, all business, no heart." Python slapped her chest as she spoke, her eyes flaring.

Mark could see dense mana surging through her limbs, naturally suppressing the web produced by her shackles. Though she didn't have enough mana to be A ranked, she was clearly stronger than Harrow, putting her at the upper end of the B rank. A palpable sense of power radiated from her muscles. Mark could only imagine what a nightmare it would be to try to fight her in close combat.

"Viper Clan is a much better choice. Besides, this neighborhood borders on our territory, and so it'd be a natural thing for you to join us. We control three of the four neighborhoods around here." There was a veiled threat in her words, but she continued without spelling it out. "While we only control two of the other warehouses, it also means that you'd have a higher position in joining us. After all, alchemical supplies are a big business, and being one of three is better than being on the bottom of a pile of five."

With a low growl, Harrow stepped forward, his fists clenching involuntarily. Python turned and met his gaze squarely. "What? You want to fight me? I'll eat you for breakfast."

Not wanting to see his warehouse wrecked, Mark coughed. "Excuse me. If you're going to fight, please take it outside. I'd be happy to continue this conversation with whoever's left once you're done."

"Ha! Hear that, Harrow? It sounds like he doesn't want you around."

The men around Harrow spread out hesitantly, their hands going to the mana blades at their waists. Python didn't seem afraid at all, simply crossing her arms across her chest as she stared at Harrow. Neither wanted to move, that much was evident, and Mark could feel the growing tension.

Thinking quickly, he stood up and gestured in the direction of Mr. Robot's shop. "Ah, just so you know, there is a specific requirement if you would like me to come under you. Again, I'm not completely opposed. Though I must say, I was warned that once I turned down an invitation to either of your organizations, I would never get a second chance. Incidentally, I have turned down those invitations. Still, if you would be willing to take me in and the conditions are good enough, it's possible I'll change my mind. However, before any of that, you're going to have to talk to my current sponsor."

Mark could tell from the way both of them tensed that he had their full attention.

"The only reason I got this business in the first place was because of my employer, Mr. Robot. So if you're interested in getting a piece of the action, which, let me stress again, I don't particularly care about one way or another, you're going to have to talk to him first."

Harrow frowned, and Python's expression turned ugly. Realizing he had hit on a key factor, Mark stood up and doubled down.

"You know, I do respect both the Syndicate and Viper Clan, but I'm currently employed by Mr. Robot. And since he's the one who signed off on this business, it feels like it would be disrespectful for me not to take his opinion into consideration. If you can get his approval and your offers meet my minimum requirements as far as conditions go, I'd be happy to pick this conversation up. But until you talk to him, I'm afraid I just don't have anything else to say. Still, I appreciate you coming to visit and the interest you've shown in my business. I do have a couple of things to take care of this afternoon, so you're welcome to hang around and peruse our goods. But if you'll excuse me, I won't see you out."

Smiling and nodding at each of them, Mark left Harrow and Python standing in the middle of the warehouse as he headed back toward his room and makeshift office. As he walked away, he caught sight of Mime on one of the shelves, lurking between two boxes. Her eyes were fixed on Python, and Mark saw a flash of pink as Mime licked her lips. Afraid his cat would attack, Mark called out to her softly. With a reluctant look at the large woman, Mime hopped down off the shelf, landing on his shoulder.

"We can't eat her in broad daylight," Mark said, taking Mime off his shoulder and holding her in his arms.

When Mime gave him a serious nod, the absurdity of what he had said struck him. The implication of his words was that so long as it wasn't daytime, Python was fair game. Taking a deep breath and pushing aside the ravenous impulses that tugged at him, Mark stepped into his office and began to consider his next plan.

In truth, he had suspected this day would come, and he was just hoping that Mr. Robot would play along, providing some cover from the two gangs. Mark didn't want anything to do with either of them, but they both had too much influence in the Tomb for him to avoid them.

An hour later, when he came out of his office, both Python and Harrow were gone, and after checking the street to make sure they weren't lurking, Mark hurried to visit Mr. Robot. He was half afraid he'd run into them in Mr. Robot's shop, but thankfully it was empty save for the seven-foot-tall metal man lurking behind the counter. When he walked in, Mr. Robot's eyes lit up, and he addressed Mark in his heavy voice. "My master would like to meet you. Will you follow?"

This was the first time Mr. Robot hadn't spoken in a declarative statement, and it caught Mark off guard. Hesitantly, he nodded, and Mr. Robot strode out from behind the counter. "You will follow me now."

This was much more in line with what Mark was used to, and with relief, he hurried after Mr. Robot. They headed through the back door of the shop and down a hallway, and soon they arrived at an old cargo elevator, which took them deeper into the Tomb.

Mark had no idea how far they had dropped when the elevator rattled to a halt, and he emerged with Mr. Robot into a dark and grungy tunnel. Flickering mana lights lit their way forward, breaking up the deep darkness with dim pools of yellow. Mr. Robot strode through them with purpose, his long limbs carrying him quickly down the passage. Mark had to jog to keep up.

They moved in silence, save for the heavy thump of Mr. Robot's feet, until they came to another passageway, this one painted a bright, soft green. Mr. Robot halted abruptly, his body rocking slightly as he came to a stop at the very edge of the passage they were in. "You will proceed to the right and will find the master at the end of the hall."

Glancing down the hallway curiously, Mark was reminded of the research facility hidden in Felwer Mine. Though the colors were different, much of the construction looked similar, and hesitantly he walked out into the passage to continue on his own. As soon as he did, he could feel the mana in the walls starting to shift, locking onto him, as if the gaze of a giant eye had been fixed on him. Feeling his breath catch in his chest, Mark continued down the passageway, but with every step, the feeling of being observed grew stronger, and he could sense the Exlian side of him shrinking.

Normally, the new and monstrous instincts he had awakened lurked in the back of his mind, continually prodding him to eat everyone around him. It wasn't a particularly strong feeling, but Mark had grown used to it, so its absence now was deafening. Licking his lips as nervousness flooded his system, Mark kept going, one foot in front of the other, until he reached a large set of double doors at the end of the hall.

As the doors parted, Mark found himself face-to-face with a strange-looking man sitting in a curious six-legged chair. The man's body was tiny and his head huge, making him look almost cartoonish. A thick pair of goggles covered his eyes, and Mark could see mana flashing across them. The man's small body was strapped into the chair and had tubes and wires extending from it in all directions. Apart from the goggles, his massive skull, which was covered in wisps of white hair, had multiple devices bolted directly into it. But as strange as the man looked, what Mark felt deep in his core was absolute terror.

Physically, it was clear that the man in front of him was weak. His bony arms had no definition to speak of, and the flesh Mark could see looked soft and fragile. And it wasn't as if the mana in or around the man in the chair was particularly strong. In fact, Mark had seen stronger mana readings off C- and D-ranked empowered. So he genuinely had no idea why a shiver of pure fear raced down his spine. Like a mouse caught in a snake's gaze, he stood frozen in place until a speaker on the man's chair crackled to life.

"You must be Mark. Welcome. I've been wanting to meet you for some time. Please come this way."

With a series of mechanical clicks, the six legs on the chair spun the man around, causing his large head to sway in the air. And then, just faster than a walk, the chair lurched off, and Mark, drawn as if by an invisible tether, followed him.

"You'll have to forgive me. It's hard to turn my head. A bit of a physical impairment, you see. Please, come up here where I can see you."

Swallowing, Mark complied, speeding up until he was half a step ahead, where the man on the chair could see him without having to turn his extra-large head. Like a spider, the chair crawled forward and shifted slightly sideways, proceeding at an angle so that the man in the chair could stare straight at Mark.

"There's no need to be frightened," the man said, "but I do realize I've been remiss. My name is Maestro. I am the master of the Tomb. Oh dear—that isn't its name, you know. But I'm afraid that that's what everybody calls it, and so it has become a habit. With fair reason, of course. But still, I do prefer its real name, the Cradle of Perpetual Progress. In a sense, you could say that the Cradle and the Tomb are two separate entities, enmeshed together in a complex web. One above, accepting those who have died to society and whose bodies have been assigned as the fertilizer from which the flowers of progress bloom. One below, absorbing and maximizing that fertilizer for the good of the whole.

"But the inner workings of the Cradle have nothing to do with why you are here. Rather, I find myself fascinated. Fascinated by you. And so I asked Mr. Robot to bring you down here so that I could meet you. After all, you are something of an oddity among the individuals sent to the Tomb, and there is nothing I love more than an oddity. One might say that such a desire is born of my subconscious. After all, as an oddity of the greatest magnitude, I often wondered how I fit into the greater whole. But you didn't come here to listen to me prattle about my childhood angst."

With a series of clicks, Maestro's spider chair turned again to face forward, and he scuttled down the hall, forcing Mark to speed up to keep pace. The solid walls of the passage soon gave way to large, reinforced glass windows. Mark's eyes couldn't help but drift to the rooms behind them, filled with all manner of scientific equipment and dozens of strangely shaped robots watching over it. If Maestro noticed Mark's looks, he didn't give any indication. He continued swiftly down the passage until they arrived at an elevator.

"We're on the outskirts of the Cradle, so we'll need to take the elevator up one more time."

A mechanical arm extended from his chair and scanned something at the elevator door, causing it to hiss open. As Mark and

Maestro entered, there was a soft beep. Then the doors shut, and a moment later they were hurtling upward. The abrupt acceleration forced Mark to grab onto the wall to keep from being knocked to the floor. Maestro didn't react at all, his chair absorbing the g-forces without trouble. Only a few seconds later they slowed to a halt, forcing Mark to stabilize himself once again. Then the door sprang open and Maestro was off again, moving swiftly down the hall. Rather disoriented, Mark gathered himself and rushed after the robotic chair, soon finding himself in a large laboratory. Maestro moved over to a big chair that looked strangely like the one Mark had sat in when his power was assessed.

"Go ahead and take a seat," Maestro said as his spider-leg chair bustled about, the arms extending from it manipulating everything around him.

As nicely phrased as Maestro's words were, it was clearly not a request. The faint sense of danger he had felt when coming face-to-face with Maestro had only deepened the farther into the facility he got. So, rather hesitantly, Mark climbed into the chair. "Do you mind if I ask what exactly we're doing?"

Maestro paused for a moment, the legs on his chair shuffling so he could turn and face Mark. "Did I not mention already? I apologize, sometimes my mind gets a bit ahead of my mouth. Let me see, what was I saying? Ah, right, I was expressing my curiosity about you—or, more specifically, your powers. First, I would like to take some blood. This is a fairly standard procedure anytime we assess a prisoner, in part so we can understand the genetic makeup of the individual. After all, empowered all share some specific genetic keys, with some subtle but important differences.

"Much of my research revolves around understanding those key differences. By isolating distinct genetic structures, we increase our awareness of how powers actually work, which is quite important. After all, we are playing a losing game here, and any edge we can get will hopefully allow humanity to not only survive but thrive in the face of the Exlian threat. Second, I'm quite curious about your interaction with the shackles. Your powers, in particular, have proved rather resilient in the face of the disruption the shackles provide."

Maestro must have seen the look of horror on Mark's face, because he paused, blinked at Mark, and then laughed. "Oh, yes, we have been tracking you. We're not actually foolish enough to allow prisoners to run around unmonitored. Far from it. Your shackles provide a tremendous amount of vital research data. They feed all sorts of information back to us, but the most important is mana usage. You see, genetics is only one part of the equation when it comes to powers. How an individual's body interacts with mana is another. Now, your shackles, in addition to generating a subtle flow of mana intended to disrupt your powers, also record feedback naturally generated by your body, as well as the shifts in feedback when powers are activated.

"You know, it's interesting—empowered are naturally incredibly adaptable, and anyone who makes it to the Tomb has adjusted to the shackles, to the point where their bodies begin to suppress the mana web, allowing them some access to their abilities. Normally, that's just speed and strength. Seeing how quickly your body adjusted, I find myself intrigued, and so I thought it would be a good idea to run some tests."

As Maestro spoke, he walked around Mark's chair, attaching a variety of sensors to him with his six mechanical arms. "This won't be painful. I mean, it's not like I'm going to cut you up or anything, though from what I understand, you have a particularly potent regeneration power, so maybe some cutting wouldn't be so bad. Ha, you don't have to look at me like that. Today, we'll stick to a regular assessment, and drawing some blood, of course. You know, you're only the third person to overcome the disruptive effects of the shackles this fast, and I find myself absolutely fascinated as to why that might be. In the case of the others, it was because they were extremely close to S ranked. Of course, being close to S ranked and being S ranked are two entirely separate and distinct things, and it may as well be an uncrossable chasm."

Pausing, Maestro stared into the distance for a moment. "That is the problem we truly need to solve. How do we strengthen our empowered, allowing them to grow their abilities until they are in the S rank? But enough about this. Go ahead and close your eyes, and I'll begin the tests."

17

Swallowing, Mark complied, closing his eyes as the sensors all over his body began to deliver tiny shocks. They weren't painful, and he could feel mana flowing from each sensor into his body, producing ripples that extended through his form. He had no idea what exactly Maestro was testing for, and he couldn't help but be worried that the strange empowered scientist would dig out all his secrets. Mark could feel the Exlian nature that normally roared loudly in his mind had retreated deep within his body, clearly frightened of the massive-headed man who strutted around on his spider chair.

Close to an hour passed before Maestro began removing the sensors. "You can get up."

Mark could tell that the scientist wasn't very happy, and opening his eyes, he saw Maestro frowning as he stared off into midair. Realizing Maestro was looking at a holographic screen, Mark rubbed his arm where one of the sensors had sat. There were no marks on his skin, as his regenerative ability had healed the slight burn the sensor had made. As Mark stood up from his chair, he found himself surprisingly fatigued.

"There's a stamina potion on the bench."

Looking around, Mark spotted the potion Maestro was talking about, and flipping open the lid, he quickly downed it. Maestro had already taken Mark's blood, but clearly, whatever he was seeing wasn't what he had expected.

His large eyes narrowed, Maestro shifted his chair around and stared at Mark for a moment. "Well, it appears your body is full of secrets. I'll need more time to assess what I'm seeing. What I do know is that your blood is quite potent. It has fascinating characteristics, which might explain your unusual regeneration. It's as if you have an incredibly mana-dense healing potion running through your veins. It makes me wonder if your blood could be bottled, used to heal others. You could be an endless source of healing potions. Ha, don't let any of the noble families find out. Otherwise, the scum will chain you up in a basement and bleed you dry for the rest of eternity."

The vehemence in Maestro's voice caught Mark off guard, and he sensed there was a story behind Maestro's words.

"Come with me. I'll walk you out."

Maestro scuttled with surprising agility through the laboratory, Mark following close behind. He could feel the stamina potion working, sending energy flooding through his limbs. For the most part, Maestro was silent on the way out, though he did stop and turn to face Mark just before they got onto the elevator.

"I'm going to use your blood to try and synthesize another serum. One of my main goals, as I stated earlier, is to discover ways to improve the abilities of empowered. And while the prisoners are not permitted to leave the Tomb, they do benefit from my attempts. You will be no different. Once the serum is done, I will contact you. You'll return, and I'll administer it. At which point, I'll monitor you for a while to determine whether or not the serum is effective in allowing your powers to grow. We will then repeat the process, looking for a way to generalize it. I'm pleased to say that I have a very high success rate, nearly twenty percent. As I said, I'll contact you when the serum is ready. Have a good day."

When Mark's elevator arrived at its destination, Mr. Robot was nowhere to be seen. The lights flickered ominously, and Mark's senses began to tingle. He took a step out into the dim hallway and heard a faint buzz from his watch. As he glanced down, Maestro's voice sounded in his ears.

"Oh, I forgot to mention. In order to properly build the serum, I need to collect some baseline data on a variety of your upper limits. I find the best way to do this is through high-intensity situations rather than simulation. Do your best to survive."

With those ominous words and a click, the message ended, and the passage returned to a deep silence. It was a good minute before Mark moved, and when he did, it was slowly. He walked down the hall, his eyes darting from side to side as he checked for danger. Eventually, he emerged from the tunnel and found himself in a narrow alleyway. This was not the way he had come in. His eyes narrowing, Mark scanned his new surroundings. Somehow, the exit had been moved, and not seeing any immediately identifiable landmarks, Mark found himself lost somewhere in the dense streets of the Tomb.

Not daring to close his eyes, he started to scan the network to see if he could spot any enemies, then hesitated. Now that he knew information was being fed back to Maestro from the shackles, Mark wasn't sure that he wanted to reveal his powers. Then again, as he reviewed the conversation, it seemed clear that the S-ranked empowered hadn't actually understood the source of Mark's abilities. If he had, Mark was fairly certain that he wouldn't have been allowed to walk out of the facility at all.

He wasn't sure exactly what details were being sent back to Maestro, but since he hadn't absorbed anyone's power since leaving the mine and returning to New Emery, Mark was confident his secrets were safe.

By this time, he could sense at least a dozen people around him. Hidden from view, but watching him nonetheless. Taking a deep breath, Mark moved swiftly toward the end of the alleyway.

Just before he stepped out, he heard a faint sound from his left. A whisper of a shoe scraping against concrete. Ducking, Mark spun, his leg lashing out as someone jumped from around the corner, whipping a pipe toward his head. Mark's foot slammed into his attacker's leg, and with a yelp, the woman fell, her forward momentum causing her to tumble past Mark. He saw a snake tattoo wrapping around the woman's arm.

Sensing an attack coming from behind, Mark placed a hand against the ground, tucked his shoulder, and rolled forward, barely avoiding the slashing mana blade that hacked down on his back. A pipe was one thing, and had it hit, Mark would have been badly wounded but able to heal. A mana blade was entirely another, intended to kill, and any compunction Mark felt in fighting off his attackers evaporated.

Coming out of his roll, he rose smoothly to his feet, spinning to face the startled Viper Clan gang member, whose mana blade had just bit into the concrete. Before the man could retreat, Mark moved forward, his hand tearing through his attacker's arm, causing him to scream and drop the mana blade. The scream choked off as Mark's fingers hacked through the side of his throat.

There was a shout, and Mark saw a group of Viper Clan thugs racing toward him. With a kick, he sent the dying man's body into the path of the woman who had first attacked him, and then he turned and ran. While he was confident in his ability to fight, Mark had a strong suspicion that getting tangled up with the Viper Clan here would be a death sentence. The particular ferocity of their gazes unnerved him, so he sprinted down the alleyway as fast as he could.

He soon outdistanced most of them, though two were keeping

pace and one was even catching up. Judging that the man closing in on him had B-ranked speed, Mark realized he was going to have to fight soon. Spotting a corner ahead, he reached out to the psychic network, hoping to determine whether anyone was hiding around it. It always took him a moment to lock on to non-Exlian figures, but sure enough, he spotted three individuals waiting to ambush him.

By this point, Mark was almost at the corner and didn't have a choice. Rather than just running around it, however, he jumped sideways into the air. His foot caught the flat wall, and he kicked off, managing to gain considerable altitude as he navigated the corner. The Viper Clan thugs waiting for him were left dumbfounded as he soared over their heads, and two just stared. The third reacted the quickest and, with a shout, gave chase, even as the B-ranked empowered lunged around the corner.

Mark landed hard but managed to keep his feet and continued his mad dash through the alleyway. He could feel his biofuel being depleted. As he maintained his peak speed, dashing around a large garbage can, Mark saw the alleyway split to the right and left, and once again, he took the left turn, even as he heard the B-ranked thug shouting behind him.

Mark had no idea where he was, and for all he knew, he was simply driving headfirst deeper into Viper Clan territory. He wasn't sure what the thugs had been promised, though it was likely they hadn't been promised anything. All Maestro would have had to do was order them to ambush him, and they would have had no choice but to comply. Hearing the pounding of feet behind him, Mark risked a glance back and saw the B-ranked thug was only a few arm lengths away. Gritting his teeth, Mark tried to move faster, but his opponent put on a sudden burst of speed and caught up in an instant.

Spinning, Mark thrust out his hands, but at the last second

the empowered thug jerked to the side, avoiding Mark's sharp fingers. Unable to stop his momentum, Mark slammed into the wall of the alleyway, driving the breath from his lungs and causing his bones to rattle.

The thug slammed into the wall a moment later but still managed to get a hand on Mark's shoulder. Feeling the crushing grip, Mark ignored the pain as he moved in toward his opponent, his hands slashing through the thug's chest. With a gasp, the thug backpedaled, releasing his grip on Mark's shoulder as blood began to pour from the wounds on his chest. Mark could hear the heavy pounding of feet coming down the alleyway, so he turned and ran once again, even as the bleeding thug reached for his belt. Just before he went around the corner, Mark caught the red flash of a healing potion, and a sinking feeling filled his chest.

Mark had been successfully fighting swarms of enemies in his dreams for over a year. Recently, however, those dreams had shifted, and he spent most of his nights battling against Exlian screamers and hulks wandering around the valley outside Felwer Mine. But fighting against empowered was very different. Not only were they smarter, but they had access to a wide range of tools to assist them, things like healing potions that could repair the damage Mark had done to their bodies.

Of course, Mark wasn't without his own advantages. As he ran, he could feel his crushed shoulder rapidly repairing itself. Continuing to flee through the tangle of alleyways, he did his best to pick passages with fewer enemies waiting to ambush him. Still, soon there was a crowd of nearly twenty Viper Clan thugs chasing behind him.

Seeing another set of alleyways breaking off from the one he was sprinting down, Mark spotted thugs in two of the three passages. Instinctively, he took the empty alleyway, realizing a moment later how foolish that was. He had been running on instinct, always taking the easier, less crowded path. Now he had been funneled into a long, narrow alleyway.

He was just considering turning around when the swarm of thugs came around the corner, blocking the way back. With no choice but to move forward, Mark fled as they chased close behind. Glancing up, he saw the buildings rising high on either side and could faintly make out a roof that sealed the alleyway at the top, meaning he couldn't even climb out.

Mark was starting to grow frustrated. Now that he wasn't near Maestro, his monstrous nature had returned in full force and was urging him to turn around and face his enemies. He reached the end of the alleyway and found himself in a wide room, with four passages leading off from it that twisted farther into the labyrinth.

As soon as he entered the room, Mark skidded to a halt, spotting a large figure in front of him. Python. The massive woman's arms were crossed over her chest, and she had been leaning against the wall, clearly waiting for Mark to arrive. Straightening up, she looked him up and down. "Huh, I thought it would have taken you longer."

Mark's senses were screaming at him that he was in trouble. The mana density in Python's body told him that she outclassed him by a full rank. Worse, the disruptive effect of the shackles hardly seemed to impact her. As she took a step forward, spreading her arms as if she wanted to hug Mark, he could sense just how dangerous it would be if he allowed her to grab him. The Viper Clan thugs who had been chasing Mark were rapidly closing in, and Mark found himself neatly sandwiched between enemies. There was no retreat, and even as his eyes darted to the passages behind Python, she laughed and shook her head. "They're all dead ends, kid. I'm afraid you won't be getting out of this one alive."

Part of Mark wanted to ask why she was so intent on killing him, to negotiate, to see if he could reason a way out. But the look in her eyes told him that would be hopeless. He took a step back, and Python took a step forward.

"You know how I got my name?" she asked, a vicious smile on her face. "Because the thing I love more than anything else is slowly squeezing my opponents, watching the hope fade from their eyes as they realize death is inevitable."

Letting out the breath he had been holding, Mark nodded. "I guess it is," he said, as much to himself as to her.

As she cocked her head to the side, unsure exactly what he was talking about, Mark abandoned all intent to hide his abilities. He pushed his fear aside, relegating it to a back corner of his mind, and instead expanded his senses. He could feel everything around him jumping into sharp relief, but what he focused on was the dim mana lights in the passage behind him. He could feel the mana running through the walls, and though he didn't feel confident in disrupting it completely, he could pause it for a brief moment.

Whether Python sensed something, Mark wasn't sure. But she chose that exact moment to attack, surging forward, her hands darting for Mark's throat. As he leaned backward to avoid her grab, the lights faltered and then winked out, plunging the room into darkness.

Mark was only able to disrupt the lights for a moment before the weight of the mana flow tore free from his grasp. That brief moment, however, caught Python completely off guard and allowed Mark to launch a counterattack. His hands, transformed into bone blades, lacerated the inside of Python's right arm, and as she jerked to the side, Mark managed to bring himself back to a standing position, taking advantage of her shifted arm to slip through her grasp and tuck himself in close to her body.

Though her skin seemed to be covered in a dense scalelike substance, it wasn't enough to keep Mark's fingers from tearing it open. He targeted her throat, jabbing his fingers deep into the side of her neck, but at the last moment, she jerked back, her arm slamming into Mark's side and sending him tumbling across the room as she swiftly retreated.

As the lights came back on, Mark saw, with a sinking stomach, that the wound he had caused on her neck wasn't as deep as he'd thought. She was glaring at him, her hand clasped tightly over the bleeding gash, even as she fumbled for a potion. Realizing that he couldn't afford to let her heal, Mark sprinted toward her, leaping the last few feet to try to disrupt her movements.

As fast as he was, she was even quicker, and with a sinuous twist of her upper body, she retreated, managing to avoid his attack, even as she poured the potion into her mouth. The Viper Clan thugs were only a few steps away, and Mark's situation was turning from bad to worse. Knowing that his only option was to eliminate the woman in front of him, Mark laid all his cards on the table. Lunging toward her, he launched an attack straight for her heart, and with a sneer, she threw the empty potion aside and met his attack with a heavy punch.

While she'd been drinking the potion, her eyes had been turned toward the ceiling, and now, when she looked down at Mark, her fist passed straight through him as his body popped like a bubble. Having activated his quantum clone ability, Mark had actually stepped around to her side, where he launched three rapid strikes into her ribs. He felt his hands cutting through her skin, but she twisted powerfully, nearly taking his head off with an elbow as she shifted her body to face him.

This was the first time Mark had ever fought a brute so flexible and quick, and he was realizing that his normal strategies simply wouldn't work. For a moment, they traded blows, but Mark found himself on the losing end, despite the fact that every touch of his hands caused blood to spurt from Python's skin.

With a growl, she used her bulk to force him back, even as the Viper Clan thugs raced into the room. Mark reacted immediately, retreating toward one of the passageways. Staggering as he quickly pulled back, Python straightened up and let out a roar.

"Get him! Don't let him get away!"

As he retreated, Mark reached out once more with his mind, disrupting the mana to the lights and causing the room to plunge into darkness again. Under the gaze of so many people, it was impossible for him to use his quantum clone ability. But in the darkness, it was different. His brain screamed, a sharp pain lancing through his skull as Mark split into four copies, sending them in different directions.

Three fell upon the approaching thugs as Mark continued to back up, heading into the tunnel. His skull pounded. He could tell that he would only be able to keep up so many clones for a few seconds. But a few seconds was all he needed, and his clones, each just as powerful as him, executed their orders flawlessly and threw themselves in a mindless fury on their opponents. Like a Reaper in the darkness, Mark's clones tore into their opponents, and screams rang out. Bone blade arms cut through throats and limbs alike, bringing death upon the thugs.

Still backing up, Mark felt the corner of the passage and turned and bolted, or at least tried to. The pain in his mind was growing stronger by the moment and was so intense that he staggered, barely catching himself against the wall as his body failed to obey his commands. It was impossible for him to keep up so many clones and his mana control any longer, and with a gasp, he hurled himself into the passage as the lights flickered and came back on.

He could feel the clones popping behind him, waves of relief filling his mind as he stumbled around the corner. Left in his wake was a scene of absolute devastation, but Mark had no way to pay attention to it, as he was currently trying to keep from falling unconscious on the spot. He had no potions, and even if he did, he wasn't sure that they would help.

Finding a doorway, Mark lunged through it, the world fading in and out around him. He could hear sounds in the distance but didn't have the presence of mind to pay any attention to them. Desperately fighting off the darkness creeping ever closer, he leaned against the wall, his breath coming in ragged gasps as he tried to clear the excruciating pain from his skull. Falling unconscious was a death sentence, but Mark could feel himself slipping away.

With superhuman effort, he gritted his teeth and started to try to pull himself up. But then something softly tapped his forehead, causing him to slide down the wall into a seated position. Through the haze that seemed to cloud his vision, he saw Mime's head peek down over him. She regarded him curiously, then looked up toward the door. Seeing her brought relief to Mark, a calm that spread throughout his body, despite the pounding pain in his head.

"Nice of you to come by," he mumbled, and then darkness overtook him.

Life as an underboss in the Viper Clan was never particularly pleasant, but Python was having an especially bad day. She had been forced to waste two potions, and what should have been an easy job was turning into a genuine nightmare. She had been instructed to trap and kill a prisoner released into Viper Clan territory. This wasn't the first time she had done such work, and when she'd found out who the prisoner was, she had agreed with relish.

From the moment she had first seen the scrawny young man in the warehouse, she had wanted to squeeze the life from him, so she had happily gathered her men, instructing them to block off the passages in a way that would lead the prisoner on a merry chase through the labyrinth of alleyways, until he was brought directly to her. The plan was simple: force him into a dead end, and then take her time, breaking his limbs one by one, while she carefully crushed his hope.

Yet as soon as he appeared, things started to go wrong, and when he finally showed up in front of her, he proved to be a more slippery fish than she had accounted for. The blasted lights kept going out at the most inopportune times, and he seemed to be able to split his body into multiple figures. The first time the lights had gone out, he had nearly succeeded in catching her off guard and cutting her throat open in a single moment, a level of lethality that seemed entirely out of step with his supposedly C-ranked abilities.

Now, observing the results of the second time the lights had gone out, Python couldn't help but shudder. Of the twenty-five men who had entered the room, nine were dead or mortally wounded. A further three were missing limbs. How he had, in only half a dozen seconds, managed to kill so many of them, Python had no idea. But what she did know was that no matter how this situation turned out, her head was on the chopping block. Losing this many gang members, all for the sake of taking down a single opponent, was a sin punishable by death. Her only chance at survival now lay in eliminating the young man without losing anybody else.

"Check the passages. Move in groups. Do not let yourselves be caught off guard."

Even as she issued the commands, Python could feel her heart constricting. Sending her men into the passages by themselves was a death sentence. She knew it, and they knew it too. She could see the fear in their eyes, and even after her voice faded, none of them moved.

Gritting her teeth, Python pushed her way to the front and stared at the three potential passages Mark had disappeared into. "You lot, move slowly down the passage on the left, and be ready to retreat if you need to."

The five gang members swallowed and then carefully began to edge their way into the passage. She couldn't blame them, as the stench of blood filled the air. Sending five more down another passage and leaving the remaining two gang members to try to patch up the wounded, Python gritted her teeth and entered the third hallway. It twisted to the right, and as she stepped around the corner, Python heard sharp yells quickly choked off by a faint crunch.

Spinning around, she darted for the main room, arriving at the same time as one of the groups of five. The two gang members she had left behind and all the wounded were staring in horror at the third passage, where the sounds had come from. One of the gangsters, lifting a trembling hand, pointed at the ground, where a limp hand lay. There was another faint crunching sound, and the hand was slowly pulled around the corner, vanishing from view.

Unable to keep their composure any longer, the gangsters turned and fled, abandoning their wounded companions as they ran out of the room back toward the labyrinth of alleyways. Python was just considering joining them when she saw a figure step around the corner.

Immediately, her senses went wild. It was Mark, standing calmly in the passage, yet at the same time, it wasn't. With a sort of languid grace, Mark walked forward, a detached curiosity in his eyes that gave off a deeply inhuman feeling. Her breath strangled in her lungs, Python stepped backward, nearly stumbling over one of the limbs scattered about the ground. As she recovered her balance and blinked, Mark arrived next to her, his fingers flicking four silver slashes that shot straight through Python's body, meeting no resistance as they tore through her heart and spine. As she began to fall to the ground, Python's last thoughts were of Mark's three crimson eyes and the black tail lashing behind him.

Mark snapped back into consciousness with a gasp. His piercing headache had been reduced to a dull throb, and it took him a moment to recognize where he was. Somehow, he had returned to the room where he had faced down Python. With a start, he realized that she was lying right in front of him. It took only a glance to recognize that she was dead. The four massive gashes in her chest were testament to that. There was no one else in the room, save for Mime, who was sitting on the other side of Python's body, licking her lips.

Mark could sense his shadow wriggling behind him, and he could tell that it was quite satisfied. There were no other Viper Clan gang members in sight. Mark's heartbeat began to slow, and he started to calm down. Mime, seeing he was alert, tapped on Python's thick arm with a paw.

"You want me to eat her?"

Shaking her head, Mime tapped on the corpse again.

"You want me to take her power?"

This time, Mime gave a sharp nod. Mark's first impulse was to agree and begin immediately. However, catching sight of the shackles on his arms, he hesitated. He had no idea what sort of information they fed back to Maestro, and he wasn't sure that he was keen on the mad scientist learning about his ability to absorb other people's powers. Seeing his hesitation, Mime rolled her eyes. Her paw rose, and a single claw flicked out, sending a beam of silver light straight toward Mark's throat. It approached so quickly he had no time to do more than jerk back. But strangely, as soon as it reached his skin, Mark felt the razor-sharp mana blunt and then dissipate.

He fell back on his butt, his eyes going wide, and he realized that his body was covered in a thin film of strange energy. When he concentrated, he could feel the back of his neck pulsing slightly. His null field was active, but for some reason, it wasn't spread out around him in a wide field like every other time. Instead, it had been withdrawn and held close to his skin. It extended just far enough from him to cover the shackles and the rest of his body, forming an antimana shield around him.

Then Mark realized that the web of disruptive mana normally generated by the shackles was no longer active, and the mental clone he had peeled off to keep control of it was now occupied in keeping his null field close to his body. In an entirely uncatlike gesture, Mime lifted a paw and tapped her opposite wrist, reminding Mark that they didn't have much time.

Jerking upright, Mark quickly stretched out his hands to touch Python's corpse but received a smack on the forehead from an exasperated Mime. Unsure why she had just smacked him, Mark saw her body shift, her fur waving, as she pointed to his shadow.

"Oh, obviously. I can't absorb her power and keep the null field active at the same time. Sorry."

Even as he spoke, Mark's shadow leaped forward, tendrils of darkness wrapping around the corpse. Quickly, the hints of remaining vitality began to drain away. Mark felt the now-familiar sense of something in the corpse tearing free and flowing into him. As soon as he had finished absorbing her power, Mime jumped onto his shoulder, and she pointed with a paw toward the long hallway. After slowly getting to his feet, Mark had taken a few steps when he heard a deep hum echoing through the corridor in front of him.

Around the corner, a Reaper drifted, its single crimson eye scanning the hallway. As soon as it saw Mark, it paused, as if unsure exactly what it was looking at. It was only then that Mark realized his null field was about to backfire, and he quickly canceled it. As the energy faded away, the Reaper trembled slightly, and Mark felt a hint of mana establish a connection with his now-active shackles. Realizing that the Reaper was here to pick up Python's corpse, Mark quickly spun, worried that its emaciated state would give away some of his abilities. Yet when he turned, he found it nowhere in sight, the entire room completely empty.

Not only was the corpse gone, but so was Mime. For a brief moment, Mark wondered if he had just imagined the whole thing. The Reaper drifted past him, paying no attention, and began inspecting the room, clearly looking for a corpse. Mark knew he wouldn't be able to answer any questions about what had happened, so he quickly left, heading down the long hallway and beginning to wander through the labyrinth of passages.

Occasionally, he came upon a locked door, but not wanting to create more trouble than he already had, he passed by them. After close to an hour of walking around, he found a small alleyway that emptied out onto a street, with a couple of Viper Clan thugs hanging out at the entrance.

"Hey, who are . . ."

Mark didn't give the thug a chance to finish his statement as he crossed the distance in an instant, his hand tearing through the man's throat. The other two thugs fell back swiftly, shouts of surprise on their lips. The wiser of the two turned and bolted, while the other grabbed for the mana blade at his waist. Mark disarmed him with a flick of his wrist, and a moment later, he lay dead on the ground next to his companion.

Grabbing both of their watches, Mark looked around and saw a number of individuals watching him warily. They didn't have the markings of the Viper Clan and clearly didn't want to be involved, so after retrieving two merit cards and the mana blades from each corpse, Mark left. Now that he was out of the labyrinth, it didn't take him long to figure out where he was, and soon he was standing outside the warehouse. When he walked in, Albert rushed over, clearly surprised to see Mark.

"Did something happen while I was gone?" Mark asked, placing the two mana blades and watches on the counter Albert had built.

"No, not here," Albert said, licking his lips and glancing at Mark warily. "The Viper Clan has put out a call for your head."

"They already tried to collect on it, and I'm sure they will again. Assign these to a couple of your guys. I've got work to do."

Leaving Albert at the counter, Mark left the warehouse after cleaning himself up and headed over to Mr. Robot's shop. When he walked in, Mr. Robot was in the middle of checking out a customer, but the robot paused, looked up, and said in his normal flat voice, "You will go into the workshop. I will come speak with you in a moment."

With a sharp nod, Mark walked into the back, his expression dour. It was clear to him that the current arrangement couldn't stand. All things considered, Mark had carved out a nice little space for himself where he could use his abilities to his advantage, but it would only be able to continue if Mr. Robot, or more likely Maestro, was willing to keep the gangs off his back.

A couple of minutes later, Mr. Robot walked in. "One underboss, seventeen members of Viper Clan. These are the individuals whose shackles have ceased functioning after encountering you within the last four hours."

Though Mr. Robot was talking, Mark could just imagine Maestro's voice overlaid on top of his. He had suspected that, like the robots down in the Cradle, Mr. Robot was really just an extension of Maestro, and this confirmed it.

"Is that not enough?" Mark asked, raising an eyebrow.

"That is not the issue. The issue is that if we continue tests this way, we will run out of population. Future tests will need to be adjusted."

Mr. Robot paused for a moment, his eyes flashing. Then mana flared in his chest, and opening up the casing, he retrieved a simple-looking card. "Go to Darkest Hour. Someone will find you there."

Reaching out to take the blank black card from Mr. Robot's metal fingers, Mark frowned. "What about my business?"

"I will ensure that it remains untouched. You are involved in a more important business now, the very salvation of humanity. Albert Johnson and the others you have selected will continue to run the business on your behalf. Merits will be added to your account. Consider them payment for services rendered."

Done conversing, Mr. Robot gave Mark a nod, then turned and left the workshop, leaving Mark gritting his teeth. It seemed he had well and truly attracted Maestro's attention, which couldn't be good for him. The only saving grace was that Maestro seemed much more interested in progress than he did in knowledge for its own sake. Had he been more interested in the latter, Mark guessed he would have ended up on a dissection table. As it was, Maestro clearly wanted to collect more data from Mark's body.

Of course, Mark had no idea what sorts of things were being transmitted, especially when he shut the shackles down with this new application of the null field. Turning the black card over in his hand, he stared down at it, his expression inscrutable. At the end of the day, survival was first and foremost, but to survive, Mark would need to come to understand his powers a good bit better.

He had never realized just how much he relied on his activator and its status screen. Now, bereft of them, Mark found himself lost. He also wanted to figure out what had happened during the time he was unconscious. The complete lack of corpses made him suspect that his shadow had devoured them, and the four puncture wounds in the middle of Python's chest suggested Mime. At the same time, strikes to the chest weren't typically her style, as she normally aimed for necks, guaranteeing instant death.

Furthermore, Mark wasn't at all excited about the idea his shadow could move him around. What would happen if, while he was asleep, it decided that it wanted to eat somebody and dragged his body along for the ride? Regardless, Mark needed to get to the bottom of the situation. Flicking the card up in the air, he watched it spin and then grabbed it and slid it into his pocket in one smooth motion. Leaving the shop without speaking to Mr. Robot, Mark tapped on his watch and opened up the map of the Tomb. Darkest Hour was a bar only a few blocks away, and it didn't take Mark long to get there.

Along the way, he saw a couple of members of the Syndicate and a small group of Viper Clan thugs, but both groups quickly left when they caught sight of him, reinforcing Mark's realization that no matter what sort of power the gangs had, Maestro truly was the ruler of the Tomb. There were three bodyguards at the door, and when they saw Mark, the largest of them stepped forward. When Mark held up his watch, the bouncer shook his head. "Not in here, pal. If you don't have a recommendation, you can't come in."

Mark's eyes narrowed, and a voice in the back of his mind whispered that he'd probably be forgiven for cutting the bouncer's heart out. Taking a deep breath, Mark fiercely suppressed the murderous impulses and reached into his pocket to produce the black card. Unaware of how close he had come to biting the dust, the bouncer nodded and stepped out of the way.

"You can go in," he said, jerking a thumb toward the door.

Stuffing both hands into his pockets, Mark walked into the bar. It was a long, low room with a faint haze of smoke and a counter that took up one entire wall, with thirty-five stools arranged along it. There were three bartenders, despite the fact that only two other people were in the bar, so Mark took a seat near the door and placed the black card on the counter in front of him. Mr. Robot had said that he would know the person who came to talk to him. So Mark simply waited.

After almost five minutes, one of the bartenders wandered over and picked up the card. He tapped it against his watch and then shoved the card in a small slot in the bar. "I've digitized it for you, so you'll be good to go. Can I get you a drink?"

Mark shook his head, remaining quiet, and with a shrug, the bartender left. For the next fifteen minutes, Mark just sat on his stool, lost in thought. His main concern was the changes that had happened to his body after he'd absorbed Python's ability. He could feel new power running through his tendons, strengthening them and allowing him to produce a tremendous amount of crushing force. At the same time, his body felt increasingly flexible, which would provide a tremendous boost to his martial arts.

Mark's greatest weapon, without question, was his bone blade hands, empowered by his Cutting Palm technique. And now, thanks to the power he had just picked up, both the amount of force he could exert and his body's flexibility had jumped. If Mark had to guess, the power he had absorbed was only B ranked and, on its own, likely wasn't that strong. For him, however, it was one of the best strengthening-type powers he could have received. Mark was just wondering how much force his fingers could produce when a shadow fell over him and someone slid into the seat next to him. Glancing up, he saw Joker's signature wide smile.

"Hello, Mark."

Joker lifted a hand, motioning to the bartender, who nodded and brought over two cups and a bottle of liquor. No sooner had the first glass been poured than Joker grabbed it and threw it back, his face twisting as he swallowed the harsh alcohol. Mark ignored the cup that was put in front of him.

"You can leave the bottle," Joker said, blinking back tears. With a smirk, the bartender put the bottle on the bar and wandered off as Joker poured himself another, much more generous glass. "I have to admit, I didn't quite think our next meeting would be under these circumstances, but from what I hear, you've been making quite the name for yourself. The Tomb's new wonder kid. Sharp as a blade, but useful. The best kind of prisoner."

Detecting a hint of bitterness in Joker's voice, Mark slowly reached out and picked up his glass. Joker downed another shot, grimacing as he wiped his lips. "This stuff's murderous, but it's good for you. At least so they say."

Holding his glass loosely with three fingers, Mark looked Joker over, noticing a still-fresh scar on his chin. "Are you the one I'm supposed to be waiting for?"

"That would be me. Normally, they would have approached you differently, but considering we had already run into each other, Asa thought it was a good idea if I came to say hi."

"Who's Asa?"

"You'll meet him soon enough. First, though, I'm supposed to explain some things to you. You've already met the big boss himself and run afoul of the gangs. Congratulations, you are officially no longer a rookie. All you'll need to do now is spend some time drenching the sands in blood, and you'll have completed the trifecta and earned the right to be a conductor."

"I'm sorry? What are you talking about?"

"I'm talking about the arena, of course. The glorious and sacred battleground of the Tomb."

"That's not what I'm asking about," Mark said. "I'm asking about being a conductor. Does this have to do with those tickets you were mentioning before?"

Stretching out his glass, Joker clinked it against Mark's and flashed his signature grin. "You're a sharp one, I'll give you that. Why, yes, it does."

"And being a conductor can get me out of the Tomb?"

"No, not really," Joker said, waving his hand before downing another shot. His face screwed up, and he poured himself yet another, splashing liquid on the bar as he did so.

"The way it works is simple," he said. "So long as you perform well enough in the arena, there's a chance you can get recruited. Of course, you can only be recruited if you fight and survive enough times. But if you do get recruited to the conductor program, it'll give you the chance to get some fresh air every once in a while. When you saw me, I was being transferred back from one of my little excursions."

"And why are you called conductors?" Mark asked, his eyes narrowing.

"Why, because we conduct all sorts of business. Though I must confess, the majority of it involves sending dangerous elements on the train to the underworld. We could have called ourselves Reapers, but the big robots with scary arms already took that name."

While Mark didn't have any particular desire to throw himself into the arena, he wasn't sure if he had a choice. Maestro hadn't explicitly commanded him to enter the arena, but he clearly wanted more data and seemed to favor fighting as the best way to get it. Making his decision, Mark nodded, braced himself, and tossed off his shot. The anticipated burn never materialized, and it was with some surprise that he stared at first his shot glass, then the bottle, which contained nothing but water.

Joker let out a delighted laugh, patted Mark on the shoulder, and then stood up. "Come, I'll introduce you to the arena, and Asa, who's in charge. He's the guy you'll mostly be chatting with if you participate in the fights."

Standing, Mark followed Joker out of the bar, and the two headed toward the center of the city. They arrived just before night fell and darkness claimed the streets. Even as the lights began to wink out, Joker led Mark to a well-lit building, right at the center of the Tomb, that rose up into the darkness.

"Welcome to the arena," Joker said, gesturing to the massive building.

Scanning the seemingly endless wall, Mark saw it met the roof.

"Does it go all the way to the surface?" he asked, and with a laugh, Joker nodded.

"It does. What's more, there's an elevator."

There was a sly quality to Joker's voice, as if he hoped to tempt Mark into some sort of action. But Mark ignored him—sure enough, there were robots everywhere, as well as empowered guards in blue-and-silver mana suits. This was by far the most heavily guarded place Mark had seen in the Tomb, and he could understand why.

As they headed inside, Joker gave Mark a quick overview. "The arena is split into three distinct areas. The first is the betting hall, where bets are laid. The second is the cages, which is where fighters are held before their matches. Last, but of course not least in the slightest, is the arena itself. It seats close to ten thousand."

As they walked through the open foyer, Mark saw a tremendous number of empowered coming and going, and when he mentioned it, Joker nodded. "The arena is where most empowered spend their time. After all, this is where the greatest benefits are. You'll notice that there's a divide in each of the rooms."

Following his pointing finger, Mark saw a thick wall that appeared to be made of glass that cut the room in half. The side he was on was thick with prisoners. The other side was entirely empty, save for half a dozen guards who stood silently at their posts.

"The entire facility is two areas. The first can be accessed from the Tomb. The second is accessed from up there." Joker pointed up, toward the surface. "Depending on your circle in New Emery, you may have heard of the underground death matches, blood sports, or maybe special clubs where you can do drugs or fulfill any of your desires."

With a sharp smile, Joker spread his arms wide. "Welcome to the arena. Of course, those of us on this side pay the price in blood so that the people on the other side can get their kicks. Come on, let me take you to Asa."

Joker led Mark through the betting hall and down into the area known as the cages. Rather than actual cages, it looked more like a prison, with hundreds of cells.

"Prisoners are held on the first level," Joker said. "Down below is all the beasts."

"Beasts? Wait, you mean Exlian?"

"And then some. Both Exlian and native creatures, all mutated by mana. All deadly. Hey, there's Asa."

The man Joker was talking about was thin and stooped, though Mark was confident that if he had straightened up, he would have stood at least six feet seven. Dressed in expensive clothing, Asa lacked shackles like the other prisoners, causing Mark to do a double take. He was currently hunched over a large book and writing in exceptionally small letters.

Walking over, Joker tapped on the desk, and Asa looked up. His eyes were deep and piercing, and his head was so gaunt it reminded Mark of a vulture's.

"Always good to see you, Asa," Joker greeted the thin man with exuberance, but Asa didn't respond.

He carefully placed his pen down and kept his eyes fixed on Mark, as if curious about the secrets he might find underneath his skin.

Undaunted, Joker slapped Mark on the shoulder. "This is Mark."

"Ah, yes. I was told to expect you."

Asa's voice was rich and deep, carrying an expansiveness that was at odds with his appearance. Mark nodded in greeting, still unsure of what to make of the situation. Asa flipped his book shut and opened another, quickly skipping through the pages. Then he ran a long finger down one of the small columns before snapping the book shut. "We're about to start a standard exhibition. Joker, why don't you take our friend here to go and view it? It'll give him a good idea of what the arena is about."

"Sure." Joker gestured for Mark to follow and headed back past Asa's desk, farther down the passage. "There are stairs up here that'll take us up to the arena level."

As they walked, Mark saw a large clamp drop from the ceiling and grab a cage that held a dispirited-looking prisoner. The man didn't react as he was hauled into the air.

Noticing Mark's gaze, Joker grinned. "Well, it looks like he's the poor sap we'll be seeing. Come on, we'll have to hurry if we don't want to miss it. These normally go quick."

Up the stairs, a hallway led to a set of double doors that opened into a wide arena. There were enough seats for almost two thousand spectators, though only a few were filled. The arena floor was hard and sandy, covered in dark spots that could only be bloodstains. The circular arena was surrounded by a massive, clear wall that gave a full view of everything happening inside.

While the prisoners' side was packed with seats, the other was divided into numerous small boxes, each holding anywhere from one to a dozen comfortable-looking lounge chairs or couches. Mark could see people standing in the boxes or sitting in the chairs, talking. These must be the visitors from the surface who had come down to watch the blood sports of the arena.

He was about to ask Joker when there was a sharp blast of a horn, and one of the arena walls shifted. The despondent man in the cage came stumbling through. He didn't go far from the doorway, which closed with a hiss behind him, forming a perfectly smooth wall with no breaks. Instead, his eyes darted around, clearly looking for threats. In the air above the arena, an image appeared, showing a close-up of the prisoner's face next to a picture of a robot.

"Wow, talk about bad luck."

Glancing over at Joker, who was shaking his head, Mark gestured to the prisoner. "Is he going to have to fight a robot?"

"Yes. So, the standard exhibitions are a simple roulette system, randomly assigned from a pool of opponents. The opponent could be other prisoners, could be Exlian, could be robots. In a second here, you'll be getting a betting link, which will allow you to bet on whether or not you think the prisoner is going to win. In fact, there's a bunch of stuff you can bet on. How long he'll last, whether he'll survive, you know, pretty much anything."

"And this is just entertainment?" Mark asked, his eyes narrowing as he turned to gaze down at the pale-faced prisoner.

"Just entertainment? No, though it is often quite entertaining," Joker said with an unsettling smile. "No, the point of this is to gather data and generate some money at the same time. Funding doesn't come from thin air, you know."

In the arena, the prisoner took a few hesitant steps forward, continuing to scan the walls. As Mark felt a buzz at his wrist, notifying him that the betting link had been sent over, he couldn't help but frown. According to the information listed on the window, the prisoner was C ranked and had a power related to the creation of energy weapons.

"How is he going to be able to fight the robot with his shackles on?" Mark asked. "It seems guaranteed that he's going to lose."

"The arena is just about the only place your shackles can be undone, or at least deactivated," Joker said. "As much as the scum over there enjoys seeing bloodbaths, it doesn't produce much data if one side just steamrolls the other. As soon as the robot enters, his shackles will be deactivated, giving him access to his powers again."

"Isn't that dangerous? I mean, what if he tries to escape?"

Looking at Mark with a faint smile, Joker shrugged. "I won't say it's never happened before, but I don't know of anybody who's succeeded."

Just then, another horn sounded, and the wall across from the prisoner slid open. A large robot stomped out. Barrel chested, with long arms, the robot carried a stench of blood. It was entirely red, but the metal around its hands was darker, as if they had been soaked in blood. As soon as he saw the robot, the prisoner leaped back, landing in a crouch. Mark could see mana gathering under his hand, pulling dirt together, and as the robot let out a roar and charged forward, the prisoner lifted a dark-yellow sword from the dirt. It glimmered, but Mark wasn't sure how effective it would be against the robot's armor.

As the two combatants clashed, the sword turned out to be quite effective, tearing through the underside of the robot's arm, sending sparks flying. Unfortunately for the prisoner, the robot seemed to be expecting just such a thing and allowed his arm to be torn apart so that it could land a strike of its own.

Overall, the prisoner was much more skilled than Mark had originally anticipated, and over the next few minutes, he watched with increasing interest as the prisoner methodically took apart the robot. Joker, on the other hand, grew bored and restless. Finally he stood up abruptly. "Fights like this are just such a waste of time."

Unsure whether he should follow, Mark was just starting to get up when the situation down in the arena suddenly changed. The prisoner managed to score a strike against one of the robot's legs, and it fell over on its side with a screech. As it did, however, its back suddenly split open, and half a dozen darts launched themselves into the air. Joker's eyes lit up, and he sat back down. "Ooh, this is new."

Sinking back into his seat, Mark watched as the darts were propelled through the air with small jets of mana. They locked onto the prisoner and shot toward him, darting erratically as they homed in on his position. The prisoner managed to block the first two, but the other four slipped through his guard, their points separating into four blades that stabbed deep into his body. With a scream, the prisoner tried to tear them free, yet even as he pulled one out, it exploded, destroying his hand. At the same time, the dart that had struck his leg exploded as well, and he collapsed to the sandy arena floor.

The robot, little more than a pile of scrap at this point, used its one working arm to begin dragging itself toward him. Mark felt his stomach churn. The screams were largely blocked by the thick barrier that separated the arena from the seats, but Mark could still hear them, and they sent a shiver down his spine. Joker, on the other hand, watched with morbid fascination as the robot dragged itself to the prisoner's side and began hacking away at him. It took entirely too long for silence to arrive, and by the time it did, Mark's fists were clenched tightly.

"Those exploding darts were new, sort of scary if you don't know they're coming," Joker said, leaning back.

Mark could see the vague figures in the boxes across the arena beginning to move around, and a large timer sprang up, counting down until the next match.

"So anyway, that's the arena," Joker said, jumping to his feet.

Though nobody had explicitly told Mark why he was being shown this, he had a pretty good idea, and as he followed Joker out of the stands, he couldn't help but look back. "Do you fight in the arena?"

"I do," Joker said, rather enthusiastically. "So long as you can survive, it's actually a pretty good gig. Of course, I don't fight in the standard exhibitions anymore. Like I said, they're pretty much a waste of time. But there are other kinds of exhibitions as well. Group fights, special challenges, you know, things like that. I participate in the special challenges, which I'm guessing is what you're going to be participating in as well."

Glancing back, Joker laughed at the ugly expression on Mark's face. "Oh, come on, it's really not so bad. Asa will be able to give you more information."

Heading down to the cages, Mark and Joker arrived just in time to see the now-empty cage being returned, and Mark noticed there was no reaction from the other prisoners sitting in their own cages.

Though he had already experienced the brutality of the Tomb, the arena was a whole other level, and Mark wasn't sure he could stand it. Not that he had much of a choice.

Seeing them walk over, Asa closed his large book and peered at Mark. "In order to qualify for the special challenges, you must take part in at least three standard exhibitions. If you attempt to run, you will be retrieved and put in one of the holding cages. Is there a need for that?"

Swallowing, Mark shook his head.

"Good. In that case, Joker will show you to room C32. That will be your entry point into the arena. Please proceed there now. You will be fighting in three matches that will take place over the next few days."

With that, he waved his hand, dismissing them, and went back to work. Joker took Mark to his assigned room, little more than a windowless cell with a simple bench built into the wall.

"Good luck," Joker said. "I'm really looking forward to getting to fight with you in the special exhibitions, so make sure you don't die."

With a less-than-reassuring grin, Joker waved, and the door closed on Mark, locking him in the cell. Sitting down on the bench, Mark could only sigh. The longer he stayed in the Tomb, the more clearly it was impressed upon him that he simply no longer had control of his life. Any attempt he made to get control, to establish some sort of normalcy, like the alchemy job, was thrown out the window almost immediately. Sitting in the dim light, Mark could feel the walls pressing in on him, as if at any moment they might come crashing down, crushing his body completely.

It was so very different from the expansive, freeing experience of sitting on a mountaintop staring out over the wilds. And Mark couldn't help but wonder if he would have been better off just staying out there, carving out a life among the Exlian. Of course, living among monsters wouldn't have been easy, but neither was living among humans, who were turning out to be just as monstrous as any of the Exlian Mark had ever faced.

With his head in his hands, Mark felt something change in the room and glanced up as his shadow began to shift and grow. Strangely, Mark felt no fear as he saw it creep up the wall opposite him. And even when three crimson eyes blinked open and stared at him, Mark's heart didn't jump.

No matter where you go, you're surrounded.

This wasn't the first time Mark had heard this voice, but it still caused him to tense.

"Who are you?"

His whisper sounded loud in the small cell.

The edge of the shadow opened, revealing a wide mouth filled with sharp teeth that curved in a savage grin. *Who do you think I am, Mark?*

Though he didn't answer out loud, Mark knew.

I'm you, Mark. The part of you without weakness. The part of you that wants to live at all costs. The part of you that will not stop until we reach the top.

There was a calm yet savage undertone to the shadow's words, and they resonated deeply in Mark's heart, as if feelings buried inside him were bubbling to the surface. Taking a deep breath, he nodded, and the shadow grew larger until it covered the entirety of the opposite wall.

The path before us is simple. Survive or die. But to survive, we'll need to grow. And to grow, we need to eat.

Mark could feel the unbridled hunger radiating from the shadow in front of him, but he tempered it, causing a deep calm to shroud his mind.

"You're right, we'll need to eat. But we'll have to be smart about it. Right now, I'm a minnow swimming with sharks who could chew me up with a single bite. We'll have to be strategic."

A faint whisper in the back of Mark's mind warned that listening to a red-eyed shadow probably wasn't the smartest idea. But locked in another tiny cell, miles underground, about to face an unknown enemy, Mark simply didn't have the luxury of doing otherwise. Especially when, without warning, a voice sounded from a hidden speaker.

"Please select the name you will use, and choose a mask."

A virtual window popped up, and Mark saw hundreds of masks pictured on it. His gaze swept across them, coming to rest on a simple black mask with two curved points like horns rising from either side. It reminded him of the head of the humanoid Exlian he had seen out in the wilds, and reaching out, he tapped on the image. There was a hiss, and a small opening in the wall appeared, revealing the mask he had chosen.

"Select your name," the system prompted.

Retrieving the mask, Mark found that it fit perfectly.

"Apex," he said softly.

He heard a faint blast of a horn, and the wall beside him began to grind open. As light from the arena filled his cell, the shadow let out a deep chuckle and collapsed into him, setting his blood singing. His face covered by the black mask, Mark stepped out onto the hard sand. He could still smell the faint stench of blood spilled in the last fight as the announcer's voice crackled through the air above him. He hadn't been able to hear it sitting on the prisoners' side, but from the way the people in the boxes crowded toward the windows, he imagined it was for their benefit.

"A brand-new challenger has stepped into the arena, a prisoner who's only been in the Tomb for a few weeks. Little is known about his abilities or his background, but we'll come to know them soon enough. Today, we have a randomized enemy for his first challenge!"

The virtual window appeared above Mark, showing a close-up of his face and the mask he wore, along with the name he had chosen. Tension built in him as he saw the other side of the virtual image flicker, eventually stopping on a brutish-looking man with a scar running from his cheek across both of his lips.

"Ladies and gentlemen, Apex versus the Savage."

When the announcer's voice faded, there was a blast of a horn, and a cell across from Mark opened up. As soon as the door opened and the prisoner inside stepped out, Mark felt the shackles on his wrists and ankles deactivate. For a moment he was disoriented as the web of mana faded away, and the prisoner he was facing let out a loud roar, lifting his hands into the air. As he did, his muscles began to twist and thicken, fur growing on his arms and chest.

Recognizing his opponent had a transformation ability, Mark was at a bit of a loss, unsure whether he should rush over and attack or wait for his opponent to finish his transformation. The Savage had no such issues, and as soon as his transformation was done, he bounded toward Mark, running on all fours as he crossed the arena quickly.

"Our fight has begun." The announcer's voice filled the arena. "Let's see what our two challengers have in store for us."

Letting out his breath, Mark shifted into his fighting stance. Transformation abilities came in all shapes and sizes, but this prisoner had turned into a savage beast, which was no doubt where he got his name. Yet Mark could tell by the mana that swirled through the Savage's limbs that he was barely in the C rank, and though his muscles looked big, his abilities seemed to be more oriented toward speed.

Unfortunately for the Savage, Mark's speed had reached C+ even before he had returned to the city, and after he'd consumed Python's ability, his body had gained an even greater degree of flexibility and agility, likely pushing him into the low end of B rank. The difference was stark, and he felt that the Savage was almost moving in slow motion as he launched himself into the air, his arms outstretched. Mark didn't move until just before the transformed prisoner struck, and then he simply took a step forward, slipping past the prisoner's guard, and slashed.

To those watching, it looked as if the Savage pounced on top of Mark, who ducked underneath him, stepping to the side to avoid his opponent's attack. After slamming into the ground, the Savage didn't stand up, as everybody assumed he would, and Mark, with a flick of his fingers, turned and looked up at the screen. There was a moment of silence, and then the announcer, in a choked voice, spoke.

"And there's the fight, folks. The reading I'm getting from the Savage says that he's dead?"

Even though the shackles the prisoners wore were not blocking their abilities, they still transmitted, and according to the readings, the Savage's pulse had flatlined. It was only then that people started to notice the pool of blood spreading under the Savage's body. As Mark had ducked under his pounce, his fingers had brushed lightly against his opponent's throat, tearing open his jugular vein and causing him to bleed out quickly. The way the Savage had landed had prevented anybody from seeing the blood at first.

With the fight over, the horn sounded again, and Mark's cell opened back up. With one last look around the arena, he calmly walked back into his cell, ignoring the faint grumbling he was getting from his shadow. As soon as he entered, the door closed behind him, sealing him in once again. He took a seat as a virtual window sprang up in front of him, and he saw Asa's vulturelike face staring at him.

"Well, that was certainly a surprise. It seems I'll have to arrange harder matches for you. In our records, you're D ranked, so I thought that somebody in the C rank would be a challenge. Clearly, that's not the case. Are you willing to share what rank you are? It'll help me in tuning the matches."

His face still covered by the mask, Mark didn't say a word, and after a moment, Asa sighed. "I suspected you wouldn't. Fine, you can crawl your way up. Your next match will be tomorrow. Please return by noon."

The virtual window flickered and vanished, and Mark saw that the small opening that he had retrieved his mask from had appeared again. Placing his mask inside, he watched it vanish, and then the door opened, and Mark saw Joker waiting outside. There was a hint of respect along with something else that Mark couldn't quite identify in Joker's gaze as Mark stepped out of the cell.

"I always pegged you as a dangerous one," Joker said, "but that was something. The Savage has been a longtime fighter. He's been down here for years, so to see him taken out that quickly . . ."

Mark shrugged. "It was a bad matchup for him."

With a laugh, Joker followed Mark out, and the two of them left the arena. When Mark hesitated, unsure where to go, Joker gestured for him to follow. "If you need a place to stay, I can introduce you to a good spot nearby. In fact, I know that a spot has just opened up, and technically, you get first dibs."

The place Joker was talking about happened to be less than a block from the arena, a large building filled with luxury apartments. Joker brought Mark to the front desk, where they were met by a heavily built robot.

"Greetings. I am Administrative Bot 3297. You may call me Admin 97. How may I help you?"

"My buddy here needs an apartment," Joker said, leaning on the counter, as Mark took in the ornate lobby.

The strange juxtaposition between the Tomb's conveniences and luxuries and the brutal fights Mark was forced into created significant dissonance in his mind, but there was nothing he could do about either. Admin 97 looked Mark over and keyed something into the terminal at his desk. A moment later, Mark's watch vibrated.

"As a member of the arena, the Savage's belongings are forfeit upon his death. We have provided the approximate value of his belongings in merits, held in an account that will be used to pay for your stay," Admin 97 said. "Your watch has been configured and will open the door to your apartment on the fifth floor. You have been assigned unit 5D. Is there anything else I can help you with?"

Seeing Joker looking over at him, Mark shook his head. "I think that's it."

"In that case, have a wonderful day."

After taking the elevator up to the fifth floor with Joker, Mark found his unit and walked in. It was a large apartment with floor-to-ceiling glass windows that looked out over the Tomb. There was a living room and kitchen, along with a bathroom and a bedroom. Though it was almost the same layout as the first apartment he had had upon arriving in the Tomb, the finishes were a world above. Mark could imagine finding something like this in the heart of downtown New Emery.

"One of the nice things about this apartment building is that the food is free. It's part of the price you pay. Additionally, there are facilities like a gym, training room, massage, all sorts of stuff. You can read through the introduction message on your own. It'll introduce you to all the amenities. People who fight in the arena and aren't a flight risk typically stay in apartments like this. I'm actually in this building as well, on the twelfth floor."

Noticing a hint of pride leaking through Joker's words, Mark raised his eyebrows. "Let me guess, they get nicer as they go up?"

"You bet they do." Joker's smile was wide. "I've got an entire suite up there. Well, anyway, congratulations on your first fight, and welcome to the arena."

Mark was able to choose from a large menu of food, selecting up to a week's worth at a time. There was a large catalog full of clothing, furniture, and all sorts of other necessities that he could select from as well. So he spent the next few hours outfitting his new apartment while trying not to think about the mess he had gotten himself into.

Eventually, he had finished looking through the catalog and started growing restless. Knowing that just sitting around would drive him crazy, Mark left the apartment and headed out into the Tomb, arriving forty-five minutes later at Mr. Robot's shop. His next fight was the following day, so Mark spent the evening working on alchemy. His main focus was completing the four potions required by his production quota, but he also began to look over other potions.

After stopping in to talk to Albert and the others at the warehouse, Mark headed back to get a few hours of sleep but found himself tossing and turning. Finally, annoyed that sleep wasn't coming, he decided to check out the training room attached to the apartment building. There was no one in the halls or the elevator as he headed downstairs, but as soon as he stepped into the training room, he caught sight of half a dozen other prisoners all working out. When they saw him, the prisoners paused, giving him suspicious glances, and for a moment, Mark considered simply turning around and going back upstairs.

"You must be Apex."

Mark glanced over and saw an athletic-looking woman, her brown hair pulled back in a high ponytail. Though a few inches shorter than Mark, she walked toward him with the calm assurance of a high-ranked empowered, and from the dense mana running through her body, Mark could tell that she was at least B ranked.

"I'm Anna Lee, but people call me Winter Wolf."

Seeing Anna Lee holding out her hand, Mark hesitated for a moment, then stretched out his own. As soon as their hands touched, the flesh on the back of his neck crawled, and his senses nearly went haywire as he realized how dangerous she was. Thankfully, she just shook his hand lightly and let go. As he was trying to calm his heart, Winter Wolf turned and gestured to the various machines that dotted the training room.

"You're welcome to use whatever you want. Joker mentioned that you'd be around, said you're a promising newcomer," she said.

Frowning, Mark didn't say anything. He wasn't sure why Joker seemed to be paying so much attention to him, and he was even less sure if it was a good thing. Just then, another prisoner walked over to introduce himself. He was large, carrying a good bit of weight around his middle. Yet despite that, it didn't make him look particularly fat. He peered at Mark through beady eyes and moved with a strange awkwardness. When they shook hands, Mark found his grip to be incredibly light, as if he were simply going through the motions of a handshake without actually knowing how to perform the action.

"I'm Servo."

"Nice to meet you, Servo." Hesitating for just a moment, Mark used his arena name. "I'm Apex."

"That's a curious name," Servo said, tilting his head to the side. "Does it have something to do with your power?"

"I guess you could say that."

"Fascinating. I look forward to seeing your performance in the arena."

As Servo walked away, Winter Wolf flashed a smile at Mark. "Don't mind him. Servo's one of the good ones, but he's awfully awkward. Come on, I'll introduce you to everybody else."

Most of the prisoners who were training weren't particularly friendly, but all of them stopped what they were doing to say hello. Mark was rather surprised to find that he was by far the weakest of everyone present. Even though he suspected he was close to B rank, simply shaking hands with the others alerted him that almost anyone here could probably crush him without much trouble.

Noticing how he got quieter with every new introduction, Winter Wolf chuckled. "I know they can be intimidating, but you don't have to worry about it. Penalties for fighting outside the arena are too high, so most of us keep our conflicts inside the arena's walls."

"Is everyone here a fighter in the arena?"

"Sort of," Winter Wolf said, with half a shrug. "Most of us only fight in special exhibitions."

"Joker mentioned those, but he didn't say exactly what they were . . ."

"Pretty typical for him—he loses interest fast. Come here, give me a spot."

Leading Mark over to one of the machines, Winter Wolf adjusted the weight and lay down on the bench. As she began bench-pressing the bar rapidly, she spoke in an even voice, leaving Mark standing there awkwardly.

"Anybody below B rank typically fights in the standard exhibitions. Those of us B rank and above usually don't bother, because most of the fights would be over too fast. Instead, we fight in special exhibitions arranged by the arena for the scum coming down from New Emery."

This wasn't the first time that Mark had heard the people in the viewing boxes referred to as scum, and in truth, he felt the term fit.

"So it might be a team of us fighting against a horde of Exlian in a ruined city, or a straight arena match versus a team of mercenaries from the surface. Occasionally, they'll even throw in some mutants. It really just depends on what they think will be an interesting enough spectacle."

Sweat was beginning to bead on Winter Wolf's skin, but she still raised and lowered the bar swiftly, her breath even and her face calm.

"At the end of the day, the point of the special exhibitions is entertainment rather than just death, so as soon as you can break out of the lower ranks and make it to the special exhibitions, the better. Of course, they're no less dangerous. In some ways, they're more dangerous, but the advantage is that you get to run with a team, at least normally."

With a click, she set the bar back on its rests and sat up, gesturing for Mark to toss her a towel that was draped over a nearby bench. After she had wiped herself off, Winter Wolf stood up and looked Mark up and down. "From what Joker tells me, you should be able to join us in only a few more rounds. He wasn't quite sure what rank you are, though."

Mark took a moment to respond, unsure what to say. His official rank was still D, at least according to his paperwork, but he could tell he was already starting to push into the B rank. At the same time, fighting against someone in the B rank was beyond him, at least at the moment. With an uncomfortable shrug, he gave an evasive answer. "I'm not quite so sure myself. It's been a while since I last had an activator. I think I'm somewhere in the high C rank, but I'm not sure."

"Well, they'll find out soon enough. Expect your next two matches to be tough. If Asa doesn't have a precise read on your strength, he'll resort to throwing you against harder and harder enemies until he finds your limit."

Just as Winter Wolf predicted, the next day, Mark found himself facing off against a group of C-ranked devil hounds. There were three of the monsters, and Mark almost laughed when they appeared. Of course, a normal C-ranked empowered facing off against three equally ranked Exlian with no suit would be done for. But to Mark, such a fight was little different from his first one the day before.

Of course, while he could have gotten through the fight without taking any wounds, Mark knew that if he didn't show some of his power, things would only get worse. Suppressing his instincts, Mark threw himself against the devil hounds in a fierce brawl, suffering more than one devastating bite to his arms and legs, but each time managing to kill one of the Exlian in return.

The first tore a massive chunk of his shoulder off, but the wound allowed Mark to land a blow on its throat, nearly severing its head. As the other two devil hounds launched their own attacks, Mark threw himself backward, rolling across the ground. He could hear the announcer's shouts up above as his shoulder began to heal. The next devil hound managed to latch onto Mark's legs but suffered a blow to its spine that left it dead. Struggling to his feet, Mark took a halting step forward, then another. By the time the third devil hound launched its attack, his leg had healed completely, and he met it with the same move he had used against the Savage the day before, ducking under its leap and cutting its throat open. Even as the Exlian landed, Mark spun and jumped on top of it, his bone blade hand piercing through the back of its skull.

As the fight finally ended, Mark felt his shackles reactivating and quickly canceled his bone blade transformation, grimacing as he pretended his power was disrupted. Of course, the shackles had no impact on Mark's powers, but he wanted to hide that as much as possible. While he had been locked in the final, desperate struggle with the last of the Exlian, Mark had felt his shadow beginning to creep toward the other corpses, but he suppressed it with a thought, ignoring its complaints as he headed for his cell.

This time, Asa only appeared after he had put his mask away. "Congratulations on another successful battle. Payment has been sent your way. I've had a request from Joker to assign you to his team for an upcoming special exhibition. Of course, you'll have to pass another standard fight before you're allowed to participate in those, but I wanted to get your thoughts first. Do you have any interest in the special exhibitions?"

Though he had already heard about them from Winter Wolf, Mark found himself curious how Asa would describe them. "What are the special exhibitions? I've heard people mention them, but I don't have a lot of information."

"Simply put, they're prearranged team fights," Asa said, glancing down at something. "Teams of prisoners who perform well in the arena are granted special leeway. However, the danger of these fights is considerably higher. If you decide to participate in this upcoming match, you and your teammates will be arrayed against two different forces, a group of Exlian and a mercenary team."

Biting his lip, Mark pretended to be worried. "I know Maestro assigned me to the arena because he wants data. If I'm not fighting in the standard exhibitions, will he still be able to get his data?"

"Yes. He doesn't particularly care, so long as you're using your powers," Asa said, his face impassive.

"If that's really the case, then I guess I'm fine with it," Mark said. "I'm not sure that I have much of a choice."

"Indeed, you don't," Asa replied. "One way or another, Maestro will get his combat data. Your last test fight will happen tomorrow. Please arrive by noon again."

After he signed off, Mark sat for a moment in the dim cell, his mind churning. Unfortunately, there wasn't much he could do about his current situation. So rather than stress about it, he decided to take things as they came. Mark split the rest of his day between selecting alchemical ingredients and working out in the training room. The next morning, when he arrived at the arena, he found Joker waiting for him, along with Winter Wolf and Servo.

"Ready for your fight?" Joker asked as Mark walked up.

"As ready as I'll ever be, I guess," Mark replied, shrugging.

"That's what I like to hear. After you crush your opponent, you get to come and join us in the fun stuff."

Just then, a young woman with bright-blue hair and faintly green skin rushed up. "Oh, sorry I'm late. Got a bit tied up back there. Hey, you must be Apex. Good to meet you. My name's Coral."

Slightly overwhelmed by her rapid-fire delivery, Mark shifted back on his heels.

"Coral is the last member of our team," Winter Wolf said. "We lost another teammate in a previous exhibition, but if you pass this fight, you'll be joining us."

"Well, hopefully Asa hasn't arranged something too hard for me."

"I'm sure you'll be fine."

Mark wasn't quite as confident as Winter Wolf seemed to be, and as he sat in his cell, an uneasy feeling brewed in his chest.

The match began like every other, with his mask appearing from a hole in the wall and the stone door grinding open. As he stepped out into the light of the arena, Mark heard the announcer's excited voice.

"Ladies and gentlemen, our new challenger, Apex, takes the stage once again. In his first fight, he eliminated the Savage with ease. In his second, he showed remarkable resilience against the dangerous devil hounds. Who knows what today's match has in store for him? Let's hope it's something pulse pounding."

Gazing up at the screen, Mark saw the image flicker and stop on a metallic figure.

"Well, we'll certainly get our wish, folks. Though I can't say Apex's luck is very good, because he is going to be facing a Deathbot!"

As the announcer's words faded, a massive section of the arena wall opened up, and a powerful robot on four legs stomped forward. Rather than being humanoid like most of the robots Mark had seen since coming to the Tomb, this one had four spiderlike legs and a heavy shell on top of it. Two sword-wielding mechanical arms extended from either side, and its head sat atop a heavy mana cannon.

As soon as he saw the massive robot, Mark honestly didn't know whether to laugh or cry. On the one hand, robots were considered one of the hardest enemies for an empowered to face, especially a Deathbot like this, which was easily able to handle most foes in the B rank. If Mark only had the powers listed in his file, there was no way he'd be able to dent the thing, let alone win. At the same time, robots were one of the easiest opponents for Mark to face. Already, he could sense the mana coursing through its metallic body, and it wouldn't be hard to disrupt it, causing the thing to go haywire. As his shackles deactivated, Mark was stepping forward, trying to come up with a good strategy, when a loud siren sounded and the announcer's excited voice filled the arena.

"In a shocking turn of events, a twist has been added to the fight. We'll have to see what it is, folks. But here we go. Will it prove a deadly challenge, impossible to overcome? Or will it be an advantage? We'll find out in just a moment."

Unsure exactly what was happening, Mark hesitated, his eyes rising to the flickering screen, which landed on a picture of four different people.

"My goodness, folks, it looks like our challenger, Apex, is about to receive some assistance."

Four doorways opened in the arena walls, and four prisoners whom Mark had never seen before stumbled out. Three of them were clearly unwilling. Upon seeing Mark and the robot, they all hesitated, then slowly began to gather. The robot started to gear up with a hum. If it had just been Mark alone in the arena with the robot, he could have dealt with it from afar. Unfortunately, with the others present, he would likely have to fight it directly. Sensing the mana cannon atop the Deathbot beginning to charge, Mark hesitated for just a moment, then threw himself to the side, timing it perfectly so the shot blazed past him, blowing a small crater in the sandy arena floor.

"It looks like our Deathbot is eager to get in on the action, folks. Let the fighting begin!"

With the announcer's booming voice ringing across the arena, the prisoners all activated their powers and charged. Mark was no different. He rolled across the hard ground and lunged to his feet, sprinting around the robot's side. Other prisoners were heading in from the opposite side, and Mark was hoping that the Deathbot would turn toward them since there were more of them. Instead, buzzing seemingly in anger, the robot shifted its bulk to face Mark. Sensing mana starting to gather once again, this time at its legs, Mark backpedaled rapidly as the robot lowered its bulk slightly and then charged, its two sword-wielding appendages held out front.

Realizing he wouldn't be able to outrun it, even with his B-ranked speed, Mark leaped into the air, dodging past one of its slashing blades, his foot catching the top of the robot's carapace as he bounded over it. Since the robot was nearly twenty-five feet tall, this maneuver left Mark hanging in the air, but as he started to fall back down, the robot slammed into the arena wall with such force that it rebounded, smacking into Mark's back and sending him tumbling. He barely managed to get his arms up around his head as he slammed into the ground and rolled over a dozen times.

Having lost sight of him, the Deathbot spun and finally caught sight of the other prisoners, just as one of them attacked with a blast of mana that skipped off the Deathbot's hard shell, barely leaving a scorch mark. This was enough to infuriate the robot, however, and it responded with a blast of its own, which tore through the shocked prisoner's chest, leaving nothing but a smoking pair of legs behind.

With one of the prisoners dead already, the others knew that the only way they were going to survive was if they managed to disable the terrifying bot, and filled with desperation, they rushed forward, evading its sharp swords and attacking its body. One of the prisoners, a heavily muscled man who wore no shirt, had skin that looked like stone, and he unleashed powerful punches against the Deathbot's side that dented its armor. Another, who appeared to be using telekinesis, picked up sand and threw it in the Deathbot's way, clearly trying to disrupt its vision and gum up its mechanical arms.

As Mark struggled to his feet, he saw the last prisoner standing some distance away, concentrating deeply as she drew her hands back, wielding a bow condensed from pure mana. Pulling the string back to full draw, she unleashed a shot that tore through the air, targeting the robot's head. At the last moment, it spun, knocking the other prisoners away. The arrow slammed into its carapace, punching a hole into it, and Mark, seeing an opportunity, sprinted forward, moving as fast as he possibly could.

The robot started to turn back around, its mana cannon charging, and Mark knew that the arrow hadn't done any damage. Still, it had managed to get through the Deathbot's incredibly tough exterior, which provided perfect cover for Mark. The Deathbot turned back around, its stomping legs forcing the rock-skinned prisoner back. As he got close, Mark, with his mind, seized the flow of mana in the center of the robot and forced it to a standstill. The mana cannon, nearly charged, suddenly faltered as the robot hesitated and then drooped, its large mana blades dropping to the ground. With a faint hum, the robot rocked to the side, and the crimson light on its head faded.

"With a lucky shot, our indomitable prisoners have taken the Deathbot down. Ladies and gentlemen, it looks as if the Deathbot is no longer operational. This sort of thing is incredibly rare, but accidents have been known to happen."

The prisoners, unable to believe their luck, looked around, realizing that they had just survived. Yet before any of them could celebrate, the siren that had sent them into the arena in the first place sounded once more, and under the announcer's surprised gasp, the virtual screen hanging over the arena began to flicker again before stopping on a large skull.

A low rumble sounded, and a section of the arena floor suddenly slid aside, making way for a massive black metal box. Mark could hear the muffled roars from inside it and see the walls of the box shaking, but at the moment, it was all he could do to keep the robot from reactivating. The other prisoners quickly gathered together as the box finished its rise. With an ominous click, the box unlatched and the walls fell to the sides, revealing a fifteen-foot Exlian that glared down at the prisoners. Shaggy, with heavy plates of armor on its chest and shoulders, six insectile limbs extending from its back, and claws that were easily a foot and a half long: Mark recognized it immediately. One of the most terrifying Exlian under the terror rank.

"Ladies and gentlemen, what a shocking twist. Our prisoners, just about to finish their match, have a new foe. The arena's dreaded Exlian war bear."

From the way the war bear immediately fixed its eyes on the prisoners, Mark could tell this wasn't the first time the Exlian had hunted in the arena. He felt a thrill run through him, even as the war bear launched itself forward. Despite its bulk, it moved with incredible swiftness, crossing the arena in an instant before its massive claws raked down toward the prisoner in the front.

With a desperate cry, the telekinetic tried to escape the hit, throwing a wall of sand and debris at the war bear. But the monster simply smashed straight through, tearing the prisoner apart with a single blow. Death came so quickly that none of the other prisoners had a chance to react. One moment, the war bear was across the arena, and the next, it was standing over the bloody, torn-apart corpse of their fellow prisoner.

The others scattered, too frightened to even think about fighting back. But in the enclosed arena, there was nowhere to escape from the war bear. Vaguely, Mark could hear the announcer shouting, but he was too focused on the monster to hear what the announcer was saying. He'd never be able to survive a direct hit, and the war bear was clearly stronger and faster than him.

At the same time, Mark felt a deep and burning hunger filling his body, a desperate need to hunt the massive creature in front of him. Throwing himself at the Exlian would be suicide, of course, and as Mark hesitated, the war bear struck again, this time targeting the prisoner with the stone skin. A paw lashed out, scoring deep marks across the prisoner's chest and shoulder and throwing him clear across the arena.

The convict let out a shriek of pain and tried to scramble to his feet. But before he could, the war bear was on top of him once more, batting him with a heavy paw to send him tumbling. Unleashing a savage roar, the war bear caught sight of the prisoner with the mana bow, who was shakily trying to pull its string.

Still sensing the threat of condensed mana, the war bear charged toward her, rearing up as it got to her position. All its limbs spread wide, but before it could bring its claws down, there was a loud hum, and a bolt of mana slammed into its back, catapulting the war bear over the shocked woman's head.

As the creature tumbled to the ground, the Deathbot hummed again and climbed back to its feet. It had targeted the woman with a mana blast before Mark had shut it down, and when it came back to life, that blast was unleashed, slamming into the war bear between them. An unearthly howl shook the arena as the war bear clambered to its feet, bleeding badly from a scorched wound on its lower back.

Though its speed was greatly hampered by the injury, it still charged the Deathbot, which met it with mana swords raised. As the two behemoths clashed, Mark sprinted toward the trembling woman, who still held a half-condensed mana bow in hand. In the distance, he could see the badly wounded rock-skinned prisoner struggling to sit up.

Across the arena, the war bear was laying into the robot, its claws tearing massive chunks from the bot's armor. Despite the robot's best efforts, its blades could hardly pierce the thick skin of the war bear, and it was quickly becoming apparent that the war bear had the advantage. Mark knew that it would soon turn its attention back to them.

"Go help him," he said, pointing at the wounded prisoner, "and stay out of the way."

"What? What are you—"

The woman's voice died in her throat as Mark took off, heading straight for the two clashing titans. Though the war bear was a good ten feet shorter than the robot, it was currently doing a number on the Deathbot's thick armored carapace, and Mark knew that his only chance to survive was to work with the Deathbot to bring the Exlian down. Of course, that was easier said than done . . .

As he ran forward, he saw the Deathbot unleash a savage slash with one of its mana swords, but as soon as the sword reached the war bear's skin, mana condensed between the blade and the Exlian's fur, forming a shield that blocked the majority of the force and prevented the sword from being able to cut into the monster's skin. Mark had been wondering why the mana cannon hadn't blasted straight through the war bear, and now he had his answer. The creature's fur carried a dense mana charge, and every time a threat approached, that mana would flood into the air, forming a natural barrier.

Rapidly, a plan formed in Mark's mind, and as he got close, he threw himself toward the war bear's back. If the war bear sensed his arrival, it didn't care, and it ignored him completely, letting out a roar as it tore another chunk from the bot's heavy frame. Just before Mark landed, he activated his null field and sensed the mana that had been gathering to block him fading away. His bone blade hands stabbed deep into the war bear's tough skin, piercing through its fur and flesh like nails through paper. The pain caught the war bear off guard, and it let out a roar, starting to twist.

Mark did his best to keep the null field tight, shrouding his own body without letting it spread farther. It was a delicate balance, as the robot ran entirely on mana, and if Mark had extended his field to its full range, it would have caused the robot to shut down again.

Mark was under no illusion that he'd be able to beat the war bear by himself, so he had to walk a fine line to disable its natural defenses while keeping the Deathbot in fighting shape.

Furious, the war bear thrashed its insectile limbs, trying to reach Mark, who was between its shoulder blades.

Seeing a large claw heading toward him, Mark climbed higher, leaving a trail of bloody wounds up the war bear's back. The robot, with no idea why the war bear had suddenly shifted its attention, took the opportunity to try to cut the monster's legs out from underneath it.

Sensing the attack, Mark relaxed his control on his null field, letting it expand rapidly. He managed to time it perfectly, with the mana-dispersing energy of the null field reaching the fur on the war bear's legs just before the mana sword hit. Having erased the mana in the war bear's fur and prevented it from forming a mana shield, Mark withdrew his null field, sucking it back up into his body, to avoid deactivating the mana blade.

With a heavy thunk, the mana blade sank deep into the war bear's leg, causing it to roar in pain. Mark had been so focused on his manipulation of the null field that he missed the war bear's scraping claw that caught him in the shoulder, piercing straight through his back and poking out his chest.

As the war bear collapsed to the side, its leg cut out from under it, Mark was flung outward, the claw tearing through his collarbone as it was wrenched free from his body. Nearly blacking out from the pain, Mark slammed into the ground a dozen feet away as the war bear began to flail.

Another strike from the Deathbot hacked down toward the war bear's neck, only to be blocked by a surge of mana. The weight of the blow, delivered with all the Deathbot's strength, drove the war bear down into the ground a few inches but failed to do any significant damage. Barely conscious, Mark struggled to lift his head and saw the Deathbot looming over the war bear, its mana cannon charging. Clenching his teeth so hard they felt like they might shatter, Mark summoned all his concentration to fight through the horrific pain in his arm and activated the null field again. For a moment, his mind trembled and he thought that he had failed, but then the null field spread, enshrouding the struggling war bear.

Confusion filled the beast's eyes as the mana around it melted away, eliminating its natural defenses. Above it, the mana cannon bloomed like a flower opening its petals. A blast of concentrated mana slammed into the war bear's head from point-blank range. The last time it had been hit, the war bear's natural defenses had diffused the blast. Though some of the mana had still made it through, burning a hole in the war bear's back, the attack hadn't done much more than superficial damage.

This time, without the defenses active, the beam of mana punched a hole straight through the war bear's face, obliterating its nose and destroying its brain. Mark's null field, which was extended just far enough to cover the war bear's upper body, cracked under the weight of the attack. He felt a piercing pain in his head as the feedback from his destroyed field rolled through him.

Groaning, he tried to clutch his head, but his shoulder still wasn't fully healed, making it impossible for him to move his arm. He could feel his biofuel draining rapidly as his body tried to heal, but he was in such rough shape he knew he wouldn't be able to move for a while. And with the war bear dead, the Deathbot strode forward, the scraps of armor still on its body rattling. Mana cannon cooling down, it lifted one of its swords, clearly intending to bring it down on Mark. But just before it could, an arrow made of pure mana punched through its arm, causing its attack to falter.

Metal screamed as the Deathbot shifted its weight to look across the arena, where the prisoner wielding the bow was crouched, her body trembling as she drew another arrow. Mark, more instinctively than consciously, did his best to crawl away, trying to get out of the bot's line of sight. Currently, he was an absolute mess, and he could feel that the shattering of his null field had done significant damage to his brain.

At the same time, the only way that they would survive against the robot was if he figured out a way to shut it down again. The problem was, he could barely muster a coherent thought, let alone focus his mana control ability. Though his shoulder was still healing, Mark let out a gasp and rolled over onto his back. A moment later, the Deathbot stomped down, clearly intending to end his life before it went to deal with the archer. At the last moment, Mark managed to twist his torso, barely avoiding the pistonlike leg that stabbed into the earth.

He had never tried to direct the healing in his body before, but now he did, using every ounce of his will to push his regenerative power toward his mind. At the same time, his hand stretched out, touching the heavy metal leg. Miraculously, his efforts seemed to work.

Yet even as his brain started to heal, Mark pushed it to the limit, focusing on the mana inside the bot. He could feel mana gathering in the cannon as it got ready to send out another blast, and though his mind screamed in protest, Mark took control of that dense ball of mana. It felt like trying to handle a sun, and he could feel his mental power burning away, even as he forced the hypercondensed ball of mana down into the robot.

Only a brief second had passed, but Mark knew he wouldn't be able to hold on. With a roar that sounded more like a groan, he pressed down on that burning sun, forcing it deeper into the robot's body before the rest of his mental energy burned away and his mind slipped into unconsciousness. Darkness only claimed him for a brief second before the intense regenerative power focused on his mind brought him back to awareness. Immediately, he rolled over, grimacing as his still-wounded shoulder brushed against the hard dirt, and began crawling away as fast as he could.

The Deathbot, unaware of what he had just done, shifted its bulk and tried to fire its mana cannon. When the blast was triggered, it abruptly accelerated, but rather than flowing out through the barrel, the mana poured downward, liquefying the bot's insides. With a loud explosion, chunks of already-shredded armor were broken apart further, transformed into deadly shrapnel that peppered the arena. Mark, trying to crawl away, felt something white hot pierce through one of his legs, and though he screamed, he didn't stop crawling.

There was a shuddering sound, the groan of tortured metal rubbing together, and then the Deathbot came crashing down, little more than scrap. Mark was running dangerously low on biofuel when he caught sight of a foot poking out from beneath the massive bulk of the now-destroyed robot.

Realizing that he would likely die from blood loss before he was able to receive medical treatment, Mark acted, his shadow stretching out to gobble up the legs of the first prisoner who had been shot. Not too far away were the remains of the telekinetic who had been killed by the war bear, and praying that the thick cloud of dirt and dust that had been thrown into the air by the Deathbot's collapse would keep him hidden, Mark commanded his shadow to consume those as well. While the lack of bodies would be noticed, Mark didn't feel safe without some backup biofuel, so it was a risk he was willing to take.

Though he felt slightly sick to his stomach doing it, his biofuel soon began to surge, bringing a new wave of regeneration that knit together his shoulder and his leg while soothing the pain in his brain. By the time the shocked announcer managed to declare the end of the match, Mark had climbed to his feet. Half a dozen guards rushed into the arena, and Mark felt the shackles on his arms and legs activating once again. The other two prisoners, both wounded and exhausted, were quickly led away, but the guards seemed strangely hesitant to approach Mark.

Casting a longing look at the war bear, whose corpse was almost completely intact save for a hole burned straight through the middle of its face, Mark held up his hands, trying to appear as harmless as possible. None of the guards bought it, and they remained a few steps away from him as he turned and headed for his cell.

Once inside, he collapsed to the bench, reaching up to take off his mask, which miraculously had remained glued to his face the entire time. Leaning his head back against the wall, Mark felt the cool stone and realized how hot his head was, a side effect of the intense regeneration. With a faint buzz, a virtual window popped up in front of him, and Mark saw Asa staring at him, a mixture of begrudging respect and confusion in his eyes. Though all he really wanted to do was sleep, Mark slowly straightened up, meeting Asa's gaze squarely.

"What was that?" he finally asked, breaking the silence.

"Something that shouldn't have happened," Asa said.

"Are you saying the fight shouldn't have proceeded like that, or I shouldn't have survived?"

Though it was subtle, Mark caught a hint of emotion that flashed through Asa's normally calm gaze, a bit of guilt, even fear. Returning to his normal calm, Asa shook his head. "Exhibition matches are unpredictable. What you experienced was someone from the boxes introducing a new variable into the fight. Variables can be any number of things, as you saw. They range from assistants to make it easier on you to additional enemies, shifting the dynamics of the fight. The individuals introducing the twists do not get to choose what type of variable they introduce. Only that a variable is introduced."

"And what about me?" Mark said. "Do I get some sort of reward for completing what was clearly a much more difficult fight?"

Asa's lips twisted into what Mark could only assume was a smile. "No, you'll be paid according to the original agreement."

Mark, who had been hoping to get his hands on the war bear corpse, shifted his tack. "Can you tell me at least what's going to happen to the war bear? This is the first time I've seen a live one, and I'd be quite interested in studying it."

"You and a long list of others. I've already gotten numerous requests, but it's not up to me to decide. Maestro will be the one who determines what happens to it."

Biting his lip, Mark thought for a moment and then nodded.

"Having passed your three-match assessment, you'll be assigned to Joker's team. Speak to him about when your next match will be."

Detecting a hint of impatience, Mark watched as Asa shut down the virtual window. After Mark had put his mask away, he left the arena. On his way out, he overheard multiple people talking about the fight that had just taken place. But he didn't linger, instead heading straight for Mr. Robot's alchemy store. When he arrived, Mr. Robot was checking out a customer, and Mark waited nearby.

As soon as the customer headed for the door, Mark stepped up to the counter. "Mr. Robot, can I speak to you?"

"You are speaking to me."

"I mean in private."

Mr. Robot shifted his gaze to the doorway, watching until the door clicked shut. "It is now private."

Taking a deep breath, Mark quickly ran over what he wanted to say in his mind before taking the plunge. "I would like to speak to Maestro about the war bear corpse in the arena."

Mr. Robot regarded Mark for a moment, and then with a nod, his eyes flashed and transformed from their normal red to a bright yellow.

"Ah, Mark, I expected to hear from you. Hopefully, you haven't called me to complain about the unexpected turn of events in the arena, because if you have, I will be incredibly disappointed."

Though Maestro's voice was light, Mark couldn't help but swallow nervously. "No, sir, I'm not calling to complain. Rather, I was wondering if . . ."

Mark hesitated for the briefest of moments, but he could practically feel Maestro's annoyance, despite the fact that Mr. Robot's expression couldn't change, so he hurried to continue.

"I was wondering if I could be of assistance with the war bear corpse."

There was a brief pause before Maestro replied. "Assistance? What sort of assistance were you thinking?"

"Well, sir, you know I'm an alchemist, but I'm also an alchemical butcher. I trained under Master Abrams. A war bear has a significant number of highly valuable alchemical ingredients in its body, and I'm wondering if I'd be able to help you remove them."

Once again, there was a pause.

"Well, aren't you just full of surprises? As it turns out, that would be helpful. Additionally, I've been meaning to call you. I have the first version of a serum I want to test on you, and given your honestly rather incredible performance and the data I was able to retrieve, I think I have a better sense of your power. No, don't tell me—I'd like to guess. A bit of professional pride, you might say. I'd like to know how close I am to the truth. I'm not quite ready for you yet, though, so tomorrow morning, take any elevator, and I'll meet you."

Mr. Robot's eyes flashed red, indicating that Maestro had disconnected. Silently, Mr. Robot reached under the counter and pulled out a list, which he handed to Mark.

"What's this?" Mark asked, taking the piece of paper and scanning it.

It was the production list for the week, and with a weary sigh, he rubbed his forehead. Somehow, the number of potions he was required to create had grown, and as much as he wanted to tell Mr. Robot that he was busy, he had a sneaking suspicion that that wouldn't be an acceptable response.

"Fine, I can get started right away, but I'm absolutely famished after my fight. I need to go find some food."

"You will begin brewing potions. I will have food delivered."

Mr. Robot's tone brooked no argument, so Mark dragged himself into the workshop, cursing his lack of autonomy under his breath. True to his word, Mr. Robot did have food delivered, and to Mark's surprise, it actually left him satisfied. Though he hadn't filled up his biofuel completely, after eating nearly a week's worth of groceries for a normal person, he was mostly full and had also turned out close to half of the healing potions on the list.

It was late when he completed enough of his quota to feel satisfied, and after hesitating for a moment, he decided against checking on the warehouse. He wanted to be well rested for his meeting with Maestro the following day, so Mark headed back to his apartment to try to get some sleep. When he arrived, he found Joker and Winter Wolf waiting in the lobby. Both of them stood up when they saw Mark enter, and with his signature grin, Joker greeted Mark. "That was incredible. Normally, a fight only has a single twist, but not only did yours have two, but it had two of the worst twists that could possibly happen."

"What do you mean?" Mark said. "I thought only one of them was bad."

"Depends on perspective," Winter Wolf said, shrugging. "After all, just because other prisoners come out doesn't mean they're going to be friendly."

"Exactly," Joker said with a laugh. "I mean, remember who is down here? A bunch of cold-blooded killers, every single one of them. And yes, that includes us. Did I ever tell you the story about how I got my name?"

"Everybody's heard that story. More times than we care to," Winter Wolf interrupted, her gaze fixed on Mark's face. "You don't look as tired as I assumed you'd be, but you should probably get some rest. The team will be meeting up tomorrow."

"I'm not sure tomorrow will work," Mark said, shaking his head. "I have an appointment with Maestro."

Joker and Winter Wolf exchanged surprised looks as Mark continued.

"I'm not sure how long it'll go, but if I'm free in the afternoon, I'll send you a message. Here, let me get your contact information."

After they exchanged watch numbers, Mark said good night and headed up to his apartment, where he collapsed into bed and soon fell into a deep sleep.

When he appeared in the dream wilderness, standing in the center of the ruined base, Mark took a deep breath. The fatigue of the day was washed away, though he could still feel a faint pressure in his head from trying to handle the concentrated mana ball. But Mark was starting to get a better understanding of both his mana control and null field abilities. Both relied on a sort of energy that he had never heard anyone talk about before: the power of his mind, or more specifically, his will. He had assumed willpower was a simple thing that determined how much mana he would be able to control and how quickly he would grow tired, but this last fight showed his power was more complex than that.

A quick scan of his surroundings showed him the screamer who normally lurked in these ruins wasn't nearby, and taking a running jump, Mark quickly scaled the side of a nearby building. Arriving on the roof, he looked around. From here, he could see much of the valley, including the large boulder hill where the screamer nest was located. Taking a seat on the roof, Mark slowed his breathing and began to meditate, doing his best to explore this strange new power he had discovered.

Mana filled the air around him in a faint haze, and he could sense traces of it in the material of the roof underneath him. It was even thicker in his body, filling his muscles and playing gently across his skin. As he sank deeper into his meditation, it seemed as if the world opened up around him. Though he had his eyes closed, immersing himself in darkness, Mark began to get the feeling that he could see just fine.

Yet mana wasn't the only thing he could sense. In the center of his mind was a soft ball of energy, gray and undulating. Another clear orb of energy was at the back of his neck, locked away in a hard marble, as if sealed. What he was sensing at his neck was the power of the null field, which could be released to spread around him, chasing mana away. And what resided in the center of his mind was this mysterious mental energy he had discovered.

Leaving the null field alone for the moment, Mark began to try to manipulate his mental energy. To his surprise, he found that it responded instantly to what he wanted, and with every change he made to it, he discovered a new use. If he spread it out in a wide globe around his body, everything became clearer, making him feel like he was tapping into the psychic network. When he condensed it, his mind felt sharper and his thoughts more nimble. He could send tendrils of mental energy out into his surroundings, forming connections with the mana around him.

Immersed in this mysterious state, Mark tried activating his mana control ability and saw multiple thin strands of mental energy spreading out around him, alerting him to pools of mana he could command. He was so immersed in his exploration that he nearly missed the screamer leaping toward him from another roof and barely managed to scramble out of the way as it unleashed a loud sound blast that melted straight through the roof of the building he was on.

By this time, Mark had been fighting screamers in his dreams so often that they hardly posed a threat. Shaking his hands free of the blood, Mark watched as the screamer's corpse faded away. In truth, there was no need to clean his hands off, as even the blood from the monster's corpse evaporated. Of course, this wasn't the only screamer who patrolled the ruins, and its death had undoubtedly alerted the other to his location.

Desiring some peace and quiet, Mark didn't wait for it to come but instead took a running leap, throwing himself to a neighboring building. He caught sight of a flicker of movement in the streets below, and as soon as he landed, he reached down, slowing his momentum by stabbing his fingers into the roof. As he slid to a stop, he ripped a chunk of the roof free and hurled it over the edge.

Down below, the screamer had caught sight of him, and when the dark mass flew toward it, it instinctively opened its mouth and unleashed a sound blast, evaporating the offending metal and wood. It hadn't even realized that it had been baited when Mark hurled himself from the roof and landed on top of it, quickly severing its spine with a slash.

As the large Exlian collapsed underneath him, Mark jumped free, his eyes scanning his environment to make sure no other enemies were nearby. He could sense through the psychic network that there were no Exlian within his range, but just as he was about to return to his meditation, a thought struck him.

Currently, his mind was burning bright in the psychic network, which had undoubtedly alerted the first screamer of his position. Remembering how, during his exploration of the Felwer Mine facility, Mime had shrouded his mind, hiding him away, Mark began to wonder if he could do the same. He had the ability to control mana by manipulating his mental energy—was it possible to use that same control to replicate Mime's shrouding effect?

After climbing back up to a nearby roof, Mark sat down with his legs crossed and began to ponder the problem seriously.

Currently, he had two forces at his disposal: mental energy and the strange null field that rejected all mana. Unlike his mental energy, however, his null field couldn't be manipulated freely. When released, it formed a wide orb around him, stretching approximately fifteen feet in each direction.

Of course, Mark had already tried only releasing it slightly, just enough to shroud his body in a thin layer, but doing so simply erased the mana around him, as opposed to the mana in him. And furthermore, mana wasn't what was showing up in the psychic network, but rather mental power itself.

Considering the problem, Mark began to manipulate his mental energy, doing his best to replicate what Mime had done. Yet no matter what he did, every time he checked the psychic network, there he was, burning bright. In fact, it seemed that anytime he used his mental energy, the light that represented his location in the psychic network flared, growing even brighter than normal.

This made sense to Mark, who remembered just how powerful the brain had appeared in the network when it had attacked Felwer Base. Realizing he was on the wrong track, he tried the opposite, condensing his mental energy as much as possible. That did decrease the size of the light representing him but also made it more potent, causing him to once again show up brightly. Despite working with dogged determination for the whole night, Mark was no closer to finding a solution when the dream began to fade.

Sitting up in bed, Mark rubbed his face, unable to shake the feeling that he was missing something key. Knowing that trying to rush it wouldn't help him one bit, Mark reached over to pet Mime, who had appeared at some point during the night. His touch woke the sleeping cat, and after giving him a disdainful look, she stretched and rolled over, exposing her belly so he could rub it.

After indulging his strange pet, Mark stood up and headed for the kitchen to get something to eat. Maestro hadn't told him when he should come, or even how he should get down to the Cradle, so with some confusion, Mark, after finishing breakfast and getting dressed, walked to the elevator to take it down to the first floor.

As soon as the door shut and the elevator started dropping, Mark sensed something was off. It was moving quite a bit too quickly, much faster than it had been the day before, and as the lights flickered faintly, Mark realized that they had long passed the apartment building's ground floor.

For close to two minutes, the elevator sank, and then it slowed to a stop. With a soft chime, the door slid open, revealing a long hallway, one quite familiar to Mark. He was certain he had never been in this particular hallway, but it looked exactly the same as the one he had taken to meet with Maestro, and as he hesitantly made his way down the hall, he heard a voice come through a speaker.

"Ah, Mark, I've been expecting you. Take your next right and then the following left. You'll find another elevator there."

Nodding, Mark did as he was instructed. But rather than rise, this elevator darted to the side. After a couple of minutes of zipping this way and that, it stopped. This time when the door opened, Maestro was waiting for Mark. "Welcome. We have much to do today, so please come with me."

Maestro didn't speak until they had arrived at a laboratory, where he requested that Mark lie down on a long silver table. A dozen probes were stabbed into Mark's body. Quite nervous, all Mark could do was lie still, hoping that Maestro wouldn't uncover too many of his secrets. Curiously, Maestro seemed to be both excited and frustrated. As he fussed around Mark, his eyes constantly darted around between the virtual windows in front of him that displayed the data he was getting. Finally, after close to an hour and a half, he gestured for Mark to sit up.

"In truth, the data your body gives off, or at least that I've been able to collect, is incredibly bizarre, but I do feel that that has something to do with your power."

Peering at Mark with his large eyes, Maestro seemed both excited and nervous, as if guessing some big secret.

"I think that you have a couple powers. Of course, you have the transformation of your arms, which was originally considered a characteristic absorption power. That seems fairly straightforward. Then there's your uncanny ability to locate Exlian, which your file says you picked up from a skill stone. Typically an incredibly useful skill, though less so down here in the Tomb than up above. Of course, what we're really concerned about are your other powers. Most particularly, this power that seems to exhibit itself rather randomly. A power which, if I'm correct, you don't even know you have, but I've managed to isolate. Tell me, occasionally, do things around you just stop working? You know, electronics, that sort of thing. Or sometimes maybe even your powers, or other people's powers. Have you ever had that experience?"

By this point, Mark's mind was spinning, but he kept his face carefully neutral as he nodded.

"See, I knew it. I knew it. Are you familiar with nulls? Individuals who have a natural immunity to mana?"

"I am. A couple of them tested me at the assessment center."

Smiling widely, Maestro shifted his chair this way and that, as if he was unable to contain his excitement. "Well, you see, nulls are only one category of power that interferes with mana. One end of the spectrum. The other end, of course, is those who are perfectly compatible with mana. Some even have the ability to elementalize their bodies, transforming them into pure energy. Many of the most powerful empowered possess this hypercompatibility with mana, and the rest of the empowered are scattered along this mana-to-no-mana spectrum. There is, however, another very interesting category of empowered that has been appearing more and more recently, whose power we still don't understand. We call them glitches. Individuals who, with no conscious effort, seem to make the things around them fail to activate. Though I've gotten my hands on a few glitches before, most of them were dead or expired shortly after. This is the first time I've had the opportunity to examine a glitch over the long term, and I'm quite anticipating it."

Mark didn't share Maestro's excitement, but he still nodded along.

Maestro looked at Mark, his eyes gleaming. "Now, let's begin with a basic set of questions. First, we'll break down the fight you just participated in. It's honestly something of a miracle that you were able to survive. Nobody in the arena was higher than C rank. Yet you came out victorious against both a B-ranked Deathbot and a B-ranked Exlian known for being able to go toe-to-toe with A-ranked empowered, thanks to its natural shielding."

Hearing Maestro bring up the war bear, Mark swung his feet over the edge of the table and let them hang. "Sir, have you decided what to do with the corpse?"

Impatiently, Maestro waved his mechanical arms. "We'll deal with that later. We have much more important business to attend to."

Mark's face fell, though he tried to control his expression. And Maestro, noticing the shift, let out a sigh and relented. "Look, there's nothing particularly valuable about a war bear corpse. Though I know, for an alchemist, it is a fairly rare product. The corpse is yours to do with what you will, but only after I'm satisfied with the examination. Am I clear?"

Perking up, Mark quickly nodded. "Yes, sir. Absolutely, sir."

Five hours later, he wasn't nearly as enthusiastic and was beginning to wonder if the war bear corpse was even worth it. And for a full ten hours, Mark was grilled about the fight and the unusual readings his shackles had been sending back. Maestro didn't seem at all concerned about the gaps in the data. And though Mark was worried that he would accidentally spill his secret, he quickly found that Maestro seemed more than willing to provide alibis. When they finally ended the intense questioning, Maestro happily compiled all the information he had gathered and sent a copy to Mark's watch.

"From what I understand, your power is fairly simple. I'm calling it 'glitch,' and I've updated your file to reflect it. As your adrenaline spikes, your body produces natural null pockets, areas where mana is prohibited. The closer a mana-powered item is to your body, the more likely it is to be overlapping one of these pockets. Now, normally, tampering with a shackle would send out a signal, causing a Reaper to make an appearance. But these glitches seem to affect all the shackles simultaneously, which prevents the system from being alerted."

Looking down at the metal wrapping his wrists, Mark spoke up nervously. "Are you going to adjust them so they don't turn off?"

The S-ranked genius shifted in his seat, a sign that Mark had come to realize was Maestro's equivalent of shaking his head. "No, why would I? I'm much more interested in understanding precisely how this works. And besides, you're not going to do anything foolish, are you?"

Mark quickly shook his head, which caused Maestro to chuckle.

"What I'm even more interested in is whether your power can be directed. I have a feeling that it can. And if so, it may provide some fascinating clues as to how exactly powers work. I'm sure you're aware that powers can be trained, molded, expanded, even. Here, take this."

One of Maestro's mechanical arms retrieved a silvery potion from somewhere and held it out to Mark. Under Maestro's expectant gaze, all Mark could do was uncap the vial and pour the silvery liquid down his throat. It tasted awful and burned like acid all the way into his stomach, forcing his regeneration to kick in.

Mark, who was still hooked up to all the probes, could see information flying on the virtual screens in front of Maestro. And as he watched, the legs of Maestro's chair began their happy dance.

"Ha, this is exactly what I thought. Your body is tremendously responsive to the serum. It'll take a day or two to have an effect. And when it does, I need you to tell me what you are experiencing, particularly in your dreams."

Mark nodded, but he was barely listening as he concentrated on the strange substance he had just consumed. It was rapidly being absorbed into his body, but what confused Mark was how tremendously familiar it felt. He could feel his biofuel rapidly ticking up, and at the same time, he could feel his willpower strengthening. As the last bits of the silvery potion were absorbed, Mark had the strangest feeling, like he had just eaten a particularly potent Exlian.

Glancing up, he saw that Maestro had turned away, and one by one, the probes that were stabbed into Mark's flesh popped out of him. As the holes in his skin rapidly healed, Mark got up and followed Maestro, who took him deeper into the Cradle. Wherever they went, Mark saw robots of all shapes and sizes busily working away. He couldn't help but ask a question that had been on his mind for some time.

"Um, excuse me, sir?"

"Hmm, yes?"

"I was wondering about the robots. Are they truly autonomous?"

Maestro's chair halted, then spun around so that Maestro was facing Mark. A ghost of a smile played on the lips of the S-ranked genius. "That is the question, isn't it? I can't tell you for certain, because after all, is anybody truly autonomous? But the robots that I make can operate independently. They have full decision-making capability, but they also benefit from having access to the greatest mind this world has ever seen. Mine."

Shifting his seat back around, Maestro continued, leading Mark farther into the Cradle. Soon, he began to see cylindrical vats filled with viscous liquid. Bodies hung in these vats, connected to numerous sensors, and occasionally the figures would twitch as mana raced through the tubes connected to them.

The first bodies that Mark saw were humanoid and appeared to be prisoners, from the shackles on their wrists and ankles. But as they got farther into the facility, Mark started to notice greater degrees of mutation. Though Maestro wasn't paying any attention to him, at least on the surface, Mark had no doubt he was being observed. After all, he had a strong suspicion that every single robot he encountered was tied directly to Maestro. So while he showed interest in the various experiments, he did his best to keep the revulsion he felt locked away inside.

Maestro stopped in front of a series of six large vats, each holding the body of a prisoner. Mark only needed a single glance to know that all six of them were dead, but that glance also revealed a number of other things.

Shifting to face Mark, Maestro pointed at the first vat with one of his mechanical limbs. "You know, one of the reasons I was so interested in you at first is because your power to shift your limbs into something approximating Exlian bone blade mirrors an experiment I've been working on for years. If you'll observe this first subject, you'll notice the bone blade spurs that extend from his elbows. Unfortunately, the Exlian cells we implanted into him ended up driving him mad. Though we were successful in adjusting the majority of his skeleton, he transformed into a mindless beast whose only desire was to kill anything that moved within his awareness. What you see here are the six earliest attempts, each using a modified version of the serum I just fed you."

If Maestro noticed the way Mark's expression twitched, he didn't say anything. Instead, the genius turned his seat around, his eyes resting on the sixth and final subject, who had plates of Exlian carapace protruding from his skin, making him look as if he were dressed in a sort of insectile suit of armor.

"It took us a long time to get the mixture right, and I was particularly sad about our sixth attempt. He seemed so promising. But over time, the influence of Exlian DNA overwrote more and more of his own, eventually transforming him into a creature that wasn't Exlian but wasn't human either. That is not acceptable. Our goal, the goal you have been recruited for, is simple. To produce a fully human empowered, with select traits from the Exlian species, creating a new kind of empowered."

Maestro's chair legs clicked on the hard floor as he turned back to Mark. "Now, you might be thinking to yourself, 'Oh no, what have I done?' But you needn't have any regrets, as you really didn't have a choice: either drink the serum or end up on the chopping block. Come, walk with me."

As they continued through the laboratory, Mark began to see more and more corpses suspended in vats, all exhibiting some sort of Exlian growth on their body.

"Over the years, the serum has gotten significantly better. Our first attempts produced random results. After all, we had not yet fully mapped the Exlian genome. Not that we've actually mapped the whole thing now either, but we have identified many of the base pieces, the building blocks, if you will. What's nice about that is that it's allowed us to be more selective in what sorts of traits are manifested. The serum that you just took is the initial base, a restructuring potion of sorts that, based on your specific biological structure, will modify your DNA to allow you to accept some Exlian traits."

The more Mark heard, the tighter his heart clenched. Though he had no immediate evidence, the first thing that came to his mind when he saw the transformed figures in the vats was the strange mutant he had encountered with Sky, as well as the little that he had learned about the human-experimentation program that took place at Saint Vincent's Orphanage. This was further reinforced when he spotted a couple of figures with extra limbs growing from their backs and sides. Yet as tense as he was, a dark and shadowy part of him was growing quite excited.

Pausing in front of a vat that held a young woman, who looked completely human at first blush but actually had some scales on her collarbones and webbing between her fingers, Maestro turned to face Mark again. "All that to say, if there are particular characteristics you think would be a good fit for you, feel free to suggest them."

This was exactly what Mark had guessed Maestro was building toward, and he couldn't help the smile that slipped onto his face. At first, he had been afraid that becoming a test subject for Maestro would expose all his secrets. But now he was realizing he might just have stumbled into the greatest piece of luck he'd experienced so far in his life. Participating in the trials with the serum would provide cover for his constantly evolving abilities. Thinking for a moment, he slowly nodded. "I do have an ability in mind."

"Oh, and what is it?"

"The war bear seemed to be able to make a mana shield around its body, to prevent both physical and mana-based attacks from reaching its skin. Is that the sort of thing I could get?"

Maestro chuckled, his chair dancing. "I had a feeling you'd be interested in something like that. However, I do have to warn you, the more powerful the Exlian you attempt to absorb from, the faster its cells will take over your body. You should have just experienced it now, with the serum. Over time, unless you continue to take the serum, which acts as a sort of suppressant, the Exlian cells you absorb and integrate into your body will progressively dominate your human cells, eventually wresting control of your body from you. While we've had some success in maintaining a delicate balance, it's only really worked out when we matched high-ranked empowered with low-ranked Exlian DNA. Absorbing the war bear's mana shield ability as a C-ranked empowered means you are playing with fire."

Mark, who had fully intended on stealing the war bear's ability anyway, nodded firmly. "I understand. I think I'd still like to try it."

"Very well. I will start tailoring your serum in that direction. It may take some time to manifest that ability, but so long as you can retrieve the war bear's heart for me, I should be able to extract it."

After informing Mark that he would ensure the Exlian corpse was delivered, Maestro sent Mark back to the surface. As soon as his elevator arrived at the ground floor of his apartment building, his watch began to ding. It showed notifications that had somehow been muted while he was down below in the Cradle.

Looking through them, Mark saw that one was from Asa, a few were from Joker, and the final one, just arrived, was from Mr. Robot, informing him that the war bear corpse had been delivered to the workshop. Though he was supposed to meet up with Joker and the others, Mark was simply too excited about the war bear corpse. After sending Joker a message, he rushed to Mr. Robot's shop.

Along the way, Mark spotted a few members of the Viper Clan. As soon as they saw him, they swiftly retreated, clearly wanting nothing to do with Mark after the wholesale slaughter a week prior. The shop was quiet when Mark arrived, and Mr. Robot was in the back, standing next to a fifteen-foot-tall war bear corpse just starting to thaw.

"The corpse is yours after you extract the heart," Mr. Robot stated gravely.

Mark dove right in. This wasn't the first time he had taken apart a war bear corpse, and he was exceptionally thankful for his master's strict guidance as he carved through the tough skin on the war bear's chest, revealing its thick sternum. Unlike most Exlian, which tended to be insectile, the war bear had a full skeleton. There were a considerable number of tricks to cutting through it without damaging the rest of the corpse.

Mark worked swiftly, his hands slicing through frozen flesh, until he spotted the purplish-red flesh of the heart. Carefully peeling back the bone above it with one hand, Mark slowly slipped his fingers around the large organ, taking care as he cut it free.

"Can you lift the head?" he asked Mr. Robot, gesturing with his chin to the war bear's massive head. "We want as much of the heart blood as possible, which means I need to get that end higher up."

Without a word, Mr. Robot gripped the war bear's shoulders and easily levered them up into the air. Mark had assumed that Mr. Robot was strong, but the ease with which he pushed up the top half of the war bear's corpse indicated that Mark's assessment had been way off. The war bear weighed multiple tons, so even pushing up its head took tremendous strength.

Reminding himself not to get on Mr. Robot's bad side, Mark carefully pulled the heart free, slicing through the last few veins that tied it into the war bear's body. All the while, he was careful to keep the heart upright, trapping the precious heart blood inside. He nodded to Mr. Robot as he climbed down, and the top half of the war bear was lowered.

"Here you go," he said, depositing the fresh heart into a box that sat on the table nearby. "I should be able to get everything else myself, but it'll take me a few hours to cut this thing apart."

Picking up the box, Mr. Robot examined the heart inside and then, with a nod, closed it up and placed it in his chest cavity. There was a flash, and the box was gone. "You will be responsible for the rest of the corpse."

With those words, Mr. Robot turned and strode out of the room, leaving Mark, who was practically giddy with excitement, though he tried not to show it on his face, alone with the war bear corpse. As soon as the door shut behind Mr. Robot, Mark could feel his shadow starting to surge. It was practically salivating as it regarded the massive corpse behind him. But Mark took a deep breath and forced the surging hunger in his belly down. Slowly turning around, he ran his eyes over the corpse.

While the war bear's heart was without question the most valuable ingredient, many other ingredients could still be harvested from the corpse, and Mark was planning on doing exactly that. What he didn't know was whether he gained his abilities through consuming a specific volume of Exlian DNA or whether absorbing a particular part of an Exlian was the thing that mattered.

For example, his null field ability. Mark didn't know whether he had gained it by eating the specific part of the brain that allowed it to produce the null field, or if the ability had appeared because he had eaten the entirety of the brain. This was an important question and one Mark was determined to solve.

In order to solve it, he would start by extracting some of the more valuable ingredients from the war bear, while slowly consuming the waste scraps that were left behind. Feeling his shadow starting to protest, Mark's eyes narrowed, and he glanced down, causing it to shrink back. At some point, Mime had appeared on a table beside him, and she was staring hungrily at the war bear. Relenting slightly, Mark carved off a piece of the half-frozen flesh and put it on the table in front of her, curious to see whether she would actually eat it. He didn't see quite how it happened, but a moment later it was gone, swallowed into her mouth, and Mime was licking her lips. Seeing that he wasn't getting her more, she nudged his hands with her nose as if telling him to hurry up. With a chuckle, Mark flexed his fingers as he faced the war bear corpse, and got to work.

There were many things he wanted to pull from the corpse, including bones, tendons, and a number of internal organs. Unfortunately, its brain had been evaporated by the beam of mana the bot unleashed, but he was able to recover one of its eyes. Each ingredient was packed away carefully, while the bits of skin, bone, and flesh Mark chopped apart in order to retrieve the ingredients were discarded into his shadow or placed in front of Mime for her to enjoy.

With every bit of the corpse that was devoured, Mark could feel a faint thrill running through his body, similar in many ways to drinking the silver potion Maestro had given him earlier that day. While Maestro had warned that absorbing higher-level Exlian came with the risk of those powerful Exlian cells taking over, Mark genuinely wasn't worried about it. He wasn't exactly sure why his body was so adept at absorbing Exlian DNA, but he hadn't had any trouble with the brain or the nest, and he had a strong sense that the war bear wouldn't be any different.

Within hours, the corpse had thawed completely, and the entire area was a mess. Mark finished cutting free the last section of intestines he was planning on collecting, and after placing it neatly next to the others he had gathered, he turned to the corpse and frowned. He had managed to fill an entire table with ingredients, yet the Exlian corpse was still massive.

Though he could have commanded his shadow to eat the entire thing, Mark was wary that he was currently being watched, and unleashing his shadow would certainly invite more questions than he wanted to answer. After thinking for a moment, he began methodically dismembering the corpse, cutting it into small sections to be packed away into waste bags.

About halfway through, when he had just gotten to the creature's ribs, Mr. Robot entered the room, clearly curious about what Mark was doing. Pausing in his work, Mark flashed a smile at the tall robot and gestured to the table.

"I've gotten everything of significant value out," he said. "I'm packaging it up to preserve it, and then, if it's okay with you, either we'll use it here or I'll sell it through the warehouse."

Mr. Robot hesitated for a moment, his eyes flashing, and then he nodded and looked down at the bags of bones and flesh. Although the robot didn't speak, Mark could easily infer the question on his mind. Reaching down with a still-bloody hand, he patted one of the bags.

"Believe it or not, these are an alchemical ingredient as well," he said. "But this sort of material is normally sold in bulk, so for the time being, I'm just putting it into bags. I'll sort it later at the warehouse."

For a tense moment, Mark thought Mr. Robot might continue to question him, but despite his eyes flashing again, Mr. Robot just turned around and walked out. Turning to deal with the rest of the corpse, Mark heaved a sigh of relief and hurried to complete his task. There were so many bags he had to borrow a cart to take them all to the warehouse. When they were piled up, they made a heap almost three times as tall as him. A messy job, but having cut his teeth with Master Abrams, Mark didn't mind.

After dealing with the other ingredients, Mark came up with an excuse to send Albert and the others out of the warehouse and got down to the real business. First, he did a quick sweep of the area to make sure no cameras could see him. Then, as an extra safety measure, he activated his null field, spreading it out around him, just in case someone was trying to peek at him with a remote viewing ability. He had no idea if the null field would actually help, but he figured it was better than nothing.

Having done all he could, Mark sat down in a meditative position, his back facing the large pile of bags. He took a deep breath and unleashed his shadow. Shaking with glee, it transformed into a wave of pure darkness that rapidly crawled up the first bag. Mark felt rather than heard the shadow sending a tendril to punch through the thick plastic, and a moment later, he felt the familiar shiver pass through him as his shadow began to consume the war bear's flesh and bone.

As it munched happily, the shadow continued forward, sending more tendrils through each of the bags, and Mark felt streams of energy rushing into him. Strength, speed, fortitude, and will. The war bear's stats drastically exceeded Mark's in every respect, and as its flesh was consumed, Mark could sense his body growing in both size and strength.

He had long suspected that the fastest way to raise his strength would be to consume powerful Exlian, and this only seemed to confirm it. Of course, the chances of Mark actually being able to kill a war bear on his own were practically zero, and he genuinely didn't know if, even with Mime's help, he would have been able to survive the fight if not for the Deathbot.

The mana cannon wielded by the bot had the power of an A-ranked attack, and even it had been unable to pierce the war bear's natural defenses. Of course, Mark did have his null field, which would have let him disable those defenses, just as he had during the fight in the arena. But as power surged through him, he had to admit that it was so much stronger and faster and tougher than he was that even if he had disabled its defenses, he likely wouldn't have gotten more than one attack before it tore his body apart.

Of course, the more powerful Mark grew, the easier it would become to find and hunt high-level Exlian, and he had a sneaking suspicion that if he could consume another nest, his level of growth would be even more drastic.

It took close to twenty minutes for his shadow to completely devour the war bear corpse, and since he didn't have an activator to show him his stats, he could only rely on the faint feelings in his body to determine how he had changed.

Jumping to his feet, Mark stumbled forward, nearly face-planting, as his body moved farther and faster than he had anticipated it would. Only his new increased flexibility allowed him to get his feet under him. As he regained his balance, Mark couldn't help but let out a delighted laugh.

He could feel an intangible force filling his body, particularly concentrated in his skin, as if a web of mana had been laid over every inch of him. Holding out his left palm, Mark transformed his right arm and struck swiftly, intending to pierce through his palm.

In fascination, he watched as mana surged, forming a thin barrier that manifested right before his fingers struck. Though the shield shattered almost immediately, it absorbed enough momentum to slow down Mark's fingers so much that they only scratched his skin. As the small cut vanished, his grin widened. He had confirmed an important suspicion. All he needed was the correct volume of an Exlian's DNA in order to pick up its ability.

Almost immediately, however, his excitement faded, and worry surged through him. He had been so excited to absorb the war bear's mana shield ability that he'd failed to consider how it would appear to Maestro. He had just mentioned wanting to gain this ability, and Maestro had agreed to attempt to isolate it for him, making a serum from the war bear's heart blood. Now, however, he already had the ability. Letting out a sigh, he looked at his hands.

"I guess I just need to learn to turn it off. As long as nobody notices it before I take the new serum, I should be good."

Mime, who was sitting on a nearby shelf watching him, gave him a strange look, as if asking why he was talking to a cat. Pushing his worries aside, Mark couldn't help but smile. Whatever problems arose, he would deal with them one at a time.

Mark incinerated the bags to make sure there was no evidence left, then sent Joker a message, informing him that he was headed back to the apartment. Almost immediately, he got a call, and opening up his screen, he saw Joker peering at him.

"Rather than the apartment, come to the arena. We had a rather sudden change of plans," Joker said.

"I'll be right there," Mark said, slightly unsettled by Joker's grin.

After double-checking to make sure he had left nothing behind, Mark headed for the arena at a swift jog. When he arrived, he saw Servo waiting out front. The big man gestured for him to follow and led the way into a large waiting room, where Coral, Joker, and Winter Wolf were all seated.

"Nice of you to finally join us," Coral said, her eyes narrowed.

"Sorry, I was sorta tied up."

"How were your tests with Maestro? Nothing too strenuous, I hope," Winter Wolf asked, shooting a sharp glance at Coral, who sat back, her arms crossed.

"They were fine. What's going on here?" Mark asked.

"So I thought that we would have a few days to train together, you know, get used to one another. But Asa just informed me that we're going to be running a special exhibition in half an hour. One of the teams dropped out and is now making epic contributions to the advancement of humanity," Joker explained.

"He means half of them are dead and the other half are test subjects," Servo supplied helpfully when he saw Mark's confused expression.

"But it sounds so much better the way I say it," Joker said with a grin. "Regardless, we'll be heading into a fight within the next half an hour. It was going to be the four of us, if you couldn't make it. But I'm glad you did."

"Me too. It's always better to have an extra person," Winter Wolf said. "I think it would be a good idea to go over everybody's abilities for Mark's sake, so he can get a sense of what our team is working with and where he'll be fitting in."

Noticing how everybody else sat up straighter when Winter Wolf talked, Mark did too.

"My abilities revolve around ice. Specifically, summons. You'll get a better sense of it once I'm not restricted by these blasted things," Winter Wolf said, holding up her wrist to show the shackle on it. "But I'm an energy controller, and my spell set includes ice wolf summons, a variety of attacks, and numerous crowd-control spells. I'm a midrange fighter with a control style."

Turning, Winter Wolf gestured for Coral to go next. Though her expression was still rather severe, Coral nodded and tapped herself on the chest. "I'm an energy controller as well, water based. I get everything very wet."

Though water was not nearly as obviously destructive as earth, wind, or fire, Mark didn't underestimate Coral one bit. In the hands of a creative fighter, water was arguably the most dangerous of the elements, as it could produce many of the other elements' effects combined. It could be used to crush and smother, to cut and trap. From the faint greenish-blue color of Coral's skin,

Mark guessed that she was getting close to elementalization, a state in which she would be able to shift her body into the element she wielded, making her nearly invulnerable to normal damage.

With Coral's introduction over, Joker took up the torch next. "My name is Joker, as you know, and I am not an energy controller. I do have a number of nifty tricks, and I'm particularly good with a knife."

As he spoke, Joker produced a blade from somewhere and tossed it into the air. Mark heard a faint whistle, so quiet he almost wondered if he was imagining it, and saw the blade vanish in front of his eyes. Jerking his head to the side, he watched as it blurred past his ear, coming to rest in front of Joker once more.

"Teleportation?" Mark asked, slowly straightening back up.

"Exactly," Joker said, reaching out to grab the knife. "It's not my only trick, but it's the main one I use in combat."

"Joker is also our main scout," Winter Wolf said.

With the other three introduced, it was Servo's turn, and he stood up, bowing slightly toward Mark. "My name is Servo. I am a backline fighter and support. My main ability is constructing devices."

Flipping his hand over, Servo tapped a thin piece of metal implanted in the center of his palm, and with a hiss, a full suit of armor rapidly deployed across his body. Stunned, Mark had to scoot back as Servo, already large, transformed into an even larger, fully suited behemoth. Two thin mana cannons swiveled up from his shoulders, and a large shield appeared on his left arm.

"Servo, you don't have to deploy the whole thing," Winter Wolf called out, causing Servo to pause and sheepishly withdraw his armor. Looking quite awkward, he scratched his cheek and slowly sat down.

"Can you make devices for other people?" Mark asked.

The big man shook his head. "They only work for me."

"Which is quite unfortunate, because I would love a rapid-deployment suit," Joker quipped. "But enough about us. I'm interested in you."

"Me too," Coral piped up, her arms crossed over her chest. "What sort of abilities do you have?"

Thinking for a moment, Mark extended his hands and transformed them into bone blade. "I have the inbuilt ability to transform my body, and strong regeneration. I'm also adept at locating Exlian."

"So you're a frontline fighter, then," Winter Wolf said, tapping her chin.

"I am. I've also got another ability, but I'm just starting to learn about it. That's why I was down with Maestro today, in the Cradle. He called me a glitch, because when I get worked up, sometimes mana-powered items nearby stop working."

At Mark's words, Servo shifted backward, clearly uncomfortable.

"I can't necessarily control it, and the range isn't very far," Mark said. "If I'm fighting on the frontline and Servo is behind me, it shouldn't be an issue."

Of course, that wasn't even close to true, but Mark had no interest in completely revealing his abilities, so he used the excuse Maestro had provided as cover.

Thinking for a moment, Winter Wolf nodded. "All right, then you'll be replacing Rex, our former frontline melee fighter. That might mean you're going to be facing up against enemies more powerful than you. Are you okay with that?"

"I am."

"Good, then let me break down this fight we're about to get into. It's a special exhibition, which means that it's been requested by one of the scum from New Emery. It looks like they're trying to test a mercenary team, and that test is us. We'll be dropped into a scenario that will include both the enemy mercenaries and an unknown number of Exlian. There will be three flags set up somewhere in the field. The goal is to be in possession of at least two flags after half an hour. Of course, this is the arena, so anything goes."

"Do we know anything about what they're going to send out?" Coral asked.

With a sigh, Winter Wolf shrugged. "No, we're going in entirely blind. Any information that was provided to the previous team has not been provided to us."

With a wide grin that didn't reach his eyes, Joker leaned back, lacing his fingers together behind his head. "This is just how the scum play. Whoever it was wants their mercs to win, so they probably pulled some dirty tricks behind the scenes to get the other team disqualified. Now they're pulling us in."

"Which is a clear sign that the administration isn't pleased," Winter Wolf said, her lips curling back to reveal her straight white teeth. "Our mission is clear."

As she stood up, she drew a thumb across her neck.

With a laugh, Coral bounced up. "Well, that's what we're good at. Let's get ready."

Following the others, Mark walked over to the wall, where five masks had appeared. As he fixed his mask in place, he saw Joker putting on a harlequin mask.

"Hey, I have a question."

"Ask away," Joker said, turning to stare at Mark.

Unsure whether the harlequin mask was creepier than Joker's actual grin, Mark considered how he wanted to phrase his question. "How did you use your power, I mean your teleportation ability, with your shackles? Don't they lock down nonphysical abilities?"

"I wondered if you'd pick up on that," Joker said, lifting his hand. His fingers flashed, and the blade appeared between them. His fingers blurred, and the blade danced in the air. "If your performance is good enough, there are all sorts of privileges available. Conductors don't have their abilities stifled, but we still have to wear the shackles."

Hearing that word again, Mark wanted to ask what a conductor was, but before he could, his watch vibrated, and Winter Wolf called out, "Let's go. It's time for the match."

Following the others out of the waiting room, Mark saw another team approaching from the opposite side of the arena. The members were dressed in body armor and carried numerous mana weapons. Two of them were clearly brutes, each at least seven feet tall, their bodies heavily muscled. There was a thin man with a bow on his back, and two women, one holding a sword and shield, the other a staff. They all looked tough and moved with the calm assurance of high-ranked empowered.

But as Mark examined them more closely, he noticed something strange. He knew that most people weren't able to sense mana the way he could, but the disparity between the two empowered teams left him shocked. Of all the enemies, the woman with the staff had the strongest mana signature, but both Winter Wolf and Coral had so much mana it continually leaked from their bodies, while the other energy controller didn't even have a tenth as much.

Similarly, Joker was practically bursting with mana, though his produced an ethereal, mysterious feeling when Mark looked at him. Servo had the lowest amount of mana of the group, but Mark could see spots with incredibly dense mana signatures in his skin. These were the spots that his suit of mana armor manifested from.

Leaning over, Mark tapped Joker's shoulder. "Why are they so weak?" he asked, his voice a whisper.

Flashing his signature grin, Joker pointed up at the boxes. "The administrators want to send a message. Trying to mess around with the special exhibitions is taboo."

As the two teams drew close to each other, Winter Wolf stepped forward, as did the woman with the staff. Just then, the announcer's voice came on.

"Ladies and gentlemen, we have an exciting fight for you today. A challenger team, eager to prove their abilities, will be taking on the Tomb Wolves in a match of epic proportions."

"Tomb Wolves is such a dumb name. We totally should have been the Death Clowns," Joker muttered under his breath, causing Coral to roll her eyes.

Oblivious, the announcer continued. "The match today is straightforward. Both teams will be required to collect flags hidden around the arena. At the same time, an unknown number of Exlian will be released into the arena. The match will take half an hour, or until one team is dead. Every two minutes, Exlian will be unleashed, drawn from the randomized pool. Teams, to your places."

With a cold look at the mercenaries, Winter Wolf turned around and walked back to the others. Mark noticed a circle had appeared around them, and he saw the mercenary team retreat to a similar one not very far away. There was a loud grinding noise, and then the circle they were in slid back as buildings and vegetation began to emerge from the floor around them. Taking considerable delight in Mark's astonished expression, Coral pointed to the rapidly emerging terrain. "The arena is pretty amazing. It can simulate almost any environment."

"Focus up, please," Winter Wolf said, snapping her fingers. "The match is about to start."

"Oh, come on. This is barely even worth our time," Coral said.

Joker's hands flashed, producing numerous blades, which he clasped between his fingers. "Well, we might as well have fun. It might be a while before we get another match."

Servo simply pressed the piece of metal on his palm to activate his suit of armor. As his body was covered, he tossed out a small stack of disks that spread into the air around him, hovering in a rough arc over his head. Not quite sure what to do, Mark transformed his arms into bone blade and jogged to keep up with the others as they began to move forward.

"I'll send some wolves out to hunt the flags," Winter Wolf said. "Let's not waste any time. We'll crush them head-on."

As she spoke, Mark sensed mana beginning to gather behind her. It traced an intricate pattern in the air, one he had never seen before. A moment later, ice began to form in midair. Six large chunks rapidly grew until they were close to Mark's size. When the complex symbol finished forming, Winter Wolf snapped her fingers, and the icicles shattered, transforming into six dangerous-looking wolves.

With a swipe of her hand, Winter Wolf commanded them to scatter, and they sprinted off into the underbrush even as the team continued straight forward. Mark could sense a faint connection extending from each of the wolves back to Winter Wolf, a sort of thread that was a mixture of mana and mental energy. And as the wolves began to search for the flags, the team sprinted through the jungle. They had just gotten halfway across the arena when the psychic network suddenly flashed, and Mark sensed half a dozen Exlian emerging from a nearby building.

"There are six warrior-ranked Exlian at two o'clock," he said, pointing in their direction. "The enemy team is just beyond them."

It took a moment for the others to respond, and when they did, it was by slowing down and looking at Mark with a variety of expressions. Coral's was skeptical, and Joker's was rather confused. But Winter Wolf gave him a grim nod and patted Servo on his metal-covered arm. "Give us eyes."

The disks that hovered above Servo suddenly shot up into the air, rapidly spreading out, and with a tap on his suit, a virtual screen appeared in front of him, showing a topographical map of the arena. There, plain as day, they saw the enemy team moving carefully through the underbrush in the direction Mark had pointed. A moment later, they spotted the Exlian too. Low to the ground and covered in hard shells, the Exlian looked like scorpions with two tails, and they scuttled swiftly through the underbrush, closing in on the enemy team.

"Do we wait or engage?" Joker asked, eagerly flipping one of his knives in the air.

"We don't want to drag this out longer than we need to. But we need to make sure we get the flags first," Winter Wolf said. "I've got one, but we're still looking for the other two. Let's let them fight the Exlian. Apex, you keep an eye out for more Exlian spawns. Everybody else, stay on your toes and be ready to engage at any time. Servo, why don't you give our friends a welcome?"

"You got it."

With a hiss, Servo's suit settled slightly, rods extending from his legs to plant themselves in the ground, stabilizing his positioning. The two mana cannons on his shoulders extended above his head and clipped together, forming one large cannon. As Mark watched, it angled up into the air, and something dropped into the barrels with a clunk. Mark could see through the psychic network and the virtual screen in front of Servo that the enemy team had engaged with the Exlian scorpions. The two brutes were doing the majority of the fighting, crushing the monsters as they came.

Reaching out with a thick finger, Servo selected a spot on the map, and there was a loud beep. The two mana cannons hummed for a moment and then fired, sending a shot arcing through the air like a mortar.

Mark caught a flash of something as the cannons fired and realized that Servo had shot a blast not of pure mana but of something else. The shot moved swiftly through the air, and though the mercenaries saw it coming, there wasn't much they could do apart from scatter. It landed right in the middle of their formation, and Mark saw their energy controller thrusting out her hands, attempting to block it. Yet right before it landed, Servo issued a curt command. "Detonate."

The shot immediately exploded, blasting apart the mana shield and throwing debris into the air. One of the brutes, who was busy fighting against the scorpions, was caught off guard and was sent tumbling forward, while the other brute staggered as the force of the explosion washed over him. Seizing the opportunity, the three Exlian who were still alive leaped on the downed brute, forcing the rest of the mercenary team to rush over and assist him.

"I've got the second flag," Winter Wolf said. "Let's go crush them."

Mark had just taken his first step forward when he sensed more Exlian appearing in another one of the scattered buildings, this time off to the team's left. "Three Exlian, a good bit more powerful than the scorpions, at our seven o'clock."

"Mark, you and I will take them down," Winter Wolf said, her eyes narrowing. "Joker, Coral, Servo, take down the enemy team."

Without a word, the team split, and Mark and Winter Wolf headed toward the Exlian. As they moved swiftly through the underbrush, Mark could tell that Winter Wolf was assessing him. He was pretty sure that his speed had already shifted into the B rank, but she kept up without any trouble whatsoever, further cementing his suspicion that she was an A-ranked empowered. As they moved, he could tell she was manipulating the six threads that extended out from her, no doubt commanding the ice wolves.

The Exlian had started stomping through the woods toward them. As they got closer, Mark could identify more characteristics. They were a type of Exlian he had never seen before—apes with an extra set of arms and white fur. Large tusks extended from their jutting lower jaws, and as they burst through the trees, Mark saw heavy plates of armor covering the majority of their bodies.

"Be careful. Arctic apes are known for incredible bursts of speed."

No sooner had Winter Wolf finished speaking than the ape in the lead let out a roar, and his body surged, becoming a white blur that shot straight at Mark as if it had been fired from a cannon. Thanks to Winter Wolf's warning, Mark dodged to the side, taking two quick steps back at an angle to avoid its grasping hands.

At the same time, Mark struck, carving slashes on the monster's arm, before taking a quick step back into its range. His foot lashed out, knocking one of the ape's legs out from under it. As the creature twisted to try to regain its balance, Mark pressed forward, his hands darting in and out. With a cry, the ape suddenly collapsed, six deep holes in its chest.

The other two apes, about to charge, were stunned as Mark jumped over the body of their companion and raced forward almost as fast as they had. Moving more on instinct than anything else, he leaped at the first Arctic ape, ignoring a heavy punch that slammed into his ribs. He could feel them shattering, but he ignored the pain as his fingers dug deep into the Arctic ape's arm, punching through the armor plating as if it weren't even there.

Caught off guard by the ineffectiveness of its punch, the ape didn't have time to react as Mark's hand tore through its throat, sending its head tumbling from its body. Though his side sent lances of pain through him every time he moved, he could feel the shattered bones knitting back together, and with a growl, he launched himself toward the last ape. Faint fear caused the creature to freeze, and a moment later, Mark was on it, his hands tearing through the Exlian with ease.

It had only been half a dozen seconds since they had encountered the apes, but all three lay dead at his feet as Mark straightened. As he turned to look at Winter Wolf, she took a small step backward. Her expression was impossible to make out behind her mask, but there was clear shock in her gaze as she slowly lowered her hands. Mark, however, was already looking past her.

"The enemy team is headed this way," he said. "Only two remaining."

Winter Wolf nodded and turned. They couldn't see anything but jungle, but that didn't stop her from lifting her hands. Mana surged behind her, and Mark watched in fascination as another intricate pattern appeared. Cold wind surged around them, and ice suddenly sprang up from the ground, forming a thick wall that shot straight out from Winter Wolf, crashing through the jungle to intercept the enemy. Less than thirty seconds later, a horn sounded, and the announcer's voice rang over the match.

"And with that stunning blow, this fight is over. What an exciting match, ladies and gentlemen. Less than five minutes long, but packed with incredible displays of power. The Tomb Wolves have once again secured a victory, their forty-sixth since their formation. Will we ever see a team able to compete? Who knows, folks, who knows."

As the announcer continued to prattle on, Mark and Winter Wolf joined up with the others. Joker was sitting on the corpse of one of the brutes, pulling a dagger from his neck, when they walked up, and Coral was standing over the dead archer, whose head was drenched in water. Around the same time, Servo stomped out of the jungle. It was clear that in his suit, he was a good bit slower than the others. But judging by the utter devastation behind him, that didn't reduce his effectiveness.

"How'd it go?" Joker asked, jumping up, when he saw Mark and Winter Wolf.

"Smoothly," Winter Wolf said, shooting a glance at Mark. "You'll all get to see the replay, but I think we found a good replacement for Rex."

"I'll have to see it to believe it," Coral said, giving Mark a skeptical glance.

Winter Wolf didn't reply, and Mark didn't bother with the provocation, but Joker laughed delightedly. "You know what we need? We need to schedule some sparring time. I must admit, I'm excited to see Mark in action."

"I think that's a good idea," Winter Wolf said. "I'll put in a request."

Something in her tone of voice caused the others to pause, their attention gathering on her. But she just shook her head slightly and gestured for them to follow.

After leaving the arena, the team went to a small restaurant attached to the apartment and settled down for a hearty meal. As they dug into their food, Winter Wolf pulled up the footage of the match they had just endured. Before she started it, she looked around. "As easy as that was, I think it's worth assessing. We made two major mistakes. The first is that we didn't fire the disruptive shot early enough. The enemy was weaker than I anticipated, and if we had hit them at the same time as the Exlian, we could have disrupted them even more than we did. As it was, we gave them the opportunity to stabilize by killing three of the scorpions before the shot arrived. That's my fault. Next time, I'll be quicker to assess the situation.

"The second mistake is that we split incorrectly. I should have just sent Apex after the Exlian. If I had done so and had Servo provide remote support, we could have trapped the enemy instead of it turning into a running fight. As I said, neither were particularly significant errors, but we don't want to make these mistakes again. Now, I'm sure you're all interested in seeing this."

As she began to run through the footage of the arena fight, Winter Wolf shifted through the cameras until she found one that followed Mark. The camera, which was really a compilation of hundreds of cameras covering the arena from every conceivable angle, focused on Mark, and Winter Wolf skimmed through until right before the fight with the three Arctic apes. Even though Mark was the one who had fought, he found it rather fascinating to watch himself from a third-person point of view as he engaged with the Exlian.

Joker, Coral, and Servo all paid close attention as well. As they watched Mark dodge the first ape's dash, Joker's eyebrows rose. When they saw Mark leap over the dead body to attack the second ape, Coral carefully put down her fork, shooting an astonished glance at Mark. And when Mark, having taken the punch to the ribs without blinking, chopped the head from the second ape and attacked the third, Servo gave three short claps.

"Textbook," he said, picking up a roll and shoving it into his mouth.

"Yeah, maybe if you're an Exlian. You sure you don't have a berserker power? How'd you just carve straight through them? And what about that punch? That should have sent you flying." Coral, clearly astonished by what she had just witnessed, unleashed a waterfall of words, leaving Mark no time to respond between her frantic sentences.

"Enough," Winter Wolf said, causing Coral to fall silent. "We'll have plenty of time to get to know Mark's abilities better, as Joker suggested. I've asked for use of the training rooms. In the meantime, I think it's only fair to celebrate. We're getting a competent new teammate."

Lifting his wineglass, Joker stood up. "Hear, hear, to the worst-named team in the arena."

Everyone else lifted their glasses as well, though Coral rolled her eyes again.

As the evening wore on, talk turned from the match to how each of them had ended up in the Tomb, and Mark was once again reminded that even though his new teammates seemed perfectly reasonable and sane, apart from Joker at least, none of them were without a history.

Winter Wolf had been a member of the military, court-martialed after a fight with another military unit that turned deadly. Similarly, Servo had been a member of the Engineering Corps but had made some sort of mistake, causing the deaths of a few dozen soldiers. When Mark looked at Joker, the rather goofy-looking man held up his hands and shrugged. "I like to kill people."

That simple statement confirmed what Mark had heard before being sent to the Tomb, but since Joker didn't want to elaborate further, the conversation shifted to Coral.

"Some scum messed around with my little sister, so I wiped out him and his family."

Though Coral spoke rather flippantly about it, Mark could sense the deep emotions her words contained.

As everyone's attention turned to him, Mark suppressed his desire to claim innocence. "Someone was sent to kill me. I killed him back. His friends had more sway."

"Huh, you make it sound so cut and dry," Joker said, flashing a dangerous grin. "I don't know, from the look of that fight, I think you might like killing too."

Ignoring Joker's needling, Mark looked at Winter Wolf. "I'm getting a bit tired, so I might head back to sleep. Do you know when we'll be training?"

"No, they'll let me know in the next few days. Using the training room is a pretty significant ordeal, since they'll be deactivating our shackles outside the arena, which always has some level of risk."

Getting up, Mark said good night and then headed back to his apartment. As he flopped down on his bed, he tucked his hands behind his head and stared up at the ceiling as Mime crawled up onto his chest. "It's sort of crazy how fast everything changes. At least you're still the same." Mime just stared at him, eyes bright, as Mark let out a sigh and slowly drifted off to sleep.

The next few days passed quietly. Mark met the rest of his

teammates to work out in the gym while they waited for access to the training room, and he spent the rest of his time at Mr. Robot's alchemy shop or the warehouse. On the third day, Mr. Robot handed him a vial of silver liquid with thick brown streaks running through it, almost like threads of lightning. Without hesitation, Mark opened the vial and poured the concoction down his throat, feeling the familiar burn as it settled in his stomach.

He wasn't sure what to expect, since he already had the ability to produce mana shields, but as the potion spread through his body, Mark could feel the ability strengthening, and he had the sneaking suspicion that that small vial had achieved an even greater effect than eating an entire war bear. Unfortunately, with no way to check his status, he was at something of a loss.

"You will report to Maestro when the ability manifests."

Not trusting his voice, as his regeneration was still repairing his burned throat, Mark nodded. He took the rest of the day off and headed back to his apartment to meditate, trying to get a better sense of the changes taking place in his body. Finally, rather frustrated, Mark sent Winter Wolf a message, asking if there was a way to get an activator. Winter Wolf called him almost immediately. As the video window popped up, he saw that she was in her exercise clothes, sweat dripping freely from her face, and realized that she was in the middle of a workout.

"What do you need? I saw you sent me a message."

"Sorry, I didn't mean to interrupt."

"Don't apologize." Winter Wolf cut him off with a shake of her head that set drops of sweat flying.

Bemused, Mark lifted his right hand. "I'm having a lot of trouble understanding the changes that are happening to my body without an activator. Is there a way for us to get one down here in the Tomb?"

"No, the only way to get a good sense of our stats is by getting a formal assessment. I don't recommend it, as they'll use it to tune your shackles."

Mark nodded. "All right, I'll just muddle through, then. Thanks."

After hanging up, Mark decided to head down toward the gym. He said goodbye to Mime and walked out of the apartment, making it halfway down the hall before he remembered he hadn't locked his door.

Rather than walk back, he turned and extended a tendril of mental power, easily triggering the lock. Thinking nothing of it, he headed for the elevator, only to stop in front of the door and look down at his arm, then back at the door he had just locked.

An idea had begun to take root in his mind, and at first it seemed like pure madness. But the more he thought about it, the more he wondered if it would be possible . . . His ability to control mana remotely allowed him to interact with any object that had mana in it. This was true for anything from the door lock behind him to the elevator in front of him to even more complex systems like the Deathbot whose mana cannon he had disrupted.

Slowly clenching his fingers, Mark examined his empty forearm. If he remembered correctly, the activator was a simple band that wrapped tightly around his skin, producing a specific flow of mana that projected a virtual screen directly into his mind. If so, wouldn't replicating that same stream of mana produce the effect he wanted?

Rather than calling the elevator, Mark practically ran back down the hallway, entered his apartment, and shut the door tightly behind him. He began to pace back and forth, his mind spinning through possibilities, as he tried to figure out if this crazy idea was actually possible. Remembering the complex symbol that had manifested before Winter Wolf's ice wolves had appeared, Mark froze. He had no idea how she had created them, but he had a feeling they might hold an important clue. Under Mime's bemused stare, Mark rushed out of the apartment again, this time taking the elevator down to the gym, where he found Winter Wolf in the middle of her workout. Seeing Mark fidgeting nearby, she finished up on the machine she was using and wiped the sweat from her face with her towel. "Do you need something?"

"Yes. I . . ."

Mark faltered, not quite sure how to phrase his request. But then, remembering how she hated beating around the bush, he just plunged ahead. "I was really impressed by your abilities, and I've never really gotten the chance to talk to a high-level energy controller, apart from my brother. But his use of abilities was completely different than yours."

As she listened to the words pouring out of Mark's mouth, Winter Wolf picked up her water and took a sip.

"Let me get changed," she said, interrupting him, "and then we can talk."

Mark felt like he was on pins and needles as he waited, but after a while, he slowly started to calm down. Fifteen minutes later, when Winter Wolf walked out of the changing room, her hair still wet from the shower, Mark had returned to his normal, even-keeled self.

"Sorry about earlier," he said as they left the gym and headed down the hall toward one of the lounges. "I got a little bit overexcited."

Winter Wolf didn't say anything until they had taken their seats and placed their orders. Then her eyes narrowed dangerously, and she leaned forward. "Your brother is Joseph Fields, right?"

In the tense atmosphere, Mark's breathing slowed, his heartbeat evened out, and his mind grew ice cold.

"Yes," he said, watching her carefully for any sign of danger.

With a mirthless chuckle, Winter Wolf sat back, draping an arm over the back of the couch she was sitting on. "He's the one they called in to catch me." Her voice was matter of fact, devoid of any hint of emotion.

Despite the calm she projected, Mark could see the surging feelings in her eyes.

"I don't know why I didn't put two and two together earlier, but as soon as you mentioned your brother was an energy controller, I knew it had to be him. It's ironic, isn't it? One brother dumps me in this pit, and the other . . ."

Her words trailed off as she shook her head. She didn't seem to be that angry, and Mark's tension slowly subsided, transforming into awkwardness.

"I'm sorry," he said, but she waved him off.

"It's not your fault—your brother's abilities just so happen to counter mine perfectly. Now, I got us off track. What is it that you wanted to know?"

Still feeling rather awkward, Mark scratched his nose as he began to speak. "When we were in the arena, you used a couple different abilities, the ice wall and those ice wolves. Both times, I saw a strange pattern that looked like it was made of ice appearing behind you. I was curious about those, what they were. I've never seen anything like that before in my life."

"It's just a specialized form of energy control. Most people who control mana directly do so with a specific attribute. There are seven of them: four elements—wind, water, fire, earth—then light, darkness, and arcane. If you ever see somebody slinging plasma bolts, that's usually arcane, which is just a pure manifestation of mana. However, as you go higher up the chain of power, energy controllers divide into a couple different paths. One is direct control, which would be like your brother, Joe. He can directly control fire and even manifest it. Like him, I can manifest ice, but the way I control it is different. I use what are called spells, which are specific arrangements of mana that produce a far more intricate effect. As good as Joe is, he can't make fire wolves who can operate independently. But thanks to my ice wolf summoning spell, I can."

Soaking in her words eagerly, Mark leaned forward. "And how did you learn that spell? Did somebody teach it to you, or did you figure it out yourself?"

"A little bit of both," Winter Wolf said as their drinks arrived.

Picking up the martini she had ordered, she took a sip. Then, dipping her finger in the alcohol, she drew a complex symbol lightly on the table.

"This is the base for the summon spell. I didn't figure this out. What I did is add all my own flairs. The fact that it's ice, the fact that it's wolves, how many of them there are, and all sorts of other particularities that give them their abilities. As for how spell constructs actually work, it's just a matter of concentration. You don't actually have to manifest them out into the world. You can just keep them up here." Winter Wolf tapped her temple. "And in fact, that's how they're actually cast. What you're seeing manifesting behind me when I activate a spell is just an echo. I can't demonstrate for you right now, but I just got word that we'll be getting access to the training ground in about a week. When that happens, I'd be happy to demonstrate for you, so long as you're willing to serve as my sparring partner."

Despite the fact that Mark knew he was edging into B-ranked territory, the thought of sparring against an A-ranked empowered caused him to hesitate. At the same time he could sense that understanding how spells worked would help him take a big step forward in this new theory of his, so he nodded in agreement.

"Good, I'll hold you to that," Winter Wolf said. "Now, can you tell me why you want to know?"

Mark froze, unsure what to say, and Winter Wolf suddenly let out a peal of laughter. "Ha, you should see your face. Don't worry, I don't actually care."

Polishing off her martini in a few swift gulps, she wiped her lips with the back of her hand and stood up.

"Thanks for the drink," she said, and headed for the door, leaving Mark to pay.

It was a long time before Mark got up, and when he did, he realized that he hadn't touched his drink even once. The annoyed server glared at him, but Mark just paid the check and slowly walked back up to his apartment. Winter Wolf's words had opened up numerous new angles for him, and Mark felt like he was starting to close in on a concrete idea. Of course, having a theory and being able to execute it were two different things, and Mark quickly realized that no matter what solution he came up with, it wouldn't matter if he wasn't actually able to control the mana in his body well enough.

His goal was simple: to replicate the pattern of an activator inside his own skin, creating his own activator that could be used at any time.

The shackle he wore sent a fine web of mana through him, and though he had pushed it to the side, Mark was curious as to whether he could use it to create the same effect as the activator. His first attempts went poorly, and no matter what he did, the mana always seemed to slip out of his control. This was where the concept of spells started to come in handy. From what Winter Wolf had said, she activated a spell by projecting the symbol in her mind. It was then reflected into reality, gathering mana into a certain pattern in order to activate a very specific power. Though it lacked flexibility compared to the direct control that someone like his brother or Phoenix wielded, Winter Wolf's spells were much more efficient and produced an incredible amount of power for a relatively low amount of mana.

It was at this point that Mark hit his first major snag. His mental energy was strong enough that he had no trouble imagining symbols. However, he didn't actually know what sort of symbol could replicate the effect of an activator. Realizing that he was going to have to figure out how to get his hands on one, Mark put that problem aside for the moment and instead pulled up an image that he had taken on his watch. Barely visible on the brown wood of the table were the lines that Winter Wolf had traced out. This was the base of the spell she used, and though Mark didn't expect it to actually work, he began to use it as a practice tool, forming the strokes in his mind as best as he was able.

He practiced for almost an hour before an uncomfortable feeling began to grow in his chest. At first, he thought it might be a result of the mental training he was doing, but very soon he realized that it didn't have anything to do with that. Instead, it was as if something were squirming inside him, like worms burrowing through his body.

The discomfort grew more intense. Mime, who had been resting on the couch, sat up and hopped down to the floor. She trotted over in front of Matt and sat down, her gaze hard as she stared at him. Almost immediately, the discomfort faded, but Mark could tell that the squirming power was still there, simply too afraid to move. The thought sent a shiver down his spine, and he suddenly wondered if the serum he had taken contained living organisms, some sort of parasite, rather than the war bear's cells.

After a long moment, Mime blinked, and her claws suddenly flashed, slamming into Mark's chest. Three silver beams pierced into his skin, causing spurts of blood to scatter across the carpet in between them. He was so shocked by the sudden attack that he didn't have time to react. And then he heard a mental scream, like the shriek of a creature caught in a deadly trap. The clumped energy inside him began to thrash, causing intense pain with every movement. But the damage had already been done, and as Mark blacked out, slumping down on the carpet, his mind fell into a strange state.

He felt as if he were fighting the war bear all over again. But this time, the two of them were locked in a fierce struggle. Intense pain racked his body as the bear gnawed through his leg, and Mark knew that if the bear ate too much, he would lose himself. Yet unlike a physical fight, where he had an enemy in front of him, Mark found himself unable to fight back. He couldn't even see the monster chewing on him because it was hidden inside his body.

With a growl that masked the pain he felt from being eaten alive, Mark forced himself into a seated position, his limbs trembling. The pain was indescribable, but it didn't weaken Mark, instead catalyzing his mind into absolute focus. Normally, with an enemy of this caliber, Mark would have thrown himself into battle, trusting his regeneration to keep him alive as he cut his enemy to pieces, but that wasn't an option with an enemy that didn't actually exist.

Snippets of his conversations with Maestro flashed through Mark's mind as he tried to figure out what was going on. The war bear's essence had been distilled down into an elixir and fed to Mark in an attempt to forcefully impart the Exlian's power, but it carried with it a trace of the monster's mental power, which was now trying its best to devour Mark's spirit so it could take over his body. Or at least that was what it seemed like . . .

Mime's attack had not only revealed its presence but wounded it, forcing it into a desperate situation. If it didn't consume Mark, it would die, so its survival instinct had kicked in, causing it to attack desperately. Mark, caught off guard by the sudden change in circumstances, nearly lost the battle before it began. It was only at the last moment that he managed to stabilize his spirit by forcing himself into a meditative state.

Even as Mark's soul was consumed in large chunks, he could feel it being repaired, and he quickly realized that the wounds Mime had caused were causing the war bear's soul to bleed out, transforming into a thick mist that, in turn, nourished and fortified Mark's soul. Of course, this process was so painful Mark wanted to scream, but he was afraid of alerting Maestro, so instead he clenched his teeth so hard his gums started bleeding.

The war bear, sensing its demise, threw itself at Mark in a frenzy, but rather than quail, he matched its intensity with his own. Instead of waiting for the Exlian spirit to bite down, he began shoving himself forward, throwing himself into the monster's mouth as if he couldn't wait to be eaten. A blind aggression grew in Mark, and soon, the ferocious feeling that filled Mark's mind grew so strong that it numbed the pain of the monster's teeth. At the same time, the bear seemed to grow weaker and weaker until, suddenly, it completely fell apart with a terrible wail.

The thick mist its body had produced surged inside Mark, healing the damage the war bear's attacks had caused until his spirit was good as new. In fact, as Mark examined himself, he could feel a strange sort of weight that hadn't existed before, as if he had become more real.

Rising unsteadily to his feet, Mark let out a loud roar, venting the burning pain that had racked his body. Hunger consumed him, so intense that he began to cast his eyes around for something else to eat, only to freeze when he caught sight of a cat sitting in front of him. It was only a fraction of his size, but its three crimson eyes shocked him back into a rational state of mind. The hunger that had plagued him was gone, and instead, a voice reverberated in Mark's mind.

Those who cannot master the hunger are nothing but slaves. Those who can wield it tread a limitless path.

The next thing Mark knew, his watch was vibrating, and with a faint groan, he sat up from where he had slouched down on the carpet. Blinking, he looked at the watch and realized an entire night had passed as he lay unconscious on the carpet. When he felt his watch buzz again, Mark glanced down and saw Maestro was calling. Realizing he had a few missed calls from the mad genius, he quickly accepted, and Maestro's massive head popped up in front of him.

"Oh, good, you're still alive. I've been trying to call you for a while, because that serum had likely taken effect, and your shackles were telling me that you were still alive. At least, your body was. Not so sure about your mind, but the fact that you can accept the call is a good sign. So how was it? I told you that trying to blend with an Exlian that ranked above you was going to be hard."

Mark felt as if he hadn't had a drink of water in years, and his throat was swollen and raspy. Still, he managed a reply. "I'm fine."

"Ooh, you sound, like, decidedly not fine. But still, you're talking, which is good. Most of the time when I feed people serums like this, they just transform into the very creature they were trying to absorb an ability from. It's absolutely fascinating how aggressive Exlian cells are. But I am glad to see you're alive. Though, of course, had you died, I just would have used your body to further the research. But the fact that you're alive is a testament to how powerful your willpower is. Unless it was a defective serum, which is also possible . . . But there is a good way to find out—answer your door."

Still a little woozy, Mark struggled to his feet and wobbled to his door as there was a knock. The virtual window still hovered in front of him as he grasped the knob and opened the door, and a mana blade stabbed straight toward his heart. Thankfully, Mark's instincts kicked in, and his upper body leaned back as his leg snapped out, slamming into his attacker's hip, causing the man's body to twist, bringing the blade up short. At the same time, Mark could feel mana gathering in the path of the blade, forming a thick shield that diverted it from its course. His mind still hadn't caught up to exactly what was going on, but after countless hours of practice, his body knew exactly what came next.

Slapping away the attack with his left hand, Mark straightened, his body rebounding as his right hand shot toward his startled attacker's throat. At the last moment, Mark was able to shift the trajectory of his hand, barely slicing the man's skin. With a shriek, the man stumbled backward, his hand reaching up to touch the wound.

Though Mark's impulse was to go in for the kill, he forced himself backward into his apartment and slammed the door, panting as he tried to figure out what had just happened. Maestro, still on a call with him, was looking over the data coming in.

"Well, that didn't go as I thought it would, but we have

confirmed the ability is working. It'll likely need a little more practice, honing, if you will, but I understand that you're going to be doing some training with the Tomb Wolves. While their name is a bit silly, they're undoubtedly skilled, so you should be in good shape. Do your best to get your skill working, and let me know if there are any side effects. I'll be watching closely."

With a beep, the screen vanished, and Mark let out a groan. Maestro's telling someone to stab him in the heart in order to test his new abilities was pure madness, but on the other hand, it made sense in a twisted sort of way.

About to turn away, Mark suddenly grabbed the door handle and opened the door, only to find the hallway empty. Clearly, his attacker had run away, not wanting to stick around and fight Mark for real. Shutting the door, Mark glanced down at his hands, trying to understand what had changed about his ability. He vaguely remembered the strange struggle against an ethereal bear, but what dominated his thoughts was the last two sentences he had heard: the idea of wielding hunger as a weapon rather than being consumed by it.

While the principles behind this idea weren't new to Mark, for the first time, he sat down on the couch and began to seriously consider what was becoming of him. His descent into the Tomb had necessitated a change in his outlook, but Mark was starting to notice a level of haste to grow strong that hadn't existed before. He was walking a thin line, and the more often he gave into his hunger, the more powerful it became. At the same time, he couldn't shut it out completely if he wanted to get out of here alive.

His goal was to climb to the top, to establish himself in a

way that could not be ignored, and personal power was one way to do that. Yet this mad rush, the scramble to gain as much as he could as fast as he could, was clearly reckless. Had Mime not interfered, Mark no doubt would have lost himself twice in the last twelve hours. First, he was almost positive that he would not have been able to resist the war bear's devouring mental energy on his own. Only Mime's wounding it had given him the edge he needed, to consume rather than be consumed. Yet in doing so, in winning the fight, he had been entirely overtaken by his hunger, and without Mime's steadying censure, he likely would have suffered a terrible fate.

Glancing over at Mime, who was sitting on the back of the couch, watching Mark carefully, he gave her a weak smile. "Thanks, you saved my life twice there." A slow smile spread across Mime's lips, and her tail lashed back and forth. Suddenly, she lifted her paw and swiped lightly. A silver flash, much like the ones that had hit Mark the night before, tore across the room, slamming into his shoulder. Yet just before it hit, Mark felt dense mana gathering, and the silvery blade broke apart, shattering into tiny glittering pieces of dust that faded quickly into the air.

When Mark had absorbed the ability from the war bear, it had been so thin that even one of his finger strikes could break through it. Now, the ability produced a thick shell, with mana so densely packed even Mime's claw couldn't penetrate it. Of course, it was just a casual swipe. Mark had no doubt that if Mime really wanted to cut through it, she'd be able to chop him into little pieces. Still, his improvement was astounding, and letting out a low chuckle, Mark couldn't keep the grin from his face. "Winter Wolf and the others are going to be in for quite a surprise."

Sticking to his new commitment to slowing down, Mark spent a lot more time over the next few days meditating as he tried to understand his abilities better. Eventually, the training day came, and Winter Wolf called Mark and instructed him to meet them down in the lobby of the apartment building. Everyone else was already there when he arrived, and looking him over, Coral flashed a smile that reminded Mark of Joker's. "Ready to get your face beat in, kid?"

"First of all, I'm not that much younger than you. And second of all, we'll see who's beating whose face in."

Laughing, Joker slapped Mark on the shoulder. "That's the kind of attitude I'm talking about, kid. Now come on, we can't afford to waste any time."

As they headed toward the training room, Winter Wolf explained how it worked. "It's pretty much a small version of the arena. There are a lot of different ways that you can manipulate the environment and a lot of different scenarios that you can set. What's nice about it, though, is they'll deactivate the shackles, which will give us freedom to use our abilities. Of course, that means we have to be extra careful, since there are no safety buttons."

When they arrived at the arena, Winter Wolf led the way, taking Mark around to a part of the building he had never been in before and into a waiting room. They were a few minutes early and had to wait until the doors to the training room opened up and three other prisoners left, barely sparing them a glance. The five of them hurried into the room, which had the same hard-packed dirt floor as the arena. While Winter Wolf went to set their training conditions, Mark looked around and quickly spotted some observation windows. Seeing him examining them, Coral walked up beside him and pointed. "That's where the scum sit to watch as we train. Unlike the arena, they can't affect anything down here, which is nice."

"Why would they want to watch us train?"

"So they can make better bets, of course," Joker said, tossing a knife up and down. "Come on, Winter Wolf, I'm getting antsy. Who's first?"

"Doesn't matter to me," Winter Wolf said with a shrug, but Coral's hand shot up immediately.

"Ooh, I'm first."

"All right, take your places," Joker said. "Don't embarrass her too badly, Apex."

Rolling her eyes, Coral sauntered out to the middle of the training room and gestured for Mark to follow. "Come on, let's see what you got."

Bouncing up and down on his feet, Mark rolled his shoulders to loosen them and then nodded to show he was ready. Joker lifted his hand, but before he dropped it, Coral was already moving as water manifested around her. She slid back, her feet barely touching the ground as water began bubbling up around her. Mark, not wanting to give her too much distance, launched himself forward, sprinting toward her as fast as he could.

If she was surprised by his speed, she didn't show it, and pointing two fingers at him, she made a shooting motion. From over her shoulder, a bullet of water flashed toward Mark, but he dodged, allowing it to whiz past his head. Two more followed quickly, but Mark avoided both. Despite all three shots missing, Coral smirked and quickly blasted off two more.

As soon as he saw her smile, Mark realized he had fallen into a trap, and he lifted his hands around his head, protecting his neck. Moving incredibly swiftly, the three balls of water that had passed him slammed into his back and neck. Yet though he braced himself, they didn't hit much harder than a water balloon, leaving Mark a bit confused. He had just taken a step forward when the two new water bullets slammed into his chest, and he realized what was going on.

As each bullet hit, his mana naturally manifested as a shield so only the water itself splashed lightly against him. Coral's smile was replaced with an ugly expression, and it was Mark's turn to grin as he rapidly closed the distance. Unable to believe her attacks weren't working, Coral reached out and formed a whip of water that lashed at Mark with tremendous force. Yet as soon as it touched him, it broke against his shield, and he passed through unscathed.

By now he was only a few steps from Coral, and as his fist drew back, she quickly threw up her hands. "I'm done! I give up!"

Holding his punch, Mark slid to a stop. As soon as he did, the water behind Coral surged, heading straight for his head. The sight of the archer she had taken down, whose head was soaked with water, flashed through Mark's mind, and he realized that Coral was trying to trap him in a bubble of water. Because that attack didn't rely on force, his mana shield wouldn't do much against it.

But instead of backpedaling, Mark lunged forward, unleashing his null field. As the energy washed over her, Coral lost control of all the water, which immediately dropped to the ground, drenching her completely. As quickly as the field had flickered on, Mark deactivated it, and then his fingers wrapped around Coral's neck, causing her to freeze in shock.

Part of Mark wanted to squeeze. He had already anticipated that she would try some sort of dirty trick. After all, that was life in the Tomb. But he also knew that the voice in the back of his head, screaming that everyone who attacked him should die, wasn't worth listening to. Taking a calming breath, he slowly opened his hand and took a step backward, then another. The entire time, his eyes were on Coral, who was still frozen in place, her face bloodless and her eyes wide.

Once he felt like he was under control, Mark turned and looked at the others. Joker's smile was gone, and instead, he stared at Mark with a strangely bright gaze. Winter Wolf looked slightly confused, and only Servo seemed pleased that Mark had won. He had a smile on his face as he lifted his big hand into the air. "Can I go next?"

"There's no point," Joker said. "He'd cut you to pieces. His hands can punch through the metal of your suit."

Faltering, Servo slowly lowered his hands as he looked over at Mark, who nodded and wiggled his bone blade fingers.

"Well, that's not fun," Servo said with a frown.

"I'm definitely next." Flipping his knife, Joker was about to walk forward when Winter Wolf stopped him.

"I think I'd like to test out our new teammate before anybody else, just to get a good understanding of where his limits really lie."

Though Joker clearly didn't like it, he still backed down and watched with an annoyed expression as Winter Wolf walked out to where Coral was standing and tapped her on the shoulder.

"There are all sorts of fantastic abilities out there," Winter Wolf said quietly. "If you get caught off guard like this, you'll eventually end up dead."

Once Coral had joined Joker and Servo at the side, Winter Wolf faced off against Mark. "Do you want a weapon?"

"No, thanks," he replied, shaking out his hands. "I'm better with my fists."

"You say fists, but it looks to me like you use a palm art. Cutting Palm, right?"

Raising his eyebrows, Mark nodded. "It is."

"Huh. I thought the people who practiced that were all really old or gone. Though I did know someone, a Ranger, who used to use it. His name was Jason, I think."

Taking his stance, Mark smiled. "Jason's the reason I started learning the Cutting Palm. I used to work as a dishwasher at his restaurant."

"Jason has a restaurant? Man, things really change, don't they?"

As she spoke, Winter Wolf drew a triangle with her fingers in the air in front of her. Mark had seen this spell activate already, and he quickly leaped to the side as a wall of sharp spikes rose from under his feet to impale him. Barely avoiding the ice, he'd started to dash forward when he saw Winter Wolf flick her fingers sideways. Even though he was already leaning forward, Mark forcefully twisted his body, throwing himself back as more ice split off from the wall, shooting out to block his advance. If he had continued forward, he would have impaled himself neatly on the spikes.

At the same time, Mark could sense mana starting to gather around Winter Wolf, spinning together to form large chunks of ice. Realizing that if he didn't stop her spell, he'd end up facing off against multiple ice wolves, as well as an A-ranked empowered, Mark threw caution to the wind and advanced as rapidly as possible, dodging past spears of ice that shot out of the wall toward him. A few managed to hit him, but each was blocked by a shimmer of brownish-gold mana that manifested above his skin.

With each blow he took, the furrow between Winter Wolf's eyes deepened. To his surprise, only three of the large chunks of ice transformed into wolves, while the others began to spin around Winter Wolf at high speed, forming a whirling shield. Though he wasn't afraid of getting hit, the massive chunks of ice would certainly slow him down, and after seeing the ice wall sprouting spikes all over the place, Mark was fairly sure that getting hit by a massive block of ice would only be the beginning.

The three wolves rushed around Winter Wolf, charging toward him, and Mark met them squarely, slamming a palm into the side of the first one's head as it tried to bite him. There was a flash of cold air, and Mark felt his palm starting to freeze as the outer shell of the wolf was cracked. It quickly collapsed to the ground, but its death caused Mark to slow down slightly, allowing one of the other wolves to latch onto his leg. As its teeth crunched down, they were met with a mana shield as well, giving Mark the opportunity to crush its skull. Unfortunately, that released another blast of cold air, slowing him down even further.

Rather than wait for the third wolf to attack, Winter Wolf lunged forward, stretching out her arm as she did so. A chain of ice shot out, wrapping around the rapidly spinning ice crystals, transforming them into a makeshift morning star. With a shout, she brought it crashing down on Mark, whose body had slowed so all he could do was block what was in front of him. The ice crystals slammed into Mark's body, sending him tumbling across the training ground. But a moment later, he was back on his feet, shaking the frost from his arms.

Joker let out a low whistle. "That kid's tough."

"It's the mana shields," Servo said. "They're blocking the majority of the damage. The only reason he was thrown back is because he doesn't have the weight to stay stable."

Mark didn't have time to consider why the massive flail had thrown him back. A deep frown had formed on Winter Wolf's lips, and as she tossed the crushed crystals to the side, Mark felt his heart clench. He had been under the impression that she was a pure spellcaster who used her power from a distance. He was wrong.

A complex pattern appeared in the air behind her, and black ice rapidly began to form over her arms, torso, and legs. Mark could see the cold air coming off it. As Winter Wolf launched herself forward, he realized why he always saw her in the gym. Her punches were fierce, and she used elbow strikes and knee strikes liberally as she rained down a storm of blows on Mark. Even worse, the cold air coming off her suit slowed Mark's reactions, causing him to quickly fall behind.

Winter Wolf was clearly a league above him in hand-to-hand combat, and as she rained down blows, Mark felt like little more than a punching bag. The only saving grace was that no matter where she punched or how quickly she struck, his mana shield ability would activate, severely blunting the force of her blows. Yet Mark knew that that wasn't a long-term solution, as every time she hit him, he could feel a sliver of his biofuel being carved away. Estimating that he could only survive a few dozen more blows, Mark moved forward, abandoning any pretense of defense.

As he struck at Winter Wolf's waist, she didn't even bother blocking. Instead, she took the opportunity to punch him twice in the face, or at least try. Gritting his teeth as the cold air assaulted him, Mark was stunned when his fingers bounced off Winter Wolf's icy armor.

For the first time in a long time, Mark's bone blade fingers had failed.

With a shout, he launched another strike, aiming at exactly the same spot.

When he saw her twist, Mark's eyes sharpened, and he realized that his attack had done more than he thought. Of course, he still had other abilities, and he was confident that he could probably catch her off guard using them. But he was also quite aware that doing so would expose his secrets. Instead, Mark resigned himself to his fate and traded blows as best he could, trying to target the same spot on Winter Wolf's waist as often as possible.

Annoyed, Winter Wolf jumped back, unleashing a side kick that slammed into Mark's ribs. Though mana started to gather, the shield was considerably thinner than it should have been, in part due to Mark's desperate attempt to restrain his power. The majority of the force of her kick slammed into his side. The crack of ribs echoed in the training room as Mark was sent tumbling backward, barely managing to stop himself after rolling nearly twenty-five feet.

Gasping in pain, he pressed his hand tightly against his side. As he got to one knee, his eyes fixed on Winter Wolf, who was staring at him with an inscrutable expression. Mark tried to get to his feet, failing the first time but then succeeding on his second attempt. He took a deep breath, trying to assess the damage to his ribs, but his regeneration was already knitting everything back together. Still taking a step forward, he staggered slightly.

"Are you not going to give up?" Winter Wolf asked, crossing her arms over her chest.

"I can keep going . . . for maybe two more hits," Mark lied, pretending he didn't want to give up.

In truth, had he not forcefully deactivated his ability as the mana shield was forming, Mark could have lasted another fifteen or twenty hits. But by this point, his wariness about revealing his full abilities was bone deep. Whether his act fooled Winter Wolf, he wasn't sure, but she lifted her hand and waved for him to go to the side and join the others. Walking over to stand in front of them, Winter Wolf was lost in thought for a moment, before seeming to make up her mind.

"Apex, you're a lot tougher than our last melee fighter was, but I'm not quite sure what to do about that glitch ability of yours. That was what activated when Coral tried to bubble you, right?"

Taking a slight step forward, Mark looked at Coral before responding. "It was. It tends to only activate if I'm in a really dangerous situation, or at least if I feel like my life is in danger."

"I see. It's unfortunate that you couldn't activate it against me. Is there a cooldown on it?"

"No, not that I'm aware of. I've used it multiple times in short order before."

"Then what we need to do is have you figure out how to manifest it reliably. That power is too dangerous to leave untrained. Combined with your mana shield, it would make you nearly unstoppable on the battlefield."

"You forgot his regeneration," Joker said. "He also heals if you actually manage to get through."

Slowly, a smile spread across Winter Wolf's lips. "You're going to make a lot of people really mad, but you're perfect for a close-range melee fighter. Especially if you can learn to turn people's powers off at will. What'd you say your rank was again?"

"The last time I checked, somewhere in the C range."

"Huh. Imagine that. A C-ranked defender who can take punches from an A-ranked brawler. All right, well, we have a training path for you. You'll trade off working with each of us, but I'd like you to start by training with Coral to understand how she controls her water."

"Oh, come on, why don't I get to fight with Apex? I've been looking forward to it this whole time."

Ignoring Joker's complaint, Winter Wolf pointed to the middle of the training ground. "Get out here. We're going to show these kids what an actual fight looks like."

"Fine. You know, you're no fun. All I wanted to do was have a friendly spar."

"Joker, the last time you had a friendly spar, someone lost nine of their ten fingers, and it wasn't you."

Tapping his teeth with the tip of his blade, Joker chuckled as he sauntered out to the middle of the training yard.

"I guess that's true. It would have been even more fun if you hadn't stopped the fight. What did I say about you always ruining my fun?"

Winter Wolf still had her armor active, and now she drew another symbol in the air, and ice spun together to form a shield and a mace. Grabbing both, Winter Wolf bounced up and down on her feet a few times, then suddenly darted forward. Joker moved at the exact same moment, tracing a path sideways as a fan of knives appeared in the air behind him and shot toward Winter Wolf.

To Mark's surprise, she didn't bother lifting her shield as the knives came close, and for a moment it looked as if she were going to ram right into them. At the last possible second, her shield tilted up slightly, deflecting only one of the five knives flying toward her. At the same time, she stomped and spun, her mace swinging in a wide arc behind her. The sound of clashing weapons rang out as the knives that had originally been heading straight for her vanished.

"It's illusions," Servo said helpfully, his arms crossed over his chest. "Joker is adept at illusions, combined with his minor teleportation power. It's pretty annoying."

"Hey, stop giving away my secrets, at least until I've shown them to him."

By this point, Winter Wolf had caught up to Joker, but every time she smashed down at him with her mace, he would shift out of the way. At the same time, his knives continually plinked off her armor, gouging bits of ice out. She sped up, increasing the rate of strikes she unleashed. But Joker, appearing completely relaxed, continued to teleport around. Sometimes he would move closer, sometimes farther away. And twice, he appeared to drift in the air for a moment, borrowing the wind from one of Winter Wolf's swings to float away from her.

To her credit, Winter Wolf didn't seem to grow frustrated, despite the fact that none of her attacks hit. For Joker's part, though he seemed completely relaxed, Mark could tell he was concentrating fully. And Mark couldn't blame him. Had he been the one facing Winter Wolf's mace, he likely would have been crushed into the ground by now.

Stomping forward, Winter Wolf suddenly thrust out her shield, slamming it to the side. As she did, her mace stabbed the opposite direction, completely exposing her front. Yet rather than attack, Joker did three rapid back handsprings, his body moving with abnormal grace. With a grim smile, Winter Wolf let out a shout and brought her mace up over her head, slamming it into the ground with tremendous force. All around her, ice crystals sprang up into the air, forming a forest of sharp spikes.

"Oh, come on, that's totally cheating," Joker said, shifting at the last second to keep his stomach from being impaled.

"You have your powers; I have mine," Winter Wolf said.

She lifted her shield in front of her and raised her mace, holding it to the side. When he saw the stance, Joker let out a dramatic sigh. "Oh, we're going all the way, are we?"

"You wanted a fight, didn't you?"

Though the two combatants were allies, Mark couldn't help but feel a slight chill. Licking his lips, he glanced over and saw that Coral didn't seem worried at all. When she noticed the faint anxiousness in Mark's expression, she chuckled and patted him on the shoulder. "One of Winter Wolf's rules is you always fight for real. She says it's the only way you can truly hone yourself."

Out on the field, Joker snapped his fingers, and all his knives teleported behind him. He turned and waved his hand in the air, as if erasing them, and one by one as his hand passed over them, they vanished. When he turned back around, he only had a single knife remaining, which he gripped in his hand and ran lightly over one of the crystals.

"You know, I've never managed to peel that armor off you, but every time I think about it, I can't help but get quite excited."

"Get excited about this."

Winter Wolf accompanied her reply with a slam of her mace into her shield. A loud chime sounded, and both her weapon and shield shattered, unleashing a torrent of crystals in every direction. As each crystal struck one of the spikes, the spike exploded as well, forming an ever-expanding blast of ice. Mark flinched back, but seeing that the other two onlookers didn't move, he sheepishly took his position again. The ice spread rapidly, until it was around thirty feet from Winter Wolf, at which point it began to swirl around her, rapidly transforming into a storm of sleet and razor-sharp ice.

Joker spun his dagger in his hand and, with a laugh, dove right into the storm. Every step he took carried him half a dozen feet, his body randomly appearing and disappearing with his rapid-fire steps, as he dodged his way through the storm to close in on Winter Wolf. As soon as the crystals had started exploding, Winter Wolf had clasped her hands together and closed her eyes, concentrating tightly. A symbol began tracing itself out behind her, and though some pieces of it looked faintly familiar to Mark, he couldn't quite see it because of the swirling ice.

Joker was still ten feet away from Winter Wolf when she let out a shout and thrust her hands forward. A savage look crossed his face, and he immediately hurled his dagger as a massive wolf maw made of ice flew at him out of the storm, biting down fiercely on his body. Joker, caught in the teeth of the ice wolf, screamed, and his body vanished, appearing above the ice wolf's head. A dagger flashed in his hand, and as he stabbed down toward the wolf, another ethereal wolf appeared, its maw snapping down on his arm.

At the same time, the dagger he had thrown reached Winter Wolf, who casually lifted a hand to brush it aside, only for her fingers to pass straight through it. Too late, she realized the dagger was an illusion and barely managed to jerk her head out of the way as the real dagger sliced across her jaw. Had she not jerked back, it would have planted itself directly in her mouth, but as it was, it left a bloody cut.

Almost immediately, the wound began to ice over, the blood freezing in place, and Winter Wolf clenched her teeth and made a hurling motion with her hand. Everything was moving so fast Mark was having trouble keeping up, and then he saw Joker's bloody body come flying out of the ice storm and slam into the dirt floor of the training room.

Joker bounced three times and somehow managed to regain

his feet. One of his arms hung limply, and there were major gashes on his stomach and chest and back where an ice wolf's teeth had bitten into him. A crazed expression was plastered on his face, and he started to crouch, clearly intending to run straight back into the storm. That was when Winter Wolf's voice rang out.

"Servo, wake him up."

Punching his fist, Servo took a big step forward, his armor rapidly forming around him. The two mana cannons on his shoulder swiveled to face Joker, and both began to hum as they charged up. Almost immediately, Joker froze and then quickly lifted his one good arm. "Ha ha, no need for that, I'm fine, totally fine."

"Joker's a good fighter," Coral said quietly, "but he suffers a bit from battle madness. As soon as blood is drawn, he can't help but go for the kill."

In the center of the training ground, the storm of ice began to settle, and Winter Wolf walked out, two large ice wolves by her side. Watching her as she dismissed her armor, Mark suddenly missed his brother, Joe. He had never seen his brother operating at full power, but if this was how powerful a normal A-ranked energy controller was, Mark could only imagine what his brother must have looked like.

"We'll be facing off against powerful enemies, and though it may have looked as if I had the overwhelming advantage there, the lesson you should be taking away is that anybody, no matter how weak, can be dangerous. Though I outrank Joker by two ranks, he was still able to draw blood."

As she spoke, Winter Wolf lifted her hand to her cut cheek, and Mark glanced at Joker, unable to believe that he was only C ranked. Joker's body seemed to hold significantly more mana than other C-ranked individuals—even more than Coral, who was a B-ranked energy controller. Then again, the amount of mana Mark's body held was significantly more than normal too, even though officially he was still only C ranked. Starting to feel as if the ranks didn't have nearly as much meaning as he'd originally believed, Mark heard Winter Wolf clear her throat.

"Mark, if it had been you and Joker fighting me together, I would have been hard pressed. If you were able to control this glitch ability of yours, I'd probably lose. It's hard to overstate just how much of a cheat your glitch ability is, especially fighting people who don't have a purely physical power set. Go ahead and split off with Coral and start practicing your control."

Though Coral wasn't exactly thrilled to be Mark's new teacher, she still took her role seriously, bringing him over to the other side of the training room and beginning to demonstrate how her abilities worked. Mark had originally thought that she created water out of thin air, but he noticed that every time she wanted to manipulate it, her hand would drop to her waist, and a few floating bubbles of water would escape from a contraption on her back.

Seeing Mark's curious gaze, Coral turned around and showed him a small pouch with a series of tubes that allowed her to extract drops of water in almost any direction. Swiping her fingers through the air, she pulled a drop out, and Mark saw it expand, doubling from a single drop into two and then four and then eight.

"I only need a little bit to start, and from there, I'm able to expand it. I don't understand exactly how this process works, but while I can't pull water from nothing, as long as it exists in a drop form, I can create an almost endless amount of it. As for how I actually control it, that's a tricky question. I can sort of sense all the water in my surroundings, and as long as I can imagine a shape, water can take that shape. Of course, it still has the properties of water, but I can sort of morph it into anything I want."

As she spoke, Coral demonstrated for Mark, rapidly transforming the ball of water floating in front of her into a dozen different shapes.

"For energy controllers, the most important thing is our will. It determines not only how much of the world we can impact but, more importantly, how far our imagination can go. The most important thing, for me at least, is believing that I can do it. For example"—with a snap of her fingers, Coral transformed the water in front of her into a translucent pane—"I can make this shape, but it'll still maintain the properties of water."

To illustrate, Coral poked a finger through it.

"If I want this to be a shield, then I have to believe that nothing can get through it. Here, you go ahead and poke."

Reaching up, Mark tapped the water. Instead of his finger passing straight through with a splash, as Coral's had, it felt as if he were hitting a tough piece of glass.

"Even though the water has its own properties and can't be made as hard as, say, a piece of metal, using my willpower, I'm able to reinforce it to create more of what I want. That's how I make the water bullets. That's how I make the whip. And there are a significant number of other things that I can do with water. Really, I'm just limited by my imagination and how firmly I believe that I'm able to do what I'm setting out to do."

Waving her hand, Coral collapsed the water shield back into a ball.

"I think the best way to train your glitch ability is to see if you can activate it through your will. We can play a game. I'll be practicing my control, trying to rotate between complex shapes. Your goal is just to disrupt me. Remember, you have to genuinely believe that it's going to work. Otherwise, it never will. How you do that is going to be really personal, though, so it's not something that I can directly help you with. You're going to just have to figure it out on your own. But these are the basics of how energy control works. All right, you ready?"

Nodding, Mark watched as Coral spun three drops of water up into small balls, which hung in the air in front of her, and began rapidly rotating them through different shapes. At first, Mark just watched, observing how the balls changed shape. There seemed to be a specific pattern that Coral rotated through, staggering the timing, so she was always transforming each water ball into a different shape.

What Mark was most interested in, however, was how she was actually manipulating them. Each water ball contained a bit of mana, but Coral wasn't manipulating the mana directly. Instead, she appeared to be sending out small flickers of mental energy that flew to each of the water balls, activating their transformations. Occasionally, one of them wouldn't arrive in time or would fade before it reached the water ball, causing a transformation to be a moment late or not happen at all. When that happened, Coral would close her eyes for a moment, allowing the balls to revert to their normal round shape before she began again.

As he watched, Mark considered his own ability. In truth, it was a simple enough thing for him to activate the null field. He could do it at will and maintain it for as long as needed. But what intrigued him most was the idea that he might be able to project the field rather than centering it on his own body. He had already discovered that through intense concentration, he was able to manipulate the size of the field so long as it stayed fixed on him. But he was curious as to whether there was a way to project the null field beyond him.

Though the null field was a tremendously powerful ability, Mark didn't like the fact that it conflicted with his new mana shield power. In an ideal world, he would be able to use both simultaneously. But his mana shield manifested on the outside of his body, and as soon as the null field activated, it prevented mana from gathering near him.

The way he saw it, there were two potential paths forward. The first was to figure out how to project the null field at a distance, using it in the way that everyone else believed it worked. The second was to pull his mana shield back into his body, forming the shield inside his skin. Mark genuinely wasn't sure that either of these adjustments could be achieved, but that was what practice was for. He started by imagining as best he could that his null field was going to appear outside his body. Just to be safe, he picked a spot a dozen feet away. But no matter how hard he focused, the null field marble that sat at the back of his neck didn't move one bit.

Almost immediately, he realized the problem. In order to move the null field, he needed to use mental energy. But in order to project mental energy beyond his body, he needed a trace amount of mana to act as a catalyst. He had first noticed this with the lines of mental energy Winter Wolf used to control her ice wolves. For most empowered, the amount of mana needed to project mental energy was so small that it was invisible, but in order to maintain the quality of her connection, Winter Wolf's threads were reinforced rather heavily.

Mark hadn't even realized that in using his mental energy, he was also leveraging mana. But it made sense and explained why he could see the mental energy at all. Unfortunately, as soon as his mental energy touched the null field, the mana that carried it evaporated, causing the mental energy to fade away as well. This left Mark rather stumped. Of course, it wasn't the end of the world if he could only use his null field centered on his own body. But still, Mark didn't want to give up. And for the next few hours, he tried his best to figure out a way around the issue.

Three hours into their practice, Winter Wolf called him and Coral up, and they began some light sparring. Mostly, that meant using Mark as a punching bag, since his mana shield prevented almost all damage. But Mark didn't mind one bit, and as they practiced, he quickly found himself getting better and better at leveraging his new ability.

Between his regeneration and the mana shield, Mark was realizing he could be much more aggressive than before. Most attacks simply failed to make it through his new shell, and those that did were quickly healed, meaning that as long as he had biofuel, Mark was an almost unstoppable tank. Of course, he wasn't completely immune, and as soon as Servo got involved in the sparring, Mark learned that a healthy dose of caution was a good idea.

The mana shield blocked almost any attack B rank or under, but A-ranked attacks would shatter it, reaching Mark's skin below. Additionally, there was a slight lag time between when a shield shattered and when it re-formed. Winter Wolf seemed to think that the best way to test the extremes of Mark's ability was to simply throw him into deadly combat, and though Mark had more than one scare, by the time their training was done, he felt he had a comprehensive understanding of how his ability worked.

Gathering everybody together, Winter Wolf glanced up at the windows, where a few people from New Emery were watching them. His eyes glowing with excitement, Joker looked up at the windows as well. "Do we have a new mission?"

Taking a breath, Winter Wolf slowly nodded. "We do. Two days. Mark, come with me, please."

Joker seemed to be the only one who was excited, and Mark found himself slightly apprehensive when he saw Servo's and Coral's grim expressions. Winter Wolf led Mark out of the training room and into a small room that only contained a simple metal table and two chairs.

"Take a seat," she said, walking around the table to sit down. His apprehension growing, Mark sat down and scooted his chair in. Winter Wolf tapped her watch, projecting a virtual screen across the table in front of them.

"As a member of our team, there's a couple of things you need to know. The first is that we don't really do special exhibitions very often. The one you were just involved in was an edge case, a message from the administrators that the scum can't do whatever they want in the arena. In truth, we're a conductor team."

Opening her palm, Winter Wolf summoned a sliver of ice that spun, rapidly forming a dagger. When they had walked out of the training room, Mark had felt his shackles reactivate. So seeing Winter Wolf use her power caused his eyes to narrow.

"As conductors, we have some special privileges. First and foremost, our abilities are not locked off. Of course, we're not supposed to use them outside the arena or the training room, but they are active. From the lack of surprise you're exhibiting, I imagine you've heard of conductors before."

Leaning forward slightly, Mark shook his head. "Only a little. Joker's mentioned the term a couple of times."

Her eyes flashing with a cold light, Winter Wolf frowned. "Joker's got a loose mouth. I'll have to have a chat with him. Simply put, the conductors are a special organization that exists to escort individuals to the Tomb."

"You mean you go above the surface, to New Emery."

Hearing the disbelief in Mark's voice, Winter Wolf cracked a smile. "We do, though don't get too many ideas, because we're always escorted. Our job is simple. When there are individuals who are not good for New Emery, we invite them to the Tomb."

"What if they don't want to come?"

"Then we send them."

Sitting back in his chair, Mark wasn't quite sure what to think. He was starting to get used to the fact that everything in the Tomb happened abruptly, with no warning, and that nothing he thought he knew was quite accurate. Finding out that the group he was joining wasn't a team that would fight for the enjoyment of New Emery's powerful elite but instead a hit squad didn't stir much emotion. The thought that he'd be able to go back above the surface and see New Emery again did. Mark hadn't quite realized just how important getting to see the sky was to him. But as soon as Winter Wolf mentioned it, Mark couldn't help but feel a tremendous surge of emotion.

"The missions we undertake are dangerous because, on the record, we don't exist, which means that the majority of what we do in New Emery, if exposed, puts us in direct conflict with the authorities. That means that we have to operate with the utmost secrecy."

"Hold on," Mark said, holding up his hand. "Were you responsible for those two politicians that went missing a couple of months ago?"

"Yes," Winter Wolf admitted, her voice heavy, "and more than a few besides. However, it's not just politicians that the city wants to get rid of. There are empowered who aren't following the rules. There are mutants and other people who disrupt social order. Recently, we've been sent after the so-called Green Line terrorists, though we didn't manage to find them or their base. Now that you're a member of our team, I'll be submitting your information to the handlers. They're the ones who plan the missions and make sure that we don't get off the train halfway through. If you perform well, the advantages are innumerable."

"And if I don't?" Mark asked.

With a small smile, Winter Wolf pushed her chair back from the table and stood up. "I think that goes without saying. Follow me—I just got word that you've got a visitor."

Twenty minutes later, Mark found himself sitting in an uncomfortable metal chair in a small room with a thick glass window in front of him. As had become his habit, he'd scanned the room for any sort of camera or observation device when he entered, and was surprised to find nothing. Through the glass, he could see another chair, which looked much more comfortable than his, and a door beyond it. Winter Wolf hadn't mentioned who wanted to see him, so Mark could only sit quietly and wait.

A few minutes went by, and then the door on the other side of the glass opened, and Mark's eyes went wide as Noah stepped through. There was a certain paleness to Noah's face, and his jaw was clenched tight as he walked to the chair. Through the door behind him, Mark caught sight of two large men who looked like bodyguards. Though whether they were there for Noah's protection or to monitor him, Mark wasn't sure.

The door shut, sealing the two of them in together, and Noah sat down in the chair on his side of the glass. For a long moment, neither of them spoke, and then, offering half a smile, Mark lifted his hand. Instead of replying, Noah, maintaining his white-knuckle grip on his armrests, leaned forward, his eyes running over Mark, taking in every detail.

"You okay?" Mark asked, surprised by the scrutiny.

"What's the code word?" Noah asked, his tone sharp.

It took Mark half a second to figure out what Noah was talking about, and he noticed that Noah got increasingly tense with every moment that passed.

"Did you see the image I sent?" Mark said quietly, and Noah expelled all his tension in a shuddering breath.

"I can't believe you're alive. They told us you were dead, that you had been executed."

Shrugging one shoulder, Mark gestured to his surroundings. "I'm in the Tomb, Noah. To some degree, I am. Though I did just find out that I might be able to see the surface every once in a while."

"That's what I'm here to talk to you about," Noah said. "But before that, what happened?"

"You know how I was sent out to Felwer Mine, and how you told me that it was likely a trap? Well, you were right. The whole mission was a fiasco. We got out there, and the Rangers left. On the way, there was a rockfall. More of a landslide, really. Half the mountain came down, blocking our road back, which delayed our reinforcements. We got attacked by a swarm of Exlian. Our fearless leader, Captain Calder, and his bodyguard, Rogers, tried to bury me and two other members of our unit in the mine. I barely managed to survive, hunkering down in the mine until I had gathered enough strength to return to the city."

Pausing for a moment, Mark leaned forward, resting his arms on his knees as he considered how much to tell Noah. Though he and Noah were good friends, Mark couldn't help but hesitate. After all, Noah's father had likely been the one who had a hand in putting him in prison in the first place.

"The long story short is that when reinforcements did arrive,

Sergeant Rogers came with them. He tried to kill me and died in the process. When I got back to the city, they arrested me, rammed the case through, and tossed me down here. Since then, I've just been trying to figure out how to keep my head attached to my body."

Some color had returned to Noah's face, and his expression had calmed down, a clear indication that his mind was working overtime. Mark didn't rush him, letting Noah process his thoughts.

"We have a couple avenues that we can pursue," Noah said eventually. "My family has considerable influence, and I might be able to pull some strings to get you assigned as a bodyguard. It's not unheard of that noble families use reformed prisoners, which is really just a code word for people from the Tomb who are too valuable to let die."

"That's a dead end," Mark said, shaking his head. "One thing I didn't mention is that your dad already offered me that option, and I turned him down."

A flash of fury raced through Noah's eyes, but it quickly vanished. "That sounds exactly like my father. In fact, the more I think about it, the more likely it is that he was the one who engineered your plight in the first place."

Taking a deep breath, Noah spoke in a calm and measured voice, but Mark could tell his friend was only a hair's breadth away from exploding. "My father has been making a concerted effort to separate me from everyone I know. He preaches ideals that I do not agree with and has been desperately trying to convince me that friends are not worth my time. His motto these days has been 'Use, don't give.' If you've already turned him down, then you're right. That's a dead end. But it's not the only path we can take. You mentioned that you might end up coming back to the surface, to New Emery. Can you tell me a little bit more about that?"

"I'm not sure it's something I'm supposed to talk about," Mark said, shaking his head.

"Don't worry. Nobody can hear us in here. These rooms are specially designed to allow for negotiations between noble families and potential bodyguards. Considering that the vast majority of deals end up with the exchange of something unsavory, the nobles don't want their agreements tracked."

Sweeping the room once more, Mark still didn't detect any sort of observation devices, so he explained what he knew. "According to Winter Wolf, who's the leader of my team, we're a hit squad, dealing with individuals New Emery doesn't like, which, if I had to guess, means people who get on your dad's bad side."

"I had wondered what was going on," Noah said, sitting back in his chair. He chewed on his lip for a few seconds and then sighed. "It made no sense that people were disappearing into thin air. But if the teams attacking them were coming from the Tomb, well, it'd be easy to hide their tracks. After all, this place doesn't exist. And who would believe that the attacking teams were coming up from underground? This makes a lot of sense. Don't do anything drastic for now. I'll make some calls and see if there's a way to leverage this new position of yours."

Glancing down at his watch, Noah sighed. "We're running out of time. But if anybody asks, I'm trying to recruit you as a bodyguard."

Seeing Noah was about to get up, Mark held out a hand to stop him. "Before you go, have you heard anything about Master Abrams?"

From the way the skin around Noah's eyes tightened, Mark knew the answer, and his heart plummeted into his stomach. Hesitantly, Noah nodded. "Master Abrams passed away," he said.

Even though he had half expected that answer, Noah's words sent a shock through Mark, and his breath caught in his throat.

Mark stood up from his chair, reaching out to touch the thick glass as Noah continued. "The official narrative is that he died of old age. There was a funeral for him, and he was buried in the Martyrs' Cemetery with first honors."

"Did you see his body?" Mark asked quietly.

Shaking his head, Noah rose to his feet as well. "I didn't, but his warehouse was seized by the council and turned over to a couple of different businesses. Jason's restaurant has been shut down, and I haven't been able to find him. Things have been getting tense."

Calming his surging emotions, Mark dropped his hand to his side. "Thanks for telling me."

"It's only right you should know," Noah replied with an uncomfortable shrug. "Once we get you out of here, I'll show you where his grave is. Until then, stay alive."

Watching as Noah adjusted his coat and walked out of the room, Mark slowly sat back down in his chair, waiting in silence to be let out. It was clear he had missed much during his time trapped down in the Tomb, and though he wanted nothing more than to rush back to the surface to find out what had happened to his master, Mark knew he didn't have a choice but to remain where he was. Sorrow gripped his heart, bringing a pain that reminded him of the cold claws of an Exlian, but it soon gave way to deep, burning anger that threatened to overwhelm his mind. When the door opened behind him, Mark rose, leaving behind deep dents on the chair's armrests where his fingers had been squeezing.

To try to still the turmoil he was feeling, Mark threw himself into his training with such intensity that he earned himself more than one strange look from the others. He divided his time in the training room between trying to gain better control of his abilities and fighting brutal brawls with Winter Wolf.

Since she wouldn't let him spar with Joker, and Servo and Coral were no match for him in a one-on-one fight, Winter Wolf was forced to take Mark on herself, and their fights became increasingly dangerous as Mark stretched the limits of his abilities. When he wasn't fighting, he meditated on his null field ability, trying over and over again to figure out ways to manipulate the energy. His ability to see and control mana was of absolutely no use, and more than once he nearly gave up.

Yet each time he decided it was impossible and he should focus on something else, he was drawn back to the problem. Eventually, he changed his goal, trying to control the distance the null field spread from his body rather than project it.

It took a tremendous amount of mental control to keep the null field close, and more than once, his concentration slipped, causing the ability to swiftly expand to its full range. Anytime it did, Coral, who was practicing nearby, would lose control of all the water around her, drenching the ground. A couple of times, Servo was caught in the bubble as well, causing his suit to lose power momentarily. Each time, Mark made sure to withdraw his ability as fast as possible to ensure the disruptions weren't that significant.

Despite the difficulty, Mark's consistent practice soon paid off. He started to learn the trick of keeping his null field right around his body. This piqued his interest in seeing whether he could do the same with his mana shield. He began to practice, forcing the ability to activate.

It quickly became apparent that doing so was not only difficult but also a tremendous drain on his energy levels. *Unlike* when he wasn't thinking about it and the shield would activate naturally, blocking anything that came close that could potentially harm him. What Mark found fascinating was that the ability seemed to be able to discern what was dangerous and what wasn't. His mana shield would manifest to block a knife, no matter how slowly it approached his skin, but not a pat on his shoulder. Of course, the mana shield wasn't foolproof. More than once, Winter Wolf managed to trick it by reaching out with what seemed like harmless fingers and then manifesting ice spikes as soon as she touched Mark's skin.

Since he no longer was running the alchemical warehouse directly, when Mark wasn't at the training room, he spent his time continuing to practice through meditation, and occasionally, he would go down to the Cradle for checkups with Maestro. During one of those visits, Mark asked if there was a way to learn to control his abilities better.

"Specifically, the glitch ability," he said.

He was sitting on the side of the examination table after a rigorous two-hour exam, during which Maestro had cut multiple chunks of flesh from his body to test both his regeneration and the conditions for activating the mana shield. It had been exceptionally painful, but Mark bore it, mostly because he simply didn't have another choice.

Considering Mark's question, Maestro used his robotic arms to manipulate a machine that was currently synthesizing a new serum for Mark. "Control, huh? In truth, we don't know much about glitches, but I do know that some people can learn to control such powers. It seems to be a bit random, but from my preliminary research, I'd wager it has something to do with the mind. I know you're already doing will training with your team, and that's probably where I would focus. The problem is that null energy can't be manipulated via mana, which is how abilities work, so you'll have to figure out another way to give the null field commands."

Nodding, Mark thought about his recent training and then decided to bring up the problem he had been struggling with.

"The main issue I'm facing," he said, hoping he wouldn't regret disclosing his idea to Maestro, "is that when my glitch activates, it normally activates around me, and when that happens, my mana shield doesn't work, so the two abilities clash. Of course, I still have my regeneration to back it up, but it would be great if I could use both my glitch and shield abilities simultaneously."

Though Maestro's facial expression didn't change, the legs of his chair bounced up and down quickly, producing a rapid tapping noise. "And this is exactly why I am so excited to work with you, Mark. You're correct—such a combination would be incredible, nigh unstoppable, so long as your physical abilities grew as well. You're what, edging into the B rank in terms of your stats? You know, as an aside, it's pretty incredible that you've made it this far considering where your potential was ranked during the assessment. But then, their equipment is outdated and hardly accurate. The more I study your body, the more I understand that it is a treasure trove of new discoveries."

Mark was starting to regret speaking up, but now it was too late, so he could only try to smile and nod along.

Turning his chair toward the machine, Maestro grabbed the serum and turned back to Mark. "This will help stabilize some of the side effects from absorbing Exlian cells. You'll want to take half now and half tomorrow. By that point, you shouldn't have any issues with rejection."

Mark hadn't had any side effects after Mime had helped him destroy the echo of the war bear, but he still took the potion and dutifully swallowed half of it.

"To answer your question, though, it's not a matter of biology but rather the mind. Unfortunately, I don't have anything that will allow your control of your abilities to improve. I will say, though, that the greater your physical attributes, the easier such control will likely be. That said, your mental control, represented by the willpower stat, is something you'll have to develop independently."

It was a frustrating answer to hear but also, to some extent, reassuring. Ever since he had swallowed the Exlian nest, Mark had been able to feel his willpower growing stronger, and every time his physical stats increased, his willpower jumped up as well. It appeared that each stat had an effect on the others, making it incredibly hard to raise one without also improving the other three.

Though it was going to be slow and laborious, Mark did at least have a path forward, namely increasing his physical stats as much as possible. Currently, he was fairly sure that most of them were in the low B range, and his fights against Winter Wolf had demonstrated clearly just how much of a gap there was between A-ranked stats and his low B-ranked stats. This meant he had a tremendous amount of space to improve.

After leaving the Cradle, Mark headed for the training room, where he met up with the others. Rather than start their normal training session, however, Winter Wolf brought Mark to a warehouse filled with all manner of gear. A number of robots were working quietly among the shelves, organizing all the items, and a grizzled prisoner with a large potbelly perched on a stool behind a counter. When he saw Winter Wolf come in, he quickly straightened up, flashing a smile that revealed his broken teeth.

Wasting no time, Winter Wolf jerked a thumb at Mark. "Got a new team member to outfit."

Getting up from his stool, the prisoner looked Mark over carefully, his forehead furrowing. "I thought you guys lost a melee fighter, but he looks a lot more like a scout."

"Looks can be deceiving. You should know that better than anyone, Paul."

With a sheepish smile, Paul scratched his cheek and nodded. "That's true. All right, what sort of gear do you want?"

Instead of answering, Winter Wolf gestured for Mark to step forward. Mark knew he was going to be taking on a frontline role in the new team, acting as both a tank to absorb enemy damage and a damage dealer. At the same time, considering that they'd be operating quietly, he needed to ensure that he had gear for infiltration. Rather than try to come up with a comprehensive list, Mark turned the problem over to Paul, explaining the role he had been assigned to. This earned him an appraising glance from both Winter Wolf and Paul.

"Sure, I got some stuff that might suit you. Come along."

Following the potbellied prisoner back into the warehouse, Mark heard Paul call out a steady stream of codes. Every time one left his mouth, the robots would hurry to a specific position on the shelves. Soon, a small pile of gear materialized in front of Mark, and as the robots brought the last few items over, Paul began to introduce everything.

"Given the nature of what you're doing, you're not going to be assigned a mana suit, unfortunately, since that would make all of this a lot easier. But you'd be too conspicuous, so instead we're going to go with a standard set of combat gear. First, armored jacket, pants, and boots. There's no mana reinforcement, but you do have a weave that'll stop most blades. Second, standard-issue vest to carry your gear. Third, mana blades. We've got a couple different kinds here. You can decide what you want. For breaking and entering gear, we have a full kit, including smart rope, a glass cutter, wedges, spikes, a number of other things. You can explore this at your leisure, and Joker can show you how to use them, if you don't already know. Next, we've got a variety of masks. You can pick any one you like, or you can use your own. To go with them, communication devices. This is a secure band that only works with the other members of the team. It's locked to that channel. Don't even try to shift it to another. All right, let's see. What else do we have here?"

Rifling through the gear, Paul spotted a short rod, and his eyes lit up. "Oh, right. Death stick." Lifting it carefully, he showed it to

Mark, pointing out the button on one end. "Press this up against your skin, hit the button, and you'll be dead within a few seconds."

Taken aback, Mark looked at the device and then looked at Winter Wolf, whose face was impassive.

"If you get captured, it's better to end up dead." Her voice was cold but serious and gave Mark pause.

Reaching out, he took the rod from Paul and examined it carefully, noting the small hole where he assumed a needle would stab out once the button was triggered. Noticing how gingerly he was holding it, Paul laughed. "You don't have to worry about it right now. It's not actually active until you're outside the Tomb. But once you are, be careful with it. It's naturally capped, so unless you deliberately press the button, it's not going to work. Just make sure you're holding it flush against your skin. Otherwise, the needle won't penetrate."

Scratching his cheek, Paul looked at the pile of gear. "I think that's about it. Everything else should be relatively straightforward and self-explanatory. If you have any questions, you can ask Winter Wolf or one of the others. Go ahead and gear up. We'll make sure everything fits properly."

Carefully putting down the suicide rod, Mark got the rest of the gear on. It reminded him of what he had worn when raiding the mercenary base with Noah. And that got him thinking about his friends and wondering if Noah had managed to figure out a way for him to escape.

Once he was all dressed, Mark let Paul fuss over him for a few minutes, adjusting the various straps to ensure that everything fit. Noticing that Winter Wolf kept checking her watch, Paul quickly finished and patted Mark's shoulder. "There you go, all outfitted. Anything else you need?"

"No, this should be good," Winter Wolf said. "Come, it's time to get going."

When they returned to the training room, Mark saw that the others were already outfitted, wearing similar black uniforms. While he chatted with the others, Winter Wolf disappeared to dress in her own gear. When she emerged, the others fell silent and quietly followed as she led the way to a small room.

"I hate this part," Servo said heavily, looking with distaste at the metal walls.

The room was barely more than six feet wide and only about eight feet long. Made of smooth metal, it was more like a box. After the door shut behind them, Mark suddenly felt a rapid acceleration. He had assumed they were walking into a normal room, but it turned out to be a special elevator.

For the next half an hour, they rose steadily through the ground. When they finally arrived, the door opened up and the others walked out, with Mark following last. The first thing he noticed was the sense of oppression in the air, and the second thing was the fifteen mana-suited soldiers watching them warily from the edges of the room. Mark and his teammates were only dressed in their tactical gear and didn't look nearly as imposing as the soldiers did. Yet it was obvious that the soldiers were much more afraid of Mark's team than vice versa.

One of the soldiers took a step forward and held up his hand. "Stop there."

When Winter Wolf complied, the others did too, and with considerable relief, the soldier continued. "Special Agent Callaghan has your mission details. She'll be in in just a second."

With a sharp nod, Winter Wolf turned and scanned the team, her eyes lingering on Joker for a long moment before passing on to Mark. "Special Agent Callaghan is our handler, or at least one of them. She's the only one who talks to us, so don't waste your time trying to speak to the others."

The door hissed open, causing a few of the guards to shift

nervously at the unfamiliar sound, and a woman dressed in a mana suit walked into the room, leading a team of six others. Unlike the soldiers, who wore the heavy knight suits of the Defense Force, the special agent was dressed in a sleek black mana suit that appeared to focus more on stealth than brute force.

Struck by a sudden temptation to unleash his null field, Mark drew in a slow breath, calming himself down. He still had no idea where he was, and until he was out in the city, it was unlikely that he'd be able to escape. Rather than giving away his advantage on impulse, he decided it would be better to bide his time.

"April! It's so good to see you again!"

As he called out, Joker stepped forward, his arms stretching toward Special Agent Callaghan, who didn't hesitate for even a second before tapping her wrist. Mark felt a flare of mana and saw Joker jerk as the shackles on his wrists and ankles unleashed a powerful electric shock. Instinctively, Joker tried to muster his ability, but the activated shackles prevented it, and instead he flopped to the floor, losing control of his muscles as electricity coursed through him. Special Agent Callaghan, ignoring Joker's twitching body, stopped in front of Winter Wolf. As she peered through her darkened faceplate, it was clear that the special agent wasn't happy to see any of them.

"Hello, Special Agent," Winter Wolf greeted with a slight bow, which Callaghan didn't bother returning.

"Your mission is simple," the special agent said, still ignoring Joker, who was writhing on the floor. "There is an entertainer who has been caught taking advantage of his position to abuse the trust of the city. The office believes that he's being manipulated by seditious groups. You're going to invite him down to the Tomb for a conversation. You'll find all the information you need has been sent to your watches."

Hearing a muffled groan near her foot, Special Agent

Callaghan tapped her wrist, and Joker's shackles finally deactivated. Panting heavily, he started to get to his feet, and one of the other special agents took a quick step forward. The kick caught Joker in the chest, flipping him over and sending him tumbling across the floor.

Mark started to move, but Winter Wolf's hand clamped down on his shoulder, keeping him in place. Realizing that Special Agent Callaghan was staring at him, Mark felt a cold sweat break out on his neck. He had no doubt that if Winter Wolf hadn't stopped him, he would have ended up on the floor as well.

"Your new member?" Callaghan asked, still staring at Mark.

Though he, like the others, wore a mask that covered his whole face, Mark had a suspicion Special Agent Callaghan could see right through him, and he did his best to appear meek. He had already been warned about the handler's dislike for them, and watching from the corner of his eye as Joker struggled to his feet, helped up by Servo, Mark knew better than to step out of line.

Clicking her tongue as if disappointed, Special Agent Callaghan turned and led the way out of the room. The six agents she had brought with her spread out, forming a loose net around the team as they entered what appeared to be an underground garage. A large van was waiting for them, and after piling into the back, they took off.

Seeing that Winter Wolf was studiously reading the details that had been sent over, Mark scanned them as well, his forehead furrowing the further he read. It appeared that the target was an actor, one Mark had seen in a number of different shows. Though the mission report did not explain why the actor was being targeted, it didn't take long for Mark to catch the abnormalities. The first thing he noticed was that the mansion where the actor was staying was heavily guarded. According to the report, there were fourteen guards, including three empowered. It was rare for public figures to have such strong security details, which seemed to indicate that the actor was hiding something.

The first few minutes of their journey passed in silence before Winter Wolf sighed and shut her virtual screen. "All right, has everybody had a chance to look over the details?"

Hearing no one say otherwise, she continued, her voice heavy, "He's got entirely too much security. And the three empowered he hired are members of a mercenary team of fifteen. If they manage to sound an alarm, we're gonna be in for a rough fight. So we need to do this as quickly and quietly as possible."

Looking up from her watch, Coral raised a hand. "Are we sure that this guy's actually bad? I mean, what if he's just paranoid?"

"Nothing to do with us," Joker said with a shrug, a dagger appearing briefly between his fingers. "The only shame is that we're not trying to kill him. I hate these capture missions. It's so much easier just to eliminate everybody."

"But we're not going to," Winter Wolf said in a frosty voice, glaring at Joker. "We're going to run this one according to the mission."

"Fine, I get it. You don't have to glare at me like that. But what about the guards?"

Hesitating for a moment, Winter Wolf shook her head briefly and made a slashing motion across her neck.

"Ha, that's more like it," Joker said, his eyes sparkling from behind his mask. "I call dibs on the three empowered."

"It'll take too long. We need to take them out as quickly and quietly as possible. Try not to touch the nonempowered guards if you can. Joker, you'll take one of the empowered. I'll take the other, and Mark, you're on the third. Servo, I want you to set up and jam all communication in and out of the mansion. Coral, you're snagging our target. Can you do it?"

"Yes, though if he has a panic button, it might be a problem."

"I can handle the panic button," Servo said, "as long as I have a couple minutes."

"Good. Once we're there, we'll move quickly. Joker, Mark, you'll be with me. Remember, if we have to go loud, there can be no witnesses."

Trying his best not to think about what they were about to do, Mark nodded, and the rest of the ride passed in silence. The mansion was located on the outskirts of the downtown district and consisted of a large building surrounded by a garden thick with trees to give the mansion privacy. There was a heavy wall around the entire property, and after the van pulled up, Winter Wolf led Mark, Joker, and Coral over it swiftly, while Servo stayed behind.

Hopping over the wall, Mark took a moment to get used to the dim light. Nighttime, and though the lights of Center City were bright, he could still see a few stars overhead. Their twinkle sent a thrill racing through him and produced an ache in his heart that he didn't know what to do with. Such a small thing, to be able to look up and see stars . . . But even that had been forcibly stripped away by Mark's unknown enemies. The sight only deepened the ache in his heart and made him desire to once more look out over the wilderness.

"Let's go."

Hearing Winter Wolf's command, Mark moved forward quietly.

Joker floated along like a wraith next to him, and Coral moved with smooth steps that left wisps of water behind.

Feeling a faint vibration on his wrist, Mark looked down and saw Servo had uploaded a map that was updating in real time, captured by the small flying disks that Servo had launched into the air. They were approaching the east side of the mansion, and Mark saw a couple of figures moving on the wide porch. Calling for them to stop, Winter Wolf sent a quick message.

"Two guards chatting on the porch. Our target is going to be on the top floor and should be asleep. We haven't located the three empowered guards yet, but I'd suspect they're close by our target's location."

Waiting quietly, Mark watched as Joker and Winter Wolf crept forward to incapacitate the two chatting guards. They were completely oblivious and had no idea what was about to happen to them.

With the way cleared, Mark and Coral crept up onto the wide stone porch and made their way to the large windows that ran the length of the building. Checking the door, Winter Wolf found it was locked and reached for her glass cutter. Wary that breaking the glass might alert their target, Mark touched Winter Wolf's arm lightly, gesturing for her to wait.

She looked at him oddly but still shuffled aside as he approached the door. Grabbing the handle, Mark closed his eyes and focused, sending his mind into the lock. Though it had mechanical components, including the bolt itself, this lock, like most others, was mana driven, which made it susceptible to Mark's abilities.

Using his mana control, Mark fiddled with the lock for a moment, and then there was a soft click as the bolt disengaged. Carefully, so as not to make a noise, he turned the handle and slid the door open. He was just about to enter when he realized that the others were staring at him, clearly caught off guard. They were all wearing masks, so he couldn't quite see their expressions, but he could tell from their body language that they were quite surprised. After a moment Winter Wolf gave Mark a short nod, and together they crept inside. Almost immediately, Mark noticed the cameras pointed at them. But when he paused and looked up at one, he realized that whatever Servo was doing to jam the communications in and out of the mansion, it had turned off the cameras as well.

On quiet feet, the team made its way up to the top floor, avoiding two other guards who were idly patrolling the halls. Now that she knew Mark could open locked doors, Winter Wolf put him to work, taking a circuitous route that kept them entirely out of sight. It only took five minutes for them to make it to the door of their target's bedroom. Mark used his connection to the Exlian psychic network to scan the area.

Noticing that he wasn't moving, Winter Wolf gestured, but Mark still didn't get to work. He had located the empowered guards, who were positioned in the rooms on either side of their target. Though Mark was confident he could open the lock, he wasn't confident about doing so silently, which meant there was a chance that it would kick off a fight. As he updated the enemy's location on their map, he earned himself another curious glance from Winter Wolf. To his surprise, however, she didn't question him and instead circled the map's representation of the room with two empowered guards, sending him and Joker to take care of them. Entirely too eagerly, Joker hurried to the door and gestured for Mark, clearly impatient to start fighting.

Glancing over his shoulder, Mark saw that Winter Wolf had set up at the door to the other room where the third guard was, and Coral was waiting to enter their target's room. At Winter Wolf's command, Mark undid the lock and threw the door open, catching the two empowered inside off guard. One of them was watching a show, facing away from the door, and failed to hear them enter at all, while the other, who had just stood up to stretch, froze, his eyes widening.

The guard's mouth opened, but a blade buried itself deep in his throat, cutting off the words he was about to say. Mark jumped forward even as a soft alarm rang out, likely triggered by Joker's use of his teleportation power. Before Mark could cross the distance, Joker had already appeared next to the second guard's seat, another dagger appearing in his hand and stabbing into the guard's temple.

Mark heard a muffled thud from another room as Joker wrenched his dagger free and spun it, causing blood to splatter across the room. Turning, Joker couldn't hide his excitement, and Mark took a step back. For a moment, he thought that Joker might launch an attack at him, but then his unpredictable teammate seemed to calm down. With the two guards dead, Mark and Joker quickly retreated to the hall, where they found Winter Wolf and Coral, who was carrying an unconscious man over her shoulder.

"Is that our target?" Joker asked, bending down to get a good look at the unconscious man's face.

"Yes." Winter Wolf opened her mouth to say something else, but before she could, Servo's voice echoed in everyone's ear.

"You've got incoming. Whoever used their power set off an alarm, and the rest of the mercenary group is on their way. You've got less than a minute."

Shooting a swift glare at Joker, Winter Wolf pulled up her map of the mansion and groaned. "They're coming from the front gate. They must have been stationed nearby. We'll go out the back and cut across the garden. I'll escort Coral to the van. Joker, Apex, the two of you will run cover for us. Do your best to slow them down, but don't engage. The last thing we need is to get caught up in a major fight like last time."

Even as she spoke, Winter Wolf was already moving, and the others followed her back into the bedroom. It was large and opulent, with gilt-edged wallpaper decorating every inch of it. Heavy, luxurious wooden furniture, inlaid with precious stones that glittered in the faint moonlight, spoke to just how much money the actor had.

Racing over to the balcony, Winter Wolf didn't bother with stealth anymore, her foot smashing the lock as she broke through the doors. Reaching back, she grabbed Coral and leaped from the third-story balcony. Just before she hit the ground, ice rose to catch her, and she slid along it into the forest.

"It's always impressive every time I see it," Joker said to Mark, before he, too, jumped off the balcony. The madman fell through the air for a second and then vanished, appearing fifteen feet ahead in a flat-out run.

Not sure if he'd be able to withstand a three-story drop like the other two had, Mark opted to jump from the balcony to the side of the building, catching himself on the windowsill. Letting go, he dropped down to the second-story window, then jumped to a railing of the wide porch below. As soon as his foot touched it, he threw himself forward, transferring the majority of his momentum as he hit the ground in a roll. He could feel bruises form on his back, but they quickly healed as he raced forward.

The others had already disappeared into the forest, and Mark followed swiftly. As he passed between two trees, he felt his senses tingling and quickly ducked his head. With a hiss, a blade buried itself in one of the trees. Mark's reaction was instantaneous; he activated his null field as he lunged up from his crouch, his fist slamming into Joker's side, sending his teammate tumbling. There was a hint of surprise in Joker's eyes as he struggled to his feet, lifting a hand to keep Mark from attacking again.

"Sorry," Joker wheezed. "I got a bit too excited, thought you were one of the enemy."

Mark didn't buy it for a second, but there was no time, as he could sense that the mercenaries were quickly closing in on their position. Leaving Joker gasping for breath, Mark moved farther into the woods. As he did, he pulled his mental energy around him, doing his best to shroud himself as he had seen Mime do before.

It took some concentration, but it seemed to work, and he felt his shadow starting to merge with the darkness around him. It wasn't nearly as strong as it would have been if Mime had been the one doing it. But it was good enough: An empowered mercenary burst through the trees nearby and ran straight past Mark without seeing him.

The empowered was moving quickly, heading in the direction of the van, where Winter Wolf and Coral were loading their unconscious target. But Mark was even faster, launching himself at the mercenary's exposed back. At the last second, the mercenary, realizing he was under assault, spun around, swinging a mana blade in his right hand, while his left hand was wreathed in flames.

Mark blocked the mana blade, deflecting it with a jab, and thrust two fingers toward his opponent's heart. Sneering, the mercenary shoved his burning palm forward, only for his eyes to widen as Mark's fingers stabbed straight through his palm, pressing his hand back to pierce into his chest. Mark's momentum carried him inside his opponent's range, and his other hand flashed, slicing the mercenary's neck. As the mercenary started to collapse, Mark grabbed his opponent's body and commanded his shadow to envelop it, before rushing farther into the woods.

A few seconds later, Joker appeared, sprinting along beside him. Though not quite as fast as Mark, Joker made up for it by teleporting every few steps. It wasn't long before the two of them had reached the wall. Joker teleported through, while Mark vaulted over it and landed lightly on the roof of the van. There was a thud from inside, and the van took off, nearly knocking Mark loose. His fingers pierced into the metal roof, and he swung himself over the back before opening the door and slipping inside.

Feeling the tension in the air, Mark took a seat quietly, his eyes darting between Winter Wolf and Joker. Though he expected Winter Wolf to explode, the entire ride passed in silence. The van drove for almost half an hour before turning and heading underground, likely entering a garage. Mark was pretty sure that it wasn't the same one they had left before, and after the van had turned off and the doors had opened, he saw Special Agent Callaghan and the others waiting for them. Two of the special agents hauled away their prisoner, and Callaghan tapped her wrist, reactivating the shackles. Feeling the uncomfortable web of energy running through him, Mark took a deep breath, pushing the discomfort aside.

"Well done," Callaghan said. "You can head down below."

Joker seemed to want to say something, but before he could, Winter Wolf silenced him with a glare, and the five of them headed back into the small metal elevator that was waiting. As the door hissed shut, the tension was thick enough to cut with a knife.

"Look, it's not my fault," Joker said. "They caught sight of us as soon as we entered the room. I didn't have a choice but to use my power. Apex can confirm it. There were simply no other options."

His words seemed to cause Winter Wolf's restraint to snap, and she spun, her arm shooting out and wrapping around Joker's neck before anybody could react. At the same time, the temperature in the elevator plummeted, dropping so rapidly that the metal walls began to warp, and ice began to form in the air with every breath.

"The last time you did something foolish like this, we lost a teammate," Winter Wolf said through clenched teeth, "and I swore that if you did it again, you'd owe me your head."

Though Joker clearly wanted to respond, his airway was

completely obstructed, and he couldn't do more than wave his arms, his teeth chattering. As the cold continued to intensify, Mark was about to activate his null field when he saw Servo place a large hand on Winter Wolf's wrist.

"What is done is done. It's not worth fighting about, especially in such close quarters. I don't know about you, but I don't fancy dying in an elevator."

With supreme effort, Winter Wolf got herself back under control and let go of Joker's neck. She took a deep breath, and all the cold vanished as if it had been sucked up into her lungs.

"Someday, calmer heads won't be around," she said, still glaring at Joker.

Her threat hung in the air for the rest of the ride, and Joker barely moved once, his eyes never leaving Winter Wolf. Shuffling into the corner to get as far away from both of them as possible, Mark lamented his life until the elevator finally reached its destination. The door opened, and Winter Wolf stalked out, not saying a word as she left. Coral hurried after her, leaving the three men in the elevator. With a sigh, Servo gestured for Mark to go ahead. "I'll make sure Joker gets treatment."

It was only then that Mark realized that Joker had been frozen to the wall of the elevator, genuinely unable to move. With a new appreciation for just how powerful an A-ranked energy controller was, Mark nodded and left the elevator, heading out of the training center and back toward his apartment.

Mark was so busy thinking through everything he had just experienced that he failed to notice the woman stepping out of the alleyway in front of him until he had almost run into her. At the last moment, he paused and then quickly stepped back, staying at arm's length. He recognized her immediately: the strange woman who had stopped him previously to inform him that someone named the Prophet wanted to meet with him.

This time, she didn't have anybody with her, and when Mark noticed her, she bowed. "The Prophet respectfully wishes for your presence. Would you be able to spare some time to come and meet him?"

Still rather unsettled, Mark immediately shook his head, but the woman persisted. "I understand your hesitation. However, it is very important that you meet the Prophet."

"If the Prophet would like to meet me, he can just come and meet me," Mark said, his eyes narrowing.

To his surprise, the woman shook her head. "Unfortunately, the Prophet cannot, though he has expressed that he would very much like to. The Prophet does not live in the Tomb."

Something about the way she said it and the way her eyes flicked upward gave Mark pause. "If he doesn't live in the Tomb, then where is he?"

Silently, the woman pointed up toward the surface, where Mark had just been.

"It is the Prophet's great desire to meet you in person, but for the moment, a virtual screen will have to suffice," the woman said, correctly identifying Mark's question.

"I thought it was impossible to set up a connection with the surface."

"It is impossible for most, but I have a way of circumnavigating it. Please, allow me to connect you with the Prophet."

"I told you I'm not interested," Mark said, waving his hand. "Don't bother me again."

Without another word, he walked around the woman and continued on his way home. When he had reached the end of the block, he looked back over his shoulder, but the woman was gone, and with a shrug, he headed for his apartment and, more importantly, his bed.

He had just lain down when he got a message informing him they would gather the next morning for their mission debrief. Mark felt trepidation. But when he arrived, he found both Winter Wolf and Joker pretending nothing had happened. The only sign of any issue was the faint cold burns on the backs of Joker's hands.

Sitting at a small table in a room by the arena, Winter Wolf called up the details of their mission. "For our first mission as a new team, we did fine. Despite some clearly avoidable mistakes, everything was executed well. More importantly, Servo found some interesting information."

Servo stood clumsily, resting his hands on the table as he nodded to everyone. With a swipe of his fingers, he pulled up a virtual screen, revealing an image of the man they had kidnapped.

"While you guys were breaking in, I did a bit of digging. As I was jamming their systems, I managed to crack into the data vault in the mansion. There was enough dirt inside to get our target locked away for years. Most of it seemed to be blackmail. My guess is either he blackmailed the wrong person, or the people he was blackmailing decided they had had enough, which is why we were called in."

Sitting back in his chair, Mark glanced around, watching the faces of everyone else at the table. Joker looked bored, as usual. Winter Wolf had an impassive expression; she had likely seen the information before. Coral, on the other hand, looked relieved, and Mark guessed that their mission had been weighing on her.

He wasn't quite sure how he felt, which was unnerving in and of itself. He had to admit his belief in the goodness of humanity had been eroding quickly, even before he had been thrown down in the Tomb. And at the moment, it was at an all-time low. He was surrounded by murderers and madmen, and the people who controlled them were clearly no better. At the same time, just how unaffected he was by their mission the previous night left him feeling unsettled. He had killed one of the mercenaries without blinking, never questioning whether it was the right thing or the wrong thing to do. Then again, in the heat of battle, he was sure that the mercenary would have returned the favor, had he been strong enough to do it.

Of course, this wasn't a new struggle. Ever since his powers had awoken, he had been fighting against the gradual deadening of his emotions and his new disregard for human life. It was a fight that he was clearly losing. Whatever instincts Mark was operating on had only been reinforced by his time in the Tomb . . . which left him fearing he would soon become just another cold and calculating killer.

Realizing Joker was staring at him, Mark shifted his gaze away, but not before Joker grinned and winked.

Their meeting didn't last much longer, and as they finished, Mark's shackles beeped, and he felt the restrictive mana web fade away. Looking over with a grin, Servo gave Mark a thumbs-up. "Congratulations, you're officially a conductor."

"Thanks, I guess," Mark said, flexing his wrists as he looked down at the now-deactivated shackles.

"Word will spread soon, and people will start avoiding you," Joker said. "So if there's anybody you want to kill, you better do it now, before they go into hiding."

"Don't pay any attention to him," Winter Wolf said, shaking her head. "It's now more important than ever that you avoid fighting."

"Oh, come on, it's not like there's anything they could do to him. We're already at the bottom of the heap, and besides cutting his head off, there's not much they can do to punish him. Besides, given his regeneration, it'll probably just grow right back. Actually, now I'm really curious . . ."

As he spoke, a knife appeared in Joker's hand, and he leaned forward slightly, insane eyes burning bright. Mark raised his eyebrows but otherwise didn't respond, instead turning to Winter Wolf. "Am I allowed to practice my mana control in my apartment?"

Having failed to get a reaction, Joker huffed and sat back in his seat, crossing his arms over his chest as his knife disappeared. Winter Wolf, quite pleased at Joker's annoyance, nodded. "Just don't do it out in public and you'll be fine. Any of the training rooms or your apartment will work."

"All right, thanks."

"Of course. That's it for today's mission. I've no idea when the next one will come, so we'll run it like normal. We'll take a week off, except for Joker. You and I have some training to do on your emotional control. Anyone else who wants to train is welcome to, but I won't expect to see you back until the break is over. Unless, of course, another mission comes up."

When Mark walked out of the training room, he paused for a moment, his eyes turning up toward the deep darkness above. Thanks to the lights from the Tomb, he could see the solid earth that hung over their heads, and a choked feeling rose in his chest, carrying with it a deep, dark anger. Up until this point, he had been able to suppress it, to keep his anger and frustration at the injustice of his situation in check. But having tasted the sweet, fresh air of New Emery again, he found it much harder to contain his anger.

As he took a deep breath to calm himself, his thoughts flashed to Noah. It hadn't been long, in the grand scheme of things, since his friend had told him that he'd help Mark find a way out. But already, Mark was starting to grow antsy. Forcing his mind into a state of calm, he slowly made his way back toward his apartment, only to find the strange woman who had spoken to him the day before standing in front of it.

The slow rumble of anger that had been building in him threatened to explode, and he could hear a dark voice in the back of his head screaming at him to tear her throat out for daring to bother him again. Instead, Mark curled his twitching fingers into a fist and stopped a dozen feet away.

"It'd be really good if you could stop bothering me," he said quietly, "for my sake and for yours."

The woman looked at him for a moment and then shook her head. "I'm very sorry, but I cannot. The Prophet needs to meet you."

"Will you stop bothering me after I meet him?" Mark said after a long moment of silence.

"Yes."

"Regardless of the outcome?"

"Yes."

"Fine. Then lead the way, and I'll see your prophet. But don't blame me if the outcome isn't to your liking."

With a relieved smile, the woman quickly bowed and gestured

for Mark to follow, leading him through the streets until they reached the outskirts of the Tomb. There, she led him into a dark maze of passages, similar in many ways to the labyrinth of hallways he had run through in Viper Clan's territory.

Finally, she stopped at a T-junction and pressed the wall directly in front of them, and it slid aside, revealing a hidden doorway. There was silence beyond, but Mark could sense that it was the silence of a suddenly stilled conversation, and when he stepped into the room after her, he found four bizarre people staring back at him.

One had a set of insectile eyes on his forehead. Another appeared to have partially transformed into a scaly lizard, while a third had an exceptionally long neck and a faint yellow-and-brown spotted pattern. The fourth looked the most human, with fair skin that sparkled every time she moved, as if covered in a faint shimmer of fairy dust. None of them seemed particularly strong, and they quickly retreated when they saw Mark, staring at him warily. The woman who had led Mark said something he couldn't make out and waved her hands, and the four quickly shuffled into the corner.

As the door slid shut behind them, hiding the room once more, the woman turned to Mark and bowed. "My name is Clara. I am one of the Prophet's messengers. Thank you for being willing to follow me."

Drawing a knife, Clara abruptly slashed her arm, releasing a spray of blood. Yet rather than fall to the ground, the blood began to morph, droplets spinning in the air in front of her to form a large mirror. Clara sagged, her face pale, as blood continued to drip from the wound. Each drop joined the others, causing the mirror to grow brighter and clearer. Finally, Clara sank to the ground. Immediately the man with the insect eyes rushed forward, wrapping Clara's wounded arm with a long strip of cloth he had just torn from his shirt. The others, clearly frightened of

Mark, crept forward to try to help, but the insect man waved them back with a hiss.

"Her dedication is commendable, is it not?"

Though the voice that emanated from the mirror was gentle, it still made Mark jump. He took a step back, gazing at the man who had just appeared on the blood mirror's surface.

"Clara is one of my most devoted servants, and you need not have any worry. Those who serve me prosper."

While the man spoke, Mark examined him closely. A strange familiarity hung around the man, but Mark couldn't place it no matter how he tried. Of average height, with dark hair and intense dark eyes, the man looked like one of the millions of workers that filled the streets of New Emery, going about their labors every day, working to keep the city running. If the man was offended by Mark's close scrutiny, he didn't show it. Instead, he quietly examined Mark in return.

"I wonder if you would be able to do something for me. There is something I would like to confirm, but it requires a drop of your blood. All you have to do is drip it onto the mirror."

With a shimmer, Mark's arms transformed into bone blades, and he cautiously took a step back, his eyes scanning the other people in the room.

The man in the mirror grimaced, holding up his hands. "I have no intention of forcing you. All I wish to do is verify that you are, in fact, the Savior."

"Okay, so you really are insane," Mark said, taking another step back.

Again, the man grimaced, shaking his head. "I'm sorry, my enthusiasm often gets the better of me. My name is Dallas. Most call me the Prophet of Salvation, for my rather unique ability. Like you, I am empowered. Like you, I am a special sort of empowered. My uniqueness has allowed me access to a realm no other human could dream of: the realm of time. And through my connection with time, I have seen a grand vision. A future in which human and Exlian no longer squabble. A future in which the world is brought to harmony."

"It's a nice thought, but far fetched. And what does it have to do with me?" Now standing by the door, Mark was ready to retreat through it at any moment.

Sensing this, the Prophet lowered his voice even further, speaking as calmly as he could. "While I am able to tap into the flow of time, peering ahead to see visions of what might be, there are others whose powers are different. Whose powers allow them to connect with their own kind. Clara is one of those. She has the unique ability to identify people whose powers share a similar source. Some years back, I had a dream. A dream that the Savior, the one who would lead us to the glorious future of unity, would appear from underground, clawing his way up through filth, yet untainted by it. As pure as the lotus that blooms from the muddy water, he would grow until he encompassed all things. Clara and other members of Salvation have been waiting in the Tomb for this day." Though Dallas was trying to keep his voice even, Mark could hear the faint tremble of intense excitement in his tone.

Tapping himself on the chest, Mark asked the question that had been bothering him up to this point. "Why do you say I'm this Savior? How do you know it's me? And what do you mean by unifying all things?"

Slowly, the fervor faded from the Prophet's gaze, and he gave a little half shrug, lifting only one shoulder. "There is much that I cannot tell you. There is much that you must learn on your own, lest the prophecy be left unfulfilled. However, as a thank-you for being willing to meet with me, for being willing to trust, Clara has something to give you."

As he glanced down at the woman, who was clearly only minutes away from death due to blood loss, Mark's jaw clenched. It didn't take a genius to figure out the play Dallas was making. Clearly he wanted Mark to help Clara, as there was no way in her present state she could give anything to Mark. Further, if he did heal her, it would create a psychological weak point for him, because he would be less willing to see her die in the future. As far as schemes went, it was simple and straightforward, and though annoyed, Mark couldn't help but appreciate it.

Keeping his eyes on the Prophet, Mark took out a potion, one he had already upgraded by mixing in a bit of his blood, and tossed it to the insect-eyed man. "Pour half of it on the wound; feed the other half to her."

Fumbling for the potion, the man with insect eyes hurried to comply, spilling a bit in his haste. Almost as soon as the potion was poured on the bloody gash, it began to knit back together, skin bonding with skin, until Clara's arm was just as smooth as it had been before she marred it. The rest of the potion was poured down her throat, and color soon returned to her face. Both Mark and the Prophet waited in silence, until Clara staggered to her feet. It took her a moment to figure out what was going on, but as soon as she did, she quickly bowed to Mark. "Thank you, Savior."

"Cut that out." Mark frowned. "We don't need any of that stuff. I'm not your savior."

Clara just turned toward the Prophet's mirror to give him a smaller bow.

"Serve the Savior as best you can," Dallas said, lifting his hand into the air and making a motion with it.

"Yes, Prophet."

Looking at Mark, Dallas smiled. "This blood mirror will fade soon, as the strength of Clara's blood is not yet of peak quality. She won't be able to form another blood mirror without dying, for at least a year, maybe two, but she can answer at least some of your questions. I'm sure you have many. As for me, I'll see you when you make your triumphant return to the surface."

With that, the Prophet clasped his hands together in front of him and bowed, leaving Mark with an ugly expression on his face as the drops of blood suddenly came apart, crashing to the ground. Just when he thought they would splash, they suddenly evaporated, transforming into mana that filled the air.

Clara, who was still slightly unsteady, leaned against the table as she faced Mark, doing her best to bow again.

"I said cut that out," Mark snapped, causing Clara to freeze. "I think it's high time somebody explained exactly what is going on."

Still holding on to the table, Clara nodded, clearly fighting off dizziness as she tried to focus on Mark. He pointed at one of the chairs the others had vacated, and with a grateful smile, she took her seat. Mark elected to stand, but not because he felt threatened. In fact, he couldn't help but wonder at just how weak the others seemed. His standing was rather to help him maintain his detachment from the whole situation. Once Clara had caught her breath, she half rose from her seat to bow once more before beginning to speak.

"We are the salvation of mankind, seeking true unity and peace in the world. Many years ago, the Prophet arose, speaking of his grand vision and the inevitable destruction of humanity."

Clara's gaze had taken on a faint fervency, and Mark saw from the corner of his eye that the others had similar expressions. Clearly, they believed what Clara was saying, with an intensity that made the hair on the back of his neck rise.

"In his wisdom, the Prophet found a path forward, a path that could lead humanity out of the darkness, into the great light, a path that could save us all. We are humanity's salvation. We are the ones ushering in the new age when humanity will no longer need fear the threat of the Exlian swarm but instead will be able to walk through this beautiful world freely."

Holding up his hand, Mark frowned irritably. "But what does this have to do with me? Or this so-called Savior figure?"

Far from being annoyed that Mark had interrupted her, Clara gazed at him with a smile blooming on her face. "The Prophet saw more than one vision, and in his vision, during the great wave, when humanity stands on the precipice, forced to choose between darkness and light, between continuing to reject the trend of the world and stepping forward to embrace it, a being appears. A being of tremendous power who can walk not only among the humans but among the Exlian as well, speaking to the souls of both with ease. A true king, born of one race but accepted by all. In the Prophet's vision, the Savior commands both human and Exlian forces, purging the world of darkness, eliminating those with selfish motivation who seek only to benefit themselves, and rebuilding this world into a world of peace."

By the time she finished, Clara was practically shouting, and tears had started to form in the corners of her eyes, leaving Mark unsure what to do. The whole thing was rather ludicrous and honestly made him quite uncomfortable. He had no desire to be a savior in anyone's insane prophecy. But it was obvious that both Clara and the others believed in it wholeheartedly. Glancing at the mutated humans, Mark rose to his feet, intending to make an excuse and leave. Before he could, the man with bug eyes caught his glance and stepped forward, dropping to his knees.

"Greetings, Savior," the man said, holding out his hands, almost as if praying.

The others quickly did the same, and Mark froze, his hands flat on the table in front of him, unsure what to do.

"Savior, we are at your service," Clara said, her eyes filled with fanatical light.

Grimacing, Mark straightened up and walked to the door. "I'm not anybody's savior."

Reaching out, he grasped the door handle and started to pull it open.

"I can't even save myself," he added under his breath.

One of the others looked as if he were about to stand and chase after Mark, but Clara waved her hand. "I understand that this might be a lot to take in, a lot to process, but we will support you regardless. We will be here when you come to see the truth of your situation, the truth of this world. We will be waiting."

Suppressing another shudder, Mark stepped out into the hallway, and a moment later the doorway was gone, sealed once more. For a long moment he didn't move, shuddering again, as if it would help him shake off the strange experience he had just had. Then Mark headed for his apartment. He didn't know what to make of the situation, and he had no desire to be responsible for everyone else, no desire to play savior or hero of the world. There was also something about Dallas, the so-called Prophet, that rubbed him the wrong way, setting his teeth on edge and raising his guard.

At the same time, Clara and the others clearly believed that Mark was this so-called Savior, to the point of fanaticism.

When he reached his apartment, Mark opened the door and saw Mime sitting on the couch, staring at him. All of a sudden, the absurdity of the situation struck him, and he couldn't help but laugh. He gave Mime a mock bow, lips twitching as he tried to suppress his laughter. "Well, hello, Mime. Maybe you didn't know, but I have moved up in the world. Not only am I an experimental test subject, but I'm also an assassin and the savior of this world. Ugh."

With a defeated sigh, Mark plopped himself on the couch. "You know, this is all just too much."

Mime didn't say anything. But she did jump off the back of the couch to sit next to him, placing a paw on his knee. Finding it strangely comforting, Mark scratched behind her ears and then took a breath and held it as he began to eliminate each of his worries from his mind, producing a state of meditative focus.

When he had re-centered himself, he gestured a command to his shadow. A moment later, a small device sat on the coffee table in front of him. A simple band of metal, similar to the device Mark had been given when he first registered as an empowered. During the frantic escape from the mansion during their mission, when Mark had killed one of the mercenaries and had his shadow gobble up the body, he had instructed it to keep the activator.

Picking it up, Mark looked the device over, a slow smile gracing his lips. While he could put it on, activators were tied to the individuals they were made for, which meant that this one wouldn't actually work properly for him. Of course, had he absorbed the mercenary's abilities, he would have been able to make it work, but he had no particular interest in the flame power the mercenary wielded, and instead was much more interested in understanding how the activator actually worked.

Leaving it on the table, Mark sent a strand of mana into the activator and watched as a mana circuit appeared, extending down from the band along the table. The mana circuit remained active as Mark continued to send bits of mana into the activator, even as he traced out the pattern of the circuit. He had already determined that he could build mana circuits in his body. His only problem had been not remembering how the activator's mana circuit was arranged, but that wasn't an issue anymore.

By the time morning had come, Mark had spent almost fourteen hours obsessively learning every inch of the mana circuit, and he felt as if it were burned into his memory, to the point where when he closed his eyes, the bright lines would immediately spring to mind. Rather than rushing to try to form the mana circuit on his arm, Mark deactivated the device and stored it in his shadow again before crawling into bed to get a few hours of sleep. Six hours later, when Mark woke up, both his mind and his body felt refreshed, but he didn't move, instead simply staring at the ceiling as he let out a shaky breath. He felt incredibly fortunate.

He had used his time in the dream world to test out activating the mana circuit. His initial attempts had resulted in the near-complete destruction of his arm. The first time he had tried it, the mana had gone berserk, causing his arm to explode and forcefully resetting him as he bled out. The second time, the mana had burned permanent scars in the shape of the circuit into his arm. This caused the mana to slip from his control as it rotated through the circuit, and once again his arm exploded.

Though his first two attempts shook his spirit, Mark gritted his teeth and kept at it, brute-forcing the problem until he figured out the trick of allowing the mana to circulate properly. The issue was that if the circuit deviated in the slightest, it would transform into a raging torrent of mana that would continue to build until it exploded. What Mark had found was that he needed to continually siphon mana from the circuit to prevent it from going wild.

With a sigh, he slowly sat up and glanced down at his forearm, trying to decide whether it was worth taking the risk. Swinging his feet off the bed, he sat there for a moment and then, with a wry smile, pulled mana together, sending it spinning through his arm. With but a thought, the mana circuit formed, and Mark winced as the mana burned a channel through his arm.

Of course, if mana control were the only determining factor, it would have been easy to create the circuit. The problem was that Mark's body healed too quickly, erasing the channels he built almost as fast as he built them. This forced him to circulate the mana much faster than normal, and while that meant the activator could work more quickly, it also meant that he had to withstand constant pain.

Still, he gritted his teeth and focused, and a moment later, for the first time since he had been thrown into prison, he saw his status window pop up.

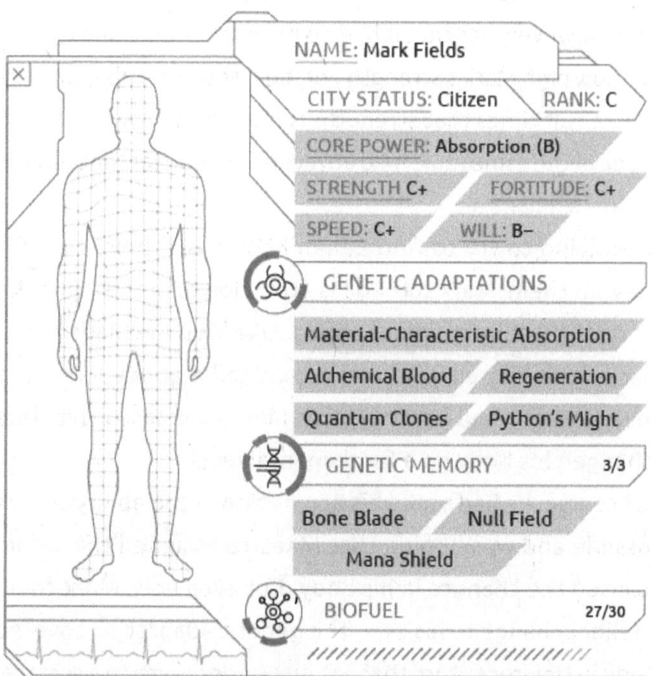

Though on the surface, his stats hadn't gone up much, Mark could feel that they were all increasing. What interested him more, however, was the new abilities he had picked up. Specifically, the ability he had absorbed from Python.

Python's Might: Your muscles have grown stronger, carrying latent power and innate flexibility, giving your body the strength of a giant python. You can exert one and a half times your normal strength.

On the surface, the ability wasn't particularly powerful, but the more Mark looked at it, the better he liked it. This was a high B-ranked power, as it only boosted a single stat. What was curious about it, however, was that it had no restriction, meaning that no matter how high Mark's strength got, he'd always be able to exert one and a half times that strength. This meant that when facing someone in the same rank, he'd always have an advantage, unless they had a similar skill.

Resolving to try to find Exlian known for their strength and devour them, Mark turned his attention to his new genetic memory, the war bear's mana shield. Like his bone blade transformation and his null field, Mark could tell that devouring the war bear's corpse had not only given him an increase in his stats but changed his body on a fundamental level.

Of course, he had timed his acquisition of the ability as well as possible and was hoping that Maestro assumed the serum had caused the changes in his body. But even now, Mark could feel a slight change to his skin. The genetic adaptation covered his body in tiny receptors that sat just underneath the surface.

As soon as they sensed any sort of danger, they would flare, gathering mana to form a thick shield. The ability was incredibly powerful and gave Mark considerable confidence.

With a sigh, he dismissed the windows, letting the mana circuit fade. A moment later, all traces of it were gone as his body healed back up. Getting up from the bed, Mark headed for the kitchen to make some breakfast, considering his future as he prepared food for himself and Mime. There wasn't much to do except wait, which made him feel quite uneasy. Until Noah contacted him, Mark's life would consist of training with Winter Wolf and the others, practicing his alchemy, and continuing to serve as Maestro's experimental subject. While all those things were outside Mark's control, he soon settled on a couple of personal goals. The first was to figure out how to control his null field.

Though the war bear's mana shield was a powerful ability, it paled in comparison to the ability to turn off mana use. And Mark had a sneaking suspicion that if he could figure out how to freely control his null field, there would be few opponents, Exlian or otherwise, who could stand against him. Of course, that was easier said than done, and Mark had no idea how to go about controlling the null field. But just because he didn't know didn't mean he was out of options to try. Once he'd cleaned up after breakfast, Mark left Mime at the apartment and headed toward the training room.

When he got there, Winter Wolf and Joker were already engaged in sparring. Though it looked more like Winter Wolf was delivering a one-sided beatdown to Joker. She seemed to have pulled out all the stops, and every single one of her moves was potentially lethal. Joker was in a sorry state, his body wounded in a dozen places, but he still threw himself at Winter Wolf with manic glee, ignoring the burns and cuts all over his body as he tried to stab her with one of his teleporting daggers. Wisely deciding it wouldn't be a good idea to get involved, Mark headed to the side of the room and sat down, beginning his daily practice controlling his null field.

Recently, he had been focusing on figuring out how to adjust the size of the field. And now, having had some success in fixing it a few inches from his body, he began to attempt to shift the field to one side, extending it from his right hand but not his left. At first, it seemed impossible, and the field didn't move one bit. Mark tried over and over, but nothing seemed to work.

Hearing a loud bang, he looked up and saw Joker impaled through the stomach on a lance of ice that Winter Wolf had summoned. Blood streamed down the silvery-white spear. Yet despite his grievous wound, Joker let out a laugh that caused blood to bubble up on his lips.

"I got you," he said with much difficulty.

Looking across the room, Mark saw that one of Joker's daggers had pierced almost all the way through Winter Wolf's palm. Impassively, she waved her hand and the ice spear melted away, causing Joker to drop to the ground with a groan. Without any change in expression, Winter Wolf grabbed the dagger and pulled it from her palm, staring at the blood that began to pool on the wound. She tossed the dagger to the side and turned to Mark.

"My apologies, but it looks like we'll have to go get treatment. Feel free to stay here as long as you'd like."

With a snap of her fingers, Winter Wolf sent one of her giant ice wolves forward. Seeing it coming, Joker tried to get to his feet, but his legs failed him. A moment later, the wolf's jaws closed around him, hoisting him up into the air and following Winter Wolf, who headed for the infirmary. Shaking his head, Mark was about to go back to his meditation when he suddenly realized that the null field around him was strangely lopsided. Blinking, he looked down and saw that the field was extended from his right hand, stretching out an extra two and a half feet, while barely covering his left side.

With no idea how he had managed to produce such an effect, Mark blinked, and suddenly, the null field snapped back into place, forming its normal sphere around him. Resisting the urge to curse, Mark canceled the field, took a deep breath, and stood up, shaking out his limbs. He found it strange that when he had focused on wielding the null field, it barely responded to him, but when he hadn't focused on it, it had naturally fallen into place.

Once he had shaken his body loose, Mark decided to try a different tactic. Instead of trying to force the null field to obey him, he began to move through his Cutting Palm kata, allowing his mind to fall into the calm of familiar action. As his mind and body relaxed, he continued to try to shift his null field into a new shape, but this time without spending all his attention on it. His hope was that he could use a more passive, instinctive sort of control on the null field. Though he had little success, Mark could tell that he was starting to move in the right direction, and he threw himself into practice with unmitigated fervor.

The next three days, he spent all his time, both awake and asleep, practicing this subtle form of control. And on the fourth day, he only stopped because he was called down to the Cradle by Maestro. Mark was always nervous meeting the supergenius, but this time, he found himself excited as well. After the normal examination, Maestro looked quite pleased, and as Mark sat up from the examination table, Maestro handed him a new serum. "It seems that you've been doing a lot of practice with your glitch ability. Have you had any luck controlling it?"

"I haven't," Mark said, shaking his head, "so I've been taking a new approach."

"Oh, and what is that?"

"I've been working on indirect control," he said, scratching his head. "I started to think about the way my other ability works, specifically the mana shield. When I try and control it directly, it is incredibly draining. But when it activates naturally, the mana drain is negligible. I started to wonder if part of the problem with my glitch ability is that I'm trying to activate it. If instead, I allow it to become an instinctive thing, then maybe I'll begin to nudge it in a useful direction. Right now, it's operating as sort of a defensive ability."

"True, it's just unfortunate that your two defensive abilities cancel each other out."

"Exactly."

Mark drank the serum and wiped his lips with the back of his hand. Taking the empty vial with one of his robotic arms, Maestro shuffled his chair around. "It turns out that our thoughts coincide. The serums that I've been feeding you should help you subtly build your instinctive control over your body. I have noticed that your glitch has been activating more often than normal, which means that we're probably on the right track."

"That's how I feel as well," Mark said, standing up and putting on his shirt. "The glitch seems to activate when I feel the threat of danger. So far, I've been trying to manufacture that feeling, but I'm confident that if I ever am in danger, it will activate."

"That's good. Well, we'll keep working on it. And in the meantime, I hope you could help me test something else."

Maestro must have seen the nervous look that flashed across Mark's face because he chuckled. "It probably won't be too dangerous for you, but I have a new Exlian sample, and I've been having trouble properly assessing the threat level. I'd appreciate it if you'd assist me."

Mark had interacted with Maestro enough to know that this wasn't actually a request. So, steeling himself, he nodded. "Sure, I can help."

"Good, come along."

With his usual hurried gait, Maestro led the way, taking Mark down a series of long hallways to a large observation lab. Even before Mark arrived, he could sense a number of Exlian in the room beyond. They stopped at a large observation window, and Mark saw an arena down below. Almost a replica of the one in the Tomb, just smaller.

"The elevator will take you down," Maestro said, pointing at a door to the right.

Mark should have felt some nervousness, but the presence of Exlian had only awoken his hunger, and rather than feeling unsettled, he was forced to suppress his excitement as he walked to the elevator and took it down to the arena floor. Emerging into the large space, Mark looked up and found himself staring at nothing but a wide blue sky. There were no arena walls, or anything else for that matter, save for the cracked dirt of the arena floor. Looking around, he appeared to be standing in an endless plane.

"What you're currently seeing exists to help us keep the Exlian in check. After all, if they could see us, they would undoubtedly go mad, which wouldn't be helpful for our testing."

Hearing Maestro's voice over the speaker, Mark held up a thumb to show he understood, and a moment later, he sensed an Exlian moving closer. At first, he thought he'd be facing a particularly powerful one, but then he realized that it was actually a group of Exlian, all bunched together, making it hard to distinguish between them.

With a grinding noise, half a dozen jellyfish-like creatures fell from the sky, landing with squishy thuds on the arena floor. Hisses began to break out as the tentacled creatures raised their gelatinous bodies and began to lurch toward Mark with surprising speed.

Mark's first instinct was to summon his shadow and devour them wholesale, but he ruthlessly suppressed that impulse and instead transformed his arms into bone blades, throwing himself forward. As soon as he got into range, one of the jellyfish lifted its body, slapping out with two of its tentacles. Mark evaded the first one and hacked through the second with the edge of his palm, causing the creature to shriek. Yet despite the pain, it didn't pull back but threw itself forward, its limbs converging on him. At the same time, the other five launched their own attacks, swiftly surrounding Mark.

Dodging a few, Mark let one of them hit his shoulder, fully expecting his mana shield to activate. Yet as soon as it started to, there was a faint sizzling noise, and the flailing tentacle produced a faint purple light that ate through the mana shield with ease before hammering into Mark's shoulder with enough force to send him tumbling. The monster's strike hadn't been that powerful, all things considered, but when the mana shield failed, it caught Mark off balance, and he couldn't help but roll across the ground.

Bouncing back up, Mark retreated to gain some distance, outpacing the rather slow creatures. His shoulder had already healed, but he couldn't help but glance at it. The fact that his mana shield had failed set his mind abuzz, and as two of the jellyfish Exlian closed in, Mark watched them carefully, paying particular attention to the flow of mana in their limbs.

They lashed out at Mark, and he blocked one of the attacks with his hands while allowing the other to slap into his side. Once again, the faint purple light flashed across the tentacle, and Mark's suspicions were confirmed. The creature was wielding the same strange energy that formed his null field, but rather than creating a completely mana-free zone like the brain could, it was using only a few threads of null energy that originated from its core and spread out along the surface of its tentacle, allowing it to bypass Mark's shield.

Grimacing as his skin was ripped open by the tentacle's fierce lash, Mark drove forward, stabbing his hand through the Exlian's bulbous body. As his hand approached, he could feel the null field beginning to bloom around the creature as it desperately tried to protect itself, but his bone blade hands were simply too sharp and didn't require any mana.

After cutting straight through the monster, Mark opted to remain in place rather than retreat as five more frantically came after him. Soon, three more corpses lay at his feet, most of them chopped into tiny pieces. With his shields not working, Mark elected to trade blow for blow, wound for wound, trusting in his excellent regeneration to keep himself on his feet. Now that there were only two left, both of them had grown wary. Rather than charge him from the front, they circled to the sides, clearly intending to try to pincer him.

Mark, taking a moment to breathe and allow his wounds to knit, tried to keep an eye on both. He found it hard as one of the creatures had circled behind him. With a shriek, it launched itself forward, intending to completely entrap him, even as the other attacked from the front. Rather than wait passively, Mark jumped aside, ducking a stabbing tentacle and throwing himself into the grasp of the monster attacking from behind. Planting his foot, he spun, his hands shredding through the rubbery skin of the Exlian's flailing limbs. Blood splattered and chunks of flesh rained down around him as his hands wove a deadly net, shredding everything that came close.

Too late, the monster realized it was in trouble and tried to retreat, but Mark burst forward, his body slamming into the monster with enough force that its gelatinous body exploded. Almost immediately, he turned around and threw himself at the final creature, allowing his instincts to control him. With no concern for the wounds piling up on his own body, Mark tore the Exlian to shreds, letting out a loud roar that echoed through the arena. The last jellyfish only lasted half a dozen seconds before it collapsed into a great pile of goo. Mark, panting, looked around with bloodshot eyes, as if seeking another enemy. There was a soft click, and then Maestro's voice came over the speakers as the illusion that transformed the arena into a wide, empty plane began to fade.

"Well, that was enlightening," Maestro said. "I was curious about how the jellyfish's antimana attacks would interact with your shields. Come on up, and let's talk about your experience."

Taking a moment to calm himself, Mark stepped into the elevator, desperately hoping that Maestro hadn't noticed his shadow stealthily enveloping the only complete Exlian corpse in the pile of bodies. He had done his best to chop the rest of the monsters into as many pieces as possible, hoping to disguise the fact that he had stolen one of the corpses. Mark was just as interested in the jellyfish's strange ability to control null energy as Maestro was, and he was eager to study the creature's body.

By the time the elevator had reached the observation room, Mark had composed himself, at least as well as he could when covered in Exlian gore. When he stepped out of the elevator, Maestro took one look at him and shook one of his robotic arms. "I'm not normally squeamish, but that's honestly disgusting. We can talk as you're getting cleaned up."

Leading Mark to a shower, Maestro began pacing back and forth as Mark stripped down. "I anticipated that the jellyfish's attacks would go through your innate shield, largely because the jellyfish seem to have evolved to fight against war bears specifically. You're familiar with the state of the Exlian swarms in the outside world, correct?"

"If you're referring to how they fight against each other, then yes."

"That's exactly what I'm referring to. Exlian dislike each other as much as they dislike us. Each nest seems to control its own swarms, though I have my suspicions that things are a little bit more complicated than that. That's neither here nor there, however. Instead, what I'm curious about is, in fighting against the jellyfish, were you able to identify how they were using their power?"

Soaping himself up, Mark thought for a moment and then shook his head. "Not precisely, no. My guess is that their skin was conducting the energy, because it seemed to roll across their limbs progressively, starting from the beginning of their strike and reaching the appropriate spot on the limb when it came into contact with me."

"That's in line with what I've observed. Dry off, get changed, and I'll take you to see something that I'm sure you'll find interesting."

Rinsing off the soap, Mark looked around and saw a robot with a towel standing next to another robot with a change of clothing. Unable to get over how bizarre the situation was, Mark toweled himself off, put on his new clothes, and followed Maestro back into the observation room, where the genius pulled up a screen that showed a chart of the jellyfish's anatomy.

"You'll notice these lines running along the limbs of the monsters. That seems to be where this energy is channeled. I've tested it extensively. If you break these channels, the glitch energy stops here."

Trying to memorize the anatomical chart as best he could, Mark pointed toward the center of the Exlian's body. "What about the source? I sensed that it was coming from the center of mass."

"Indeed, it appears to be originating from somewhere close to the creature's brain. Unfortunately, I haven't been able to identify the specific point. But considering we're using mana to scan, that rather makes sense."

Just then, a small beeping screen flashed up in front of Maestro, causing him to frown. "I'm afraid one of my other experiments needs my attention, so we'll have to call this to a close here. But I do hope you'll continue to think about this. Your insights into instinctive control and examining how Exlian manipulate this energy seem to me a worthwhile path to pursue. I have you scheduled for next week to come down and get another serum, but I need you to check in every day so we can gather data on how the changes are progressing. We'll continue trying to build your will stat while also pursuing these other avenues. Don't slack off in your training."

With those parting words, Maestro hurried off, and a robot that appeared behind Mark led him out of the Cradle. When he arrived in the Tomb above, his watch began beeping, alerting him to a number of missed and silenced messages. Figuring Maestro had likely had something to do with delaying the messages, Mark could only smile wryly and open them up. Most were from Winter Wolf, informing him that he had a visitor.

Hoping it was Noah, Mark hurried to the arena, where he found the team leader in the training room. When she saw him, Winter Wolf's expression grew dark. "Why weren't you answering your messages?"

Though Mark had never been expressly told not to talk about what he was doing with Maestro, he had a feeling that it would be better to share less information rather than more, so he simply shook his head and pointed down toward the ground.

Winter Wolf's expression grew even darker, and then she realized what he was indicating, and with a light groan, she gestured for him to follow. "It's not a good idea to keep the scum waiting, but some things are unavoidable."

When Mark stepped into the meeting room, Noah was already there, and his expression lit up. "Is everything okay? It took you longer than I thought it would."

"Everything's fine," Mark said, taking his seat. "I was just occupied with something."

By this time, the door had shut behind Mark, sealing the two of them in together, and after his customary scan for listening devices, Mark shrouded his watch and shackles with his null field, ensuring that it wouldn't be possible for anybody to eavesdrop through them. He noticed that Noah wasn't wearing a watch either, and figured it was for the same reason.

For a moment, the two young men just looked at each other, and then, with a sigh, Noah shook his head. "Were you involved in the recent incident?"

"If you're talking about the actor being kidnapped, then yes," Mark said, his voice calm.

"Did you kill the mercenary too?"

Mark simply shrugged.

"Either way, it doesn't matter," Noah said. "What does matter is that people on the surface are starting to take notice."

"That explains why Winter Wolf was so mad. One of our team members is a bit wrong in the head," Mark said, tapping his temple. "He intentionally set off the alarm, likely to pull the other team in so that he could fight more people."

Lost for words, Noah rubbed his forehead, and with a chuckle, Mark waved his hand. "Believe me when I say that's the least crazy thing about this place. So if you have any ideas for how I can get out, I'd love to hear them."

Straightening up in his chair, Noah nodded. "I actually do. Though it'll be pretty dangerous."

"Noah, I'm not joking when I say that my life is on the line every single moment while I'm down here. So no matter how dangerous your ideas are, let's hear them."

Standing up, Noah began to pace back and forth, though it only took him two steps to cross the room. Mark sat back, giving Noah time to organize his thoughts.

"The simplest way to get you out of here is for you to die while on a mission."

"Umm . . . dying is exactly what I'm trying not to do."

"I don't mean die for real, I mean appear to be dead. There are more than enough ways to change your identity. We've done it for enough other people that we can do it for you."

"Okay, I'm interested. What are you thinking?" Mark asked.

Crossing his arms, Noah stood by the clear barrier between them, his gaze resting on Mark. "The most important thing is going to be figuring out how to get those shackles off you. Once we can do that, then it'll be a simple matter of having you caught in an explosion or something that would destroy your body. From there, as long as we know where your mission is, it won't be hard to smuggle you out. Then we set you up with a new identity, potentially even a new face, and as long as you lay low, you should be fine."

Thinking for a moment, Mark nodded. "I can deal with the shackles, and I can probably do one better than being caught in an explosion. I have a way to fake my death so long as I can get the appropriate supplies. The real challenge is going to be coordinating all of this. After all, I don't know when our missions are going to come up. And even if I did, we don't find out what the mission is supposed to be until we're actually deployed aboveground."

"What if I could smuggle in a communication device?"

"I mean, can you?" Mark asked, intrigued.

As Noah thought over the question, his face fell. "It'll be hard. Getting things into the Tomb is notoriously difficult."

Mark had an idea. "Hold on. Do you have any sort of communication device that's very simple? Something that's like a two-way channel?"

"We have a bunch of those."

"Do you have it on you?"

Thinking for a moment, Noah reached up and undid his collar. On the inside, Mark saw a small metallic disk. "You mean something like this?"

Peering at it through the glass, Mark could see a faint thread of mana forming a circuit. "Yeah, exactly like that. Any chance you could get me a copy of that mana circuit?"

"Do you have the material to build a communicator on your side?"

"I think so," Mark replied, half lying. "I'm sure I can find some way to make one. I just need to understand how the mana circuit works."

"Unfortunately, I can't help you at the moment, but I'll make sure to bring that with me next time," Noah said. "If you truly can build a communicator like this, you'll be able to get in touch with me directly, which means that the next time you go out on mission, you'll be able to alert me to your location."

"We'll have to be careful, though, because one of my teammates is really good at jamming. But this whole thing is high risk, high reward, and I don't know that we have any other options."

"In that case, I'll focus on getting you the circuit," Noah said. "I'll be back soon."

Watching him leave, Mark couldn't help but rub his forehead. He knew that he was playing with fire, and if anyone caught wind of what they were trying to do, he wouldn't be surprised if he ended up scrapped for parts in Maestro's lab. Still, Mark was determined not to spend his life down here in the Tomb, and at this point he felt that practically anything would be better.

To his surprise, Noah was back the next day, and when Winter Wolf reported that Mark had a visitor again, she gave him an odd look. Ultimately, she kept silent, and Mark soon found himself facing Noah again. True to his word, Noah had a printout of the mana circuit, which Mark dutifully copied down.

"I'll make sure things are good to go on my end," Noah said, putting the drawing of the circuit away. "Once you have that ready and you go on a mission, all you have to do is activate it, and I'll know exactly where you are."

"Sounds good. And Noah?" Seeing Noah pause at the door before walking out, Mark grinned. "Thanks. I really appreciate this."

Flashing a quick smile, Noah shrugged. "What are friends for if not risking their lives breaking you out of a high-security prison?"

With a wave, he vanished through the doorway, and Mark headed back to his apartment. With a rough plan in place, he was feeling more optimistic about his chances to escape, and he began practicing a new mana circuit. Ever since he had succeeded in creating the mana circuit for the activator, Mark had been thinking of how else he could leverage this ability, and creating a simple communication device seemed absolutely perfect. Though he was confident in his ability to form the mana circuit, Mark didn't want to take any chances, and he started his practice in the dream world. That had the added benefit of not accidentally alerting anyone to what was going on, and slowly, Mark's life fell into a simple routine.

He split each day into three different sections. In the morning, he would train, working on his mana control and trying to puzzle out a path forward to control his null field. Between bouts of mental training, he would spar with Winter Wolf, engaging in increasingly ferocious fights that often left him bloody and battered. Then, after a massive lunch, he would head to Mr. Robot's shop, where he would practice his alchemy and alchemical butchery. After an equally large dinner, he would take one of the hidden elevators down to the Cradle to meet Maestro.

There, he would spend the next six or so hours undergoing countless examinations and experiments, often being thrown into the arena to fight Exlian of various kinds. Mark found these parts of his day the strangest of all, and slowly, he began to develop a strange sort of appreciation for the mad genius who lurked under the Tomb.

Maestro's focus was absolute, and he seemed to care little for the world outside his laboratory. He had no particular concern for anybody, including Mark. It was also clear that he fully intended to improve Mark's abilities as much as possible, sparing no expense as he treated Mark's body. At this point, even if Maestro knew his secrets, the genius simply didn't care. He only valued Mark as an experimental subject who could help him in his quest to understand the world better.

Rather than continuing to hold back, Mark threw himself into the experiments with gusto, intending to maximize his benefits as much as possible. Noah hadn't come again since handing over the mana circuit, and Mark found himself worrying about what might have happened to his friend. Unfortunately, there wasn't much he could do to find out, so he pushed his concerns to the back of his mind.

Occasionally, Mark would run into Clara or other members of the Salvation cult, and each time, they would stop and greet him, causing Mark considerable annoyance. Thankfully, his aggressive training schedule helped him keep his emotions firmly in check. Otherwise, he was afraid that he would be sorely tempted to simply wipe them out, ensuring that they couldn't bother him again.

During the nights when he was back at home, Mark also worked on taking apart the corpse of the jellyfish Exlian he had swiped, trying to figure out how it was wielding its null energy, but to no avail. Eventually, tired of the smell, he fed the remains to his shadow.

Four weeks after his last meeting with Noah, Winter Wolf finally called them all together, her expression grim.

"Do we have another mission?" Joker asked, sprawling in one of the seats in the meeting room.

"We do."

"Oh, good, about time. I have been getting so bored."

"Do we have any details?" Coral asked, a frown gracing her lips.

"No, and we're leaving now. Everyone gear up."

With an annoyed groan, Servo pushed himself to his feet. "I hate that they spring them on us like this."

"Me too, but it's the position we're in. Everyone, make sure you have all your gear before we head up."

Following the others quietly, Mark did his best to suppress the nervous excitement bubbling up in his chest. He kept himself calm as he slowly got his gear on, trying to avoid Winter Wolf's gaze. After getting dressed, the five of them gathered together and stepped into the elevator that would take them to the surface. Apart from Joker, who carried on a conversation with himself, the others were silent. And even Joker fell quiet as they approached the surface.

"Why do I have a really bad feeling about this?" Coral suddenly said. "Something about this feels off."

Winter Wolf, standing at the front of the elevator, had her eyes closed and her hands placed on the small of her back. "It's not unusual for us to get a mission on short notice."

Despite her reassuring words, Mark could see her reflection in the polished silver of the elevator door, and it was considerably colder than normal. Clearly, he wasn't the only one feeling on edge.

A large group of mana-suited soldiers was waiting for them outside the elevator, just like last time. As Mark and the others stepped out, they also saw Special Agent Callaghan. To Mark's surprise, Joker didn't have a quip, and it seemed that even he was sensing the strange air.

"We found a mutant nest," Special Agent Callaghan said, wasting no time. "We need to clear it out now."

"Will we have any support?" Winter Wolf asked, looking at the report that Callaghan sent over.

"No, but the mission is a lot easier. The target this time isn't a particular individual. Instead, we found a group of mutants hiding out in a hospital. We've locked down the area, and we want them cleared out. No need to keep any of them alive."

Looking up from the file, Winter Wolf stared at Special Agent Callaghan with narrowed eyes. "And you've confirmed that everyone inside the facility is a mutant? Not just empowered?"

Callaghan, completely indifferent, shrugged. "All the ones we've seen have strange limbs growing out of their bodies, so you can treat them as if they are. Bodies will be sent to the Tomb. No need for live specimens."

The callous way that Special Agent Callaghan spoke of killing indiscriminately set Mark's teeth on edge, but the others seemed used to it, and soon they were bundled into a waiting van. Worse, Mark's pulse hadn't jumped at all when the topic of mass murder came up, and he found that his companions were equally undisturbed. Joker was in a great mood and hummed quietly to himself as he played with a dagger. Servo busied himself with his gear, while Coral sat quietly in the corner, her face expressionless. Only Winter Wolf showed any sort of expression, but even that was just a mild frown as she combed through the details again and again. Opening his mouth, Mark hesitated, unsure how to voice his qualms. He wanted to protest, but this seemed to be par for the course, and he wasn't even clear on how he felt about killing mutants. So far, every single mutant he had met apart from Clara had been a raging lunatic. Then Winter Wolf looked up, and the moment was gone.

"We'll do a direct sweep, starting from the bottom floors and working our way up. We'll enter through the front and engage in direct assault. No need to sneak in. Mark, you'll be leading the charge. Joker and I will watch your flanks. Coral, you're on crowd control, and Servo will bring up the rear."

"Can I deploy my suit?"

"Yes," Winter Wolf said, causing the large man's eyes to light up with happiness. "However, don't go bringing the building down on top of us."

"You got it, boss."

"Once we're inside, we'll have to split up to make sure the floors are cleared. Mark, you'll be in charge of the hallways. I'll sweep rooms on the right, Joker the left. The layout of the building is fairly straightforward, with a single long hall and two shorter hallways coming off it in a rough U shape. It looks like there are two staircases, one on either side of the building, that go from floor to floor, as well as a staircase closer to the middle. We'll pick a random entrance as we reach each floor. There are five total floors, and I would expect that we'll find the fiercest resistance on the second or third."

"Why don't they just bomb the building?" Coral asked, causing everybody to look at her. "I mean, it wouldn't be hard to level the whole thing, kill everybody inside. Isn't that what they did at the Green Line?"

Shooting Coral a cold glance, Winter Wolf lifted her finger to her lips. "Hush. This is a civilian facility, so the less infrastructure damage, the better. Obviously, don't hold back if it's a matter of life or death, but try to keep things as clean as possible."

Mark's mind was racing, but before he could ask the questions on his lips, the van came to a stop, the back door opened, and Winter Wolf ordered them out.

"Get in there. The mutants are probably starting to suspect something."

Joker was the first out of the van, and he sprinted for the front door. Mark was close behind him, with Winter Wolf keeping pace and Coral and Servo following behind. As they headed for the building, Mark got a glimpse of it. Five stories tall and painted a soft blue, it looked like any other hospital, and he couldn't help but feel a flash of guilt as he imagined what it might become by the time they were done.

Taking a deep breath of the fresh night air, Mark concentrated, and a hint of mana traced out a pattern on his throat. Behind him, he could hear the buzz of Servo's drones deploying, and knowing he only had a brief moment before the jammer kicked in, Mark quickly activated the mana circuit he had just created. He could feel it establishing a connection, but before he could say anything, he felt a wave of static forcefully cutting it off. Hoping that he had managed to give Noah enough, he let the circuit fade, his skin quickly healing to hide that it had ever existed.

Joker, teleporting forward, had just reached the door, and rather than burst through it, his body flickered and he disappeared. Mark was a step behind and blasted through the door to find Joker already on the other side. A large orderly in the hall saw him, but before he could shout, one of Joker's daggers materialized in his throat, causing him to gag and drop to the ground. Mark brushed past Joker and headed straight for the front desk.

Two people were sitting there. One of them screamed and hunched down, while the other let out a mad roar and hopped over the desk, his body beginning to twist. Mark, still running full tilt, slammed into him, planting an elbow in the man's chest, even as his transformation finished. Thick chitinous plates formed on the mutant's sternum, but they weren't strong enough to stop Mark's elbow, and they cracked open, causing the mutant to scream as it was blasted backward to crash into the desk it had just jumped over.

As it broke apart, the woman who had ducked down emerged partially transformed, let out an angry hiss, and lunged at Mark, a scorpion tail stabbing toward his leg, its tip glistening with venom. There was a low growl, and a large ice wolf bit down on the tail before it could reach Mark. Though this was the first time that Mark and Winter Wolf had directly coordinated in an assault, they had fought with each other enough that their movements were perfectly timed.

Mark stomped forward, delivering two rapid strikes to the scorpion mutant, while at the same time, a blast of cold air flew past his shoulder, and an ice lance impaled the armored mutant. With a flash, Joker appeared next to Mark, his dagger stabbing down into the scorpion mutant's neck, severing its spine.

Mad with excitement, Joker raised his head, only for his smile to falter as he met Mark's cold gaze. Without a word, Mark pointed to the left. Though he hesitated, Joker managed to control himself and gave a short nod, vanishing to comb through the rooms on the left side of the hallway. Winter Wolf had already moved to the right, leaving Mark to guard Servo and Coral.

There was a shout, and a door burst open, revealing five muscular men and women, faces twisted with fury. As they got closer, they began to shift into a variety of twisted monstrosities, and Mark stepped forward to meet them. Behind him, Servo, dressed in a massive suit of armor that forced him to crouch in the hallway, tossed out a few devices, beginning to set up his defenses. Coral pulled water from her backpack, sending drops whizzing like bullets at the charging enemy.

Shaking ichor from his fingers, Mark strode to the center of the hallway and faced the mutants directly, meeting the first one with a straight punch. The mutant's gaze held a hint of derision as it slashed its claws at Mark's chest, clearly intending to rip his heart out with a single strike. When the mutant's claws slammed into the mana shield and bounced off, its derision turned to shock, and then Mark's fist hit, and that shock turned to horror as the mutant was blasted straight back down the hallway it had just run down.

In the last few weeks, Mark had been experimenting with his python's might, trying to understand how best to leverage it, and he had realized that short, sharp bursts of power were the answer. His strength, which was extremely close to B–, then multiplied by one and a half times thanks to the python's might. This meant that when he unleashed it directly, it was the same as a low A-ranked strength, making his fists practically unstoppable in direct confrontations. He hadn't yet figured out how to keep it active all the time, however, and after he unleashed his magnified strength, it took a moment before he could use it again. That didn't matter particularly, though, as even when he wasn't using overwhelming strength, he still had his Cutting Palm techniques.

Withdrawing his fist, Mark struck one side, then the other, disrupting the movement of the other charging mutants and pulling them all into a scrambling melee. He attacked with abandon, allowing them to hammer away at his body as they pleased. Every second blow was blocked by his shield, and though the ones that weren't left deep wounds on his body, those wounds rapidly healed, leaving the mutants at a loss.

One of the mutants, whose arms had transformed into giant claws, tried to rip at Mark's throat, but just before its claws landed, a whip made of water wrapped around its neck, yanking the mutant backward and throwing it into the wall. Mark used the opportunity to press forward aggressively, his hands ripping through the mutant's chest and his fingers piercing into his opponent's heart. With a twist, he tore a massive gouge out through the side of the mutant's chest, at the same time delivering a fierce punch to the side of its head, dropping it to the ground.

"Aw, looks like you're having all the fun out here!"

Joker's words were accompanied by blades that stabbed into another mutant from multiple directions. There was a flash, and Joker's foot slammed into the mutant, knocking it to the ground. With a wave of his hand, he recalled his daggers, then launched them again, stabbing it repeatedly until it lay still. Mark could feel a hint of bile rising in his throat, but he ignored it and threw himself at the last mutant, swiftly cutting it down. Winter Wolf arrived a moment later, indicating that the floor was clear, and the team moved to the end of the hall, where they found a set of double doors leading to a stairwell. They could hear shouts from above: Clearly the other mutants had already been alerted.

"Any injuries?" Seeing everyone shaking their heads, Winter Wolf pointed up the stairs. "Then let's get going. Mark?"

Mark took the stairs two at a time, anticipating an attack at any moment. The first attack came in the form of an ambush, a mutant who appeared out of midair, slamming into Mark with enough force to send him tumbling over the railing. There was madness in the mutant's eyes, and it was clear he was hoping that the fall would kill Mark. Unfortunately for him, Mark's reflexes were too quick, and he grabbed the railing even as they went over, keeping ahold of it as they dangled in the air.

With his arm clutched in the mutant's grip, Mark used his knee, lifting it sharply to hammer into the mutant's stomach. With a groan, the man's grip slipped slightly, giving Mark the opportunity to free his arm. Just before he could cut through his opponent's throat, the man let go, a strange expression in his eyes as he stared at Mark. Twin daggers whistled through the air, flying toward the mutant. But a moment later, the air folded around him, and he was gone.

Recalling his knives, Joker had an ugly expression on his face as Mark climbed over the railing back onto the stairs. "They've got a teleporter. Everybody be careful."

"Is that different from what you do?" Mark asked as they resumed moving up the stairs.

"Yeah, I just blink. I can move myself, and I can move small objects. That guy can actually fold space."

When they arrived at the second floor, Mark was a bit surprised to see that the landing was empty. He had assumed that the commotion would have brought everyone to this stairwell. As soon as he opened the door, however, he understood why it hadn't. Instead of pushing out into the narrow stairwell, the mutants were waiting for them at the end of the hallway. As soon as Mark stepped through, he was hit from three directions at once. Two of the attacks were energy blasts that failed to penetrate his shields, while the last was a thick glob of acidic spit that lingered on his shield, burning through it. The force of the three attacks sent Mark stumbling back, but he felt a broad hand steadying him as Servo surged through the doorway.

Dressed in a massive mana suit, Servo was almost too big to navigate the hospital, but he used his thick metal armor as a shield for the team as he threw himself into the enemy. Mark was only a step behind, and soon a frantic fight had broken out in the hall. Though the mutants were numerous, they weren't very strong individually, mostly E and D ranks. The result was an absolute massacre. But despite that, they still threw themselves at the team with abandon, no doubt understanding that they wouldn't survive regardless.

Just as the fight was winding down, Mark felt something shift behind him. Instead of spinning to face the threat, he threw himself forward to try to avoid the attack, but before he could get away, he felt a hand lock onto his shoulder, and then the world shifted again. By the time the twisting air around him stabilized, Mark had reached up and grabbed the hand, keeping it pinned in place as he spun. There was a sharp scream as his fingers tore through the teleporter's forearm, slicing his arm clean off just below the elbow. The mutant stumbled backward, and Mark moved in for the kill, but a soft sigh caused him to freeze.

"I really wish we could meet under better circumstances."

His senses going wild, Mark ignored the teleporter, who was desperately clutching at his arm and groaning as he rolled around on the ground, and slowly turned. His eyes narrowed as he stared at Dallas, the self-proclaimed prophet of Salvation.

"I did mention we'd meet soon, didn't I? Well, here we are. Unfortunately, the circumstances are worse than I thought. Then again, it's his fault for not explaining the situation to you. I imagine anyone teleported against their will would be a little bit upset."

Mark was only half paying attention to what Dallas was saying. Instead, he was sweeping the area, trying to see if there were any hidden threats. Though their psychic signatures were not as bright as normal Exlian's, he could sense dozens of mutants scattered nearby and even more down below. Peeking out one of the windows, he saw a building in the distance and realized that they were probably on the fifth floor. The room they were in looked to be an operating room, or at least some sort of examination room, and was filled with numerous devices, all clearly well used. It was quiet, the sounds of the battle below muffled by the floors between them, and as Mark slowly gathered himself, preparing for a desperate fight, Dallas held up his hands. "I know it's hard to believe, but we really don't want to fight you. In fact, we won't. After all, we exist to serve you, not get in your way."

Mark's lips twisted into a grimace, and he shook his head slightly, taking a step toward the Prophet. Two big mutants, who still looked entirely human, quickly stepped forward, but Dallas held up his hand, stopping them.

"We do not move against the chosen instrument of salvation," he said sharply, causing the two mutants to pause. "I assume that Clara spoke to you about your role in the coming ascension of mankind?"

Taking another wary step forward, Mark shook his head again. "She only said some nonsense about me being the Savior. I didn't stick around long enough to listen to any more."

"In that case, allow me to enlighten you," Dallas said, spreading his hands out in a welcoming gesture. "We are Salvation, an organization dedicated to the ascension of mankind. After all, humans are a fundamentally flawed species, a species stuck on the ladder of evolution, forever frozen in a weakened state. Compare that to the Exlian, for instance, who have the ability to grow and evolve endlessly. It is that ability that has allowed them to overrun this world. Yet humanity foolishly continues to fight against the inevitable."

Though Dallas spoke softly and his gaze was warm, Mark couldn't help but shiver as he listened to the Prophet's words.

"There are those among us, however, whose bodies have ascended beyond mere humanity." Pausing, Dallas gestured around at the mutants, all of whom stood a little bit straighter, clearly filled with pride.

"You're not serious, are you? You really think that your bodies are superior to humans'?"

"Are they not? Faster, stronger, imbued with abilities, even without becoming empowered? What else can we say except that this new race is superior? But it is not enough for some to rise. All must join us."

"You want to turn everybody into mutants?"

"Of course not," Dallas said, rolling his eyes. "That would be entirely unfeasible. And besides, very few people are truly worthy."

Rather confused, Mark glanced at the nearby mutants, trying to figure out how many of them he'd be able to take down once the fight started. To keep Dallas talking, he threw out a question. "So what is this ascension, then? If it's not to transform everybody into mutants, what exactly did you see in your vision?"

"I saw glory!"

For the first time, Dallas's voice took on the fanatical excitement Mark had first heard in Clara's words.

"It was an endless wave of perfect beings. The pinnacle of evolution. They crashed against our city, purging the weak, destroying any resistance, stripping away the frailty of humanity, and inviting all of us to join in the perfect harmony of the swarm."

The Prophet's soft tone and insane words left Mark unsure how to feel. "So where do I come in? Am I going to save the city from the swarm?"

"No. Haven't you been listening?" Dallas said, his eyes narrowing ever so slightly as he took a step forward. "You, or rather what you will inevitably become, stood at the front of the horde, led the charge into the city, slaughtering defenders right and left. The absolute pinnacle of perfection."

"That doesn't sound like salvation to me."

"Ah, but you were not there. You did not witness the end!"

Unconsciously flexing his fingers, Mark shifted forward slightly, his body ready to burst into action at any moment. Yet the Prophet paid no attention and instead lifted his hands, gazing up toward the ceiling as if he could see the night sky beyond. "You called the Mother up from the depths, enveloping those deemed worthy, those pure enough to survive. And all fell under the Mother's sway, carrying us to the pinnacle of perfection."

The Prophet's words faded slowly, and with a happy sigh, he turned to look at Mark. "I do love that vision. It's much better than the other, in which humanity mounts a puny defense and this city is overrun, obliterated by the unstoppable swarm. But all of that is for the future. What matters now is that we've met and that you know what your future holds. I don't expect you to believe, at least not yet. It'll take a few more meetings before you accept your destiny. I've seen that too, the moment when you submit yourself to fate, taking up the mantle as the one destined to bring humanity to its peak. Unfortunately, though I would love to stay and share a few more words, we're running out of time."

Following the Prophet's gaze toward one of the windows, Mark heard a faint crackling sound and saw ice beginning to creep up the windowpane. Without hesitating, Mark lunged for the Prophet. But a bloody gash appeared, hanging in the air behind the Prophet. Even as Mark reached for him, it split open, and the Prophet stepped back into it, his gaze now locked with Mark's.

"This is the second meeting," he said, and his words echoed strangely in Mark's head. "The second of five. I look forward to our next."

With a sharp crack, the bloody gash sealed up, leaving Mark grasping at air. At the same time, an explosion shook the building, nearly throwing him from his feet, and two of the mutants who had been standing nearby rushed toward him, their bodies morphing into monstrous forms.

One of them grew four thick tentacles from its back, and its mouth transformed into a sharp beak. Flailing tentacles tried to wrap Mark up and pull him close, but Mark tore through them with a few flicks of his fingers. The other mutant grew in size, its shoulders and torso expanding rapidly, as two more pairs of legs wormed their way out of its lower back. With a roar, the mutant smashed down a massive fist at Mark, who dodged. The force of the mutant's punch shattered the floor, and all three of them tumbled down to the floor below.

A few large chunks of concrete slammed into Mark as he hit the ground, but his mana shield activated, sparing him from the majority of the crushing force. Losing sight of both mutants in the collapse, Mark scrambled backward, trying to find stable footing, but before he could, a tentacle wrapped around his ankle and jerked him up into the air, flinging him toward the opposite wall. Mark could only wrap his arms around his head, hoping his shield had recharged.

When he hit the wall, it was with enough force to blast straight through it, and Mark went crashing into the machines on the other side, shattering one of them completely. There was a loud roar, and two hands gripped the hole he had made, ripping the wall apart so that the giant mutant could force its way in.

Groaning, Mark scrambled to his feet, his mind racing furiously as he tried to figure out a way out of this predicament. Both of the mutants were at least B ranked, and their abilities were purely physical, which meant that his secret weapon, null field, wouldn't have any effect. Thankfully, they didn't seem to be able to easily bypass his mana shield, and he still had his regeneration, which meant that in a direct fight, he'd at least be able to survive for a while.

As the mutant forced its way into the room, there was another loud explosion, and the building shook again, making both Mark and the mutant pause. Remembering the ice that had started to form on the window, Mark could only imagine just how dangerous the fight down below was. Though it was risky, he figured his best bet would be to lead the two mutants down to meet up with the others, hopefully borrowing Winter Wolf's strength to kill them.

Unfortunately, the mutant, who was bent over to squeeze into the room, was between him and the door and clearly didn't want to let Mark go. Worse, behind the large, multilegged mutant was the mutant with tentacles, waiting to grab Mark if he tried to slip by. With no choice but to mount a desperate defense while he waited for an opportunity to crop up, Mark focused his mind, forming the communication circuit on his throat to see if he could connect with Noah. To his surprise, it connected almost immediately, and Mark heard Noah's voice in his mind.

"You're at Morning Glow Hospital. We're about five minutes out. Sky should be there within the next thirty seconds."

Taken aback, Mark nearly missed the mutant's punch and barely managed to duck, letting it slam into the wall behind him. He took the opportunity to dart forward, intending to stab the creature in the ribs, but before he could, a whipping tentacle forced him back. The large mutant's fist opened, and it grabbed for Mark, roaring in pain as Mark slashed its palm.

Furious, the mutant tried to push farther into the room, its hand slamming at Mark. Once again, Mark dodged, and the hand smashed through the wall, sending chunks of concrete flying. Seeing an opportunity, Mark darted toward the opening, but before he could slip through, the mutant's other hand slammed into him. The majority of the force was blocked by his mana shield, but it still caused Mark to stumble through the gaping hole in the wall.

Empty air flashed before his eyes, and he realized he was four stories up the side of the building. His hand scrambled against the wall, gouging the cement, as he tumbled down the side of the building. Vaguely, he heard what sounded like someone calling his name, and then a force punched him in the gut so hard he lost his breath, slamming him through a large window and back into the third floor.

Barely able to process what was going on, Mark instinctively closed his hand over his attacker's throat, but before he could squeeze, a displeased hiss echoed in his mind, and his hand jerked open as awareness came flooding back in.

Sky threw her arms around Mark, choking back tears as she hugged him. "Noah! Noah! I've got him!"

"We'll be there in three minutes. Stay alive."

Hearing Noah's voice from Sky's watch, Mark took a breath and quickly pulled her to her feet, his heart pounding. The first thing he noticed was that her body had filled out and she was even prettier than he remembered. A dozen different questions rose to his lips, but then he caught sight of the wounds on her neck, and he winced. "Are you okay?"

Sky's fingers brushed the marks on her neck and came away bloody, but she just grinned and blinked past the tears in her eyes. "I'm fine. I'm fine. We need to get you out of here."

"That's going to be a tall order," Mark said.

Seeing that he was gazing past her, she spun around and saw the octopus-limbed mutant climbing through the window. Faltering at the sight, Sky shifted until she was slightly behind Mark. "Uh, he doesn't look friendly."

Calming his breath, Mark shook out his hands and got ready for a fight. "Not even a bit."

The lights flickered intermittently, adding a sinister air to the ruin of the hospital. Mark's attention, however, was firmly placed on the monstrous mutant coming toward them. But before he could step forward, he felt a hand pat his shoulder. He turned to see Sky moving past him.

"Mark, we need to get you down to the bottom floor. I'll distract him. You start retreating. Noah will be here with reinforcements and an escape vehicle in a few minutes."

"What? No, I'm not gonna leave you to fight this thing by yourself."

"I'm not gonna fight it."

As if to illustrate her point, Sky lifted from the ground, hovering a few inches above the white polished floor. Though her face was pale, her eyes were bright with determination. With a smile, she suddenly zipped away, moving faster than Mark could react. The mutant let out a roar, swinging its tentacles toward her, causing Mark's breath to catch. Yet Sky twisted her body and accelerated, darting between the monster's swinging limbs, managing to get behind it in an instant without ever being touched.

The mutant spun to chase her, but she danced back out of reach, and with another roar, it lumbered after her.

"Go! I'll see you downstairs."

Though Mark hated the idea of separating from Sky so soon after finally seeing her again, he had to admit that she was much better suited for this sort of thing than he was. She moved through the air with practiced ease and had clearly mastered her power in a way that left him dumbfounded. As she lured the mutant toward the window, Mark took a step back and then another. The mutant paid him no mind, all its attention focused on trying to swat Sky out of the air. Yet despite the close confines, she had no trouble avoiding its arms and even managed to hit it with a few light attacks. Mark knew she was right and that the best thing for him to do was to rush down to the first floor to meet up with the other reinforcements, but it took him a considerable amount of willpower to leave her.

"Mark, go!"

Taking a deep breath, Mark spun on his heel and darted out the door, finding himself in a long hallway. At the end, he could see a few mutants guarding the stairs. One of them caught sight of him, letting out a shout to alert the others. Frustrated at having to leave Sky behind, Mark lowered his stance and accelerated, slamming into the first mutant a few seconds later. The force of his charge sent the mutants stumbling backward, and Mark pressed his advantage, even as another transformed into a gelatinous substance and struck out at him.

With a growl, Mark hacked at the attacking mutant's body, his fingers tearing a large gash in the mutant's chest. With a shriek, the mutant tried to wriggle backward, but its way was blocked and its sudden lunge sent it slamming into the wall. Its jellylike body bounced off, and Mark was forced to drop to the ground as the mutant stumbled forward, its flailing limbs slamming into one of its companions. Now flat on the ground, Mark dug his fingers into the floor and pulled, shooting across the smooth surface even as the mutants erupted into a vicious melee behind him. Because of their companions flailing, none of them could see Mark, but thinking he was in the hall, they all started fighting with each other.

By this time, Mark had already gotten past them, and with a kick, he broke open the door to the stairwell they had been guarding. Grabbing the railing, Mark vaulted over, holding himself suspended four floors up for a moment. Behind him, the mutants had finally figured out that they were fighting each other and separated. As they all surged toward him, Mark's eyes narrowed. Feeling a particular eagerness bubbling up in him, he glanced at his shadow, which was splayed out on the landing of the staircase.

"None of them can survive."

Mark let go, and his body plunged down into the stairwell as the first of the mutants stepped out onto the landing. His shadow trembled and rapidly coalesced into a small cat that sat perched on the edge of the rail. Mime's tail lashed back and forth, her eyes glowing red. Unnerved by the sight of the small cat and the ever-widening smile that stretched across her mouth, the mutant tried to pull up short, its instincts starting to go haywire, but its companions behind it were moving too quickly, and they forced the mutant forward, directly into Mime's growing mouth.

As Mark fell through the air, he heard a short scream and a soft crunch but had no time to assess what was going on above. His hands shot out, grabbing the railing of the floor a story down. This was where he had left the others, and rather than continue down, he jumped over the railing and darted into the hall. The signs of battle were everywhere, and Mark saw almost a dozen scattered corpses. A few of them had been cut to pieces, while others sported large holes torn through their bodies. There were patches of ice here and there, and Mark saw more than a few heavy burns.

Yet his eyes were drawn as if by a magnet to a large figure

slumped against the wall, and with his breath catching, Mark hurried over. He only needed a glance to see that Servo was dead. A long cut, starting under one ear and ending at the other, traced its way across Servo's neck, drenching his chest in blood. There were no other wounds on the large man's body, and Mark felt intense anger and more than a bit of sorrow filling his chest as he clenched his teeth.

"Mark."

He lunged to his feet and saw Coral standing in a nearby doorway with a strange look on her face.

"Joker, he . . ."

Coral's body jerked slightly, and she never finished her sentence, as the light in her eyes dimmed and she fell face forward to the ground, revealing dozens of wounds in her back and a knife planted in her spine. Though Mark had never been particularly close with either Servo or Coral, the anger that burned in him swelled, threatening to obliterate his rationality.

"You know, it's not kind to talk about me behind my back."

With a flippant smile, Joker stepped over Coral's body. He flicked his finger, and the knife, which had been buried in Coral's neck, wrenched itself free and flew up into the air. Mark would have expected Joker to look insane, yet curiously, the madman looked calmer than Mark had ever seen him before. Slowly standing up, Mark measured the distance between them. Joker's abilities worked within a thirty-foot range, and in that space, he could freely control both himself and the knives. There was currently around forty feet between them. Barely able to contain his rage, Mark took a step forward.

"Ooh, you look angry. Which is strange, you know, because I'm pretty sure you weren't friends with them."

Mark didn't say a word and simply took another step forward.

"Hey, hold on, hold on. Don't tell me you're actually going to try and fight me." Joker broke out into a laugh and reached up to wipe imaginary tears from his eyes. "You really are an idiot, you know that? Both of them were stronger than you, and look how easily I killed them. Come on, you don't actually believe that you're going to be able to fight me, do you? You should be running, fleeing as fast as you can in the hopes that I'll find a better target to go after. Besides, don't you want to know why I killed them?"

Mark paid no attention to Joker's babbling and took another step forward, his stance lowering slightly as he got ready to charge.

"Oh, you're serious about this? Well, in that case, before I cut you to pieces, why don't we have a conversation?"

Now thirty-one feet away, Mark frowned. "Where's Winter Wolf?"

"The boss? Oh, she's—"

Halfway through Joker's response, Mark sprang forward, his body blurring as he crossed the distance. Yet Joker simply rolled his eyes and snapped his fingers, teleporting thirty feet back to widen the space between them. At the same time, two knives appeared in midair, flying toward Mark, only for him to pull up short outside Joker's zone of control. The two knives stabbed into empty air before reappearing above Joker's shoulders with soft pops.

"As I was saying before I was interrupted, Winter Wolf is off fighting the mutants. She is probably trying to rescue you, which is ironic, because you're down here now, and she won't be fast enough to keep you alive."

Holding out his hand, Joker summoned one of his knives and licked the blood from the blade, his gaze never leaving Mark.

"You know, two of the enforcers wanted you dead. Paid me quite a bit just on the off chance I'd have an opportunity to take care of you. And look, the opportunity has come."

Mark grimaced and shifted his weight as he watched Joker's knives dancing in the air. "What about Servo and Coral?"

"I've been meaning to clean them up for some time. Dead people don't get any funny ideas, and the scum here on the surface were tired of them. What better way to deal with them then pinning their deaths on Salvation?"

The all-consuming fury that had burned in Mark had begun to cool, transforming from a raging desire to tear Joker into pieces, into a calm, cold, but no less murderous mood. In truth, it wasn't just because of Coral and Servo's deaths that he planned on killing Joker, though they did play a part. He was also worried that when Noah and the others arrived, they would become Joker's targets. Rather than let that happen, Mark preferred to clear this unpredictable obstacle first. Unfortunately, that meant he had to figure out a way to catch the teleporting madman, and he had to do it quick.

Risking a glance back at the bodies of his two companions, Mark feigned as if he were going to charge at Joker, but instead he turned and began to run, heading back to the stairwell. He heard a delighted laugh behind him, and a dagger slashed toward his leg. The first one was blocked by his mana shield, but in the moment before the shield recharged, a second dagger stabbed into his shoulder. Feeling the biting pain, Mark grabbed it and wrenched it free, but it vanished from his grasp and appeared in front of his chest, flying straight toward his heart.

Slapping it aside, Mark redoubled his efforts to reach the stairwell, only to see Joker appearing in front of him, a fan of knives hovering above his head. With a growl, Mark lifted his arms, blocking the daggers that shot toward him as he barreled through the doors into the stairwell. He was moving so fast he couldn't stop himself, and he slammed into the rail, snapped a number of the posts, and lurched over the edge. At the last moment, his hand grabbed the broken railing, and he managed to twist himself around, but Joker's foot stomped down on him. The blow was blocked by Mark's mana shield, but that allowed two daggers to stab into his arm, causing him to grunt in pain as he let go.

Joker teleported a few feet away as Mark tried to grab his opponent's leg. His hands closed on empty air, and Mark fell to the floor below, dropping twenty feet to slam into the concrete. With a groan, he rolled over, avoiding the daggers that punched into the spot where he had just been lying.

"Come on, kid, I thought you were better than this," Joker taunted.

As Mark struggled to get to his feet, Joker appeared in front of him, perched on the railing of the stairs, his eyes bright as he stared at Mark. "Where's that glitch ability of yours? Or maybe you're not feeling threatened enough. But that's okay. I'll stab you a few more times, and we'll see if we can get it going. I really do want to see it work."

Slowly standing up, Mark shook out his limbs, his eyes never leaving Joker, who was content to wait for him to get up. The wounds on Mark's body had already healed, and he could hear a commotion in the distance, an indication that Noah and the reinforcements had arrived outside the hospital. Seeing Joker was about to say something, Mark shook his head slightly and activated his null field, enveloping the entirety of the stairwell. The field only stretched a dozen feet at its full range, creating a bubble around him. In the hallways above, this wasn't enough space, and it would have been easy for Joker to move outside it, using his teleportation to stay well out of reach. In the stairwell, however, Mark's null field covered the entire space, and there was nowhere for Joker to hide.

Joker still reacted instantly, his body jerking as he tried to activate his teleportation. When it failed, his eyes widened in surprise. He hopped down from his perch, even as his daggers dropped to the ground, no longer able to float in the air. He swiped for three of them and rapidly hurled them at Mark, targeting his stomach, throat, and eyes.

Lifting his hands to block the daggers heading for his face, Mark pressed forward and felt the third dagger bite into his stomach. He ignored the pain, even as Joker scrambled backward, trying to escape up the stairs. Though Joker was a C-ranked empowered, none of his stats were that high. He wasn't as fast or strong as Mark, and before he could get away, Mark caught up.

Joker, realizing he couldn't escape, produced two more knives and lunged forward, his blades dancing. Mark met him head-on, and they exchanged a flurry of blows. Though Joker's knife work was exquisite, it quickly became obvious Mark had the advantage. His bone blade arms acted as offense and defense at the same time, blocking Joker's cuts and stabs while leaving wounds scattered across his body.

Mark pressed forward aggressively, and as the seconds ticked by, Joker's breathing grew more and more labored. He was incredibly hard to pin down and kept trying to distance himself, but Mark stuck to him aggressively, continually battering at Joker's defenses. The longer the fight continued, the uglier Joker's face became, and Mark saw him try and fail to activate his ability over a dozen times.

When it finally began to sink in that Mark's glitch ability wasn't going away, Joker tried to negotiate, but every time he opened his mouth, Mark increased the intensity of his attacks. Finally, unable to keep up with the rapid pace of the fight, Joker abandoned his defense and threw himself off the stairs, allowing Mark to score a nasty hit to his back that tore through his tactical suit, leaving a wide gash on his skin. Landing hard, Joker staggered and then sprinted for the door. Mark had been expecting something like this and dove after him, slamming into him from above and carrying him to the ground. Not giving up, Joker tried to stab Mark in the neck, but Mark jerked his head back just in time, the blade leaving a bright-red line on his throat.

Mark could feel the blood welling up and spilling from the cut even as his regeneration kicked in, a clear demonstration of just how close he had come to dying, but his focus was single minded. Rather than killing Joker immediately, Mark hacked down with the edge of his palm, tearing into the muscles on Joker's arm. With a muffled scream, Joker tried to roll away, but Mark pinned him to the ground and stabbed him in the shoulder, disabling his other arm. The madness that had filled Joker's face had given way to pure fear, and his inability to escape caused something in him to break loose. Mark first noticed it as a sort of heat building up in Joker's chest. He was unsure what was happening but instinctively sensed the danger. Even as he tumbled backward, away from Joker, an intense flash of mana burst out of Joker's chest.

Freed from Mark's grip, Joker struggled upright and shot a glare at Mark, his mouth opening to say something. The surge of mana burning in Joker's chest gave Mark pause, but he still stepped forward, intending to finish the job. Flinching, Joker took a step back, his body blurring slightly as he instinctively activated his blink ability.

Mark could feel the heavy mana that surged from Joker's chest, burning away at the null field for a brief moment, allowing him to vanish. Stunned, Mark realized what was going on. Joker's power had overcharged in a desperate attempt to keep him alive. Normally, such a surge in power would have given him a tremendous advantage, but because it had happened while inside the null field, the majority of the mana the overcharge produced had been used up fighting the field, leaving only enough for Joker to teleport away.

Fear raced through Mark at losing sight of Joker. The man was insane and dangerous, and Mark couldn't afford to let him live. Not wanting to lose his opponent, Mark dashed through the door into the hallway, only to come skidding to a stop as he saw a frozen standoff in front of him.

At the far end of the hall, he could see Noah in his custom mana suit, with half a dozen guards nearby. They were armed to the teeth, and from the dead mutants at their feet, it was clear that they had already been attacked. But despite having cleared the threat, they didn't dare enter farther into the hospital, as White Wolf was standing in their way, along with four of her giant ice wolves.

The area around Winter Wolf was frozen solid. Everything within thirty feet had been covered with ice. What drew Mark's attention, however, was Joker's body, impaled on half a dozen ice lances. Though he was still alive, the intense surge of mana had faded from his body, and the lances, having pierced him through from multiple directions, prevented him from speaking.

"What an absolute mess."

Winter Wolf's voice was as cold as the ice that surrounded her, and the raw power her words contained sent a shiver down Mark's spine. Quietly deactivating his null field, he took a hesitant step forward. Joker was clearly on his last legs, and Winter Wolf paid the dying madman no attention as she turned to look at Mark. Though she exposed her back to Noah and the others, they didn't dare step forward, given the four massive wolves staring at them.

"Servo and Coral?" she asked.

Mark gestured to Joker. "They're up a floor. Joker killed them. He said that the enforcers put a bounty on me and that the scum put one on them."

Sighing, Winter Wolf rubbed her forehead, clearly annoyed. "I knew this was going to happen."

"Wait!"

Joker managed to squeeze out a single word before Winter Wolf pointed a finger at him, and the ice spears that were stabbed through his body suddenly sprouted more spikes. One drove through the side of his neck, piercing through his jaw into his brain, and his words were choked off. As the light faded from his eyes, Winter Wolf smiled, though it didn't make Mark feel any better. Feeling his palms grow clammy in the cold air, Mark shifted backward, but if Winter Wolf noticed, she didn't say anything.

"I've been wanting to do that for a long time," she said, and with a snap of her fingers, frost rapidly rose around Joker's corpse, encasing him in ice. "Now, tell me, what's all this about?"

Seeing her jerk a thumb over her shoulder toward Noah and his men, Mark took a deep breath, thousands of thoughts racing through his head. He could lie, try to come up with some sort of excuse, but regardless of what he did, Mark knew he was in for a fierce fight. So instead, out of respect for Winter Wolf, he told the truth.

"They're here to break me out. My plan was to pretend to die here in the hospital and then retreat with them instead of going back to the Tomb."

As he spoke, Mark reached out with his mind, triggering the locking mechanism on his shackles. With a click, they popped open, clattering to the ground, and Winter Wolf's eyes widened. Mark saw the mana around her starting to flare and readied his null field. Winter Wolf was quite a bit faster and stronger than he was, and he knew that he didn't have much of a chance, even in a direct physical confrontation. But that was better than facing her ice, against which he had no defenses. On the other side of the hall, Noah and his men lifted their weapons, getting ready to throw themselves into combat, but before the fight started, Winter Wolf suddenly let out a loud laugh. "Ha, you're lucky, kid."

With a wave of her hand, the field of ice surrounding her began to rapidly melt, retreating into Winter Wolf, leaving only the four large ice wolves and Joker's frozen body behind.

"It's a trick others have tried before, but I think you might actually succeed," Winter Wolf said. "The administrators aren't going to be happy when I'm the only one who comes back alive, but it's not like there's anything they can do about it."

Chuckling as if she had just told a funny joke, Winter Wolf walked toward Mark. Though he had relaxed his stance, he didn't let down his guard completely, and his tension began to build as she got closer. He was just about to activate his null field when she stopped, her eyes dropping to Mark's feet. Glancing down, he saw

Mime sitting calmly next to him, licking her paw as she watched Winter Wolf with an impassive gaze. Holding her hands up, Winter Wolf slowly moved forward, until she was standing only an arm's length from Mark. With Mime beside him, Mark found himself completely relaxed, and he didn't react as Winter Wolf held out her hand, revealing a glittering coat button in the center of her palm.

"Take this," she said, "and then retreat with your friends. There are still a few mutants to kill, and I'll clear them out."

Hesitating for a moment, Mark nodded and picked up the button, holding it tightly in his hand as Winter Wolf closed her eyes for a moment.

"I'll deal with the handlers, but make sure you stay out of sight. They're going to be awfully suspicious when your body doesn't turn up. You're a good kid, Mark, and I'm glad you're getting out of here."

Walking past Mark, Winter Wolf patted him on the shoulder, then paused, her hand resting lightly on his shoulder. "Oh, and do me a favor? Tell your brother, Joe: Ambrosia exists."

With those cryptic words, she continued past Mark into the stairwell. He felt a blast of cold air, and she was gone. The wolves had vanished at some point, leaving Mark alone in the hallway with Noah, his men, and Joker's frozen corpse.

Rushing forward, Noah grabbed Mark by the shoulders. "You okay? Are you hurt?"

Mark could tell Noah had been deeply shaken by the display of Winter Wolf's power. Carefully removing his friend's hands, he nodded. "I'm fine, but we need to get out of here. What's the plan?"

Taking a deep breath, Noah gestured, and one of his guards stepped forward, unclipping his helmet. He was almost exactly the same build as Mark, and as he stripped off his suit, Noah explained, "You'll take this suit, and you'll walk out of here with us. We're going to simulate a fierce fight and retreat."

"What about him?" Mark asked, pointing at the guard.

"He'll leave on his own," Noah said, giving the guard a nod. He saluted, and his body began to fade, turning insubstantial before drifting down into the earth. "He's got a wraith power that lets him move through solid objects. He'll be fine. Hurry up and get suited, and let's get out of here."

It only took Mark a minute to get the suit on, and when he had clipped on the helmet, he looked no different from any of the other guards, who were throwing attacks around, hacking at the walls and unleashing blasts of mana. As soon as Mark was dressed, they began to retreat, heading for the door as quickly as possible. A moment later, they burst out of the hospital as if they were being chased.

In the distance, Mark could see more guards, along with two large vans. The guards were facing off against Special Agent Callaghan and five heavily armored soldiers. However, fighting had yet to break out. Seeing Noah and the others rushing toward them, Special Agent Callaghan took a step back, her eyes narrowing. She was clearly furious, but before she could speak, there was a loud rumble from the hospital and an accompanying roar of pain that echoed through the night.

Everyone's eyes turned back to the massive building, watching as jagged chunks of ice began bursting out through each of the windows. The walls cracked as frost raced over them. Under Mark's astonished stare, the entire building froze solid. There was another roar, and Mark saw a massive figure hurl itself from the roof, trying to escape the rapidly spreading cold. But before it could, the ice expanded, freezing the very air itself and halting the massive mutant.

A tiny figure darted up from the roof, her hand brushing past the frozen mutant, whose body shattered into a million pieces, sending bloody shards of ice scattering into the air. As frozen chunks of flesh rained down, the small figure began to grow larger, and a moment later, Winter Wolf was hovering in front of them. Behind her, the hospital had transformed into a frozen tomb.

"The mutants are all dead," she said, her voice glacial as she raked her eyes over Noah, Mark, and the helmeted guards.

Special Agent Callaghan, clearly nervous, kept one hand on her wrist as she stared at Winter Wolf. Mark had no idea how Winter Wolf was flying, but slowly she lowered to the ground. As her foot touched the earth, it trembled faintly, and the hospital, unable to bear its own weight, crumbled in on itself. The collapse was surprisingly orderly, but by the end, it was little more than a giant pile of rubble.

"Where are the others?" Special Agent Callaghan asked, her voice strained.

For a moment, Mark thought Winter Wolf might not answer, but then the glacial expression on her face thawed. "Everyone else is dead. Joker went mad and killed Servo and Coral. Apex probably fell to the mutants."

"And Joker? What happened to him?"

"I killed him myself. The mutant threat is gone, so it's time to retreat before anybody else shows up."

Special Agent Callaghan was clearly unhappy with the situation, but Winter Wolf was done talking to her. Instead, she turned to Noah and nodded. "Thank you for your assistance. Without you, a group of mutants may have slipped away."

Opening his faceplate, Noah placed his fist on his chest and bowed to Winter Wolf. "I'm only sorry we couldn't do more. If we had arrived earlier, some of your companions may have been able to survive."

A cloudy look appeared in Winter Wolf's eyes for a brief moment, but it disappeared so quickly Mark felt that he might have imagined it.

"They laid their lives down for the sake of their duty," she said coldly. "There's little more they could ask for."

Turning, she walked past Special Agent Callaghan, who shot a glare at Noah and then, with gritted teeth, followed Winter Wolf. The entire time, Mark stood quietly behind Noah, pretending to be one of the guards. When Noah gave the command, he piled into a van with the others, and soon, they were pulling away.

As soon as they had left, Mark unbuckled his helmet. "Where's Sky? Is she okay?"

In the front seat, Noah turned and nodded. "Yes, she withdrew just before we ran into you. We'll meet up with her in a moment."

As it turned out, it was closer to half an hour. The vans wove their way through the city, taking numerous twisting turns, before arriving at a small out-of-the-way mansion. After turning into the driveway, they headed down into an underground parking garage. Everyone got out and walked through a set of fortified blast doors into a training facility, where they stripped off their suits and changed their clothes. The first thing Noah did after getting out of his suit was give Mark a hug, a grim smile on his lips. "I'm glad you're out."

"I am too," Mark said, shaking his head, "and I have to admit, that went entirely smoother than I thought it would."

"You and me both," Noah said, his expression turning dark. "That Winter Wolf, there's no way she's A ranked. She's clearly an S-ranked empowered. If she hadn't decided to let you go . . ." His voice trailed off, and Mark could only nod in agreement. If Winter Wolf had wanted to, she could have killed all of them easily. But instead, she had helped Mark escape, leaving him with the burning question of why.

The level of power that Winter Wolf had just displayed was leaps and bounds beyond anything she had ever revealed before, and Mark knew for certain that if she had wanted to stop him, there was absolutely nothing he could have done to escape. The amount of mana control she'd revealed was so strong that he was pretty sure that even his null field wouldn't have been able to prevail against it.

The thought sent a chill down his spine, and he realized that he had been treating his null field ability as absolute, when in reality, it could be countered just like any other ability. His encounter with Joker had proved that. Of course, doing so was only possible for someone whose mana was overwhelming. But clearly, those people did exist and were more prevalent than Mark had thought.

Thankfully, Winter Wolf had decided to let him go. Though remembering the way her mana had suddenly paused and she had seemed to change her mind, Mark couldn't help but feel there was more to the situation than met the eye.

He followed Noah out of the training room and up into the mansion, and a minute later, Sky burst in, still dressed in her tactical suit. Throwing herself at him, Sky wrapped her arms around

Mark's neck, squeezing tightly. As her legs wrapped around his waist, Mark's first thought was that she was light. So light it hardly felt like she was there. Then he realized that it was her power at work. He hugged her tightly for a minute and then loosened his grip, but she didn't want to let go.

"All right, enough of that. If we do this right, we'll have plenty of time for this sort of thing later. But right now, we're on a time crunch."

Blushing faintly at Noah's words, Sky reluctantly unwrapped herself from Mark and pushed back, her body floating in the air.

"What happened with the mutant?" Mark asked.

Losing her blush, Sky gave Mark a smug grin. "I danced around with him for a little while, and then, when I figured you had gotten enough distance, I retreated. I'm way too fast for a clumsy oaf like that to catch me."

As if to illustrate her point, Sky zipped backward, then zipped forward again, crossing the entire room in a flash. She let out a delighted laugh when she saw Mark's stunned expression. "I've been practicing hard."

"She earned herself a nickname," Noah said, tapping on his watch. "'Queen of the Sky.' Even Exlian can't catch up with her."

The virtual screen on the wall shimmered, and a picture of someone who looked almost exactly like Mark, with a few subtle differences, popped up.

"This is going to be your new identity, Mark. Jonathan Leeds. You're a former guard who's just applied for a hunter's license. I've arranged for an apartment and a bank account. For the moment, it's best that you lay low. But once things have calmed down a little bit and we're sure that they're not tracking you, I can get you a job too."

Reading over the information, Mark nodded. "Thank you, Noah."

"Don't thank me until we're actually sure that they're not coming after you. All right, are you hungry? Let's get some food."

"Sounds great, because I am famished."

Sky led the way to the dining room, navigating the halls with an easy familiarity. Soon, they were sharing a simple meal. To Mark, it was rather surreal to be sitting in a dining room with two of his friends, and he couldn't help but wonder what crazy turn his life was going to take next. Rather than worry about it, though, he figured it was better to enjoy the moment, so he immersed himself in the food and conversation.

As they finished up, Sky tucked her feet under her on her chair and peered across the table at Mark. "So what actually happened? I've heard a little bit from Noah, but only bits and pieces."

Still unable to believe that he had managed to make it out of the Tomb, Mark picked up his glass and took a drink. "The deployment went poorly, and while I was out there, I ended up having to kill someone who was trying to take my head. But when I got back, they turned it around, and using the testimony of people who were there, they accused me of murder. I doubt that the two people who they claim testified against me were actually saying anything bad. After all, the guy I killed set off a bomb in the base in an attempt to wipe out an entire Engineering Corps battalion. Regardless, they framed me for murder and sent me straight to Gray Rock, then the Tomb."

"Gray Rock I know about," Sky said, looking between Mark and Noah, "but what's the Tomb?"

"It's an entire city down below our feet, like a smaller version of New Emery, but everybody there is considered highly dangerous or useful for experimentation. It's run by this supergenius named Maestro, who does all sorts of experiments on people."

"Doesn't sound like a pleasant place."

"Not so bad once you get used to it," Mark said, "but I'm happy to be out. Anyway, after getting sent to the Tomb, I got caught up in all sorts of crazy stuff, but then they stuck me on this team, part of what they call the conductor program. Conductors are deployed to the surface to carry out missions. Noah found out I was down there, and we were able to arrange this meetup. Originally, I thought I was going to have to fake my death. I even made myself a Dead Man Walking potion."

"Isn't that the potion you gave to me when we were outside in the dead zone?"

"Yes, same one. Originally, the plan was for me to fake my death, and then after everyone left and the cleanup crews came in, I could sneak away. Turned out I didn't need it."

"It sounds like you've had a pretty rough time," Sky said. Rising from her seat, she walked around the table, sat on the arm of Mark's chair, and leaned her body against his. "I'm really glad you're out, though."

"Me too. Hopefully, I can stay that way."

"Well, that's what we're going to work on next," Noah said. "In order to verify this identity, we need to go visit someone, but we can't go until tomorrow. So why don't you get some sleep? I think we could all use some rest."

"I think you're right," Mark said, pushing his chair back.

As he stood up, Sky did as well, her expression slightly frustrated. "I'm supposed to be on patrol, so I can't stay, but once you get a watch, send me your number, all right? I have some free time coming up, and it'd be nice to hang out."

After giving Mark a hug, Sky pushed off with her foot, drifted into the air, and then a moment later was gone, flying out of the open window into the dark sky. Seeing Mark looking after her, Noah grinned and patted him on the shoulder. "It's quite the power, huh? Are you sad you gave it away?"

Smiling, Mark shook his head. "Does anybody else know I'm alive?"

"No, and I wanted to talk to you about that." Noah gestured toward the door. "Come on, let me show you where you'll sleep. Currently, it's only me and Sky. Phoenix, Danny, and the others have no idea."

"Let's keep it that way for the moment," Mark said, his expression calm. "It's probably better that fewer people know. Though I'd like to tell Phoenix at some point. I think she deserves to know."

Giving Mark a long look, Noah nodded. "All right. If something changes, let me know, but I think you're right. It's better to keep this quiet."

After showing Mark to his room, Noah left him alone, mentioning that they'd have to be up in a few hours to get Mark's secret identity finalized. Sitting down on the bed, Mark flopped over backward and stared up at the ceiling. "Mime?"

The bed shifted near Mark's feet, and he heard the soft thump of Mime's paws as she jumped up next to him. She climbed up onto his chest, her paws producing a comforting weight, and looked down at him curiously.

"Thanks for your help back there."

Licking her lips, Mime nodded and lay down on him, her head resting just below his collarbone. He could feel the faint tickle of her breath on his neck, and he felt much of the tension he had built up over the last day drain away. For the next thirty minutes, Mark simply lay there, with Mime resting on top of him, his mind blank. The fact that he was no longer in the Tomb was almost overwhelming, and rather than try to deal with the mixture of excitement and fear racing through him, he just let the feelings roll around in his chest. It was only when he heard a soft beep from the console in the room that he sat up, earning himself an annoyed look from Mime, who moved to the pillow. Mark's attention was completely fixed on the console, and when the virtual window popped up without him doing anything and a familiar face appeared on it, Mark wasn't surprised.

"Ha, I thought you would be shocked," Maestro said, peering at Mark through the screen.

Moving from the bed to the chair, Mark shook his head. "It wasn't particularly hard to figure out that you were behind Winter Wolf letting me go."

"Have I mentioned that I like dealing with smart people?" Maestro said, his lips twitching into a smile. "I like it a lot. It saves me a tremendous amount of time, and you'd be amazed. Most people with power sets like yours are dumb as a rock, so this is quite refreshing. But congratulations on earning your freedom."

"Did I earn it?" Mark's eyebrows rose. "Here I was under the impression that I had you to thank for it."

"Well, of course you do. You wouldn't have gotten free if I didn't think it was a good idea. But I do think it's a good idea, which is fantastic for you. Now, I will miss our time together, and I'm already starting to regret not taking more samples. But I think that you can do more good out there than you can do in here."

As Maestro spoke, Mark's forehead furrowed. "What is it you want?"

The edge to his voice caused Maestro to pause for a moment, his abnormally large eyes peering at Mark. Though there was a virtual screen between them, Mark couldn't help but tense, wondering if he had offended Maestro. After a long moment, the genius spoke, his expression revealing none of the anger Mark was worried about.

"Mark, after a great deal of consideration, I have decided that you are the appropriate person for a specific and incredibly important task. Even if you and your friends hadn't hatched your scheme, I would have suggested something similar, though probably after a few months. But the fact that you got to it before I did is an indication that our minds are aligned, and the simplicity of your breakout plan is, in fact, genius. Very similar, though slightly inferior, to the plan I would have used. We don't have a tremendous amount of time, as I'm currently preventing anybody from seeing this interaction. And if it goes on too long, they will start to grow suspicious.

"But what you may not realize is that I, like you, am a prisoner as well. The constraints placed on me are significantly stronger than those shackles they bound you with. And I'm sad to say that there isn't a way for me to escape, at least not yet. So my only option, if I want to grow and improve, is to make investments. Investments in empowered who don't see eye to eye with my captors. You are one of them. Not the only one, by a long stretch, but one of the most promising. And so it was my intention to arrange for your release. At least, eventually. I admit, I was having a little bit more fun than anticipated examining your body."

By this point, Mark's anger had started to bubble up, and he was having trouble hiding it. Whether Maestro noticed it or not, he suddenly switched the topic, holding up a silver serum that looked similar to the ones Mark had consumed. "One of my primary responsibilities is understanding how to improve empowered, and I admit I've had some luck. From what Winter Wolf has told me, you got a glimpse of what I am able to do."

"Are you trying to say that her abilities are the result of your potions?"

"Technically serums, not potions, but yes. Her power, which used to barely qualify as A ranked, has been fascinating to study. The improvement to S-ranked power that you witnessed was the result of my efforts. I don't like the idea of relationships based on threats. In fact, it rather infuriates me, so what I propose is an even exchange. You help me with what I need, acting as one of my agents on the surface. In return, I will continue to help you improve your powers and learn to control them better. I've even got some ideas about how to help you manage that symbiote of yours."

Maestro's words had yet to finish when Mark felt the hair on the back of his neck rise. Glancing over his shoulder, he saw Mime sitting up on the pillow, her three eyes glowing red as she stared intently at Maestro. The genius didn't seem to care as he continued.

"Your ability to consume matter is a fascinating one, one you should be leveraging more often. Combined with your nearly unstoppable defenses, you have the makings of a perfect warrior. You know, I was genuinely surprised the first time I saw that ability, because I've never seen anyone able to do that outside of Exlian nests. It was also rather amusing how you tried to hide it."

With a sinking feeling, Mark tried to review his time in the Tomb, looking for when Maestro might have noticed something. "When did you discover it?"

"Almost as soon as you entered Gray Rock. I have access to the biological samples taken during the intake process. Your body has an unusually high level of mutation, a level beyond anything I've ever seen before. Certainly beyond the level of mutation in the failed products currently running around New Emery. Closer to the level of mutation one would find in a nest. That's why I arranged for you to come to the Tomb, so I could take a closer look. Since then, I've been paying particularly close attention to you. Why do you think that no one seemed to care about the bodies that constantly went missing around you? I'm well aware of your powers, Mark. I'm well aware of everything about you."

Though the expression in Maestro's eyes didn't change, a slow smile spread across his lips, and he looked at Mark the way one might look at a delicious piece of meat grilled to perfection.

"I think you might be laboring under a misconception, young man. I am not simply smart. I am the smartest. The only things I don't know about New Emery, and the people in it, are things I don't care to know.

"You cannot hide anything from me."

Raising his eyebrows, Mark leaned forward. "And yet you're trapped in the Tomb."

Maestro's smile vanished. "Exactly," he hissed. "This city was built upon my back, and yet I'm trapped underneath it, chained to this place, forced to churn out weapons of war. But like you, I am unwilling to submit to my fate."

Maestro's eyes flicked sideways, and with a sigh, he calmed down. "We're out of time for the moment, but I will be in touch. You don't have to worry about contacting me. Any device connected to the InfoWeb is within my grasp. I can tell that you're still wary, but whether you believe it or not, I do wish for an even exchange. Occasionally, I will make requests of you, and as they are completed, I will reward you accordingly. To help start our relationship off on good footing, I've erased all records of your stay in the Tomb. Obviously, I can't get rid of the impression you made on those individuals you came in contact with, but your biometric data is no longer in the authorities' hands. Additionally, I've altered the records for your past life. Mark Fields is truly dead."

Early the next morning Mark and Noah took a car to the

outskirts of New Emery. Watching the buildings flash past, Mark was struck by a strange feeling of incongruity, as if everything he was seeing were simply an illusion. When he closed his eyes, he found his mind wandering to the wide-open spaces outside the city, as if his spirit couldn't wait to get away from the oppressive concrete buildings humanity called home.

They stopped at a rather run-down, four-story apartment building, and getting out, Mark followed Noah to a metal door. After Noah knocked, a slot in the door opened, and two bloodshot eyes stared at them suspiciously. Noah didn't say a word, but after a long minute, the slot was closed with a clang, and the sound of dead bolts being drawn back echoed in the early-morning air. The door creaked as it opened, providing just enough space for Noah and then Mark to squeeze through.

An empowered man stood on the other side of the door, clearly a brute from the way his muscles bulged, and without a word, he jerked a thumb farther down the hall, indicating that they should go in. There were doors off to the right and left, but Noah, clearly having been here before, strolled past them and turned the corner, entering a wide room that had a single desk right in the middle of it.

Behind the desk was an elderly man with half-moon glasses perched on his nose and a thick frizz of hair that traced the edge of his bald pate, sticking out in every direction. Though he looked up when Mark and Noah entered the room, his fingers didn't stop moving, each hand acting independently, as he worked on two different devices. One appeared to be a workstation, while the other was a calculator.

"I'll be with you in a minute," he said, his voice high and nasal.

Nodding, Noah stood there quietly in front of the desk, with Mark behind him. Exactly a minute later, the man abruptly stopped his rapid-fire typing and peered at the two young men. "Well, this is quite a sight. Noah Javesi, prince of New Emery, and Mark Fields, heir to the Order of Blood. I didn't expect either of you this morning, and certainly not together."

Pursing his lips, the elderly man adjusted his glasses on his face, only for them to slide right back down to the tip of his nose.

"You know who I am?" Mark asked, taking a step forward to stand next to Noah.

"Your late master was a good friend of mine. A very good friend of mine," the old man said. "Which, I presume, is why Mr. Javesi brought you to me."

Though Noah was trying to maintain a neutral expression, Mark could sense the tension in his friend's body, and the old man could clearly sense it too.

"Relax, young man. Despite how much I hate your father and his cronies, ours is a fight of the older generation. I'm not so pathetic as to take it out on you, unlike someone we all know."

Though delivered in a rather acidic tone, the old man's words were enough for Noah to relax. "Hello, Master Lemuel. I'm assuming you know why we're here?"

"Well, nobody's told me, but if I had to guess, I'd say that having sprung young Master Fields from the Tomb, you're looking to give him a false identity."

"That's correct, sir."

"What a nice friend you are."

Master Lemuel's chair scraped against the ground as he pushed himself back from his desk and stood up, leaning over it slightly to peer at Mark.

"Normally, no matter who you were trying to get an identity for, I'd have you thrown out. After all, regardless of how poorly you feel about your father, the reality is that you and I are not on the same side."

Seeing Noah open his mouth to speak, Master Lemuel held up his hand.

"However, given the exceptional circumstances and the fact that the majority of my work has already been done"—here his eyes flickered to Mark, who realized with a start that Master Lemuel was talking about Maestro—"I think it's only appropriate that I contribute as well. Young Master Fields, if you would follow me, we can get this process sorted quickly."

His body hunched from years of leaning over his desk, Master Lemuel placed his hands behind his back and walked out of the room. Exchanging glances with Noah, Mark saw his friend nod, and feeling strangely nervous, he followed Master Lemuel back through the hall into one of the side rooms they had passed. There, he found two comfortable chairs, and Master Lemuel directed him to sit down.

"What a mess. What an absolute, unmitigated mess."

Mark wasn't sure if Master Lemuel's muttering was meant for his ears, but he couldn't help but agree. "Tell me about it."

"We don't have time for me to tell you about it, but at least it's not as bad as it could be. You've got quite the spine, kid, which you'll need for what faces you. Now, let's get the trivialities out of the way. Thanks to a little assistance, your new identity will be quite a bit easier to use. Your name is Jonathan Leeds. You have a very real history as a guard working for young Master Javesi, and your biometrics are all up to date already. All you need to do is verify here."

Seeing a virtual screen pop up in front of him, Mark scanned the information and quickly realized that many of the details matched his own life. Seeing nothing concerning, he accepted the prompt below, and with a beep, the virtual screen closed.

"One of my men will deliver a watch in a moment. It will contain everything you need. Now, since we have a few minutes without Mr. Javesi's snooping, let's speak of what's important."

Though he didn't like the way Master Lemuel talked about Noah, Mark held his tongue, which earned him an appreciative look.

"So you're not entirely brash. That's good."

"No, that was beaten out of me over the last few months," Mark said calmly.

"An unfortunate way to learn an important lesson, but at least you learned it. You'd be surprised at how many fools are shown the right path and yet fail to take it. But I digress. The mutterings of an old man. You'll have to excuse me."

Waving his hand, Master Lemuel straightened his glasses, and this time, they stayed in place for a whole two seconds before slowly sliding their way down his nose. He didn't seem to notice, though, as he peered at Mark. "Did your master ever mention the Order of Blood to you?"

Thinking carefully for a moment, Mark shook his head.

"Of course he didn't. Your master, for all his strengths, could be something of an idiot and was entirely too optimistic. Did he leave you with anything in particular? Any item that you found curious?"

Again, after thinking it over, Mark shook his head.

Rubbing his forehead, Master Lemuel sighed. "Of course he didn't. You are the heir to the Cutting Palm, are you not?"

"I am."

Master Lemuel's eyes narrowed, and he muttered something under his breath. It was too quiet for Mark to hear. "Have you ever met your master's old friends? Been introduced to anyone around my age?"

"No."

Master Lemuel's expression had gotten progressively darker with each of Mark's answers. Finally, his eyes dropped to the floor, and after nearly two minutes of silence, he waved his hand. "Forget it."

Just then, there was a knock on the door, and it slid open, revealing a massive brute who poked his head into the room.

"Here's your watch, sir," he said, handing Mark a small box.

Opening it, Mark found a used watch. It looked to be in good shape, but there were a few scratches on it, and it was a few generations old. Slipping it around his wrist, he activated it and saw his information as Jonathan Leeds pop up.

"You've just been assigned a hunting license that will allow you to venture out into the wilds, either solo or on a team. The majority of hunters hide their appearances, and so I recommend you do the same. It just so happens that a small gift arrived for you before you came."

To Mark, it appeared as if Master Lemuel pulled a box out of midair before handing it over to him. Inside was a black mask, reminiscent of the one Mark had used down in the Tomb. Next to it was a small data stick. He was about to pull it out and slot it into his watch when he saw Master Lemuel hold up his hand.

"I need plausible deniability, so wait until you're alone to do that. We shouldn't leave Mr. Javesi waiting any longer."

Pushing himself to his feet, he began to walk out of the room, and Mark hurriedly stood up and followed him. "Sir, about my master . . ."

Master Lemuel cut him off with a shake of his head. "If Master Abrams wanted you to be involved, you'd not need to be asking these questions."

Hesitating for a moment before entering the room where Noah was waiting, Master Lemuel turned and peered at Mark. "You have already sunk deep into the whirlpool that is New Emery. Besieged from outside and inside, humanity fights on the brink. Someday, when you have the ability, if you have the ability, to help, I'll speak with you again."

"And when will that be, sir? How will I know?"

Though Master Lemuel's body remained hunched, Mark had the distinct impression that he had suddenly straightened and was peering down at Mark through his glasses. With a casual wave of his hand, Master Lemuel walked into the room, leaving Mark staring at a brand-new cut that had just appeared on the concrete wall.

Twenty feet away.

"He's all done. The two of you can leave."

"Thank you, Master Lemuel," Noah said.

Mark was still standing in the hallway, his mind continually replaying what he had just seen, when Noah came out.

"How did it go?" Noah asked quietly.

Snapping out of his trance, Mark smiled. "I'm good to go. My name's Jonathan Leeds."

With a not-so-subtle sigh of relief, Noah led the way back out to the car. "Do you want me to drop you off at your apartment?" he asked. "Or you could come back to the mansion with me."

"Actually, I think I'd like to go visit my master's grave," Mark said, his mind still fixated on the incredible attack he had just witnessed.

He had believed that Master Abrams had been the only living person who could wield the third and final stage of the Cutting Palm technique, Body as the Sword. Yet what he had seen Master Lemuel do completely shattered that belief.

Sensing Mark's odd mood, Noah agreed and directed the driver to take them to the Martyrs' Cemetery. When they pulled up outside the heavily guarded graveyard, Noah opted to stay in the car while Mark got out and made his way to the gate.

Dozens of guards, dressed in exquisite mana suits, stood at attention outside, honoring those who had fallen while giving their all for the safety and security of New Emery. Mark was surprisingly calm as he scanned his watch, half expecting some sort of alarm to sound. But his new identity worked perfectly, and with a soft beep, the gate opened and he was allowed to enter.

A directory allowed him to search for his master's name, and when he found it, he quietly walked to the grave, immersed in the somber mood that shrouded the graveyard. His master's grave was surprisingly large and clearly well taken care of. Flowers that looked no more than a day old were placed by the headstone, and Mark could see that there had been other flowers there before.

"Took you long enough."

Glancing up, Mark saw Jason, Master Abrams's former disciple and owner of the restaurant where Mark had been a dishwasher. Jason was standing next to the grave, dressed in the uniform of one of the grave keepers. He had a rag in one hand and a bucket in the other and had clearly just come from wiping down some of the headstones.

"I was a bit tied up."

With a knowing smile, Jason put his bucket down. "At least you're here."

"What happened?"

If he heard the hard edge in Mark's words, Jason gave no sign of it. Instead of answering Mark's question, he looked at the ornate memorial stone for a moment, then sighed. "I was a terrible disciple. Brought the old man much more trouble than I was worth. But despite that, he stuck by me. Saved my life on multiple occasions, while asking nothing in return. Unfortunately, there's not much I can do to help. So I'll stay here. Watch his grave. Make sure it's taken care of. I wish I could help shoulder your burden. Help carry on his legacy. But this, this is the most I can do."

With another sigh, Jason's shoulders stooped, as if he were carrying a massive weight, and reaching down, he picked up his bucket. "Before he left, he asked me to pass something on to you. Here." Reaching into his pocket, Jason pulled out a data stick and tossed it to Mark. "I don't know what's on it. I haven't looked. I'm not worthy anymore."

Slipping the data stick into his pocket, Mark didn't know what to say. He could feel the intense sorrow around Jason. A crushing weight that threatened to drive the man into the ground. Yet despite that weight, Jason still stood.

"As your useless senior brother, I have a present for you too. Watch carefully, because I can only do this once."

The tone of Jason's voice shocked Mark out of his thoughts. And his eyes widened as he saw Jason lift his hand, extending two fingers.

"Ha!"

With a low shout, Jason brought his fingers down in a cutting motion. And Mark felt the world around him shudder. Sweat beaded on his forehead. And though he was standing nearly fifteen feet away from Jason, he had the distinct impression that everything between them had been split in two. The feeling grew stronger and stronger until Mark realized that he was going to be split too. Unfortunately, his thoughts were entirely separated from his body, and he found himself unable to react.

Then there was a faint cracking sound, and Jason's fingers, unable to bear the strain of his own strike, shattered. Blood began streaming from his torn skin, but Jason simply wrapped his now-broken hand in his rag and turned away as the world reconnected.

"You'll find the things you left in the warehouse in your new apartment. Master practiced Body as the Sword. I aimed for Motion as the Cleaver. But I failed. I can't wait to see what you come up with, junior brother."

Mark felt his mind reconnect to his body. His breath returned to his chest. And clasping his hands together in front of him, he bowed toward Jason's back. He remained bowed until Jason had vanished among the tombstones. Then, his steps unsteady at first, he began making his way out of the graveyard.

The two strikes he had seen today, the first from Master Lemuel and the second from Jason, had opened his mind, expanded his view of the world, and fundamentally transformed his thinking. By the time Mark had reached the gate, his steps were firm, his breathing no longer shaken, and his mind focused.

Though he had made it out of the Tomb, Mark could tell that the maelstrom engulfing New Emery was just beginning to pick up speed. Change was coming to New Emery, and no matter how he felt about it, he was firmly at the center of the storm.

But Mark had no desire to run or hide. His experiences over the last months had taught him many things, but they had taught him one lesson most clearly. The only way to avoid being a pawn in someone else's game was to gain the strength to become a player.

Which was exactly what he was going to do.

To be continued . . .